C. L. EASTON
STRANGERS OF EASTWOOD

THE COMPLETE SERIES

Strangers of Eastwood

Copyright © 2023 by C L Easton

Cover Design: Black Pirate Book Cover

Publisher: Black Rose Publishing

Paperback ISBN: 978-1-998910-09-0

This book is written in Canadian English

Welcome to Strangers of Eastwood:
This is a dark romance series
Combined warnings for all three books

It includes:
Drug and Alcohol use, Temperature Play,
Public Sex, Rope Bondage, Anal play, Graphic
Sex, Orgasm Denial, Group Sex, Graphic
Murder, Torturing, Gore, Blood, Flashbacks to
childhood abuse.

Only freaks would know.
L.M.E.Y.P.T.Y.C.O.M.F

Playlist

Strangers of the Night

Strangers of the Town

Strangers of the Crowd

C. L. EASTON
STRANGERS OF THE NIGHT

STRANGERS OF EASTWOOD BOOK ONE

1

Catalina

Halloween night.

The one time of the year when the residents of Eastwood let loose.

No questions asked. The only night that I can do what I do without having to look over my shoulder. See, this town is known for two things. It's the university, and the other I don't think it's well known, but they have a Halloween purge night. I'll tell you about that later. When I enrolled at Eastwood University, I thought I would be financially stable; it turns out that's a bunch of bullshit. I had to find work, and your scholarship only covers the bare minimum. I struggled for the first couple of months before my professor noticed. He told me about an opportunity that I would enjoy.

Now at first, I didn't think I would enjoy it so much, but being a loner at this school, I didn't have a problem. I really don't have many friends. Okay, I don't have any, so my evenings are always available. After showing me the first time, I was hooked. I started digging graves and making a profit from my professor. Cadavers are a much-needed thing in medical training.

Not the most glamorous job, but when you are working on a low income in an expensive town, you need to supplement everything. I'm gathering up my gear to head out for the night. I'm told there are three bodies that need to be brought into the school. It'll be an all-night job. *Thank God*. I don't think I can handle all the drunk shenanigans or any of the shenanigans going on tonight.

I change into my uniform, which consists of leggings and my black t-shirt with my skull lovers on it. I'm classy. I grabbed my combat boots and set them by my front door.

"Ah, shit."

I dart back into the kitchen to find my satchel can't forget about this. I have all my important things in there, like snacks. After strapping on my boots, I head to my 1976 Volkswagen Beetle, my baby. I call her Johnny. Don't worry. No dead bodies will ever go in her. Can you imagine trying to get that smell out of the upholstery? No thanks. Luckily, I have a van parked at the campus for everything else.

The evening is upon us; the streets are lined with jack-o-lanterns, every yard is decorated to the max with decorations. I pity those that aren't. It'll be a free for all

having your house destroyed. That's why I'm glad I live in my shitty ass apartment building. Plus, when I'm finished for the night, I can lock myself away from all this bullshit that's beginning to fill the streets with teens and adults dressed up in costumes chasing each other, drinking and having fun.

This town is by far the *weirdest.* "I'll never understand this town," I whisper out loud.

As I near the campus, I pull into the parking lot. I park behind the shed by the east side of the medical department. The last thing I need is someone to figure out what I've been doing this past year. I race across the parking lot without getting caught by any frat boy. The last thing I need tonight is getting caught in one of their sick orgy games. That's the thing about this night. The mayor has sick fantasies, and this is a way of saying it's not cheating. Once inside, I pull my phone out, checking which cemetery I need to hit up first. Eaglewood it is. It's the furthest one out. It's only one body. The other two are in Eastwood Cemetery, which is in the middle of town.

I feel relieved to be leaving town, even if it's only for a short while. I know it won't last long. Digging up one body won't be long enough for the silence. It gives me time to think, like how a group of guys that go here are not the friendliest. More so, three of them, Dorian, Nyx, and Cole. They always seem so pissed off. I can't figure out if I did something or if it's who they are. I only share one class, and it's with Nyx. I try to stay out of their way as much as possible.

Eaglewood Cemetery gives me the creeps, and that's saying a lot considering I live for this sort of thing. Massive iron gates welcome you as you drive down the road. Oak trees guard the property everywhere you look. Guarantee they are over a hundred years old. Both sides of the road are lined with tombstones and mausoleums. Leaves that have fallen are now gathered against each tombstone. Fall is such a beautiful season, except for this night. As I said, Eastwood is fucking weird. I never understood why they went all *purge* like on this night. Well, in a way, I do, but to involve the whole town.

Following the directions to the new grave, I find it over the hill towards the back, I'll have to walk to get to it. Grabbing my bag off the front seat, I jump out of the van, heading to the back, I swing open the doors. I'm greeted with a beautiful sight. All my things are neatly placed in Rubbermaid containers on the left side. I take my shovel, to begin with. I'll come back for everything else later.

Do I feel guilty for digging bodies up? No. I probably should, but it's not like I'm doing anything horrible to them. Their bodies are technically being used for good, even if they never wanted them to. We all make sacrifices, even when we are dead.

The nice thing about fresh graves is that the soil hasn't had time to compact. It only takes me a couple of hours to dig. The best thing about this school is the gym. Can you imagine me doing this with noodle arms? I grab a baby wipe from my bag to wipe some dirt off my hands. I can't stand dirty hands. I also can't stand wearing gloves. It's a vicious cycle. I take a body bag, hooks and a crowbar

from the van. This is the part that gets tricky and where I sometimes wish I had an extra person. Before I do anything further, I make sure no one is around. I don't trust this night any more than any other night. When I'm only greeted with silence, I continue. Wrapping a bandana around my face, I grip my crowbar as I stare down into the hole housing a dirty coffin. With a deep breath, I jump back down.

I'll save you the nitty gritty. After opening the casket, I prep the body for hauling it upwards. I know this is a lot for a five-foot-two little old me. Remember, I've been doing this for a year now, so it's all repetitive motion, plus my professor only gives me certain bodies that he thinks I can handle. Climbing out of the hole, I lay out the body bag getting ready for the most challenging part. Now I'm no physics major, but with no leverage, this is taking the longest.

"Fuck me, Joe, why are you so heavy? How much shit did they stuff you with?"

Sweat pours down my back, my biceps are ready to give out, and I'm panting like a bitch in heat. This body is heavier than I expected. With a few more tugs, their feet are finally above ground. I plant my hands on my knees to regain my breath—no need for cardio. I get plenty of it. After what feels like a lifetime, I zip up the bag. It's time to drag Joe back to the van. My favourite gigs are when I can park closer. But that's also me being extremely lazy. Opening the doors, I step in the back to drag the body bag inside; with one final pull, I get it into the van. I slam the door shut, resting my back against

them; I wipe the sweat off my forehead, letting out a deep sigh. I take a deep inhale of the night's crisp air. Closing my eyes, I take a few minutes to enjoy the silence because we're headed back to crazy town. I wish every night were like tonight. There's just something about Halloween that makes my soul happy. It's too bad it doesn't last longer than one night. I wished I lived somewhere different from this place. I open my eyes, glancing at Eastwood in the distance. I guess I better get this done with.

I'm barely in town when the streets are littered with more people running in every direction. It's the most I've seen by far. Said jack-o-lanterns are now smashed everywhere. Soon crime will be ridden come midnight, and that's when the gangs fall amongst the town. The time that I need to be somewhere other than outside. Those three I spoke of earlier belong to the gang The Soul Stealers. How you might ask that I know this. It's rather fucking easy. They make it well-known around campus.

I've kept my bandana on with my dark hair in a messy bun. My disguise is working for now; making my way back to the school, I need to unload before heading to the other cemetery. The east side of the school is still vacant. Guess no one wants to hang around here tonight. Backing up to the loading dock, I get out and unlock the doors. I find a gurney in one of the anatomy labs. I wish I had more room in the van for one of these. Once the body is loaded, I wheel it back to the lab, placing it in the cooler. With a heavy breath, I begin the toughest job of the night.

Travelling down main street, it's eerie. A couple of trashcans are set on fire. Let me know; the gangs are already coming out, and everyone is running around yelling and chasing each other. I see a small crowd gathering around the alley entry; chances are it's a small orgy going on. Shop owners take precautions for their businesses and board everything up, but that won't stop most people. I hit the brakes as a group of clowns dash out in front of me. One hits the hood of the van and waves his bat at me. My heart jumps in my throat, but luckily they run off towards the park. Once I'm inside the cemetery, I'll be safe. I repeat this until I believe it. I hear motorcycles in the distance growing louder. I hit the accelerator. Like hell, I'm getting caught in that shit. I make one last turn, and I'm here. Dark stone pillars with a wrought-iron fence the entire perimeter, large gargoyles loam overhead guarding all that live here now.

Too bad it'll be losing two of its residences. I know what you're thinking. *Jesus, Cat, don't you have a fucking heart.* I do. But she's black as the darkest of night. I wasn't always the normal kid growing up, so I was built to be tougher. I guess I was a little too tough because I don't care what happens anymore. I prefer the dead over the living; they at least can keep all my secrets to themselves. Never spilling anything while I bitch to them about this miserable life I'm living.

I park next to a mausoleum, and I read over my text. I need to make sure I'm in the right area. Sometimes they all look the same, especially at night. Third on the left, but it's the fourth down. That doesn't make any fucking

sense to me. It looks like I'm not driving any further after all. There are rows and rows of mausoleums down here. I just wanted a quick night. *Fuck.* It's getting late. I knew I should've waited for these two until tomorrow. Digging took a little longer than I expected tonight.

The motorcycles revving is a steady sound in the distance. I don't think they would come here because why would they? I'm the only one here. No one ever hides out with dead things. They are all out looking for someone to shack up with or causing small riots on main street with the gangs. Giving my head a shake, I get back to work. I don't have time to worry about everybody else's business. I have other pressing matters to worry about, like finding this stupid grave. I'll have to come back for the last one. Making the final turn, I finally see the fresh grave.

As I'm digging, I feel like I have eyes on me, but that's insane. I've checked this area over occasionally to make sure I'm alone. I haven't seen or heard a peep out of anything. Even the animals don't want to be out. I can't shake the feeling, though; my skin is crawling by the time the hole is finished. Once the body bag is laid out, I can't take it anymore. I crouch low and take in the cemetery. It's a cloudy night, and thankfully the moon is hidden, letting me become invisible as well. I scan what I can take in the mausoleums, not seeing anyone or thing, squinting to ensure I didn't miss any reflection, but nothing is there. My mind must be finally catching up with me. I jump back into the hole, attaching the hooks around the body's armpits.

"I'm sorry for what I'm about to do," I mumble. Then I climb out of the hole.

As I have the body halfway out, the crunching of leaves has me halting my movements.

"Fuck," I whisper.

I slowly turn my head to see what is coming up behind me; my heart jumps in my chest when more leaves crunch. My biceps twitch from holding a body for longer than I've ever had before. If I have to do this for longer, I will drop this poor thing. Would they notice if I lowered it back down? I'll take my fucking chances. Inch by a painful inch, I lower it back down. Every time I do, I pause, and I can hear male voices to the left of me in the distance. I won't have time to clean and run. My best bet will be to dump and run and pray. It'll be a huge loss, but I can't come back once someone knows I've been here. I'm done for. I calculate the risk and say fuck it.

I take off like a bat out of hell. I make it halfway to the van when they yell at me.

"Hey, where the fuck did you come from?"

"Get her!"

"I'll cut her off."

Oh, I don't think so. Digging into my pocket, I find my keys. I know how this works; I'm not getting caught without being prepared. I can see my van in the distance. So, fucking close, I can hear the pounding of their boots quickly gaining on me. Guess I need that cardio after all.

"I'll call the cops on you fuckers," I yell over my shoulder.

The sad thing is the cops won't do anything tonight, and we all know it. I'm just wasting my breath. Once I'm caught, I'm caught. I stumble over a rock and tumble to the ground. I wince in pain when I smack my head on a tombstone. That's going to cost me time. I scramble to my feet, taking off again.

I didn't stand a chance as a body slammed into me from out of nowhere. His arms wrap around me, and a scream leaves me as we fly. We tumble on the ground, with me landing on the bottom. All the air in my lungs evaporated, leaving me gasping. Whoever landed on top of me wasn't getting off anytime. As I tried to suck air into my lungs, I got a look at the prick who landed on me.

What my eyes land on isn't what I was expecting. He's wearing a black hoodie with the hood up with a LED mask covering his face in lime green. When I look around, two more bodies come into view dressed the same way. The only difference is their masks. One is red, and the other is blue.

That's how I know I'm in deep fucking trouble.

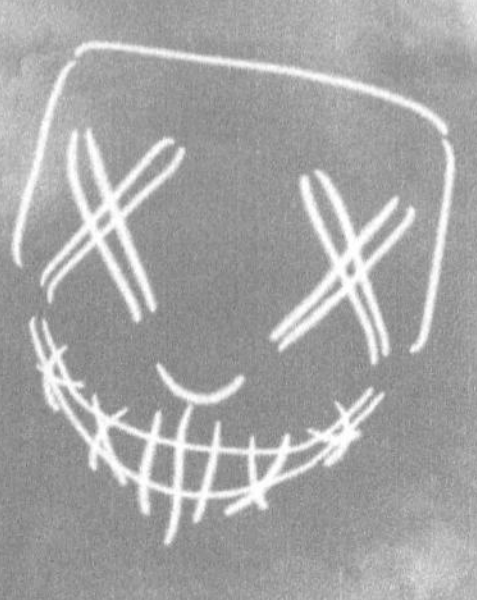

2
Catalina

The moment I laid my eyes on all three of them, I could feel their energy radiating off them. I knew I was in trouble. I'm thankful to be still wearing my bandana, and my identity is still hidden from whoever these three are.

The one wearing the red mask started laughing suddenly.

"Well, look what we caught for the night, boys. Fresh meat and no one around to save her." His voice was muffled from behind his mask, so I couldn't even figure out who he was.

The one on top of me shifts slightly, finally letting me get a deep intake of air into my lungs. He looks down at me. If only I could see his facial expression. His head

tilts to the side when his hand moves to my forehead—a spike of pain shoots before fading to an ache.

"You're bleeding, don't move."

Why he would care is beyond me. He reaches for the back pocket of his jeans when he pulls out a white paisley-printed bandana. That's when I should've had red flags going off. But my brain wasn't catching up to me yet. He goes about cleaning my cut.

"Seriously, dude, who gives a fuck if she's bleeding or not." The one in Red says. He's been a real dick this whole time. "She's only here for one reason tonight."

"I know it's a hard concept, but head wounds bleed a shit ton, and I don't need blood everywhere. So, if you don't mind, I'll get it to stop before we do anything further."

Well, so much for being a gentleman. The Blue masked hasn't said a single word. He's taking the entire scene in. I can only imagine the questions he has formed, and I ain't telling them shit. It's Halloween, so figure it out.

"Get her up, we only have a couple of hours left, and I'm not wasting any more time."

"Yeah, whatever. Don't worry. I didn't forget that you're in charge."

After the Green mask hauls himself up, his hand clamps around my upper arm, hauling me upwards. The world spins for a second before my body can catch up. My eyes ping between all three of them. Red stands the tallest. He's also the hugest. His hoodie is pulled tight around his muscles. Green looks to be a few inches shorter; although muscular, he doesn't compare. His

body felt solid while on top of me, and I'll admit it felt wrong to be turned on when he shifted his growing bulge into my needy pussy. I know he felt something because when he reached for his bandana, he moved forwards more than needed. I had to stifle a moan. They don't need to know how turned on I am for them. That's the last thing I need them to know, especially on this night. We all have a secret fantasy. Okay.

Now Blue is a mystery. He hasn't come any closer to where he currently is, so I'm assuming he's around the same height as Green, maybe taller. They are strangers of the night, after all. Do I really need to get to be besties with them? I need to get away from them and get the fuck home. I still have my keys in my hand, and I need a better opening to run.

"What do you want from me? I don't want anything to do with this night." I try to plead with them, hoping it'll be enough for them.

They all laugh, including Blue. His deep voice sent tingles through my body.

"I think you can guess, and I think you know Catalina," Blue says with venom in his voice.

My entire world shifts. How the fuck do they know me? I made sure to stay hidden tonight without running into anyone. This doesn't make sense. Green slowly lowers my bandana, giving away my facial expressions to them all.

"H-How do you know my name?"

Red only shrugs, not giving away anything. So do the other two. Wrenching my arm in Green's grip, I try to get

free, but his hand only tightens. Causing a small whimper to slip past my lips.

"Don't worry, you know us. We aren't quite strangers." Red speaks. His words brought some relief to my over racing brain.

"I don't understand any of this. How did you know where I was?"

"Let's just say we've been watching you for a long time now. We made the perfect opportunity to make our move tonight," Green speaks into my hair. Almost nuzzling close to me.

With a steady breath, I stomped his foot as hard as possible. His hold on me breaks, and I bolt. If they want me, they can work for it. I'm closer to the van than I thought. Their voices behind me yelled at me to stop. Like fuck, I'm listening to them. I've never been more nervous than I am right now, with adrenaline coursing through my body. It makes it hard to unlock anything, especially this van that will help me get away. I wish this van were equipped with remote locks, but she's older than time. My hands shake as I struggle to get the key in the hole. I can't hear anything besides the pounding of my heart. I drew in a shaky breath. I finally get the key in, only for another body to slam me into the van, pressing me flat up against the door panel.

"Didn't get very far, did we half pint?" Red whispers in my ear.

"Don't fuckin' call me that, you cunt." I elbow him in his hard abdomen. A small grunt comes out of him, making me smile. "Serves you right, jackass."

He runs his finger along my neck; goosebumps ripple along my skin. My only reaction is wanting to curl my toes and see where else he'll touch me. I can't let them know the effect they have on me. My body is a trader.

"What's wrong half pint, mad because you can't get away from us? Or mad because you like what we do to you?"

"I don't know what you're talking about," I hiss at him. "Don't fuckin' touch me again." I try jerking my head away from him, but it's hard when he has me pinned, pressing into me. His laugh vibrates against my back.

"Tell yourself what you need to, but you're not getting away from us. You'll be with us tonight. You can't outrun us. Your body wants us, no matter how much you lie to yourself."

That's when Blue comes close, taking the keys from my hand. His fingers gently caress over the top of mine, giving me a calming effect. Red hauls me out of the way while the doors get unlocked. Green rounds the back of the van producing a set of zip ties. My heart stills.

"You don't need those; I swear I'll behave." Swallowing the large lump that settled in my throat, they all stared at me. I can tell they don't want to take any chances, but neither do I. I don't want my hands restrained before I can argue anymore. Red tugs my arms behind my back. My breath hitches the second the ties touch my skin. I try to suck as much air as possible, but it's not helping. My mouth fills with extra saliva as bile creeps up my throat. I try to swallow multiple times, so I don't throw up everywhere. I can't focus on anything other than trying to calm

myself down. The last time I had a massive panic attack was when I left home. That was almost two years ago. I thought I had everything under control again. It wasn't until my vision faded that I knew I was in trouble. The pounding in my ears only grows louder by the second. When my knees buckle, large hands grab me around my biceps.

"Shit, maybe this wasn't such a good idea, man."

"It's a little late for that, don't ya think? Open the fuckin' door."

Their voices were muffled, and I couldn't tell who was talking. Strong arms lift me carrying me bridal style. I'm pretty sure it's Red. I can't help but rest my head on his chest. My entire body was spent of energy, and I lost my fight. My chest is still tight when I suck in deep breaths. It isn't until he places me inside the van that the tears start. My night is sealed.

"Don't worry, half pint. You're safer with us if you believe it or not."

I find that hard to believe, considering I have no idea who the fuck they are. They could be my worst nightmares, and I'm walking to death's door right now. Yet I feel safe, and I can't explain it. How fucked up is that? It's not until he closes the door that the other door closes, too, and I'm alone with Blue.

"You'll have fun with us tonight."

I don't say anything. I close my eyes and pray that this night goes by fast. It's only for the night. I can do this. I've lasted the other Halloweens, yet this one is turning into a nightmare. How fair is that?

It turns out home isn't my home. That would've been a dream. The house that stands in front of me is a black three-story Victorian that screams to my soul. How is it they live where I'm meant to be? This place is calling to me.

"Wow."

"Amazing, right? Come on Wednesday. I think you'll enjoy what we have in store for you."

I highly doubt that, especially with the way I'm feeling now. He helps me out of the van, and that's when I hear the bikes nearing the house. I haven't looked around; my eyes are still fixed on this gorgeous house. Hands land on mine, tugging at me backwards. My back collides with a solid chest. Their hand runs up my ribs, brushing alongside my breasts, causing a moan to fall from my lips.

"You like that, don't you, half pint?"

At the sound of his voice, I pull away. "Untie my hands. Maybe I will."

"That's okay. I rather like restrained. Gives me more control of your body." He tugs the zip ties again, causing my heart to skip a beat.

"Please, untie me," I whisper.

"One way to get over a fear is to face it," he whispers in my ear. He guides me towards the house, and when we reach the porch, I halt my moves. "Don't be scared. We'll take care of you."

I see Blue and Green enter the house, leaving the door open for us. Red's hands wrap around my waist, making me move into the house of horrors.

When I step inside, it nearly blows me away. The interior is dark like the outside; to the left of the front door stands a set of stairs leading to the second floor. To the right of me is the living room furnished with leather couches. Everything is so organized and kept clean. For a house filled with guys, I'm shocked. I'm led to another room further into the house, my body is buzzing with anticipation, yet I'm nervous at the same time.

"All the way, stand in the middle," Red tells me.

When I turn around, I'm greeted with such temptation. All three stand there, each dressed in jeans, a black hoodie and a mask. I still don't know who they are.

"She listens well. I'm impressed. Kneel." Green's voice comes out husky.

His voice makes my pussy throb the most, and it's already wet. I'm sure my panties are ruined, kneeling the best I can. I look up at them.

"Good girl," Blue says. Walking towards me, palming his growing bulge.

Sweet Jesus, that's turning me on even more.

"Tell me, have you ever done anything adventures in bed before?"

I dip my head; he cups my chin, lifting my head. My eyes stare into the blue cross stitches over his eyes on his mask.

"No need to be ashamed. We're not here to judge you."

With a deep breath. "I've only done the usual stuff, I guess."

The other two step forward, creating a circle around me. "We'll take things slow then, guide you into it."

"Into what?"

"This, you do want this, don't you? I can read your body like it's an open book, Catalina. Don't lie. How bad do you want to taste us?" Who knew the quiet one was always the freakiest? Blue runs his thumb over my bottom lip, and my eyes close, loving how my skin tingles at his touch. He pushes his thumb, past my lips, into my mouth.

"Suck," he demands.

I hollow my cheeks sucking, then stroking him with my tongue. He pulls out, giving me a groan.

"Please say you want this, Wednesday. I'm desperate to have you."

"Only for the night, right?" I look at all of them, and they eventually nod. I swallow the lump I have stuck in my throat. "Yes, I need you all. Please."

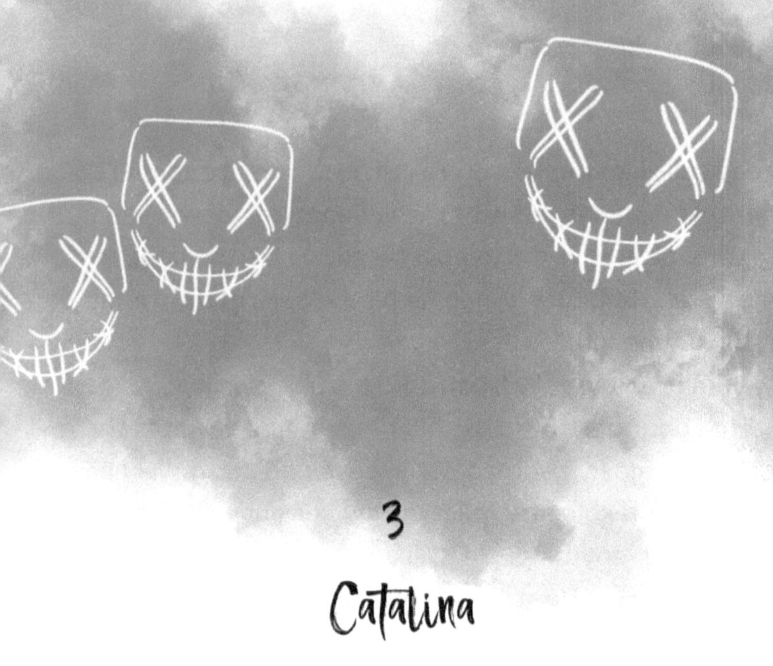

3

Catalina

All three of them undo their zippers. I grow wetter with each passing second, waiting for what's in store. I've never done anything this crazy before, and I can't believe I'm doing this. When I look over at Green, he's gripping his cock. Red's cock is hanging out, all ready half-hard. Waiting for me, when I look back at Blue, his cock is beautiful. I've never seen one like his before. His cock has a Prince Albert plus a pubic piercing. My pussy tightens at the thought of what pleasures it'll bring.

Red threads his hand in my hair, releasing it from the hair tie. Wrapping my hair around his hand, he tilts my head back.

"Open wide for him." Blue takes control of the group.

Without hesitation, I open for him, and he takes hold of his large cock, lining it up with my mouth. Holding my

head still gives him all control. I'll be the first to admit I'm not that experienced with giving head. He doesn't seem to care; he groans the deeper he goes. He's too large for me to take him fully. When he hit the back of my throat, I gag around him.

"Mmm, just like that, baby. Take it all."

He continues to thrust his hips; my eyes water the harder he goes. I spread my knees apart for more balance or to take some relief off my sensitive clit. I need something, anything. He pulls out of my mouth when Green steps up. He strokes himself, letting out a frustrated groan.

"Stick your tongue out for me."

Opening wide, I stick my tongue out. He slaps my cheeks with his cock, whipping his pre-cum all over me.

"Such a dirty girl, aren't you? How bad do you want his cock?" Blue asks while walking behind me. "Tell me, and I'll reward you."

"I want it so bad; I can taste it. Please."

"You heard her. Give her what she wants."

Blue wraps his hand in my hair while Green slides his cock into my mouth. I wrap my lips around him. Blue's other hand runs down my body working towards the waistband of my leggings. I let out a moan when his thumb caresses my stomach going inside my thong—Green grunts when Blue moves my head forwards. I take over the movements, moving until my nose touches his trimmed pubic hair. Pulling back on a gag, I take a deep inhale. As Blue's finger inches over my clit,

circling it. The sensation of both is overwhelming. His finger dips lower.

"So wet for us, aren't you, Wednesday. Enjoying yourself, are we?"

"Mmm hmm," I mumble around Green's cock. I continue bobbing as Blue's finger enters my slick core, bringing me closer to my waiting orgasm. I clench my inner muscles around him, closing my eyes when he strokes my g-spot. I can feel it nearing when he pulls his hand out of my pants. I whimper at the loss. I snap my eyes open. Green pulls out of my mouth, backing away.

"You've been a good girl. Should we get you out of these clothes?" Blue grabs my wrists, causing me to wince in pain. The coolness of a knife touches my wrist; with a flick, my hands are free.

I bring them forwards, giving them a slight rub. His hands run down my arm reaching for the hem of my shirt, and he pulls it over my head. My nipples pebble under all their stares. Even though I can't see them, I know they're looking. I'm sitting in my black lace bra, waiting. My entire body is on fire. Red extends his hand for me, placing my hand in his. I notice how he completely encloses around mine. You know what they say about large hands. Well, it's true, ladies. Cause I still can't take my eyes off his girthy cock. Swallowing the excess saliva, he pulls me up. This is it. No turning back. I'm allowed one night of craziness, right? It's not like I'll ever see them again.

"Are we doing this in here? I'm about ready to blow," Red tells the other two.

"Might as well. She's ready." Green agrees while pumping his cock.

I lick my lips while watching him. Why is that such a significant turn-on? The site alone makes my knees weak.

"Do you have any hard limits?" Blue asks.

I turn to face him. I bit my lip while narrowing my brows. "Um. I don't know what you mean?"

"Okay, for example. Fisting, breath play, double vagina or double penetration, spanking." He finishes speaking, and my jaw drops. What the actual Satan have I gotten myself into? Fisting? That's a pass. I don't need them to explain it, and I can take a wild guess. I'm also fond of breathing.

"The first two are a no." I try to say it with determination, but I'm sure my voice quivers at the end.

"That's okay. We have safe words in place anytime you don't feel safe or need to stop. Use them. We'll stop immediately. Yellow means slow and red means stop. Understand?" Blue informs me of everything.

"Please don't tie my hands anymore. That's a huge red for me."

He nods, I look at the other two, and they nod. I'll never tell them why. It's none of their business.

"Take your pants off. I want you in nothing but your underwear."

There is something about Blue that I want to figure out if only I had time. Untying my boots, I kick them off. Dipping my thumbs into my waistband, I bend down, dragging them along with me. I show my ass off to Blue.

I can hear him growl. Being the only one I haven't tasted yet, I tease him a little more. I wiggle my ass before I stand. I pull each foot out and toss them to the side as well. You'd be wrong if you think I'm wearing matching panties and a bra. Why would I be? I didn't expect to be hunted down. My thong is appropriate for the day, orange with bats.

"Mmm, these are hot." Red runs his hand over the seam of my thong, pulling the front upwards. I hiss with the added pressure to my clit. He lands a smack on my sensitive clit. I jolt from the bite.

"Oh, fuck. Yes." My knees wobble. I've never had my pussy smacked before. Holy hell, does it feel amazing? I can feel wetness on the inside of my thigh, and I'm aching for more. Red peels my thong off, revealing my naked pussy in front of him.

With a deep inhale, his finger traces my slit. "Feels amazing, doesn't it." Then he spreads my lips open, pinching my clit.

"Fuck." I gasp. The other two step up to my side, and my hands dart for their cocks. Giving me something to hold on to while I'm thrown into pure ecstasy. Red flicks my clit with his tongue before he goes back to rubbing it, causing my hips to jerk forwards. He takes hold of my left ankle, lifting my leg and placing it over his shoulder. The other two steadies me around the waist. This new position opens me up further. I throw my head back, moaning louder. I pump each cock faster the closer I get to my orgasm. As he slips a finger inside, within seconds,

he tickles my g-spot. I scream out my orgasm. I move my body back when I feel liquid squirt out of me.

"That was fucking hot. Let's do that again."

"What the fuck just happened?" I look down at him in horror.

"Baby, you squirted all over him," Green sounds excited when he tells me.

"S-Squirted? It felt like I peed all over him." I try to bring my leg down, but Red only tightens his hold.

He runs his hands up my inner thigh. "That's right. You've never experienced that before. Felt amazing, didn't it?"

I can't explain it. It was overwhelming. My entire body felt like it was on fire. My legs were still shaking from the aftershocks. "I've never had it happen before. It's so embarrassing." I fold my head into my hands.

"It's beautiful. I think she's ready for us. Where's the blindfold?"

At the mention of a blindfold, I lift my head. That's adding so much trust in these men. Can I do this? Fingers grasp my chin, turning my head to face Blue.

"Use your safe word. We already know your hard limits. Anything we do, we'll explain, and you can tell us to stop. You understand?" I wish I could see his eyes to see if he was telling me the truth. All I have to go off is his muffled voice. My gut is giving me a small warning but no huge red flags.

"Okay. Yes. I trust you all."

Electricity intensifies in the air, sealing my fate for the night. Green walks towards me, holding a black silk blind-

fold, running his hands over it. My heart jumps when he stands behind me, placing it over my eyes. My world becomes dark. I only have my four senses to go on now. Touch, smell, taste and hearing. Thankful that they won't take my touch away again.

A hand touches my neck, causing me to jump. Goosebumps trickle over my body when the hand moves alongside my arm. Another hand runs up my thigh while the last set unclasps my bra. The straps fall before someone removes it entirely.

"Oh, fuck. Baby, look at these beauties." I know that's Green from the nickname he uses. When his warm mouth latches onto my nipple, I realize why I needed the blindfold. They've taken their masks off. He bites on my right nipple while a hand plays with my clit. The moans slip freely from me now.

A tongue darts out and traces over my clit before sucking it.

"Yes, more, please." My entire body is on fire, and it needs something more. A finger is added to my needy core while he continues to suck my clit. My hand darts out to grip their hair, pushing him further into me.

"Want something else to hold, Wednesday?"

I can only nod. A hand takes hold of the one with which I'm gripping the hair, guiding it to the side. When I touch a velvet like tip, I open my hand. There's no piercing, so I know this is Green. A hand threads into my hair, turning my head to the side.

"Open for me. I need to feel you." The sound of his voice makes me clench around Red's finger.

"She loves when you talk. I can feel her tighten." Red groans.

I open for Blue while he slides his cock into my mouth. I take my other hand, wrapping it around him. I flick my tongue over his piercing, lowering my head further. When Red hits my g-spot again, I moan around Blue's cock and pump Green faster.

"I'm gonna come if we don't do something soon." Green halts my move, causing me to release him from my grip. Red removes his finger, and then Blue pulls out of my mouth.

My chin is tilted upwards, and I can feel the warm air on either side of my neck. Eventually, they kiss down my neck and my heart skitters with the sound of foil being torn open. I can't believe I'm going to have sex with three men. How insane is this?

"Walk forward. He's waiting for you on the couch." With the help of both men, they lead me to the couch where Red is waiting for me. His hands wrap around my waist when I reach him, and he has no problem lifting me upwards. I place my hands on his shoulders. He's so broad he could be a football player.

He lines himself up, and he already feels too big. "You ready? What's the safe words?"

"Yellow and Red." I barely had the words out of my mouth before he slammed me down on him. I let out a scream when he stretches me wide. I can already feel myself coming. A smack lands on my ass, and it startles me at first, then he smacks me again. I groan with hunger. He smacks me one more time, and I explode. I grind my

hips chasing my orgasm more, digging my fingernails into his shoulders. All while he pounds deeper.

"Don't stop... feels too good." I squeeze my eyes when he groans and grunts. I clench around his throbbing cock.

"Fuck, you feel so good." He palms my breasts, pinching my nipples. "I'm gonna come soon." He grunts out. The next thing I know, I'm pulled off him. I hear the condom being ripped off. "Open now." I open my mouth for him right as he comes down my throat. "Yes, I love seeing my cum in your mouth. Stick your tongue out. Let me see it all."

I show him what he wants to see and swallow it all.

"Good girl, ready for more?"

"Yes, please." I squeeze my thighs together, trying to relieve some pressure.

I'm lifted onto another body and my hands land on a set of thighs. His large hands glide up my thighs towards my aching pussy, flicking my sensitive bud, and my hips jerk forwards.

"Please, I need you inside of me."

He lets out a chuckle. "You don't even know which one I am." From his voice alone, I know it's Green. Blue's voice is deeper and holds more power than the others. Red's voice is Gruff, and Green's voice is too smooth. Especially with the nickname he gave me. Not that I'll ever let them know I can tell the difference.

I moan when he adds pressure to my clit. My lower stomach begins to cramp with an oncoming orgasm. I'm about to come when he pulls away. I let out a whimper.

"Don't worry. I've got you." He goes back to rubbing, bringing me closer once again. Only for him to stop.

I let out a small cry. "Oh, God. Don't stop." I'm frustrated all to hell.

"So needy, aren't we." He lifts me, sliding his hard cock inside of me. "Fuck, that feels good. Doesn't it? He warmed you up nicely for me." He groans from behind me. "Use me, baby," he said in a choked voice.

I rocked my hips forward, his cock hitting my g-spot every time. A hand touches my cheek.

"You're doing so well. Let's see what else you can do." Blue's pierced cock touches my lips, and I dart my tongue out, licking the pre-cum from him. His hand threads into my hair, pulling it into one hand. The other hand runs down the length of my neck. I swallow deeply when he closes around my neck. "Make me come with your mouth."

I open for him; he rams his cock in until I gag. While I rock my hips on Green, Blue fucks my mouth. Green pulls my hips back while he takes over. Sweat drips down my back from how hard he's working me. All while Blue was still rocking in and out of my mouth. Drool falls between my lips and all down my breasts. When he finally pulled out, letting me breathe deeply. Before sliding back in, groaning when I swallow around him. He thrusts deeper each time, Green thrusts deep, and with one final thrust, he comes down my throat. He stays put until I swallow, then pulls out.

"Beautiful. You did real good." He wipes my lips, releasing my hair.

Green thrusts faster when my orgasm hits me hard—milking his orgasm from him as well.

"Oh, holy shit." He moans, going still with one last thrust, and he relaxes.

My entire body is spent. I've never had this much pleasure in my life, I'm riding on a high, and I never want to get off. Warm arms wrapped around my body, cradling me into them.

"You did so good. How do you feel?"

"Mmm, like I can sleep for days. My entire body feels like jello."

A kiss lands on my shoulder. "Come, I'll take you upstairs. You can rest."

Even behind the blindfold, my eyes close. I have little energy left in me to care where I go or how I get there. Even though I should, this night is one that I'll never forget.

I'm placed on a soft surface. Fingers brush under the blindfold lifting it off my face. I turn onto my side, slipping further into darkness.

"Think she'll be pissed once she finds out it's us?"

"Oh, probably. It'll be interesting when she does."

"Be prepared for tomorrow, then. Head to bed. Get ready for a battle."

Whatever they were talking about, I couldn't be bothered to be worried about. They probably have girlfriends out there that will find out. Not my problem.

I need sleep and lots of it.

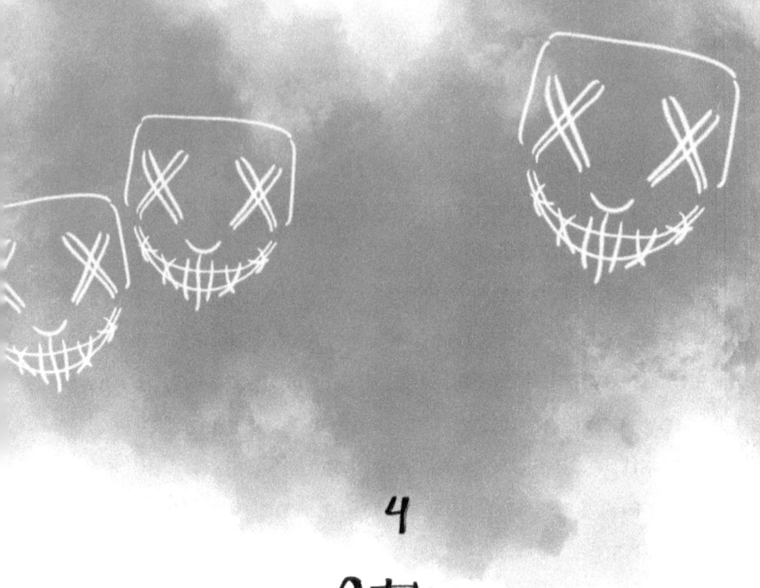

4

Catalina

My body is sore but in a good way. Three men have never railed me; I guess, technically, two. Never in my wildest dreams did I ever see this happening. The scary thing is they all seemed somewhat familiar, like I'd known them from somewhere before. Especially Green. I swear I've heard his voice daily, but that can't be right. *Can it?* I must've gotten too much cock last night. That's all.

Cracking open my eyes, I can see where I am. The room I'm in is too bright and cheery for me. The bedding is white; the furniture is white. Why does everything have to be white? The downstairs is perfect. Dark. This room doesn't belong here. I sit up for it to be worse. I swear my grandmother heaved her decor in here. There is a motherfucking afghan draped across the end of the bed.

Knitted in different coloured squares. Then on the night-stand is a crochet doily. *Who are these people?* I need to get out of here and quickly.

I find my clothes neatly folded on the dresser. All that's missing are the keys to the van. *Perfect.* Pulling on my leggings, I hear the floorboards creak outside my door. I pause my movements. When the footsteps continue, I quickly finish getting dressed. Peeking through the door's keyhole, I can't see anything. Cracking the door open, it sends out a small groan in protest. *Swing it fast, stupid.* Swinging it fast, it's quieter. The stupid brain is constantly being right. The hallway is empty when I step out. The hallway is decorated in modern Victorian. Burgundy walls, floral floor runner, gold picture frames. It takes my breath away. Heading down the staircase, I take notice of the pictures on the wall. It's filled with frames, not just any frames. There are bats pinned in one, a larger frame with three moths. The oddities only continue the further you go down the stairs. The double-headed mini skull would be my favourite.

If I were van keys, where would I be? I walk in the direction of the room we were in last night. Maybe Blue left them in there somewhere. Entering the room, I finally get a look at it. It turns out to be a den. A leather couch is angled in front of a fireplace with two accent chairs to the side, and I still don't know how I didn't notice it yesterday. Bookshelves line the furthest wall, filled to the brim. A small bar cart tucked to the side is fully stocked. This room reeks of masculinity.

As I look around, I remember what happened last night. Heat creeps up my neck with the thought of all three of them touching me, and I place my cold hands on my cheeks to cool them down a little. Leaving this room, I hunt down a different room. Maybe the kitchen. This is why I should always hide an extra set in the fucking gas cap. I could've snuck out already. I expected the kitchen to be empty when I walked in, but it wasn't.

Someone is standing at the stove.

Without their shirt on.

Without their mask on.

I'm not sure which one between Green or Blue they are. But sweet baby Jesus, the back muscle. Red is broader, so I know it's not him. But whoever this is. Fuck me again, please. How did I get so lucky for them to find me? The other question is, do they know me?

"Oh, sorry. I didn't mean to interrupt. I need my keys. I should be getting back home."

He hums in return. Not sure what that means. Is that an 'okay, sure see ya' or a 'no, you need to stay longer' hum?

He continues going about his business, ignoring me. Not sure what I should do, I back out of the kitchen. I can tell when I'm usually not wanted. Obviously, we aren't a morning person. I'll try the living room. If they aren't in there, I'll walk home. I'll ask the professor to tow the van at my expense. Even though I can't afford it, I can't leave it sitting here. It's too valuable.

The living room is still quiet when I enter, and the only thing is there are now two shirtless men standing by the

front window. I gotta swallow the drool that pools in my mouth. One is Red, for sure. I wasn't lying when I said he could be a football player.

"Have either of you seen my keys?" I'm starting to get nervous about how no one will talk to me. Footsteps fall behind me.

"Wednesday, it's been a real pleasure having you all night."

At the sound of Blue's voice, I turn around.

My world tilts on its axel, and my entire life can be seen crashing before my eyes. Atomic bombs have nothing going on with what's happening right now. How did my brain not figure this out before now?

No, no, this can't be happening. I swing my head back around again. My skin crawls, and my stomach churns. Bit by bit, I backed away from all three of the school gang members. Dorian, Nyx and Cole. Tears fill my eyes when last night plays in my mind. I had sex with two of them. I gave all of them blowjobs. My lips tremble, and I bring my hand to my mouth, shaking my head.

"This can't be happening. You knew this entire time." My voice cracks at the end.

Dorian steps closer to me. His broad shoulders over-shadowed me. "We did. Thanks for last night, by the way."

"We knew you enjoyed it; it's a shame you didn't know our names to scream them." Nyx's smooth voice washes over me.

I turned back to stare at Cole, his blue eyes darkening more. "Don't get us wrong. We enjoyed every sound you

made." He tosses something to me. When I caught it, I saw my keys.

"I hate you all!" I scream savagely. "I can't believe you did this to me. This is an all-time low, even for you, Cole." I storm towards the front door to the sounds of their laughter.

I've never wanted to die more than I do right now.

I couldn't get the van started fast enough. Peeling out of that driveway should've felt refreshing; shame, that's what it feels like. I feel like a dirty, worthless person. How could I do this? I should've said no, the first chance I had. Then again, would it matter? For some unknown reason, they aren't fans of mine. I drive back to the cemetery. I still have a job to finish, even if I want to crawl under the body that I need to bring back. I brush away the tears that continue to fall.

This is such bullshit.

They don't deserve my tears.

No one does.

With that, I pull up my big girl panties and hopefully try to move on. I can only hope that come Monday at school, and they won't try anything. I can only hope I'll be that lucky. Every day they pull something on me.

Having Nyx in my philosophy class is bad enough. I can't escape him. He sits directly behind me, not rows back or a few seats to the left. Directly behind me, breathing down my back. Watching my every move, I can't escape him until the class ends. Even then, he walks out when I do, then Dorian and Cole meet up with him in the hallway, following close behind me. The last time

they did anything was right before Halloween. I should've seen this coming.

Professor Adams kept talking, but I couldn't focus any longer. My night was a little longer than I had hoped for. I was gearing up for Halloween night, and I knew it was going to be a fucking shit show. When he finally dismissed us, the hairs on my neck raised before I could get out of my seat. I grab my bag, ignoring the dirty looks coming from Nyx. Walking past him, he sticks his foot out, tripping me before I can dodge it. I land on my knees, and my bag spills everywhere. Books, tampons, pens. Fucking everything spilled across the floor. Everyone that was left behind laughed. Heat blossomed across my cheeks.

"Sorry, didn't mean that." He walks away without helping me.

I watch him walk out, meeting up with his buddies. I try to avoid their presence when I finally leave the room. I can hear their mumbles behind me when I try to get more distance between us. If only that lasted.

"What's the matter? Cat got your tongue?" Dorian's voice was closer than I expected.

I keep walking, praying they'll leave me be.

"You know, we'll always find you. You'll never be able to escape us, Catalina." How my name slid out of Cole's mouth sent shivers down my spine.

Cole is the worst of them all. He's ruthless. He's the one that started tormenting me every chance he got. He sent Dorian and Nyx to do the job when he couldn't. Like today, it's up to Nyx to embarrass me. Maybe one day I'll figure out

what I did to cause all of their attention, but I know for one thing I don't fucking want it.

Life would've been perfect if it wasn't for them. Now I feel like my entire life is a mess. Even going to work feels like a form of violation. I look down at the open grave. The body is exactly how I left it. All my equipment was thrown around from my quick getaway. The early morning brought in a low coverage of fog, so if I'm going to do this, I better work like the speeding bullet. The last thing I need is a nosy Nancy calling the cops on me. After reapplying the hook to the body, I haul it upwards. The tarp is wet with dew, but it'll have to work. I won't have time for the other one until tonight.

As always, the campus parking lot is empty; the same can be said about my soul right now. I'm running on fumes. I only want to get home to wash away the terrible night. After leaving the body, I restock the van, having everything ready for tonight. Grabbing my keys from the cup holder, I head toward my baby. At least driving in her will boost my spirits for a little while. *Hopefully.*

The purr that comes from her is a welcoming sound. Even though she may be a little old for some, she has never disappointed me. Like almost everything else in my life, I can count on her. Johnny has gotten me out of some terrible times, moved me to this fucked up town, and after graduation, she'll be moving me again. I don't know what I would do without her. While driving back to my apartment, I can see all the destruction that went on last night. Litter lines the road, driving past the park. I can see people passed out in compromised positions. So

disgusting. That's where the kids fucking play you pigs. Now your cock and balls have literally touched all the playground equipment.

I want to throw up. This town drives me mad. You are all probably asking yourselves. 'Then why did you move here, Cat?' I'll tell you. The art program at EU is the best, it also doesn't help that I won a scholarship, so I don't have to pay back so many student loans. I would have gone to a smaller school if I knew what I was getting myself into with the three men and this backward town. Not that I have any family waiting for me or any I give a shit about anymore—the joys of writing them all off. I don't need drama. I like to avoid it any chance I can. Then what happens? Dorian Prescott, Nyx Thornton. Then Cole Valentine, a stupid last name if you ask me, he isn't filled with love. His heart is filled with darkness.

The second I unlock my door, I feel the stress leave my body. One step closer to that bed, which has been calling my name for hours, I'm a dirty fucking mess. I still needed to clean the cut on my head from the tombstone yesterday. You would think they would've fixed me up a little before they had their fun, but apparently, all they were thinking about was getting off. I can't say much. I was too. I'll never forgive myself for what I did.

"That's because you're stupid, Cat."

I flick on the light in the bathroom, finally looking at myself in the mirror. I cringe when I see my forehead. The gash is bigger than I expected. I'm surprised I didn't have a headache from it. Opening the cabinet, I dig around until I find a washcloth; I don't have a first aid kit, guess

it'll have to go unbandaged. After I clean it, I climb into the shower. Washing away all the filth and scrubbing until my skin turns pink. My mind keeps flashing back to last night after they all took me to their house, I should've known something was wrong, yet my gut never warned me unless you count the white bandana from Nyx's back pocket. That should've been a clue as to who they were.

I wanted it.

How sad is that?

Is my life so pathetic that I wanted a little action and adventure, that I was willing for strangers at the time to take me? Then the second I find out it's the three of them, I run instead of facing them and telling them how I really feel about them and giving them hell.

Loser, that's what I am. That's what I'll always be.

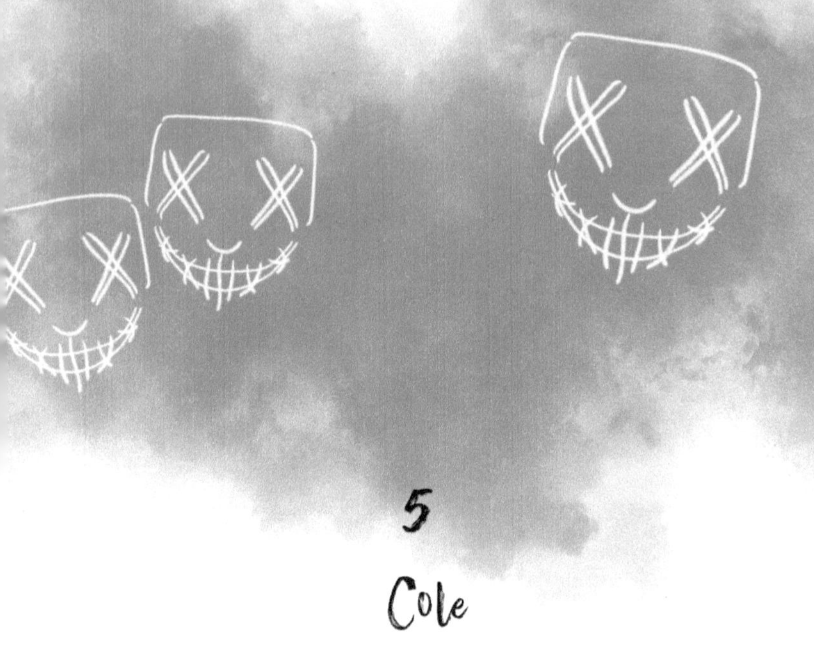

5

Cole

This morning was a whirlwind. After Catalina left, I received a phone call from the president of our gang, telling us to get our asses down to the warehouse. I didn't bother asking questions. I knew better. Belonging to the Soul Stealers, we had important roles to play. We're all enforcers, so if he's calling, it's gotta be important. No matter how much I want to relive Cat's mouth in my mind, we have to head out.

"This better be good. I have important shit to do today." Dorian grumbled as he pulled his pants on.

"*Seriously?* I highly doubt he would be calling us for a spot of fucking tea," Nyx calls from his bedroom.

I sometimes question how I'm still friends with these two. Even after all these years, we've stuck together. We've seen some weird shit, been through the worst and

yet stayed together. I have a feeling whatever we're about to get into today won't be anything different. After last night, this town is going to be a mess. After the new mayor took over, he had new ideas he wanted to try. One is no rules on Halloween night. I think it was a way for him to experiment without being called out on it, fucking pig if you ask me. Now we're responsible for cleaning up his mess.

"Hey, I need a lift to my bike," I call to no one in particular. I hated to leave it last night, but I'm sure it was safe in the cemetery. Not many people went there, and I'll admit I was a little surprised to see *her* there. We were only kidding when we said we were watching her. We were only doing a drive-by when I noticed a van parked there. I figured it was another drug van. When we saw it was her, we came up with our plan.

"I can give you a lift, and you're riding bitch though." Dorian pats me on the back before walking down the stairs. Fuckin' prick.

I throw on my hoodie as I jog downstairs. The guys are waiting for me like always, I'm not sure how I became the leader of this group of ours, but it seems fitting Dorian brings the muscles, and Nyx is the calm one of the group. Me, I'm the cruel one. I take no pity on anyone. I could give two shits about how they felt. Think anyone cares about my feelings? The answer you're searching for is no. So, the faster you learn that the world is a cesspool, the quicker we'll get along.

The first day of November is always chilly, but thankful enough that we never have to give up riding our bikes. If

I ever had to move to a snowy location, that's the day I'll visit the cemetery for good.

Dorian rides like a fucking pussy. The quicker I can feel the vibration of my bike, the better. Eastwood Cemetery is in the middle of town. Rather weird to build a town around dead people, then they have another cemetery because one wasn't enough. I'm telling you, this town is funny. Yet, people still move here. The cemetery comes into view, and I feel relieved when I see that my bike is still parked where we left it, *thank God.* I pity anyone that would've touched her. I looked around for anything that belonged to her, but you couldn't tell she was here. I have so many questions about what the fuck we witnessed.

"We better hurry before Henry loses his fucking gasket," Nyx said, gripping the handlebars of his black Harley Davidson Street Bob. Well, to be honest, we all have Street Bob's. Mine's grey, and Dorian's is red. It's the best for quick getaways. When you do what we do, you need to be quick.

"Yeah, yeah. He won't say anything until we get there, anyway. He can hold his fuckin' pants for all I care," I say as I climb on my beauty. Tilting my head, they follow when I take off. The ride to the warehouse is calming to my soul. The town is a disaster. If this is why Henry is calling, it'll be for a clean-up, as much as I love participating in the Halloween festivities. Clean-up duty is the least part of the fun. When Henry agreed to this with the mayor, I don't think this is what he had in mind. But it keeps everyone off our backs.

Our warehouse is at the edge of town, surrounded by trees. You would miss it from the road if you didn't know what you were looking for. The Soul Stealers' residence is one of a kind. The warehouse houses the office, gun room and my favourite room. The torture room. I could eat and sleep in them. Whenever a body is brought to my door, I'm ready to get answers from them. Whatever it takes, I'm down for it. A broken bone here, a stab wound there. Hell, I even go as far as shoving a metal rod up one dude's dick before. He squealed like a fuckin' pig with all the secrets we were waiting for. Men are easy to get answers from. They really value their dicks.

Behind the warehouse is a few empty sheds. Henry tried to convert them into houses, but no one wanted to stay in them. We all felt like it through off cultic vibes. So, we have our own place in town instead. Which works well, considering we all go to school. Something I wish we didn't have to do. It's Henry's wishes everyone in the gang must attend university. I think it's the most half-witted idea he's ever had. Like, what gang member is educated? Luckily, it's only one more year, and I'm fuckin' finished. With a useless degree that I'll never use.

"Come on, let's get this over with. I'm sure it has something to do with the town's mess."

"Oh, one hundred percent. Did you see the park? All those naked bodies. I only have one stuck in my head that I won't be getting out of my mind anytime soon." Dorian groans while adjusting himself.

I can hear Nyx groan behind me as well. "I'd have to agree. She was amazing. I still think we could've gone a different way this morning."

I stop dead in my tracks, turning around. "Seriously. That's what you're worried about? I didn't hear you complain when you were balls deep in that cunt of hers."

He throws his hands up. "Hey man, that's not what I meant, and you know it. All I'm saying is we could've done things differently."

See, the thing with Nyx is, although he's the calmest. He's also the nicest one. He hates when we need to teach Catalina a lesson. The reasons aren't important right now.

I head towards the warehouse door, not waiting for them. Pushing the door open, everyone in the gang greets me. Freddy sits by the office door, watching who's coming and going. He's got to be pushing ninety, but I saw him kill a guy last week. He's not one to mess with. He's also lived in this town his entire life, so he's the one to ask about anything. The boys and I usually meet with him on Sundays for coffee and small talk. It's nice to have someone older to have a decent conversation with. He waves us into the office with a dip of his chin. I dip my head in return before I find my seat at the large table.

Now you might think this is like an MC club, but no. We are far from that. We are worse were a gang. We aren't called Soul Stealers for a reason. The only rank this gang has is technically Henry. The only reason we are called the enforcers is that we aren't afraid to finish a fuckin' job. We deal in drugs, guns, prostitutes and more. When

I say we are worse, trust me on this. We don't deal with a sexual Halloween purge for nothing.

Henry clears his throat before he talks. "All right, girls, some things have been happening around town that no one can explain." He looks around at every single one of us, pausing dramatically. I can't help but roll my eyes.

"Spill it, Henry. It can't be that exciting," I tell him, trying to hold back a yawn.

"Always with the negativity, aren't you, Cole? If you must know. Someone has been playing around in our backyard. There is apparently a new dealer in town. I need to send them a little message. Give them the royal treatment, if you know what I mean. I'm sending Cole and his boys out on this one." He nods at me, and I keep a straight face showing no emotion. I can't tell him how much I'm looking forward to this. After last night, I need more of an outlet. Don't get me wrong, coming down Catalina's throat was remarkable, but I want the real thing from her.

"On it, you won't be disappointed."

He gives me a smirk. "Never am with you. I'll text the details to your burner."

With that, he dismisses us. Whoever this new dealer is, he's in for a real treat, that's for sure. I don't put up with fresh meat very well, especially ones that take food from our mouths. This town isn't big enough for more than one dealer. Surprisingly enough, it's big enough for a university, but that thing is older than time. Most of the outbuildings should be condemned. It's disgusting how far this town has let the buildings go to waste; they only

care about the medical facilities. It's what brings the most students here, not that I'll complain. The students are our biggest drug clients.

"So, what's the plan? Go in like always and ruff them up a little?" Nyx questions as we walk outside.

"Nah, I have a better idea. Dorian, do you still have those explosive packs we used last time?"

"Like you have to fuckin' ask," he says with a slight laugh. "How many packs do you think you need? Anything else?"

"Maybe a three and a couple of timers. We'll drop by, say our peace, then blow up their shit to seal the deal. If that doesn't tell them we're serious, then they really are dense."

They both laugh, but I know they are excited for tonight. Killing gets us all amped up. The only thing that would be better is a nice warm pussy to sink our dicks into. I have to stop thinking of Catalina so much; it's only pissing me off even more. I just didn't know she would respond to us the way she did. Even if she didn't know who we were at the time. She handed over all control. I didn't think she would, my dick twitches with the thought of her under my control again. With that thought, I start my bike taking off back to the house. I can't let her get under my skin, it was one thing to let her suck me off, but it's another thing to keep thinking about her.

The streets are a little cleaner, another thing about the mayor. His image is everything. Other mayors would be ashamed of him if word got around what this town did. The only saving grace is they hold a meeting here

in mid-November every year. So, he has no choice but to clean the town up. If any significant riots did break out, he would have so much explaining to do. I almost want to cause one next year just to watch him piss his pants in front of everyone. By the time we roll into the driveway, I'm already thinking of ways of destroying our competition. Let me tell you, it'll be sweet, sweet revenge when I'm finished with them.

When it's time to go, we load our bikes. When I look over at Dorian, he's all smiles when he packs his side saddles with his bag of goodies. You be surprised to learn that he isn't taking chemistry in school. He's only taking what he needs for a shitty degree that he won't use. His life is the gang and only the gang. Nyx, on the other hand, is harder to read. His face is nothing but his poker face. He'll keep everything inside until the last second. Don't think he won't blow your brains out because he speaks softly. That's how he draws his enemies closer.

It's late evening by the time we roll into the Southside of town. I have to laugh at the name they call themselves. Death Eaters. Like fucking come on. It's like they placed names in a hat, and that's the one they pulled out. I swear someone in that gang likes *Harry Potter* too much. Their house isn't anything to get excited about. It sits in the middle of two other houses. One house is abandoned

and boarded up. The other looks to be occupied. I'm not one for innocent causalities, but I can't risk a gang member living in that house if we tell them to leave.

Dorian must be on the same page as I am. "I'm going to set the explosive on the left side so the abandoned house takes the most abuse."

"I would agree. I'll keep watch. I send the single if I see anything," I tell him before he creeps towards the side of the house.

Nyx scans the area while I keep watch on the gang's house. The only sound is the thumping of bass coming out of the house. It sounds like they are having a grand old time. Too bad we're about to crash it like a bunch of pricks that we are.

Dorian comes running back, giving us a thumbs up. "I'll blow them once we leave. I set them around the back, close to the basement. I'm sure that's where they set up production."

"Good, let's head in."

For a drug house, it was kept clean outside. I guess they didn't want the cops to be showing up at their doorstep anytime soon. They should've thought of us instead. Drawing our guns out, I didn't even bother knocking. I give Dorian a nod, and with one swift kick, the door crashes down. The music stops instantly. We are greeted with guns pointed at our faces. I couldn't help but laugh.

"Seriously." I spread my arms out wide. "You all have the balls. Who's in charge here?" Looking around, I wait for someone to point out the asshole I'm about to destroy. When no one makes a move, I cock my desert eagle

and shoot the nearest person. The thud when the body hits the floor sends a flurry all around us.

Three against, well, to be honest, I couldn't even count them all. It doesn't matter cause Nyx is dropping them like flies. He's the only double-fisting his desert eagles, firing a path on either side of him, looking like a total badass. Which don't get me wrong, he really is. He may be the shortest between the three of us, but he's a killing machine. I'm still trying to find the fucking leader. Henry gave me a brief description of him, shaved head, short. Like, what kind of description is that? Anyone is short compared to my six-foot frame. Like, is he skinny like a twig, got a belly? Old or young. Nah, nothing like that. I could've shot the fuck by now.

"Where's your leader?" I grip some cunt by his shirt.

He spits on my hoodie. "I ain't tellin' you shit."

I look down at his gob of spit. Curling my lip, I look back at him. "Either you tell me, or I'll place a bullet in your dick, and you'll never be able to use it on a pussy again."

He pales, placing his hands over his dick. "He's in the basement."

"His name."

"S... Spencer, his name is Spencer," he stumbles out.

I shoot him anyway. I'm not a nice person, remember? He howls in pain. I only smile at his discomfort. "Thanks, sorry about your dick. My finger slipped."

I whistle for the boys. Letting them know where I'm headed. If you thought I would stick around for a fight, I'm about to start a new one. Apparently, with a guy named Spencer, I trust the boys to deliver a good message from

me. The basement is well-lit, with tables lined the entire length. Weed and Coke laid out, waiting to be delivered. There's a room in the back which I'm going to guess Spencer is hiding like a little bitch.

"Spencer, come out, come out wherever you are," I sing out, making my way toward the room I know he's in. I hear a crash inside. Not very quiet now, is he? Twisting the doorknob, I fling it open so fast I catch him trying to climb out the window. He slips, landing on the cement floor on his back.

"Oh, Spence. That's not how this is going to work. You see. I heard from a certain bird called the Soul Stealers that you decided to sell drugs in our town. That's not going to work for us."

He lets out a small whimper. "I swear I didn't know. I thought it was free game."

"See, now we both know that's bullshit. Eastwood is known for their gang. It's in your best interest to pack up and move out before something else happens. Compeesh?" I stand over him, hovering my foot over his hand, waiting for him to answer. When he hesitates. I step down, crunching his fingers under the weight of my foot.

He screams, struggling to remove his hand. "I asked if you under-fuckin stood. This isn't going to be an all-night conversation, so answer me."

"Yes! I get it. I'll leave," he yells while still struggling.

I lift my foot; he cradles his hand into his chest. "I also advise you to haul your ass upstairs and call you dirty men off mine. If they aren't dead by now."

Upstairs is nothing but a bloodbath. Everything is covered in red. With a shout from Spencer, his men halt their fighting. Perfect timing because I need this night to end. I'm sure Dorian is waiting to send them his big boom.

"Fuck this. Let's go. He was dealt with. If he can't figure out we're serious, that's on him."

"Good. I have some schoolwork to finish," Nyx informs us as we make our way outside.

"You always have some form of work to do. I don't know why you even try." Dorian grunts.

"It's because I don't want to be stuck in a gang for my entire life, Dorian," he spits out.

"Okay, that's enough. Fight at home." I cut in before they get too far into a fight, and we forget our actual purpose.

"Whatever. The timer will go off in five." He storms off towards his bike.

Work with your friends, they say, it'll be fun, they say. It's a fuckin' headache.

A huge boom is heard. I looked back, and the side of the house was gone. A huge fireball is shot up to the sky, lighting up the neighbourhood. You can feel the heat from where we're parked at the end of the street. I'm pretty sure we delivered our message loud and clear. Don't be doing business in our town. You won't be surviving.

By the time we get home, we're all beat.

"I'm calling it a night. I'll see you guys tomorrow." I wave at them before heading upstairs. I need to wash the night

off me. I can tell you one thing: I'm not looking forward to going to school tomorrow. Okay, that's a lie.

I'm looking forward to fucking with my Wednesday.

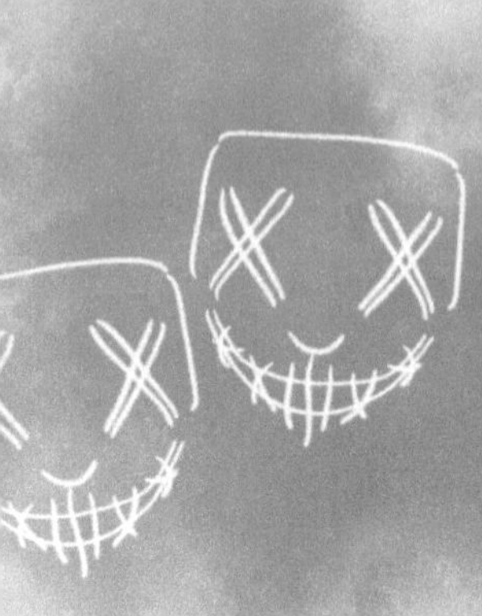

6

Nyx

I was never the one for school. I hated it, especially in high school. The only thing that keeps me going now is a certain raven-haired woman that sits in front of me in Philosophy. Yes, that may seem weird to some, but Catalina really is a beauty. Ever since the day I walked in here, I have been blown away. Then Cole made me watch every move she made. Whatever she did to him that day set him off.

I can't complain, except I can't handle hurting her anymore. I can tell by how her body stiffens that she knows I'm watching her. I'm sure she's waiting for us to pull another stunt like we did Halloween night. To be honest, I want a repeat of that night, but getting her to that point again, I don't see happening now that she knows it was us.

She turns her head ever so slightly, catching me watching her. Her eyes are what draws me in the most. I've never met anyone with violet eyes before. It wasn't hard to figure out who she was in the cemetery. I never take my eyes off her, and we continue to stare until Professor Adams' voice breaks and cuts between us.

"Mr. Thornton is Miss. Wilson more entertaining than I am?"

Catalina swings her head to the front; I can't help but smirk at her. "Sorry, professor couldn't help myself. You know how it is when a beautiful girl is around. All logical things are tossed out the window."

"Yes, well, not in my class or next time. The both of you will stay behind."

Her head snaps upwards. I'm pretty sure she wanted to say something, but she never got a chance. Professor Adams got back to teaching the class about theoretical philosophy. I still never paid attention; I went back to watching Cat. By the time we were dismissed, I had devised a plan. One that doesn't involve the other two. I watch her gather her bag, and when she stands, I damn near come in my pants. She's wearing black knee-high socks held up by a garter and a black miniskirt with chains hanging off her belt. Her graphic t-shirt is hidden under a leather jacket. Only she could make all that black look sexy. I have to hold back the groan when she locks eyes with me again. She looks nervous when she steps out of her row, and I let her get to the door before I follow.

"Hey, Catalina, wait up," I call out to her.

She doesn't bother slowing down or looking back. She picks up the pace, trying to add distance between us. That's fine. I don't mind the chase.

"Catalina, please. I only want to talk."

"Get away from me, Nyx. I don't have anything I want to say to you." She turns down an almost vacant hallway. Wrong move, baby.

Her stride is smaller than mine, and I have no problem catching up to her. I grab her by the elbow, dragging her into an empty room.

"Let go of me." She wiggles in my grip; I only tighten my hold on her.

"You're not going anywhere, baby."

"Don't fuckin' call me that, you pig. What you guys did to me was wrong."

I laugh. "Really, because you were begging for all of us from where I was standing. You said the words *yes*."

She glares up at me. I spin her around, holding her back to my chest, pinning her arms to her sides. Her chest rises rapidly, pushing her breasts out every time. I couldn't help myself. I lower my face into her nape. I breathe deeply. She smells like apples and honey.

"You smell so good, baby." I kiss her neck up towards her ear. "Wanna play a little game? Just you and me?" I can feel her body slowly melt into mine.

"Not really. I don't fully trust you. How do I know this isn't some sort of trap?"

I bit her earlobe, sliding my hand away from her wrist. "You'll have to trust me." I continued sliding my hand until I reached the hem of her skirt. She doesn't stop me when I

run my finger under, feeling the smooth skin of her thigh. "Yes, or no?"

Her breath hitches when I slide higher, and I run my other hand over her stomach, pushing her into my hard-on. I run my finger back and forth, waiting for an answer, slowly inching closer to her panties. I can tell she's holding back.

"Baby, I can feel your heat, but I'm dying to sink my finger inside you. Don't you miss how Dorian made you feel?" I place kisses along her jaw, getting a moan out of her. "Yes, baby, I love when you make that sound. Do you feel what you do to me?" I push her ass into me more, groaning when she rotates her hips. "Fuck me, that's it. Give me a yes." After a long pause, she finally answers.

"Yes, Nyx, make me feel good." Turning her body, she looks into my eyes. I can see she doesn't fully trust me. Maybe with time, she will. I only need to convince Cole and Dorian to give up their bullying. I cup her face; she flicks her gaze to my lips for a second. That's all the welcoming I need. I slam my lips to hers. Her lips are soft against mine. I nip her lower lip before I lift her with one hand. Her hands wrap around my neck, pulling me in deeper. Pinning her to the door, I slip my hand under her skirt, moving her thong to the side. She is soaking wet for me.

"So wet for me already, baby." I flick my finger over her clit.

She pulls away. "Nyx." She moans my name.

"Yeah? You like that?"

I sink a finger deep inside. "Oh, God... I like that a lot."

Her hips rock, looking for more. Placing another finger in, her core tightens immediately. She is so wet, and it's dripping down her thigh. I walk her over to an empty desk. Placing her down, I spin her around.

"Lean over and hold on."

She's a little hesitant but listens. I unbutton my jeans, and her head snaps up with the sound of my zipper.

"W-what are you doing?"

I pull my cock out and start pumping it. Her pupils dilate, watching me, licking her lips. She doesn't turn away.

"Turn around, baby." I groan.

With one final look, she lays back down. I lift her skirt, sliding her thong down her thighs. Her wet pussy glistened in the light. I pump faster when I sink my fingers back inside of her. Pulling out, I wipe her juice on my cock.

"God, you feel amazing on my cock." I run my finger over her tight rosebud. "Have you ever had anyone in here before?"

She shakes her head. I spit on her tight hole before pushing the tip of my finger inside.

"Holy shit, Nyx," she yells.

"Yes, scream my name." I run the tip of my cock along her entrance, pushing in slowly, watching as her pussy pulls me inside. "You feel so good, baby." I rock my hips forwards until I'm fully inside while pumping my finger into her tight ass.

"I'm gonna come."

I can feel her grip me. I groan and rock harder and faster. The desk moves forward, scraping along the floor,

but neither of us cares. I grab her by the waist with my hand when she screams her release. I pull my finger out of her ass and hold on to her as I move deeper.

"Nyx, don't stop. I'm coming again."

As she finds her release, she milks mine from me. It came out of nowhere. I was left breathless.

"Holy shit, baby." I lean my forehead on her back.

She hums her response. She tilts her head to the side. Her eyes are closed, but she has a smile on her face. "That felt amazing. I've never done anything with my ass before and was always too scared to try." She glances at me. "Thank you for being so gentle with me. I don't know why you are suddenly."

I shrug because, honestly, I don't know either. "Maybe it's time for a change." I pull out of her, tucking myself back into my pants.

"Well, I don't know about Cole. I don't know what I did to him for him to hate me."

I frown. How is that possible? Cole said she knew the reason. I don't understand any of this.

"We better head out before someone walks in. What class do you have next?"

She straightens her skirt, then grabs her bag. "I have an art class, but I'm sure I missed most of it. Which fuckin' sucks. So, I'll head home for the day."

"I'll walk you out."

"That won't be necessary. I'm sure you have a class to catch or whatever you do." She walks towards the door, leaving before I can say anything.

All I could think about was Catalina Wilson for the rest of the day. When I get home, Cole is on a rampage. I guess Henry is being a hardass, wanting us to pull extra duty on the town's border to ensure we don't have any other mishaps as we had. To be honest, he should've caught it sooner, he is the fuckin' leader of the gang, and really, it's his job to scout the entire town for problems. Yes, I know we're the enforcers. But we only enforce what he tells us, so if he doesn't say anything, we can't take matters into our own hands. We tried that once when a bunch of frat boys went after a girl. We handled things. Henry lost his shit on us. We never went rogue again. In a way, it's his fault this happened. If he didn't place us on a leash, we would've figured it out before all of this.

Now Cole is yelling at whoever is in his crosshairs. I should've gone for a drive instead of coming home or found Cat. Anything is better than listening to him.

He's also pissed off that he didn't get to pull anything on her today. *Oops, my bad*, guess I kept her from him. I've tried asking him why we keep doing things to her, but he only accuses me of things. I'm better off keeping quiet. He doesn't need to know that Cat trusts me, all I can do for now is keep Cole off her back, and hopefully, he'll come around. Maybe it was a misunderstanding. I know that once something is in his head, good luck getting it out. He has a way of twisting the truth to his liking.

I need a plan for him to see what I see in her. I wonder if I can think of something that will force them together somehow.

7

Catalina

I can't get what happened with Nyx out of my head. Crazy right? Am I going crazy?

"Bitch you might be," I tell myself. I lied to Nyx. I didn't have a class. I had to head home to prepare for tonight. Turns out I have another job. The dead never rest in this town. Lucky me. I need a clear head for tonight, and having Nyx weasel inside isn't helping. I don't know if I can fully trust his motives, especially when he's friends with Cole. Dorian seems like an okay person. The other night he didn't come off as he would hurt me, and the following day Dorian only said one thing to me, although he did come off as an ass beforehand. Dorian's harder to read. He also follows along with what Cole says.

Jesus Cat, get your head in the game, not Nyx's dick game. Oh, but what a dick he has, indeed.

I swiftly change out of my skirt and knee-highs, throwing on a pair of leggings. I guess the usual uniform for grave robbing, and you guessed it, messy bun. You get great at the messy bun when you usually run late. That and I'm horrible at hair. It was the one thing my mother figure lacked in teaching me. She was more interested in all the sons she produced, leaving no room for me. You tend to get lost when you are wedged in the middle of four boys.

That's all I can handle about thinking of her. Dr. Dead-bodies wanted to talk with me before I headed out. I double-checked that I packed everything, including snacks. Can never forget the snacks or wet wipes, oh and hand sanitizer for apparent reasons. Johnny always waits for me in my driveway, never letting me down. Is it sad that my car is the only one I can rely on? *Just say no.*

The drive to the school brought more memories that I didn't want to remember. I knew I should've let my mind wander into my past. I kept that door closed for a reason. My mother and her sons were not very nice people. I couldn't wait to leave that house. Whatever Cole throws at me is nothing compared to what I had to deal with in that house. When I think of the last time her sons tormented me, shivers race down my back.

They tied my hands behind my back, stuffing me inside the closet of my room. All four left me there for two days before coming to check on me. I was so dehydrated I couldn't talk; my lips were cracked and bleeding. That didn't seem to matter to them because they hauled me out by my hair, my screams going unheard. My joints were so sore from

sitting in one spot for so long that my legs didn't want to work, but that didn't stop them. I was tossed into the middle of my room; I could still see their evil eyes staring at me. I never asked why they were doing this to me; I felt it was because of Mother. She didn't want a girl; she wanted me gone. I never understood why she never gave me up or why my dad never stepped in and said something. He stood by while she let her sons do whatever they wanted. But after that night, they beat me so badly; I thought I was going to die. They kicked and punched me, all while my hands were tied. I moved out shortly after, finding whatever work I could and bought Johnny. I lived in my car until I graduated high school, received my scholarship and moved here.

What a childhood, right? As I said, I have family, just none that I give a shit about.

The campus parking lot has a few cars spread out. It's almost eight, so I'm sure most of these are for the clubs that will be ending soon. Parking in my usual spot, I walk towards the medical entrance. Dr. Deadbodies is already waiting for me outside. He flicks his cigarette on the ground before he opens the door.

"You know, professor, those things will kill you."

"Oh, probably. Then you would have the fun time of digging me back up."

"Yeah, pass. No offence, but I ain't touching you when you're dead."

He hums, then passes me. We walk down the hallway towards his office, and it's quiet. The only sound is the clicking of our shoes on the floor. I can't complain. Some-

times the quiet is nice, but with the thoughts running rapidly in my head, I kinda want some chatter.

"Did I do something wrong? Is that why you wanted to talk?" I ask as soon as we step inside his office.

He doesn't say anything. He simply sits in his seat, folding his hands on top of his desk. I readjust my bag, put it on my lap, and fold my arms over it.

"Want to tell me what happened the other night? I asked for three bodies. I received one. Then I had another one the next day."

I figured this would come up. I can't actually tell him I got railed by three men. Now can I. Clearing my throat. "Things didn't go as planned."

He raises his forehead giving me a *no-shit* look. "Explain Catalina."

"Right, after the first one, I headed into town. Things already became unhinged with Halloween *activities*. While digging up the grave, I was interrupted by a bunch of teenagers. I had no choice but to pack it in before I was exposed. I figured that was the safest thing to do."

He continues to stare; I can only hope he believes my lie. He leans back in his chair, giving me a nod.

"Let's try not to get caught again. I can't afford to lose bodies. I'm on a tight schedule this year, and I need all the ones I can get. I have two for you tonight. Think you can handle them?"

I give him a small scoff. "Have I ever come up short before now?"

"No, that's why I was concerned. If you need help, I'm here."

I stand, letting him know I'm finished. Fuck if I'm letting him help me when I don't need him. He knows which ones I can't do. I head to the van with my anticipation. At least I can get my frustration out tonight. I have no choice but to get both bodies in, or who knows what would happen. I've never actually had this happen before. I feel like a major failure. I haven't felt this way since I was living with my mother. When she kept telling me she wished I was a boy, or how she wished I could be more like her sons and less like a slut, that I'll be one when I grow up. Well, I'm not far off. I had sex with three men in one night, so congratulations, Mother, your wish came true.

The cemetery is deserted, just the way I like it. I figured I'd start with the body I didn't grab. It's located around the same area as the last one. I wish I could drive closer. The walk to the grave is quiet, a far cry from the other night. No motorcycles revving in the distance, no one yelling or cheering. Just complete silence.

"Excellent working conditions." I let out a deep sigh as my shovel sinks into the ground.

I'm laying the tarp out, getting ready to drag the body out, when I hear motorcycles in the distance.

"You've got to be kidding me." I grind my teeth. I jump into the pit and hook everything up. Fuck if I'm getting caught again. Why can't I work in peace anymore? Pop-

ping my head up, I look around, ensuring the coast is clear. I climb the rest of the way out, hauling the body once I'm situated.

I wrap everything up and drive to the following site. I don't see the point of driving back to the school for a drop-off when I can do everything at once. I can still hear the revving of engines. I'm happy that they haven't come any closer to me. Let's pray it stays that way.

The next grave is near the far back, and I'll admit this part of the cemetery is very eerie. The tombstones are older, and some are falling over, while some have moss overtaking them. If I believed in zombies, this would be the time for one to pop out of the ground. Shivers raced down my spine. Never have I ever felt like this before. Maybe it's some bad mojo going on with this body. That's what I tell myself as I continue to walk deeper and deeper. I see the fresh mound of dirt just up ahead. Relief washes over me. I don't have to get closer to the tree line. It's almost one, and I swear that's when the crazies come out. Even after Halloween, they still try to pull things. I don't fully trust the gang that runs this town. If they ever found out what I've been up to, well, I'll be afraid of the outcome.

My muscles were screaming at me to take a break, and that's when I realized I should've eaten something before I headed out—a good thing for those snacks. Wiping my hands off, I grab a granola bar. I glance around the cemetery taking everything in, and that's when I see them walking toward me. I don't have time to run.

"Don't even think about it, Wednesday. We see you." Cole's deep voice breaks the silence of the night.

My breathing stops. I've been doing this for over a year, and I've never been busted. Why suddenly are these three showing up here? Disturbing me. For the second time this week.

I lower my granola bar. "What the fuck are you guys doing here?"

"Business can't say. But this." Cole points to the grave I've been digging. "Looks to be more interesting. Do tell."

"Um, yeah, I don't trust you enough, so. No thanks." I go to pack up when a hand is wrapped around my arm.

"This doesn't look good, baby." Nyx brushes dirt off my cheek while checking out all my gear.

"Still not going to tell you," I lean on my tiptoes to whisper into his ear.

Dorian walks forwards, giving me a smirk. "I might know a way for her to tell us."

"Oh yeah, do tell, pretty boy?"

Nyx grips my waist, moving me against his chest as Dorian moves forwards, running his hands up my waist slowly, leading to my breasts. My nipples harden when he squeezes them. My clit throbs and I'm embarrassed about how fast I've gotten wet for him.

"That's it, baby, let him make you feel good just like I did earlier today," Nyx whispers in my ear. I can only nod, even though I know better, but I can't help it. My body has a mind of its own, and I can't control it anymore.

Dorian takes me from Nyx, carrying me away. "I need to feel you on my tongue again. I've been thinking of you

since that night. You tasted so sweet on my lips. Are you ready?"

Oh fuck. I clench my thighs tighter when he sets me down on the ground. Nyx and Cole watch a few feet away. Looking very interested.

His lips land on my neck I grip his shoulders. He walks me backwards until my legs hit something solid.

"Lay backwards, hands over your head." The intense stare he gives me leaves no room for an argument.

I turn to look at what I'm lying on. It's a tombstone. *Holy shit,* this is going to happen in a cemetery, of all places. When I'm fully laid down, I place my hands over my head. His warm hands move under my ass, pulling my leggings down to my ankles.

"Ankles together and push your knees open. I want to see your wet pussy."

I do what he says, and he groans.

"Cole, get over here, want to see what you're missing out on."

I tilt my head to see his eyes flare. Even in the dark, I can see how much he resents me. To make matters worse, I bit my lip and moaned. I can tell he wants this. Maybe this will help change his mind toward me.

I gasp when Dorian flicks my clit with his tongue. My fingers flex, looking for something to grab, and my fingers brush against a pair of jeans. Tilting my head upwards, my gaze landed on Coles. I watch his hands move to his waist, unbuttoning his jeans; he moves his hand inside his briefs, pulling out his hard cock. His piercing shines under the moonlight. When his thumb moves over

the tip spreading his pre-cum around, I turn my eyes to his. I slid my tongue along my dry lips.

"Make me come."

He moves closer, spreading his legs wide. Lining his velvety smooth tip against my lips, I open wide for him. He groans when he glides along my tongue. Dorian chooses that moment to plunge two fingers into my wet core. I scream around Cole's cock; he thrusts deeper, causing me to gag. His hands move to my breasts, squeezing as he fucks my mouth.

"Add a finger to her tight asshole. She loves that." I can hear Nyx tell Dorian. He slides his fingers out of my pussy and rubs them around my tight hole.

"Fuck, this is amazing. I can tell you love all of your holes being played with, don't you?" Cole said, breathless, while he slowed his pace.

Dorian pushes his finger into my ass. I grip Cole's thighs and moan around his cock. My hips tilt, looking for more. My clit is throbbing, needing release, and my entire body is on fire. Cole pumps a few more times before pulling out. He strokes himself.

"Fuck, I want your eyes on me when I come."

Dorian pulls his finger out of me, pulling me upwards. "On your knees for him."

Cole doesn't waste any time plunging his cock back into my mouth. His hand wraps around the back of my neck, holding me still. Tears run down my cheeks every time he makes me gag. He hisses when I swallow around him.

"Yes, I'm coming. Hold it all. Don't swallow until I tell you to." His hips jerk forwards before he stills. Warm cum

shoots into my mouth. He slowly pulls out. "Open, let me look." I show him, and he pushes his two fingers inside my mouth until I gag. "Mmm, good girl, swallow."

"Fuck, that was hot. Let me finish what I started." Dorian came up behind me, pushing my face into the ground. My ass is exposed to the sky. Cole places his wet fingers against my asshole.

"I'll help you push some of my cum inside that beautiful ass." Cole pushes two fingers inside.

"Holy shit!" I scream, pushing back against him. Fingers rub my sensitive clit bringing my climax on quickly. The pull in my lower stomach is intense. Explosions are all around me. "Oh shit, shit. I'm fuck—" I never did finish my sentence. The tremors hit, and I collapse. Thank God for the cool grass under my cheek. I'm on fire.

Then I remember I still have to dig up a fuckin' body.

8

Dorian

Making Catalina come is like pure heaven. Nothing else compares.

She's currently on the ground reeling in from her intense orgasm. Nyx kneels in front of her, brushing her hair away from her face.

"You okay?"

She hums, giving him a smile.

"Come on. We best get you back into the human world." He kisses her forehead before moving her into his lap. When I glance at Cole, he looks perplexed. I know he has mixed emotions for Cat. I only wish he could let everything go. When I look back at Nyx, he's pulling Cat's legging back up.

"Wanna tell us what you're doing out here now?" Cole asks.

Catalina studies him. "Cole, I still don't know what I did to deserve your bullying. I keep replaying everything over and over ever since I started here. Did I say or do something to you? I need to know." Her eyes are begging for him to tell her.

Nyx and I have been wondering the same thing. We don't enjoy pulling our stunts on her, but pissing Cole off is another level we don't like crossing.

"Fucking tell her already, don't be such an asshole. I'm pretty sure she has a right to know by now. Besides, I'm out. I'm not doing it anymore," I tell him. He can figure his own shit out. She isn't some toy to be played with. Besides, I enjoy playing a new game with her.

"Yeah, man, I'm with D. She deserves so much more from us," Nyx adds. I had my suspicion that he also wanted out.

Cole glares at us. "Why am I getting ganged up on suddenly? I bully her because she's fucking her professor."

My head snaps towards Cat. Her eyes shoot open. Nyx looks at her with disgust.

"W-What the hell. I've never done anything like that. Why would you say that?"

"Don't act so innocent. I've seen you come and go out of his office for a year, usually at night. What else goes down at night in a professor's office, Catalina?"

Her lower lip trembles. She pins him with her eyes. "You really wanna know that fuckin' bad?" Her eyes fill with tears. "See that grave over there." She points to where she was standing earlier. "That right there is the reason I see the professor every night. You think I have

the luxury like most of the students here? The professor gave me a job if you must know. One I've kept quiet about this entire time until you assholes showed up. So, no, Cole, I'm not sleeping with my professor."

She walks over to her gear, grabs her shovel, and goes back to digging.

"Why is she digging?" Nyx looks so confused. I shrug because what the fuck do I know. We stand around watching while she digs this grave. Then it clicks.

"Did you want help or anything? I feel horrible just standing by while you work so hard?"

She looks so tiny in the hole she's digging; she pops her head up, looking at me. "I'm good. I do this more than you think. I'm almost there, anyway. You don't have to dig the entire six feet, only to the top of the coffin."

"I'll take your word for it, considering this is the first time I see anyone dig up a body."

Cole stands, clenching his jaw muscle. While Nyx looks like he's going to throw up, considering he can kill a person yet, this is drawing the line. I find this fascinating, like how cool it is to have this as a job. Don't get me wrong, I enjoy beating the shit out of people, but hers. She's always on high alert to never get caught. The adrenaline must be pumping through her body. I feel myself harden under those thoughts.

Her small grunt brings me out of my thoughts. "Can someone hand me the rope and hooks? Maybe I'll use your help after all. I'm getting tired."

I move forward, searching the tarp for what she needs. When I look down at her, she's covered in dirt. She straps

the hooks up under the armpits and lifts her hand to me. Grinning at her, I hike her upwards. She's so tiny and light it doesn't take much effort.

"There you go, half pint. Want me to pull it up for you?"

She bits her lower lip. "Fine, only cause it's late, and you guys crashed my night yet again."

I've never hauled a dead body out of a coffin. Let me tell you, it was interesting.

"Are you going to tell us why you do this?" Cole demands.

"Seriously. I can't catch a break with you, can I? Why else would someone dig up a body?" She glares at him.

"I can't tell you; you are already weird. This could be a cult thing."

"I'm weird. You guys live in a house with skulls and shit hanging on your walls. So, get over yourself. Oh, and what's your gang called? *Soul Stealers.*" She rolls her eyes. "How stupid. Did a kindergartener name it?"

He's on her so fast she didn't have time to move. He grips her throat, lowering his face to hers. "You watch your mouth. That gang you speak of could do anything they want to you."

"I'm not afraid. I've been through far worse than you can imagine, so take your boys and leave me alone." She narrows her eyes.

He releases her. Never letting her move out of the way.

"You're a prick. You know that." Shoving past him, she works quickly, bundling the body in the bag and packing up her tools. She swings her satchel over her head.

Bending down, she grabs the body bag and then starts dragging it toward her van.

I swing back to Cole. "What the hell was that? We're trying to get on her good side, and you go off, and fucking grab her by the throat. Are you kidding me right now?"

"Watch your fucking mouth. Do you forget who's the boss around here?"

I go in to show him who really is the fucking boss.

"Hey, hey. That's enough, you two." Nyx pushes his body between the both of us. "Stop right now. This isn't like us. We've never let a woman get to us before."

Cole steps back, throwing his hands up. "You're right. We aren't, and she's done. Don't touch, talk or associate with her anymore. She's tearing us apart, and hells if I'm letting a woman do that to us."

"That's not what I meant at all. She didn't do anything wrong. That's on us," I tell him.

He shakes his head. "It's done. She wanted us to stop anyway, so." He walks away, and I watch as he walks right past Cat, who's still dragging her body bag. She doesn't even look at him, and I'm relatively sure she heard our fight. It wasn't like we were quiet.

"Let's go. Cole can cool off at home. Besides, we have a job that needs to be finished. As shitty as that is to say." Nyx strolls away, stopping to talk to Cat, but she waves him off.

How did this night turn into a shit storm? I stop at Cat's side.

"Did you want any help? I'm sorry for how this night ended. That wasn't how it was supposed to go."

She waves me off, too. "Don't worry about me. I'm a big girl. Go, they need you."

I know I should stay, but she's right; they do need me, but I wanted her to need me too. We need a way for all to get over our shit. I want her, Nyx wants her, but fucking Cole. He'll take the most to convince otherwise. He doesn't have a problem getting his dick sucked, but God forbid if he gets his feelings involved.

With Coles' wishes, it's been a week since we've all talked to Catalina. Nyx still sees her in class, but they both ignore each other. I can tell it's killing him. It would kill me, too. Instead, we pushed ourselves into doing what we do best. As always, Henry is still having us drive around. I have no clue why it's bullshit. We already destroyed one drug house; I highly doubt we have any more that are going to pop up anytime soon. He's just being paranoid now, like how much control does one really need over this town? We were about to call it quits when Cole's phone went off. He's reaching for his personal phone when he goes for his back pocket, and it's his burner, so we know it's a new job.

He lowers his head, pressing his palm into his eye. Great, this is going to be a shit job. I just know it. He hangs up and lets out a few mumbles.

"You're not going to like the new job."

"Why? Another drug house?" I deadpan.

He blows out a heavy breath, and his face creases with doubt. "Henry wants to know why graves are being dug up."

"Fuck," Nyx whispers.

"Oh, shit," I mumble.

"Yeah. Catalina found herself on the wrong side of the gang. I don't know what to do."

If Henry wants someone, it's only a matter of time. Especially if he calls us, he's not going to let this go, and he'll want someone brought in because what Henry wants, he wants delivered promptly. There's only one thing I can think of doing.

"We're gonna have to protect her now. You do realize that. I'm not handing her over for something that she does for work. Fuck Henry."

They both nod. The only question is how. We can't come out and tell her, can we? Her life is going to be at risk now, and Henry will know something is up.

"I'll come up with a plan—let's head home for the night. We'll try to talk with her at school," Cole says.

"Yeah, if she will. She doesn't even look at me in class anymore. I think we hurt her."

Nyx looks troubled. Shaking his head, he starts his bike. If anyone can get through to Cat, it'll be him. He's the friendly one out of the bunch. I can only hope he can get her to listen.

9

Catalina

The guys have left me alone for a week, a week of pure bliss.

Okay, that's a lie. I missed when Nyx would look at me or how Cole would dominate me and how Dorian would protect me, and they each had their own nicknames for me. Like how pathetic is that? Who falls for their bullies? It has to happen more than often, right? Or is it trauma from my childhood that I'm holding onto? Either way, I think I'm falling for each of them, and their being quiet has shown me that I've looked forward to them every day since school started. Is it normal to want three lovers?

"Jesus, Cat, you sound like a fucking pussy." Why am I always talking to myself? "Probably because you have no friends."

I really don't. I have a hard time trusting people. After what her sons put me through, I can't tell what people's

motives are. I continue with my painting brush to canvas is the best therapy around. I close my eyes as I paint. I don't need to see when you paint in abstract; I trust my hand to lead. The piece I'm working on is called *Wrath*. I wish I could show it to her sons. I'll never have the chance because hell if I'm ever going back there. I'll paint it out instead. I dip my brush into the red, creating nice long strokes on the canvas.

I've been working on my art for most of the day, this piece is due in a week, and I need to buckle down to finish it in time. It's my fault for slacking, and my mind has been elsewhere. I can't keep thinking about them, they left me, not the other way around, and it's not like we were all in a relationship together. They got me off a couple of times and vice versa. It should be easy to forget and walk away, so why can't I?

I need another job, that's what I need. The professor has had nothing in days. I can't stay inside the walls of my apartment any longer. Can't somebody die so I can get some work? I get how bad that sounds, but come on *already*. Karma is probably going to bite me in the ass for that remark. My phone dings with a text. Only one person ever sends me a text. Dr. Deadbodies. Looks like I have a job tonight. After all, see. That's what happens when you think hard enough. Things happen.

The job is out in Eaglewood; thank the lucky stars. Be a little more relaxed than in town, that's for sure. I wouldn't have to look over my back continuously. Get in, get out. I never knew I could be home early enough to enjoy a nice warm bath, and the evenings were getting a little

chillier. Packing up my art, I head out. The parking lot is almost empty, considering it's damn near four o'clock. The sun is setting, reflecting a lovely orange glow on the windshields of the few vehicles in the lot. I shield my eyes looking around to make sure I'm alone. I don't need anyone following me to the medical parking lot. No point going home just to turn around to come back again. I'll have to drop a few things off at my car first. I take a step onto the pavement, only to hear a rev of a bike entering the parking lot.

I continue making my way to my car without paying whoever is rolling in any attention, digging in my bag for my keys. The revving grows louder. I slam my keys into the lock, getting it unlocked in no time. Sometimes I wish this car had a remote.

"Wednesday, we need to talk." There was an edge to Cole's voice. I should've known it was him.

I smack my head against my car window a few times before rotating in his direction. Cole has his arms resting over his handlebars, and his jet-black hair is tousled from the wind. He never takes his icy-blue eyes off me. His biceps flex, catching my eyes. That dirty bastard knows exactly what he's doing to me.

"The fuck do you want Cole," I snap, getting frustrated with every second he's wasting.

"Where ya headed?"

"Why the sudden interest in my life? You leave me alone for what a week? Just needed to torment me, is that it?" I turn around, opening my door.

"That's not it, Catalina. Look, I'm sorry for being a real asshole to you—"

"Seriously." I storm closer to him. "That's how you're going to apologize, you take something out of context, and that's that. You are unreal." Rage roars through me, and I clench my hand into a fist. Rearing my arm back, I punch him in his handsome face. The crunching sound tells me I fucked up. The pain shoots up my arm. Yep. I broke something for sure. Too bad it wasn't on him. Sweet baby Jesus.

I stagger backwards, holding my hand to my chest. Tears roll down my cheeks from the pain that's still shooting down my arm.

"Jesus, Wednesday, what were you thinking." Cole's hand wraps around mine. I hiss when he tries to move it.

"Clearly, I wasn't thinking ass. I wanted to hurt you."

"You forget how tiny you are. Come on. We gotta get you to the hospital."

I shake my head. "I can't. I have a job I have to do tonight." Wincing when I try to flex my fingers. Maybe I didn't break anything and could've sprained them. Right?

"Don't be stupid. Get in the car, and I'll drive. Now."

This wasn't how I saw my evening going. If it wasn't for Cole, I could've been digging a body right now. He ruins everything; climbing into the car, I have to laugh. Watching a six-foot man trying to sit in my seat is the best thing ever.

"How the hell can you drive this thing?" He grunts, trying to reposition the seat.

"Well, it helps when you're short. How do you ride that bike of yours?"

"Easy, fast." He smirks as he pulls out of the parking spot.

I shake my head aggressively. "Pass. I like the comfort of four tires on the ground."

"Ahh, once you feel that vibration between your legs, you'll be hooked, Wednesday."

Butterflies danced in my lower stomach. I squeeze my thighs together when I picture what the thought of Cole and I on his bike would look like.

The drive to the hospital is quiet. I don't know what I'm going to do. My scholarship is running on my grades. If I can't complete my art project, I'll fail. Say goodbye to my funds. Then I can't work. Jesus, what the fuck was I thinking. I have to hold back tears and pray that it's only fractured or bruised. No damage, please. I send a mental prayer to whoever listens to non-believers.

✦

"Come on, you got lucky, and no more going around punching people in the face from now on."

I toss him a side-eye. "You are the lucky one, and if I ended up with a broken finger, I would be fucked right about now. Consider yourself lucky, asshole. Now go grab your bike. I can handle getting home."

"Really? That's how you want to end the night. I actually came here to tell you something, not for you to attack me."

"I wouldn't have to attack you if you weren't such a dickhole."

He lets out a groan. "You are being unreasonable. I came here to tell you to watch yourself."

"Oh, 'cause that doesn't sound threatening in any way." I shift in my seat, placing my back against the car door. My hand is in a brace. I'm looking at a sprained middle finger, but I'll sacrifice everything just to punch him again.

"I'm only trying to help Wednesday. Hand me your phone." He reaches across, holding his hand out, not letting me have a choice in the matter.

I've never noticed how much larger his hand is compared to mine. I feel like a child sitting next to him—no wonder Dorian calls me half pint. I reach into my bag and fumble around, and it's a lot harder with one hand. I slam my phone into his palm with a grin. I watch him add his number to my phone. He passes it back to me with a smirk.

"Call if anything happens." He opens his door and steps out.

I didn't even notice we were back at school. I was too busy checking him out or fantasizing about punching him still. Now for him to leave so I can get to work, this is going to take some maneuvering. I can't afford to let Dr. Deadbodies know I can't do this job. The rev of his engine brings me out of my head. I climb out of the car walking to the driver's side.

"Behave tonight, Wednesday."

"Same to you, and whatever you get up to with your gang of merry men." I salute him before getting into John-ny. I wait until he leaves before getting out and walking to my van.

I don't know why he felt the need to warn me. I haven't gotten into trouble before, and I don't plan on finding it now. *Great,* now I'm going to be paranoid all fuckin' night. Thanks a lot, Cole. If anything, they don't know I take jobs in Eaglewood. It's my only hiding spot for now.

It's later than I wanted to start. By the time we left the hospital, it was nine. I wanted to be home by now. There goes my relaxing bath this evening. Parking my van as close to the grave as possible, I try to think how I will do this. How much damage can I do if I take my brace off? Fuck it, gonna have to try it without it. I can't make a fist without it bringing me to tears. Please let this body be a lightweight.

It's been two hours, and I'm still digging; I'm not even halfway done. I don't think I have the energy to finish it. Sitting down, I stare down at the grave. How is it you live your entire life only to end up here in a hole in the ground covered in dirt? *What a joke.*

I force myself to dig. The amount of pain I'm in is making my head throb. With every sink of the shovel, my finger swells. Maybe I should've left the brace on.

"Well, no one said you were smart." I whimper when I try to continue. Finally, my shovel hits the coffin.

"Sweet fuckin' Jesus." I'm almost finished. My chest is heaving, and my left hand is working overtime, pulling

the rope. I think I'll have to tell Dr. Deadbodies that I'll need the week off, and I have no choice. With determination, I get this job done.

Wheeling the gurney into the cooler seals the rest of my night. I'm done. I can't do it anymore. My hand is throbbing in pain. I'm scared to look under the brace, guaranteed I fucked it up worse. The walk back to my car is quiet, almost too quiet. Usually, some form of bird is out flying no matter what time of day. I pick up my pace. I have better things to do than let my brain wonder. My car is only a few feet away when a black figure steps out from behind it. I stumble to a stop. A flicker of light can be seen under the hood; then, I see an LED light-up mask. Just like what the guys wore. Except this one isn't their colour, it's yellow.

I move my hand under the flap of my bag so I can get my phone.

"I wouldn't move if I were you." He spat out in a low, croaky voice.

I try to swallow the lump that's quickly forming. "Who are you?"

He steps away from my car; I see something reflect in his hand. My heart hammers in my chest, and my hand twitches in my bag, feeling the outline of my phone. If I can only grab it, I only have a few contacts. Someone will come if they figure out where I am.

"What are you doing out so late, pretty girl? Don't you know by now that strangers come out at night?"

Those words are so familiar it's scary. My boys said something almost the same Halloween night while wear-

ing the same masks. Was someone watching us? My fight-or-flight kicks in. I still have the keys to the door of the school. It'll be my best shot.

I take off, running full tilt, my feet pounding on the pavement. My breath comes out in pants as I try to get away. I hear his feet pounding behind me. I don't know who he is or what he wants, but he isn't going to get it. Running and fishing into a bag takes a lot of concentration and coordination.

"Get back here, you bitch," he yells. His voice is closer than I would like.

Who is this guy? I don't remember pissing anyone off nor talking to anyone at school lately. I always stick to myself. So why am I a target? When I'm thrown to the ground, the door is right there, only two feet from me. My sore hand smashed to the ground. I yell out in pain. Even with the brace on, I can feel everything. I give it everything I have. I throw my elbow back, connecting with his face when he falls backwards. I roll onto my knees, climbing to my feet. I take off in a clumsy run.

"HELP!" I scream even though I know there's no one around, but your assaulter never likes to be called out. I dig around in my bag again when I feel my lanyard. I yank it free from my purse. I slam the key fob onto the keyless entry system.

"Hurry, turn green." Why do the seconds seem to take forever when you're running for your life? When the red light finally turns green, I swing open the door, pulling it closed faster. The masked man slams into it, pulling on the handle. Luckily for me, it locks automatically.

He slams his hand on the window that's holding the knife. My body trembles as he stares at me, the glow from his mask lighting up his eyes. I slowly back up.

"I'll be seeing you, Catalina; you best be watching your back." The yellow neon lights flick off, submitting him to the darkness of the night.

My chin wobbles and I close my eyes, trying to calm myself down. When the first tear falls, I sink down the wall. Bringing my knees to my chest, I let them fall freely. Sometimes it's okay not to be strong. How did my life become such a rollercoaster? With a shaky hand, I grip my phone.

It rings and rings. I sniff back more tears as I hang up. Isn't that great? Now I'll have to call Dr. Deadbodies and try to explain this entire situation. I don't even know this situation. Maybe it'll be safe to go outside.

"Either you're stupid or have a death wish," I whisper. Both are up in the air.

Turning on the flashlight on my phone and griping my keys, I peer out the window. Not that I can see much, but I can see enough to know he's not hanging around. With a deep breath, I push the door open.

"And you wonder why the cat died, Catalina." Guess I'm not that smart.

Scanning the parking lot, I don't see a soul. I'm still on edge. What if he did another jack-in-the-box appearance? I quicken my pace without trying to freak myself out.

"No, the boogeyman doesn't exist, Cat." I swivel my head around, checking, anyway.

When I reached my car, I could cry all over again. I try calling Cole again.

"Pick up, pick up assho—"

"Hello," his raspy voice cut me off.

Emotion welled in my throat when I tried to talk.

"Hello, who's there?" Irritation surged through him.

"C-Cole." I gasped wetly.

"Catalina?"

"I didn't know who else to call."

"Hey, that's okay. What's wrong? What happened?"

I take an unsteady breath. "I'm still at school. Can you come get me?"

I hear him getting out of bed. "Yeah, give me about twenty minutes. Hang tight. Are you sure you're okay?"

I shake my head, then realize he can't see. "No," I whisper.

"Hold on." Then he hangs up.

I sit by my car, touching my one-slashed tire. "We had a good run, didn't we, hey?"

I close my eyes and wait. I want this nightmare to end.

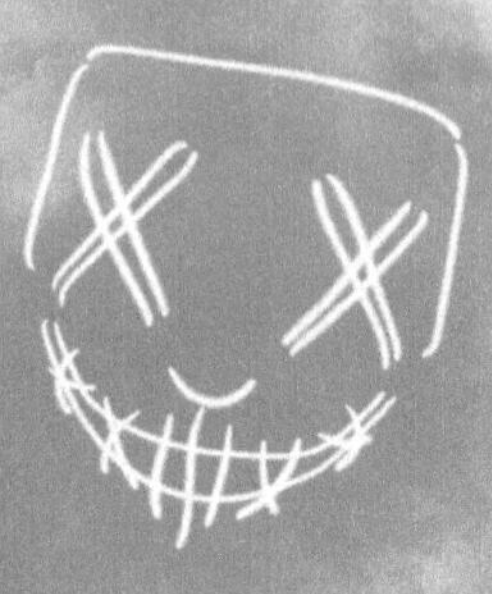
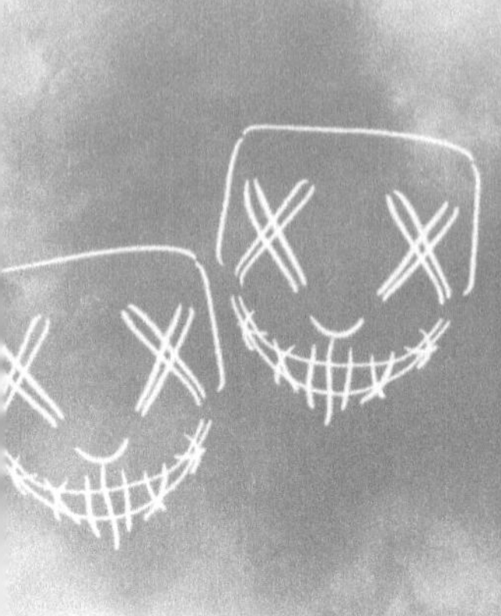

10
Cole

I stumble out of bed, pull my pants on, then knock on the guys' door, waking their asses up.

Dorian flings his door open red-faced. "What the hell, man."

Nyx stumbles out of his room, pulling his sweats on.

"No time. Catalina's in trouble. Let's go." Skipping the stairs two at a time, I run into the kitchen to grab my car keys. No time for bikes.

"What exactly happened?" Nyx asks, rounding the corner to the kitchen.

I can only shrug. "I have no idea. She didn't go into detail; she sounded scared and crying. Now I'm glad I gave her my number."

"Less talking, more action. She could still be in danger." Dorian grabs the keys from my hands, heading for the front door.

"What the hell is happening in this town, Cole?"

That's what I would like to know. It used to be so laid back, and Henry has some questions to ask that fuckin' mayor of ours. We've never had any attacks at night before, hence why we had fuckin' purge night on Halloween.

What usually took twenty minutes, Dorian got us there in ten. I knew where she was parked, so I gave him directions. The parking lot was dimly lit. Unfortunately for Catalina, she never parked under a light. Her car sat alone in the vacant lot. All I could make out was the shape of her black Volkswagen Beetle.

"Something's wrong with her car." Nyx points out. "Look at her rear tire. It's flat."

"Maybe that's why she called. Could be cause she doesn't know how to change a flat tire."

"I don't think so. No one cries that much over a tire. Besides, you would call a tow truck, wouldn't you?" I shift in my seat, trying to get a closer look at her car. I can't see her; I hope she's smart enough to be inside it.

Dorian parks behind it. As we all climb out, we take in our surroundings.

"Shit," Nyx whispered.

Shit is correct. The driver's side reveals both tires are slashed, along with the words WEDNESDAY scratched into the door panel.

"What the hell? I've only ever heard you call her that and only when we were together," Dorian utters, making sure no one could hear him.

"Catalina?" Nyx calls out quietly.

A small whimper comes from the other side of the car. Rounding the front of the car, I find her sitting against the passenger side door, knees curled to her chest, cradling her braced hand. Kneeling in front of her, I place my hand on her knee. She jerks her head up, and her eyes are bloodshot and puffy. Tears fall from her left eye. Her hair was in a messy bun sitting lopsided on her head.

"Wednesday, baby, what happened?" I stroke her cheek, wiping her tears away. Her lower lip trembles. She looks between all of us and then bursts into a heavy cry.

"I-I... tried to c-call you earlier." Her voice shook. Regret washes over me. If only I had heard my phone ring the first time. We could've gotten here sooner.

I stand only to scoop her into my arms. "Come, let's get you home." She rests her head on my chest. She looks so tiny in my arms.

"Do you need anything from your car?" Dorian questions her.

"No, just grab my bag." Her small voice answered him, pointing to the ground, where her bag lays.

I lock eyes with Dorian. He'll know to check the car for anything suspicious. Nyx opens the passenger door for me, helping me slide in. Brushing her hair away from her face, I lean down, placing a kiss on her forehead. Her body is cold. I lightly rub my hand up and down her arm.

"Are you hurt anywhere?"

She winces when she moves her hand. "I smashed my hand into the ground when I was pushed, and I haven't looked yet."

"We'll do it at the house. Relax, you're safe now with us."

She closes her eyes. Her small hand runs up my chest working around my neck, running her fingers through my hair.

I didn't think that slight movement would calm me so much, nor did I know it was what I needed at this moment. I'm the one that should be helping her feel calm, not the other way around. I pull her closer, giving her more warmth.

The front two doors slam shut, making her hand still. "Ready?" Dorian spoke faintly while starting the car. We all remain quiet on the drive home. Guilt eats me alive; I should've done more. I could've stayed with her tonight. Did I honestly have to leave her? I press my lips into her hair, inhaling her scent.

"Wanna tell us what happened?" I ask her. When we arrived home, we gathered in the living room. I'm kneeling in front of her, waiting for her answer. I grab her hand, not knowing what to expect under her brace. Undoing the Velcro, she takes a deep inhale. "If it hurts too much, we can return to the hospital."

"No, it's okay. It's just the relief of all the pressure, I think."

I continue undoing the brace, and I gently slide it off. "I don't see any more damage, but it's swollen."

"That would be my fault. I didn't wear it when I was digging."

"Here you go, baby." Nyx places a bag of ice on her hand. She tilts her head up, smiling at him. He cups her face putting a gentle kiss on her rosy lips. The sight of them kissing causes my dick to twitch. When he pulls away, he smiles. "When you're ready, can you tell us?"

"Way to kill the moment, Nyx." She laughs. He shrugs, and she closes her eyes taking a deep breath. "After I was finished tonight, someone was standing by my car, wearing the same masks you guys were wearing." Opening her eyes, tears clinging to her eyelashes. "He said some things that sounded the same as what you said on that night. It's like he's watching us."

"What the fuck?" Dorian whispers, uneasiness creeping into his voice.

Now I understand why her nickname was scratched into her car. "Did he try to hurt you?" Nyx asks mindfully.

She shakes her head. "I was able to run inside the school, and I have a key. Thank God."

I rub small circles on her knees as she lets out a small yawn. I can only imagine how tired she is. She's been through a lot tonight. All I know is I'm claiming her tonight before those two can. I have a great deal to make up for.

"Come on. I'll take you to bed." I reach for her hand. Standing, I help her off the couch.

She searches between the three of us. "Go with Cole, baby. He needs you tonight." Nyx insists, placing a kiss on her forehead before heading upstairs.

Dorian comes over, placing another kiss on her forehead. "Good night, darling. See you in the morning."

"Are you okay sharing a bed with me?"

"Of course. Thank you for coming to get me. I didn't know who else to call."

I lead her up the stairs. "We'll make sure you always have someone to call from now on, don't ever feel guilty for calling us. I only wish I'd gotten there sooner." Wrapping my arm around her waist, I pull her into my side. I lead her up one more flight of stairs to my floor. It's more so the house's attic, but it's still nice having it all to myself.

When she enters my room, it's with pure amazement on her face. "Oh, wow. This is beautiful."

My room isn't anything special. There's a queen-sized bed in the middle of the room, and across from the bed is my dresser with a tv mounted over the top. When she turns her head to the right, she gasps.

"Is that a bathtub in your room?"

I chuckle. "Ah yes, that would be my tub." She's referring to my claw-foot tub that sits for everyone to see. What I love most about it is seeing who's in it. "Don't worry, and you can try it later. Right now, I have other plans." I walk her towards my bed until her legs hit the edge, causing her to sit.

"Arms up. I'll help you get undressed." When she raises her arms, she gives me a small smile. I'm drawn to her violet eyes. I run my hands down her ribs, reaching for

the hem of her shirt. I pull it up slowly, running my hands along her smooth skin. She closes her eyes when I touch her breasts. Pulling her shirt over her head, we lock eyes again.

"Why did it take me so long to find you?"

She whispers, "Maybe cause you were looking in all the wrong places."

"I'm not letting you go. You're mine now, Wednesday."

"I'm all of yours." She wraps her arms around my waist, resting her forehead on my stomach. I thread my fingers in her hair, closing my eyes, enjoying this moment. I didn't think having her in my arms would be possible. I thought I fucked it all up when I misjudged her.

"Will you forgive me?" I ask her.

She looks up at me with narrowed brows. "What do you mean?"

"For the way I treated you, it wasn't fair. I judged you before I knew you, then we fought. I should've stayed or done something. That prick touched what's mine. He's dead when I find him."

"Cole, what happened tonight isn't your fault. Whoever followed me must've been doing it for a while. We need to figure out who it is."

I need to talk to Henry first thing. This has him written all over. Then again, he only just mentioned someone digging up bodies, so can it be him?

"Enough of this conversation. I have plans, remember." I push her on her back, dipping my fingers into her waistband. "Are you okay with this?"

"Yes," she whispers.

I pull her leggings off, leaving her in another pair of Halloween thong. I cock my eyebrow up.

She laughs. "What can I say? I love Halloween."

"I can see this. What will it take to see something sexy on this body of yours?"

"Don't know, don't own sexy underwear."

I tsk at her. "We'll have to change that. I need to see this body in something with leather." I kiss her inner thigh, moving upwards. I move past her needy pussy and work upwards her stomach. She lets out a muffled moan. I wrap my hands around her bra straps, sliding them down her arms, sliding her bra off her breasts.

I reach around her back, unclasping her bra. Her nipples tighten when the cool air hits them. Her body looks so dainty under my massive size, and I need to remind myself that she can't handle my entire body weight at once. My hand swallows her breast easily. Rubbing her nipple between my finger and thumb, she pushes her hips into my stomach, moaning as she does.

"That feels good."

I find her other nipple bringing it into my mouth, sucking it before I bite it.

"Holy fuck," she screams.

"You like that? I know you don't like being tied, but can we try something different?"

Her breath hitches. "I don't know, Cole. I need to feel like I can get away."

"Trust me." I take her hands, being careful of her sore one, guiding them to the headboard. "Hold on, don't let go, or the fun stops."

She nods. Grabbing onto the spindles of the head-board with her good hand and laying her bad hand on the mattress.

"That's my good girl."

I repeat the process to her other breast. I dip my finger into her panties.

"Mmm, you're so wet. What are you thinking of?" I swipe my finger along her clit.

"You." She moans.

"Doing what?" I swipe once more.

"Fucking me. I want to know what it feels like to have you inside of me."

God, I want to know too. I hook my fingers into her panties, peeling them off. I stand, pulling my shirt off over my head. I push my sweats down, standing naked with a throbbing dick. She licked her lips, and her pupils were fully blown out with lust and need. I grab the bag of ice that she used for her hand. Finding a piece, I kneel on the bed spreading her legs.

"Don't let go. Red is your safe word." I wait for her nod, then slowly drag the ice cube up her shin. She lets out a gasp when the ice touches her skin. Her skin breaks out in goosebumps. I only end up with wicked thoughts, and it's hard to control my inner demons. They only want to come out and play. They wanted to come out on Halloween, but she wasn't ready for them. I can smell her arousal, letting me know she's ready. After being with Dorian and Nyx, I'm sure she can handle me.

I continue to run the ice cube on her body, running it around her belly button. Her heels dig into the bed

for leverage when I leave the ice cube sitting, collecting water in her belly button. I fish another ice cube from the bag and suck her right nipple in my mouth. She squirms under my body. I draw back, watching her nipple tighten even more from the cool air. I blow warm air over it.

"Cole, please."

Her hand squeezes the frame harder, her hips grinding onto my groin. "God, you feel good." I drag the ice cube around her nipple, watching it pucker even more. Kissing down her stomach, I remove the ice cube from her belly button. Dipping my tongue into the pool of collected water, I dip my finger inside her wet entrance, curling my fingers and touching her g-spot. I drink the water from her button before moving lower.

11

Catalina

Oh, my fucking God.

My body is on fire. With every touch from Cole, I feel like I'm going to combust. His tongue dipped into my belly button shouldn't be this hot. The swipe of his tongue on my clit has me fighting my orgasm.

"Come for me, little one." His demands send me over the edge. I pulsate around his finger as I come.

He pushes another finger in while sucking my clit. My entire body was shaking, he was the only one I hadn't had sex with, and the anticipation was killing me. I understand why he hasn't. I wouldn't want him anywhere near me, but nothing can stand in our way now that we have resolved our differences.

A shiver runs up my leg, followed by wetness; he slowly slides the ice cube up my inner thigh.

"You use those safe words if this gets too much."

"Okay."

"Are you on birth control?" His lips nip at my nape.

"Yes."

He rests his head taking a deep breath. "Thank fuck, I need to feel you so bad." He sits up, spreading my legs, exposing my pussy for him. He groans, and I jump when he touches me with an ice cube. On my clit.

"How does that feel?"

"G-Good." My hand grips the spindle till my knuckles turn white.

Then he shoves the ice cube inside of me. "Hold it, don't let it fall out."

I hiss from the shock, squeezing my inner walls around something cold sends my body into overdrive. I've never done something like this before. Sex has always been vanilla for me. Squeezing as the ice melts, water drips out. Cole's sculpted body is on show for me, his deep v lines showing me precisely what I'm about to receive. Cole strokes himself, his piercings glimmering in the faint light. I've never felt a pierced cock before. He slowly leans forward, lining up.

"What about the ice?"

He smirks. "Don't you worry about that." He runs his piercing along my clit, before finding my wet entrance. He slowly nudges his way in, stretching me. "Oh, fuck, you're so tight holding that ice. I'm going to fuck this ice right out of you."

He pushes the rest of the way in. My scream is silent as I feel everything. The sensation is unlike anything I've felt

before. The warmth of his cock mixed with the coldness of the ice.

"That's right." *Thrust.* "Take." *Thrust.* "Everything." He tells me between thrusts. I reach down, grabbing his ass to get him deeper when he stops. I let out a whine.

"What did I tell you about letting go?" He pulls out, flipping me over onto my knees. "You need to listen, little one. Hands out front."

Smack. Then another ice cube is placed inside. "Cole, holy shit."

"You can take it; I know you can." Then he slams back into me with much more force. I come immediately, clamping around him with a force that he groans and digs his fingers into my hips, pulling me closer. My knees are trembling to keep me up. His thrusts become ruthless, his hands coming to my shoulders as he brings his feet onto the bed. He only becomes more savage this way. My lower stomach tightens again. I hide my head in the bed and scream, closing my eyes tight. I see stars and chase my release until I struggle to stay on my knees. Cole speeds ups before pulling out and coming all over my back.

"You look good covered in my cum." He draws swirls in his cum, and then I collapse on the bed.

My eyelids are like bricks. I can't keep them open anymore. I'm on a high. I didn't even pay attention when Cole cleaned off my back or when he pulled me into his chest. The kisses he leaves on my shoulder feel like a distance.

"Feeling okay, Wednesday?"

"Yeah, tired and sore."

He rubs my neck and into my hair. "Sore in a good way?"

"Yes, and no. My hand is starting to throb again. I need to get my brace on." He rolls away, leaving the room. I get up, making my way to the bathroom. Cole is sitting on the bed when I get back into the bedroom. He glances up and down, and that's when I realize I'm still naked.

He takes my hand, slips my brace on, kissing my exposed knuckles. "Let's get you to bed. We have a lot to figure out in the morning."

I never thought sleeping in the same bed with someone would make me feel so safe before. I never wanted to rely on anyone to make me feel this way, especially after her sons terrorized me. I felt like I couldn't trust anybody ever again. They completely ruined me.

"Shh, I got you. Everything will be okay." He wipes a tear that's streaming down my cheek. That's when I realized I'd been crying. How dare those assholes get my tears. I cuddle closer, closing my eyes.

* * *

We're all sitting around the kitchen table while Dorian cooks breakfast. Bacon crisping on the stove while he flips pancakes makes this seem a little too homey for me. This wasn't how this was supposed to be. How did we end up here, anyway? I'm looking at each one of them. They chat, drinking coffee like it's a regular morning. I've

never been around such normalcy. I'm not sure how I'm supposed to act. Is this a normal thing for people to do every morning? I've only ever seen this in movies. These three have a strong bond I've never seen before. To be honest, it's a beautiful sight to see.

"How long have you known each other?" My eyes darted around the room, looking at each one.

"Dorian and I have known each other since elementary school. Then we met Cole in junior high," Nyx says, looking at them with a heartfelt smile.

"That's a really long ass time."

"Doesn't seem that long when you think about it. We've been through a lot of shit together. I wouldn't have it any other way." Dorian smiles over his shoulder.

Guess that's what I'm missing in life, a friendship. I've always been classified as the *weird* one in school that no one wanted to become friends with. I've let it grow the older I've gotten. If no one wanted to be friends with me, that was fine.

Dorian places the food on the table before sitting next to me. His hand resting on my thigh, inching under the t-shirt that I'm wearing, he puts a pancake on my plate, followed by some bacon.

"Eat, please," he whispers, sending shivers down my spine. I have difficulty concentrating on anything with him sitting this close to me.

"All right, we need to figure out what the fuck went down last night. Do you have any enemies?"

I can feel Cole's eyes on me, but I continue to stare at my pancakes. Do I have enemies? I don't think so. Why

would I? I always stick to myself, and I bug no one. I shake my head. "No, I never talk to anyone around campus. I go to class, then back to my apartment. I never disrupt anyone."

"What about your art? Has anyone been pissed off because you've excelled more than them?" This time, Nyx asked the question. The concern is written all over his face.

"Again, not that I can think of. I wouldn't classify myself as the best painter." I hitch my shoulders. My forehead creasing as I think of someone. "I honestly don't know who this could be. What about one of you? It could be someone you know."

All three lean back at the same time when they realize that it could be them.

"Well, shit, I didn't think of that. We've pissed off so many people it's not even funny." Nyx rubs the back of his neck, bringing his hand around and rubbing his chin. "What if she's right?"

"If she's right, then we have our work cut out for us." Dorian's shoulder slumped forward.

Cole only sits there staring straight ahead, not saying or doing anything.

Only stewing.

"Cole," I say his name in a low whisper. He slowly cocks his head in my direction. His blue eyes hardened when they landed on me.

"I think it's time for you to head home. One of us will give you a ride" His voice is low but stern.

I cringe. This can't be from the same person who just took me to bed last night, who apologized because he was in the wrong. Can it?

"What the hell, Cole?" Dorian demanded. "She didn't do anything wrong. Where is this coming from?"

Cole narrows his gaze on Dorian. "I want her out."

You know what? I know when I'm wanted; clearly, this isn't it. I thought this was going to be different. I rise from the table, never taking my eyes off Cole.

"You know what, Cole, I regret everything. All of it. You, them... all of it. I thought this was going to be different. You are just like every other guy out there. Once you get it, you turn into a complete asshole." It makes him flinch, but he says nothing.

Dorian reaches for me, but I pull out of his grip. Nyx stands looking like a lost puppy. Fuck them. I'll find my own way home. I march upstairs to Cole's room, throwing on my clothes and grabbing my bag. Dorian and Nyx are waiting by the front door when I come down.

"Don't listen to him, and he's just upset, that's all," Nyx pleads.

I give him a clipped nod. "Sure, he is. What happens next time? He repeats something because something pisses him off. I'm not dealing with that. I don't need someone in my life that can't figure out what he wants or to wait till he grows the fuck up. Sorry, but I can't do this."

Dorian hangs his head. I feel bad because, in return, I have to punish these two. It's not fair, but I can't keep two knowing they still talk to him. I grab the doorknob.

"I'll drive you," Dorian tells me.

"That's fine. I called a ride." They don't need to know I didn't need to walk all this built up energy off. Pulling the door open, I step outside, saying goodbye to what I thought would be the best thing in my life.

12
Catalina

It's been a week since I've talked to any of the guys. Nothing but radio silence from all of them. I understand that's how I wanted it. That was the last thing I remember before my entire world went dark.

They haven't been at school since I walked out of their house. Not sure if that's Coles doing or mine. I've been trying to ignore them, too. I guess I'm still trying to figure out what the hell happened between Cole and me. We were fine, and all of a sudden. Boom. He went off on me. It's like he did a one-eighty.

My finger is healed, so I'm able to go back to work. It helps, so I can't think as much. I had to take an extension on my art project, and I can't express my gratitude. My piece turned out better than I could imagine. Probably because I have all this pent-up anger inside. I'm also going

to assume one of the boys had my car fixed for me because Johnny was parked right outside of my apartment a few days after I walked out of their house. Now I have to find the finances to pay them back. I don't want to owe them any favours.

I'm sitting in my Philosophy class, trying to listen to Professor Adams, but his voice sounds so dry today. Who cares about caring about people when my entire world is crashing around me. I have problems going on, too, you know. More significant than what he's trying to preach. I sound like a sad sack. They clearly got what they wanted and are now done with me, so why am I still so obsessed with them? It's not like I ever gave them the time of day before, so it shouldn't matter now. I need to either drown myself in paint or a grave. Right about now, I'd take the grave. I need to wear myself out physically.

I'm about to pass out when the door to the classroom opens. Dr. Deadbodies rushes in. I tried to avoid eye contact; we made a deal that we wouldn't pay attention to each other outside of our classroom or at night if need be. The fact that he's in my classroom right now has me nervous. I didn't think he and Professor Adams were friends. But makes sense since they work in the same place. He's exchanging words with Adams rather quickly and quietly. What do they have in common in this university? Dr. Deadbodies teaches biological sciences. This doesn't make any sense to me.

When he walks past me, he locks his eyes on me. A small shiver runs down my spine. I've never felt any threat from him before. I must be paranoid from my

attack last week. I haven't had any more weird run-ins, although I've kept my work to a minimum and only worked once if we're being honest. The creep could be waiting for me. Still, I just haven't placed myself in danger yet. He gives me a slight nod before leaving.

I do have a job tonight, and I'll have to ask what the fuck was up with this. I don't like secrets.

It's freezing tonight. I bundle up extra; I even pack a pair of mittens.

Heading to the school again, I figured I might as well confront Dr. Deadbodies and see what the hell was going down earlier today.

"Calm the fuck down, Cat." I'm a nervous wreck, and I'm going to cause one. I grip the steering wheel of my poor Beetle. I've never felt this way before. I'm scanning the entire road to ensure I'm not being followed. Once I'm in my van, no one will know it's me, and I'll feel a little safer. I knew I should've joined that stupid self-defence class constantly being advertised. But *no,* I thought nothing would happen to me in a dark, scary parking lot.

"Yeah, well, look what fucking happened, Catalina."

When I'm parked safely in the parking lot, under a streetlight, I exit my car. I wrap my coat around my body, protecting myself from the night air. My nose stings from the coldness already. I hustle my ass inside, and I find Dr.

Deadbodies inside his office typing away on his computer. I clear my throat to get his attention.

"Oh, sorry, I didn't hear you come in. Sit, sit. I have something I would like to discuss with you." He sounds extra excited to see me, which calms me down.

I have no choice but to grab the seat he wants me to claim. I lean back in the chair, crossing my right leg over my left knee, tapping my finger on my knee. I raise my chin, and I wait.

Then I wait. Like how *long* does it take to tell me some shit.

I stare at him and narrow my eyes. "Well, what is it?"

"I know you like digging up bodies, but with the weather turning colder sooner than expected, we won't be able to work as much." I nod because he is right. "I figured you could help in the lab. I know it's not the best, but it's something."

He still doesn't answer why he was talking to the professor, but does it matter why he was talking to him? Guess it really doesn't affect me. I think about what he asked. Working inside does sound fantastic right about now. "When would I start?"

"Not for a few more weeks. We need stock beforehand. I'll get everything sorted out. Until then, you have two bodies to recover. You can space it out. But I need them here by tomorrow night. We should've been on them a few days ago."

I flex my hand, giving him a nod. He looks at my hand. "Is it better?"

"Ya, it gets a little stiff in the morning, but nothing I can't handle. I got this. I'll see you tomorrow, I guess." With that, I head out.

I gather my gear, making sure the van is fully stocked once again. It's going to be weird working inside for once and around others. That's going to be difficult for me, talking to others and small talk. My skin crawls with the thought. My phone goes off with a text, and only one person is texting me these days, so I know exactly who's it from. Pulling it out of my bag, it's directions to the graves. Both are in town.

Perfect, I don't feel like driving more than I have to.

The night is peaceful, and even the wind is quiet. Nothing is moving tonight. This is how I love my mind, empty. Yet again, the grave is at the very back of the cemetery. Like always, this place gives me the chills. And I call myself a fan of all things scary.

When I open the van door, a gust of wind blows inside. If that isn't a sign, then I don't know what is.

"You need to get out of your head." True, it serves me right for watching a horror movie last night. I'll stick with true crimes as my bedtime lullabies, apparently. The leaves crunch under my combat boots when I walk to the back of the van, a sound I've grown very fond of. It's going to suck losing that as well. I'll have to take up evening strolls like an eighty-year-old just to get my intake of fall. Then again, he knows more than I do and what's best. It's his business, and I'm the employee.

Just once, I would love to sell one of my paintings. That would help substantially, and I only need to find the right

market for my work. People in Eastwood are dull and lack the taste of art, apparently. Do I need to finish school? I only came here to get away, and I received a scholarship. I could always drop out, move somewhere else, get a job, and start selling my work. It's not like I have anyone here holding me back.

Then the guys all pop into my mind. Why I can't get them out is beyond me. It's not like we spent so much time together. We only slept together, that's it. I don't owe them dick shit. But maybe it could have led to something, and I could finally have my happiness with them. Don't I owe myself that, at least? Not that it matters anymore. They made it perfectly clear what Cole says goes.

My heart sinks more, sorta like this shovel is doing when I dig in the soft earth. Am I being too weak on myself? I've been through... well, we know what that is, don't we?

Things are going at a slow pace. I'm not in a considerable hurry tonight like I was told if I get everything done by tomorrow. I'm in the clear. I don't bother straining myself, I dig slower than usual, which will take me a couple of hours longer, but it's not like I have anywhere else to be. God, I sound like a sad sap. Why can't I be a better person? I just want to be happy.

"Broken record, that's what you sound like," I sing out loud. Glad no one is around to hear my horrible singing voice. My shovel hits the coffin with a thud. Would it be wrong of me to wish for once I found treasure instead of a body? After getting out of the grave, I stand on the edge of the hole, staring down at the open coffin

contemplating things. That's when I hear it, a peal of deep dark laughter.

I swivel around, gripping my shovel tight. I know for a fact that my mind isn't playing games. I heard that I just couldn't see anything in the darkness. I crouch down low and start crawling toward my bag. If only I could get to it and grab my bear spray, I knew I should've worn it around my neck. The laughter comes again, only this time closer. With a shaky hand, I snatch the can from my bag. I study the tree line, then the tombstones behind me. The voice is in either direction. My only option is to run again. I'm taking my shovel with me this time.

I race away, almost stumbling over my feet. Why can't there be lights in the cemetery?

"Where are you running to, pretty girl?" His voice rings out in the night.

How the hell is he finding me? I thought I had lost him. I look over my shoulder in time to see a glimpse of the yellow led light of his mask dart behind a tombstone. I hide behind the closet one, my heart racing a mile a minute.

"Come out, come out wherever you are," he sings.

I go to reach for my phone, only to realize I left it in my bag. *Fuckin' stupid idiot.* What are the odds of me getting back to my bag?

"I'm coming for you, pretty girl." His voice is nearing closer to me, and I need to make my move now if I'm going to do it.

I dash out, making a zig-zag pattern making it harder for him to catch me. I hear the leaves behind me crunch-

ing under his footsteps. I peer over my shoulder to see him gaining on me. It was that moment when my foot fell further than I expected. My heart bottoms out.

I fall into the grave I just dug, smacking the side of my head on the edge of the open coffin. My vision turns blurry if I move my eyes, and I become dizzy if I move too quickly. I touch the side of my head, wincing when I brush a bloody cut. I get up slowly when I hear that laughter again, only a few feet away. I need to find that fuckin' bear spray, and of course, I never got my hooks down here yet.

"Oh, come on now. You'll have to get out of there eventually. Can't stay down there forever."

I glance upwards at him; his demeanour screams he's going to do whatever he wants with me. I need to find a way to outsmart him. He's still wearing that led mask, I can't tell what he looks like, but I can feel his eyes are on me.

"What do you want from me? I don't even know who you are?"

He laughs again. "Climb out of that hole, and I'll show you who I am," he says with a sinister voice.

"Yep, I'm good down here." I move to the side that I would climb out as if I was working. He doesn't need to know I'm currently planning an escape. I may be short, but I'm a quick climber. I scan the contents of the coffin. Why couldn't this one be buried with something special?

Like a thick book.

"Whatever you're planning, it's not going to work. Either way, I'll catch you."

This time, his voice comes from right above my head. I crane my neck to stare at him; I smile and flip him the middle finger.

"Fuck you."

13
Nyx

I'm so pissed off with Cole and can't stand being in the same room as him.

Where does he get the right to go off on her like that? Everything was going great at breakfast until she mentioned it could be someone we knew. It's not like we haven't made enemies being in Soul Stealers, but he didn't have to be an asshole to her. Here I thought we were finally making progress, and then he goes and sets us back again.

"Seriously, did you have to kick her out?" Dorian asks, looking more pissed off than me.

Cole slams his hands on the kitchen table. "Yes, if it was someone, we knew we were only causing her to be in more danger. I did what I thought was right." He bows his head, exhaling loud.

"I'm sure you could've done it a little better than kicking her out, especially after what you did last night, asshole." I glare at him, shaking my head.

He runs his hand through his already messy hair. "Fuck, I didn't think of that."

I scoff, walking towards the fridge. "Of course, you didn't. All you thought about was yourself and trying to protect you."

His hand is around my throat, pushing me into the fridge in a second. "You watch your fucking mouth; you have no idea."

"I'm pretty sure I do." I struggle to get out.

"Hey, back up, man." Dorian pulls Cole away. Once his hand is off my throat, I swing.

I get one good punch to Cole's pretty face before Dorian steps in again.

"Cool it, Nyx, we understand, but this isn't like you. We don't fight each other." He says the last part to Cole. "Now, I say we keep away from her for a week and see what happens. If no one attacks her, then we know it's us. I'm not dealing with your toddler tantrums any longer than I have to."

He storms out of the kitchen. I turn to Cole. "Figure this shit out, you have one week, and that's it." We made a deal when we were in high school. If we found someone, we all liked that it was all or nothing. Well, I'm not letting him get his way. Catalina belongs with us; I can feel it, and I'm sure Dorian does, too. If only Cole could pull his head out of his ass long enough to see it.

The next day at school, I skipped my philosophy class. I couldn't stand the thought of facing Cat. If that makes me sound like a coward, so be it. I can't look her in the eyes without breaking down and begging her to come back.

Instead, I watch her from a distance.

She strolls into the classroom with her head down, and her hair is braided to the side, showing off her beautiful neck. She wears an oversized black hoodie, leggings and combat boots. I would be concerned about the amount of black she's wearing, but this is Catalina we're talking about. I would have been worried if she had shown up wearing colour. Not that I'm not concerned. I can tell that she's taking this hard. The stupid thing is we weren't even together yet. We all felt it, though. A week is going to be torture.

I'm sitting in the warehouse while Henry tells us he has had no leads on who's digging up the bodies. We've been quiet this entire time, telling him we've been making our rounds, but haven't seen anything that looks suspicious.

They must be doing it after we leave. That is what we tell him.

He didn't like that answer. "I've given you enough time, so I hired outside help. I know you three have been busy with your schoolwork and all." Cole goes to interrupt him, but Henry holds his hand up. "Just listen. He's only here

to go out after you get back in. He's not going to step on your toes. Would I do that to you after all these years?"

Honestly, yes, I don't trust him. Especially now, why wouldn't he sit us down and talk to us? This is like a slap in the face, and it's telling us we can't do our job. We're only doing this to protect Catalina. We aren't stupid. He should know by now that we don't fail at any of our jobs. Why would we start now? I knew we should've found some fuckin' loser and brought him in.

"Do we get to meet this person or anything?" Dorian looks at Henry with disgust. I can tell he already hates the idea of someone stepping on our toes. Someone else in our territory. Hunting his half pint. I can read his thoughts.

Henry squints his eye at Dorian. "Not yet, boy." Dorian hates being called boy.

"Then when? This is bullshit." He slams his fist on the table. His chest rose and fell quickly.

"You'll meet him when he finishes the job unless you finish before him. Either way, I want it done soon. Suppose anyone hears what's going on in this town. It's game over."

Oh, yes, his charming town with the mayor. How can we ever forget? What happened to handing out drugs to college kids or the surrounding area? Those were the best times. Now he's worried about Catalina digging up bodies for the medical class, Jesus Christ.

"I do have another job for you three. It'll take you out of town for a couple of days. I need you to check production and ensure everyone is in line."

I don't like the thought of leaving, thankfully, it's only a couple of days, and we should be back before the end of the week.

"Send us the details. We'll leave first thing in the morning. I doubt you have anything to worry about if they know whose boss, that is," Cole tells Henry. Stroke his ego, and you're in the clear.

"Very well. Keep me updated, and I'll see you when you get back." With that, we are dismissed.

The three of us walk out, nodding to Freddy on our way. I would love to stay and chat, but I need to clear my mind. Climbing on my black Harley, Dorian climbs onto his red one and Cole on his grey. We start them at the same time, giving them a quick rev. My tire spins out on the gravel before it catches traction. I shoot out of the warehouse compound like I don't give a fuck. To be honest, right about now, I don't. My only concern is Catalina. If she's still digging, she might get caught, and it won't be by us this time. The shitty thing is we won't be around to help her. That's what's getting to me.

This stupid job takes us to a remote location, all because Henry wants us to check on shit. Give me a break. I call bullshit. We've never had to come out here before, so why we are starting now blows my mind.

"I hate this. Why couldn't he send someone else? Like, Royce. He's newer and needs to prove himself, we're the enforcers, and he sends all of us out of town simultaneously. This smells fishy." The way Dorian stands with his back half turned to the door; tells me he doesn't trust any of these guys.

I'm beginning to think Henry might have more information than he should. If he's been spying on our personal life, I'm having second thoughts about this gang lifestyle. This isn't what I signed up for. I don't see why it would matter if we found someone. He can't hold her over our heads.

"Heads up," Cole nods towards the far door.

I notice a group of ten enter, wearing all black, walking with a hand in their pockets. Guaranteed, they are packing either a gun or a knife. They came here looking to cause shit. Well, it seems like it's our lucky fuckin' day. If this doesn't make Henry happy, then I can't help him.

"Wait until they make the first move. We came to help, not start shit." Cole cracks his knuckles, waiting to get them bloody.

"Where's James?" The leader of the group calls out.

A few of the men standing around don't move, nor do they bother to call out for James. Guess they've done this before. Finally, one man steps forward.

"We're not doing this again, Jayce. Leave now, or you'll regret your life."

"See, that's not going to work for me this time. I was promised double last time, and you failed to deliver. I paid for it, and it never happened. Either hand it over." He pulls his gun out and clicks the safety off. "Or we'll simply... take it." He hitches his shoulder.

Oh, shit. Is James skimming his dealers? Dorian and Cole both stiffen at the realization that this is what happened. Son of a bitch. Henry brought us here so we would fight and make it, so he won. He only wants the money

and extra product. He knew someone was about to call him out on his shit.

"I don't like this at all," Dorian whispers.

"Same, but we have no choice. If we don't try, James' men will send word back to Henry." Cole dulled his voice down to a whisper.

"So, you want us to fight even though our side is in the wrong?" I ask, feeling disgusted even asking the question.

Cole's shoulders droop forward. "Yeah, unfortunately, we don't have a choice."

Before we can do anything else, a shot is fired, and it's a mess. I whip my guns out, not knowing which side to shoot. But in the end, my gang comes first.

When we arrive home, we head straight to the warehouse, and we haven't said a word to each other since we shot and killed everyone from Jayce's crew. I'm pissed, and I can tell the other two are pissed. It was so uncalled for, and Henry needs to be called out for it. There's no way he didn't know that shit wasn't going down.

Cole storms into the warehouse first. It's quiet, which is weird. Freddy isn't in his regular spot.

"Where the fuck is everyone?"

I look around when I notice a light coming from the office down the hallway. "Down there, in the furthest office."

The closer we get we can hear muffled voices coming from behind the closed door. Dorian doesn't bother knocking, and his patience is wearing thin. Pushing it open, he stalls. Blocking Cole and me from entering.

"What the fuck is going on?" he raises his voice in a thunderous tone. Coles had enough of waiting and pushes past him.

"Who the fuck is this?" he spits out.

I take notice of Henry sitting at his desk while someone else is sitting across from him. His hair is black, and his moss like eyes never leave mine. Then he smiles.

"So, these must be the enforcers." He rises, sticking out his hand. "I don't mean to be rude. I'm Conrad."

I step forward, shaking his hand and squeezing harder than usual. I hate meeting people crouching in my territory, and this guy is screaming hardcore.

"I'm Nyx, and this is Dorian and Cole."

"What the hell is going on, Henry?" Cole narrows his eyes at Conrad.

"Calm down, boys. I heard about what happened at James'. Congratulations, by the way. I'm impressed things could've gone way differently; I knew you three could handle it."

"Handle that? It was a fuckin' mess, and you know it. You knew all along that James was skimming, didn't you? You just didn't care. Any other jobs you care to tell us

about before we go." Dorian places a hand on Cole to keep him from doing anything he'll regret later.

Henry waves us off, then he simply stands. "Remember when I said I would only introduce you to the person once they caught the person responsible for digging up the graves?"

I try to keep my expression blank. The taste of bile slowly rises in my throat. If this is true, Catalina is caught.

"I did the job that you three couldn't. I caught the digger last night. It was rather easy; they didn't even hear me sneak up on them."

Them? "What do you mean them? There were two?"

"Oh yes, and they are in the torture room right now." Conrad sounds too excited; his entire face is glowing.

I send a side eye to Cole and see him dig his phone out of his pocket. We follow Henry and Conrad into the hallway.

"Anything?" Dorian asks.

"It goes straight to voicemail. Well, if they haven't caught her, then who the fuck did they catch?" I mummer.

"To be honest, I don't care as long as it isn't her," Cole grunts out.

"I still like to know who this Conrad guy is. I've never seen nor heard of him before. He weirds me out," Dorian states. I would have to agree. Where did Henry find this guy?

The door to the torture room is open. When I see who's inside, I freeze. They are both tied to a chair bloodied, and the 'them' they are referring to are Professor Adams and

Professor Davis. Two people associated with Catalina. Tortured enough, and Professor Davis will squeal like a pig.

"How do you know it's them?" Cole asks.

"I found them in the cemetery, poking around a grave. It was dug up." Conrad kicks Professor Davis.

He jolts awake, looking around with wide eyes and shaking his head. Conrad kicks Professor Adams awake next. He moans, coming too slowly. When he spots us three, he panics—pulling against his restraints, yelling into his covered mouth.

Recognition plays in Professor Adams' eyes when he calms down. He stares at me, then moves his eyes to the corner of the room. He does this a few times before I catch on. I casually scratch my head turning.

My eyes land on something, something very familiar.

A tan satchel with pins all over it. I only know one person with that bag. I turn back to the professor; he nods slightly, letting me know she's gone. Now I understand why they were caught.

The question is, where the fuck is she, and who the fuck has her?

TO BE CONTINUED...

C. L. EASTON

STRANGERS OF THE TOWN

STRANGERS OF EASTWOOD BOOK TWO

1

Dorian

My eyes must be lying to me because these men in front of me are not responsible for anything. This Conrad fuck thinks he's caught the grave digger. Little does he know he only saw the ones that were looking out for her. Where we failed, they came through. I can't let them die because of us. I knew we shouldn't have let her go.

"I'll see that they are properly looked after," I told Henry, "it's technically mine—our job, after all." I gesture between the guys.

Conrad gives me a screwed-up look, I pretty much took the candy away from the baby, and he's pissed about it. The tension rolls off him.

"I suppose that is why I made you all the enforcers, isn't it? I can't be taking away your jobs now, can I. Very well, call me when the job is finished." He nods for Conrad to follow, leaving us alone.

"What the hell is going on?" Cole demands.

Nyx walks over, pulling the cloth from both professors' mouths. While they cough, he explains.

"Catalina's bag is in the corner of the room." He points to the far corner of the room. I turn to look, and he's right. I see her satchel walking over. I bend down and dig through it. I am trying to find anything that will let us know where she is. All I see are snacks, sanitizer, wipes, some other random girl products and her phone.

Which is dead.

"Great, so no clues. Where the hell would she be? How long has it been?"

Professor Davis groans. "I gave her the job earlier tonight. We talked about another job opportunity. I wanted to check up on her because of her hand, and I became worried when she didn't answer. We went to go check on her."

"That's when we found her missing, then the next thing we know, were both hit over the head and waking up in this room," Professor Adam told us.

Great, so no one knows where the fuck she is. "There wasn't anything to hint at where she is?" Nyx questioned them.

They shake their heads.

Cole punches the wall yelling, "Fuck." Rubbing his eyes, he turns to us. "We need to try to find her, retrace her steps or something, the longer she's gone."

He doesn't finish his sentence; we all are thinking the same thing, the longer she's gone, the more time whoever has her can torture her or worse.

"What about them? How are we going to get them out of here and produce bodies for Henry?"

Cole looks at me and smirks. "Guess we're going to have to channel our inner Wednesday. How do you know which ones to dig up?" He looks back at Professor Davis.

"I usually look in the newspaper for the obituaries, then wait until the funeral to see where they are buried. It's not rocket science or anything."

Huh, I figured it was a lot more work than that, but this way makes more sense and is more straightforward.

"But she didn't finish her jobs tonight," Professor Davis said.

"What you mean is, there are two bodies in the cemetery that we can use."

"Jesus Christ Nyx, yes. Does he have to spell it out for you?" Cole snaps, losing his patience.

"Sorry," he muttered.

We need to work together, or it's going to turn to shit; I get that we're all under a lot of pressure, but it's not doing her any good. I try to ignore all the arguing that's going on and try to figure out a plan. If we do successfully dig up these bodies and somehow sneak them into the warehouse, then what? Can you even beat up a dead body? We are so far out of our element. I'm thankful that we watched Catalina dig up that one body. I'm sure we have this in the bag, but it's still a process either way.

As we leave the warehouse, we bump into Freddy.

"What are you boys doing sneaking around here?"

"Freddy, you didn't see us. You got that?" Cole emphasized. "We have shit to do, and we can't involve anyone. We trust you, old man."

Freddy gives us a nod. "I ain't seen shit. Have a good night, boys."

That's one thing I love about him. He'll do anything for us, and I don't think he fully trusts Henry either. I'm not sure why he's still in the gang.

The drive to the cemetery goes by faster than I hoped for. With directions from Davis, we find the van. Everything that we need is inside.

"The question remains, how the fuck are we going to drive this thing into the compound?" Nyx finally asks the question that I've been thinking about.

Cole ponders for a minute. "We'll tell Henry it's the new delivery van only if we get caught. We'll have to get to the compound in the morning. It should work."

I look at him. "And if it doesn't."

"I'm not sure, to be honest."

We set off towards the grave that Cat started, and when we arrived, everything was still the way she had left it. Maybe we can find a clue here. Whoever took her had to leave something behind. No one is that stealthy. Except we find nothing, just the grave. It doesn't look like there was even a struggle. I have so many questions. Did he sneak up on her? Maybe she ran, and he caught up with her elsewhere? Either way, we need to find her.

"Hurry, this gives me bad mojo. Bodies are meant to be resting. What we're about to be doing will give us bad karma." Nyx looks down at the grave, staring at the body,

and a shiver jolts off his body. He was always a sensitive soul.

Cole scoffs. "You're worried about karma? We just killed how many people? But this." He points downwards. "Is bad mojo. Get off that horse of yours. Grab the hook and get down there."

I save Nyx from heading down there and don't mind this sort of thing. Besides, I watched Cat do it, so I feel confident enough. Jumping down into a grave is the weirdest thing I've ever done.

"I can't believe half pint does this for a job. She can barely see over this thing." I strap the hooks under the arms.

"Her job is pretty interesting, isn't it." Cole waits for me to finish before he can haul the body up.

I whistle, letting him know I'm finished. The body slides out of the coffin with a thud, up the dirt, then I hear the crinkling sound of the body bag. I climb out of the hole and see Nyx zipping up the bag.

"One down, one more to go," he grunts as he hauls it up over his shoulder, walking back to the van.

"This time, we'll have to dig, speaking of digging. Where's the shovel?"

That gets us to look around, usually, all her gear is in one pile. I shake my head when I don't see it. I reach for my phone and flick the flashlight on, lighting up our surroundings. I walk away to the east of the site. Maybe she took it or threw it. Honestly, I'm grasping at straws. If some punk kids had come, I'm positive they wouldn't have taken a shovel. I'm sure they would've done some-

thing with the body. What I don't understand is when Conrad picked up the professors why he never refilled the grave in again. This whole digging-up bodies was the reason Henry was in a tizzy in the first place, so why leave it open?

"Yo, over here," Cole yelled opposite the side of the grave.

I hustle over to him, and he's bending down, picking up the shovel. We're a reasonable distance away from both the grave and the van.

"What do you think?"

"Either she tried to run, or she used it as a weapon." He looks it over, not finding any blood. We both relax a little. "We need her back, D." I can hear the desperation in his voice. We're all going to go crazy if we don't find her.

We're halfway through digging and haven't exchanged a single word. We switch off every half hour, and the only thing that goes through my head is that Cat does this alone, and she's half my size. I still can't imagine how she can do this more than once some nights.

"How far down do we go again?" Cole asked, wiping sweat off his forehead.

"Till you hit the coffin, I'm guessing." I shrug. "The other one wasn't very deep."

"I'm just hoping this plan works, or all this is for noth-ing."

I would have to agree with him. If Henry suspects any-thing, we're fucked. Before I can think more, the shovel hits the coffin. Cole looks up at me, shallows hard.

"Fuck, now I gotta open it."

"Man, the fuck up, you are a member of the Soul Steal-ers. You, torture people, remember." That's the most admirable pep talk I'll ever give.

"Crowbar, let's get this over with."

The drive back to the warehouse has me nervous. It's pushing dawn, and if we're lucky, Henry will still be asleep and be oblivious to what's about to happen. Nyx pulls the van around the back, parking at the doors that lead to the torture room. Climbing out, I stand guard while Cole heads inside. He's going to bring out Davis and Adams while we move both bodies in. Then we'll make it look like we killed and tortured them. Pray it'll be enough, and no one will see the difference. We'll have to pay special attention to their faces, that's my only worry.

The doors open again, and Davis comes limping out.

"You're going to need blood. Dead bodies don't pro-duce," he reminds me.

Ah, shit. Sorta overlooked that, didn't we? "Now what? We don't have time to head somewhere else."

"Check the van. See what you got in there. We might be able to help." Adams says from behind me.

I raise an eyebrow questioningly. "I'm sorry, you might be able to help. How?"

Adams chuckles. "Well, my body was full of blood last time I checked. What about you, Davis?"

"Mmm-hmm. Red River is a flowing."

I go to say something but come up empty. After everything they've been through, they still want to go through more. Unbelievable. Nyx climbs in the back, digging through all of the totes, trying to find something we could use. Except this van is meant for the dead and not the living. What we need is a miracle. Nyx holds up a knife. I look over at them and smile. They jerk their head no, quickly.

"That'll be a no, Nyx."

"Damn. Too bad she didn't have this on her tonight." He tosses it back in the tote and climbs out of the van. "I can't find anything in there. Unless we slice and dice something. We're fucked." He turns to Davis and Adam, raising an eyebrow.

"No, Nyx," Cole says from the doorway. "Get the bodies inside, and we'll figure something out. We can find something inside. You two in the van."

Trying to do things sneakily in a quiet building is hard. Every little sound is heightened. I swear Henry will hear us from his fuckin' shack up the road. I throw a body on the chair, and if you're wondering.

Both bodies are male.

So, our plan will work, and yes, we get the *pleasure* of stripping them naked.

"I'll go and find something we can use. You two strip them and get them tied to the chairs. I don't care what

you do to make them look abused." Only Cole would leave us with the shitty jobs.

"Dickhead, who put him in charge again?"

I can't help it. My lips pull into a slow smile. "We did. Cole's technically older."

"Pfft, he's older by two months. So, he's hardly one to give orders."

"No, but you know how he likes to have control and likes to boss everyone around."

We busy ourselves prepping the bodies, waiting for Cole to return. We strip them off their clothes and get them in position. I look at the table with all the tools. I reach for the blowtorch, lighting it up.

Here's to hoping dead flesh doesn't smell like living flesh.

I was wrong. The dead smell is so much worse. Especially when they have chemicals in their bodies. Nyx and I nearly barfed all over the place. All I did was go around their wrists and ankles. I had to make it look like they struggled in their restraints some. Cole chose this moment to walk in.

"Oh, sweet fuck. What is that?" He covers his nose with his shirt.

Nyx points to the bodies, then to the blow torch still in my hand. He places a finger over his lips, tilting his head to the side. He swallows. "He... um... burnt their flesh." He exhales, then walks to the outside doors, opening them a crack to grab some fresh air.

"You sick sonofabitch. I found this." He holds up a syringe. "It'll have to work. This place is empty for emergency shit."

"I guess they'll have to play rock, paper, scissors."

"Unless you torch them some more, then we just add some blood here and there. That should do it. Snap a picture or two. It should keep Henry satisfied."

That's true. It's Conrad that might want to see the bodies. He rubs me off like a fuckin' creep.

We spent the next couple of hours getting the bodies situated for the photos. Adams ended up drawing the short straw. He didn't seem to care, more relieved than anything, because his nightmare was almost over. To be honest, I can't wait till it's over as well. Then we can focus on Catalina.

2
Catalina

"You are a worthless whore, Catalina. You're going to mount to nothing." My mother spits in my face. All I wanted to do was go to the school dance, and I didn't think it was too much to ask for. Everyone else gets to go, so why can't I?

"Are you listening to me, girl? Or do I have to get your brothers involved?"

I shake my head. "N-no, mother. I'm listening, I swear." My voice was shaking. My nerves are on edge every time she's around. One wrong move, and I'm off to see my brothers, and it's her go to move. I just have to play nice with her. But I want to go to this dance. I don't ask for much, but this one thing I want.

"Please, can I go? I'll only go for an hour, I swear." I look up at her. Her green eyes burned into my violet eyes. Her jaw clenched like madness.

That's where I made my mistake. I looked into her eyes. Not only does she hate me, but she also hates my violet eyes. She says it's what makes me a whore. It'll bring the men in because it's my fault that I was born with them. Before I can move, her hand collides with my cheek. Heat explodes the entire way up my face. I grab the side of my face, keeping my tears at bay. If I dare cry around her, it'll only get worse.

"Don't ever ask for shit. Get to your room. I don't want to see you until I'm ready." Her voice holds a savage edge.

I scramble up the stairs, and the oldest son greets me at the top of the stairs. I freeze, and my body physically shuts down. Fear clawed its way through me. His lips twisted to the side, sneering at me. His dark, empty eyes stare into mine like daggers.

"I heard you were causing grief with Momma. This better not be true."

I felt a lump at the back of my throat. All I could do was shake my head mutely.

"I doubt you know what's expected of you."

My blood runs cold. "Please, no. I promise never to do it again." Lips were trembling around every word. When the rest of the sons appear, it makes the air in my lungs vanish. My entire body shakes, and sweat builds up on my forehead while they stare at me. I gingerly wipe it away with a trembling hand.

A hand clamps down on my wrist, dragging me the rest of the way to my bedroom. Please, no, not the closet. I can't go another round of the closet. Every time I was in there, they left me longer and longer. I fear this will be bad. The way all the sons are looking at me. They throw me in my room; once

they pile inside, they slam the door shut. Sealing in my fate. I clamp my eyes closed when the first fist meets my face.

I wake sweaty and wheezing. I haven't had a dream like that in forever. Not since I moved out of that house. I thought I was past all that, so what brought them back? I have no idea. All I know is I'm probably late for class. Rolling my shoulder around, my breastbone cracks, reminding me how sore I am. I didn't sleep very well. Guess it's time to invest in a new mattress after all. Since when did mine have springs poking out. My eyes finally take in the room. This doesn't look like my bedroom. This room is too dark, and you can feel the dampness in the air. It smells musty, like a wet dog. That's when it all comes crashing back.

"Only you are this stupid Cat." Um, yes, I am. How do you forget that some mask wearing prick knocks you out and kidnaps you? For fuck's sake, how dumb am I? I feel the weight on my wrists, my skin prickles, and my breath hitches. Now's not the time, Catalina. Rein it in bitch, and you gotta figure some shit out. With a couple of deep breaths, I slowly move my hands. The chains rattle, making a lump form in my throat. I turn to look. Handcuffs attached to a chain are locked on each wrist. I follow the chain to find it latched around a steel headboard. I shift my feet apart. Thank God. I can use them as a weapon.

Beads of sweat form along my hairline, and I become dizzy with every inch I move my hands; I hate this. I lay back down to try to calm down. I'm focusing on my breathing when the door flies open. I shift into a seating position with my back against the headboard. I take in

my captor. He's still wearing that stupid LED mask, with a black hoodie to hide his hair and other features. He stands in the doorway, commanding control. He can suck my big toe if he expects me to bow at his feet.

"Aren't you going to ask why you're here, pretty girl?" His croaky voice echoes in the small room.

"Why? If you're expecting a ransom, I'd give up now."

He walks further into my humble adobe. "Catalina, you are an important piece to this story."

Goosebumps work all over my body. What goddamn the story? Who the hell is this creep? Come closer so I can kick that stupid mask off your face, you prick. He must read my thoughts because he heads back to the door.

"I'll be back later, don't go anywhere." He walks out of the room, slamming the door closed.

"Like I could if I wanted." I mock him.

I sink back into the bed, not sure what I'm supposed to do. My hands are literally tied behind my back. I don't even know where I am, and I'm still trying to figure out what he wants from me. I have nothing, and no one will pay to get me back, so he must be really fuckin' desperate. Honestly, who pays ransoms these days? My mother wouldn't. She would laugh in his face, turn around and walk away. She'll probably yell at me, telling me I had it coming from being a whore. If she only knew. Fuck. Now I'm thinking of them. I was hoping I could go without memories of them. I can't go down that rabbit hole right now. From what I witnessed, I witnessed Cole's blue eyes and sharp jawline, Nyx's brown tousled hair and full lips, and Dorian's green eyes and tattooed skin. Come to think

of it, and I haven't actually seen Nyx or Dorian fully naked. I've seen the lower half, and I have no complaints. Ten out of ten would do it again. But I need to see the entire package.

Will I get that chance again? Cole kicked me out. Does that mean he's finished with me? Ugh. Now I'm getting pissed off again. I slowly work the cuffs, so they sit comfortably, my skin still crawls, but at least I can control my breathing. I try to distract myself; I look up at the ceiling or lack of. It consists of rafters and wires. I try to follow them but lose them halfway when it gets too dark to see. Wouldn't it be amazing if humans had built in night vision like cats? The things I would see and probably want to unsee.

Dear God, I'm going mad already. It hasn't even been that long. I furrow my brows. Or has it? I don't even know how long I was passed out for; he did hit me pretty good. Maybe this is a dream.

"You dummy, you can't smell in your dreams." Why am I so mean to myself?

I couldn't tell how long I sat here, waiting for dickface to come back. My stomach lets out a painful rumble, so guaranteed I've been here for at least a day. I close my eyes, thinking of anything besides being in this shitty basement.

A hand runs along my jaw, I'm in that weird phase of sleep where I'm somewhat aware of my surroundings, but it could be a dream. I'm pretty sure Dorian is touching me, but that can't be. I snap my eyes open, coming face to face with dickface. I pull away and growl.

"Don't fucking touch me."

He lets out a monotone laugh. "Now, pretty girl. Don't be like that. I came by with some food." He leans over, grabbing something off the floor. When he sits back up, he's holding a sandwich and a bottle of water.

I arch my black eyebrow at him. "How do I know you didn't poison it?" I question him.

I can hear him take a deep breath, yes. Remove the mask and take a bite. Show me it's not poisoned, mother trucker. Then I can see you.

"Guess you'll have to believe me." He drops the water and puts the sandwich on my lap. "Better eat that before the mice come out." Standing, he heads back for the door.

"I still don't know what you want with me. If you're not gonna–"

"Abuse you? Pummel my fist into that face of yours? Or string you up from the ceiling naked and leave you hanging until someone hopefully finds you?" His voice turns malice like. Sending chills down my spine. "As I said, you're a piece of the story, and it's just the beginning."

The slam of the door rattles my bones. If I was hungry, I'm not anymore. I need to get the fuck out of this place. I'm not sticking around any longer than I have to, espe-

cially if that's the way he thinks. The only thing stopping me is these handcuffs and the headboard.

I turn around so I'm facing the headboard. I'm a little compromised in this position. My arms are crisscrossed, but at least I can see what I'm doing. I grab the bar between my hands, and with a tight grip, I spin it to the left. I keep trying until it loosens. The nice thing about old things, they fall apart rather quickly. I grab the chain in both hands, and with a deep breath, I give a huge tug against the bar. The metal clanged together. A loud ringing sound plays in my ears. I freeze and listen for footsteps. When none are heard, I try again. This time a little bit harder, I place my feet up on the wall for stability.

Nothing. I need to bend the bar some so it can pop out of the holes.

"Work. With. Me." I grit my teeth as I pull the chain. My spirit is slowly fading when this plan of mine goes into the gutter. I try one more time because, let's be honest. I'm losing steam, and I tossed that sandwich on the floor. Poisonous or not, I would've eaten it... eventually.

With my teeth clenched, I pull, tug, and yank.

My entire body flies backwards, my back landing on a spring that's poking out of the mattress.

"Ow." I rub my back. Wait. I can rub my back.

I gather up the chain, slipping off the bed. I get a cold chill from the cement floor on my socked feet. That bastard took my combat boots and my coat. I couldn't even tell you if it was day or night out. When my hand touches the doorknob, I get a little nervous. I'm five-two. I can't fight for shit. What am I going to do if I run into

someone up there? There could be more than dickface up there.

I drag the door open, going in blind. I peer around the doorjamb. It opens to a large empty room. I creep along the walk, trying not to shake the chains. It's so dark down here I can't see a fuckin' thing. Including…

"Fuuuuck." I limp around in a circle trying to calm down. But it's safe to say my pinkie toe is done. I felt that one in my stomach. I breathe easy when I take in the stupid thing I stubbed my toe on. The staircase is right in front of me. The first step creaks a little, and I look up towards the door holding my breath. Each step is slow, my heart trying to beat out of my chest. The last step, I place my ear against the door, listening for any sound. My trembling hand reaches for the knob, slowly turning it. I push it open.

I'm greeted with silence. It's dim up here. The only light coming in is from the streetlight shining in through the front window. Looking around, I take in the sight of the run-down house. The living room is sad and grim, opening up to the kitchen that at one time may be held incredible house parties. Then again, the way it looks now, it hasn't seen anyone decent in years. I'm guessing slums have moved in, turning it into a drug house. Good to know I'm still in Eastwood. Southside from the looks of this house. The floor is cluttered with garbage and broken bottles. To be honest, I'm sure there are needles and other drug paraphernalia that I'm unable to see. The living room appears to be empty, and nothing is in my

way of that front door. *William Wallace* called. He wants his freedom back. I'm not one to stop that.

With one final look around, I step over a broken bottle, only to step into something wet. I'm not going to look or freak out; I'm glad to be wearing socks. The chains rattle together when I sway, a little fatigue setting in. After I find a way out of these stupid things, I'm getting a thick ass burger. I finish the distance without any other incident. I don't even care if someone is on the other side of this door. I swing it open so fast the cold air leaves me breathless. The cold air nips at my skin as I step out into the night. As I suspected, I'm in Southside. This will be tricky, a woman running around with handcuffs on. That just screams easy prey.

I take off down the broken stairs. On a whim, I take a right down the street. I'll eventually figure out where I am and have to get off the main road. That's my goal. I keep running until I reach the first alley, darting down just in time as a car comes down the road. I place my hand over my heart, and it's beating like rapid-fire. I throw myself into a sprint, my feet screaming at me with every step I take.

The second I cross over the invisible line dividing the town, I slow my pace. Every muscle in my body is cramped with fatigue, and I'm so dizzy and tired.

Trudging along, I go to the only place I can think of.

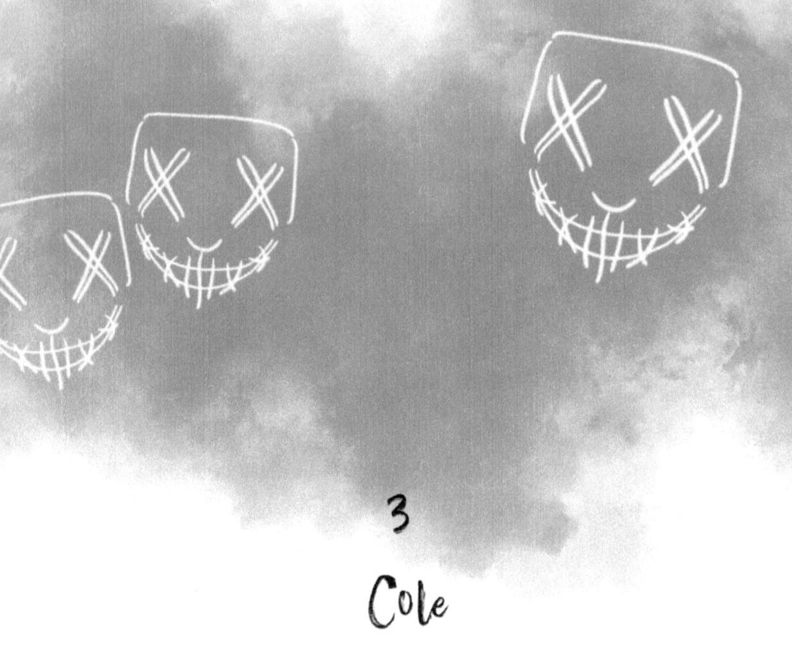

3

Cole

I'm on pins and needles, waiting for Henry to get to the warehouse. We had time to return the van and grab our bikes. He'll never be the wiser on our little stunt. Or at least, I hope. When I joined the gang, Henry wasn't this crazy. He didn't care what people did around town and only cared about others producing drugs. He was the go-to for drugs and no one else. I think that's where it all went wrong. The power went to his head.

Growing up in this town, you only had two options if you weren't leaving it: Soul Stealers or Southside. Well, considering I came from Southside, I wasn't staying there. I knew what would happen if I did. I would've ended up either dead or in prison. So really, I do owe Henry, but the last couple of months. Fuck that dick. I'm so over this. I want out. I'm sure the guys want out as well. Our views have changed recently.

"He's here. He just walked in," Nyx whispered under his breath. He's standing in the torture room's doorway.

I dip my chin. "Let's get this over with, and then we can search for Cat." We both leave, walking into the common area where Dorian is currently waiting for us.

Henry takes notice of us, smiling so big it causes wrinkles to appear around his eyes. "Great work, boys. I knew I could count on you. It's a shame I couldn't have watched it. You all know how to work some magic, that's for sure."

I'm not sure how to take that. Is it a compliment, or are we sick bastards?

"Um, thanks, I guess."

"We need to discuss Conrad. I would like for him to join and become an enforcer."

All of our heads snap at him.

"How many do you need? Three isn't enough?" Dorian raises his voice. Nyx places his hand on his bicep to calm him.

Henry raises his hands in surrender. "It's not like that. You're all still in school. Sometimes I need shit done during the day–"

I cut him off to remind him. "It was your stupid idea for everyone to go to school."

"Yes, so you would owe me when you graduate. You don't think I would pay for your schooling for free, did you?" He shoots me a grin. "By going to school, you signed up to be my little bitch until your debt is paid off."

I should've known better. There is no getting out of this gang. It might not be blood in, blood out. We did have an initiation, and if you owed Henry a debt, you bet your

ass you would have to pay it. If not, he sent the enforcers after you. We collected so many debts for him that it's unreal. I think he wants this gang to be more prominent, but his members refuse. Having that Conrad join up is a problem. Nothing about this guy screams decent human being. Not like I have a say it. We just need to find a way to bring Henry down.

"No, Henry, I know better." My lips curl around the words. "If you don't mind, we had a late night, and we're tired."

"You have balls, kid. You should show me some respect before I beat it into you." I watch as his nostrils flare. At least I can still get him riled up.

I just turn and walk away. I'm fuckin' done. I push the doors open, getting blinded by the sun. Hard to believe we worked throughout the night and early morning. It doesn't seem like it, but I guess when you're trying to disguise dead bodies to look like fresh dead bodies, it takes a lot out of you. My mind quickly wonders to Wednesday, wherever she is. I hope like hell she's safe.

"Let's get some rest, and we'll head out tonight to look for Cat. My gut is telling me she's still in town somewhere." I look at the guys as I climb on my Street Bob.

Nyx grips his handlebars until his knuckles turn white. He's staring off into the distance. I can tell he's taking it the hardest. He's used to seeing her almost every day in class, and his eyes find mine blinking slowly. He nods and fires up his bike. Dorian's face rumpled with sadness, with eyebrows perched low. I know this is hitting him

hard, too. But we're all stubborn fucks and won't talk about it.

Once she's back, I'll have a lot of begging to do, and I'll give her anything she wants if I have to. As much as this kills me to think, if she wants nothing to do with me, I'll walk away. I'm the one that keeps pushing her away all the time.

By the time we get home, we're all exhausted.

"Man, I'm so tired I can't even think straight." Dorian rubs his face roughly before getting off his bike.

"I hear ya, D. I'm about to drop dead," Nyx said with a yawn.

I open the front door for us. I always love coming home. We all purchased this house together. You could say it was love at first sight. Something about it called to us. Not sure about the darkness or how unwanted it was. Sorta like all of us.

I wave to them as I climb the stairs leading to my room. It's not the same entering here after having her in here. It smells faintly like her if I inhale deep enough. I pull off my shirt and kick my boots off simultaneously, stumbling around. Fuck it. The pants can stay on. I fall face-first onto the bed.

I wake wrapped up in my blankets. My mind is still foggy, and I'm trying to figure out what day it is. When it finally

clicks that, it's still the same day. Only much later, the sky is already growing dark. My stomach lets out a low groan. I guess it's been a while since I've eaten. I would love to just lay in bed for a little while longer, but Catalina is more important. We need a game plan. With no clues, we're in the dark about where to begin. It'll be like looking for a needle in a haystack. When I get downstairs, Dorian is already cooking.

"You know, you make the perfect kitchen bitch." I slap him on the back on my way to the table.

"Fuck off. If I didn't cook, you would starve."

"Well, you are a good cook, D. So." Nyx grins and hitches his shoulder at him. "What are you cooking, anyway?"

Dorian lets out a mumble. "Homemade macaroni and cheese."

My stomach releases another rumble. "How much longer? I'm not gonna last that long."

"Jesus, don't be rushin' me, or I'll make you two cook." He turns his back to us and goes back to cooking. Either way, he'll finish supper.

As we eat, we devise a plan and figure we'll search around the cemetery again. The thinking is that her captor might have dropped something that belongs to her, or we can determine what way they left. Not many people have been up to the cemetery between them and us. So, our chances are good.

We're all quiet as we get ready. Dressed in black, we look like we're about to get into trouble. The cops wouldn't even think about giving us any grief tonight. You couldn't tell we belonged to the gang, and we figured to

keep it all under the radar. I jerk the front door open and pause.

"Hello, boys, did you miss me?" she huffed, her lips pulled into a grimace.

Catalina, the sight of her has my knees buckling. She's leaning against the house, alive. I'm looking her over for any injuries. She's shaking, only dressed in a t-shirt, leggings, and socks. Her wrists are locked in handcuffs. I don't know how she isn't breaking down right about now.

"Half pint," Dorian whispered from behind me.

Nyx rushes out, wrapping her in his arms and getting her in the house. That brings the fire under my ass working. He sits her on the couch, his fingertips travelling down her arm for her hand.

"Baby, we'll get these off you right away." He turns to me. "Bolt cutters?"

"Hold tight, Wednesday."

When I return with the bolt cutters, she's wrapped in a blanket, drinking a glass of water. When her violet eyes met mine, they were soft as a whisper. I lose myself more and more in the depths of her. I walk over to her, and her eyes shift to the bolt cutters.

"Don't worry. It'll be over quickly."

She takes a deep breath. "Okay. Cause I'm starving."

"It also means we need to talk."

"Yeah, whatever. Hurry, Cole." She holds her hands out for me.

Fuckin' little shit. I make quick work getting these off her. The metal hits the floor, and her entire body relaxes. Her wrists have bloody red marks from being rubbed raw

against the cuffs. I gently take them in mine, running my thumbs over them.

"How do you feel?" I look up at her, and she's staring at her wrist with a grim expression.

"I don't understand why all of this is happening to me." Her voice is wavering.

Nyx moves next to her, placing a hand on her thigh, while Dorian stands behind the couch, placing a hand on her shoulder. We're all giving her a little bit of our strength.

"I'll grab you something to eat, and then you can fill us in." I stand, placing a kiss on her forehead. It takes everything inside of me to leave her side. I eventually go and head to the kitchen. I pull open the fridge, trying to think what to get her. This should've been Dorian in here, not me. What was I thinking? I delve into the fridge to find some leftovers. I can't fuck that up. Placing her food on a tray, I carefully walk back into the living room. Small chatter greets my ears before I take in the scene in front of me. Nyx is laid out on the couch with Cat in between his legs, and Dorian looks at her feet. I walk around, placing her food down on the coffee table.

"What's wrong with your feet?" I grab a bowl of reheated macaroni and cheese for her.

"That masked prick took my boots. I'm glad I had socks on, but running sorta did my feet in." She wiggles her toes, then groans.

"Hold still, half-pint. You still have some slivers in there."

"Sorry," she mutters around a mouth full of food. "This is good. Who cooked?"

We all laugh. "The only decent cook in the house is Dorian, don't get me wrong, I can cook, but it's questionable." Nyx discloses his dirty little secret.

She looks at me. "Same."

"To be honest, I haven't eaten in a while, so that it could taste like dog shit, and I would still eat it." She shovels another mouthful of food into her mouth, not caring about manners.

I hate to kill her good mood, but I think it's time for her to tell us what the hell happened. If I'd ever taken someone, they usually didn't look like themselves, so why the hell did this person take her? I need answers, and I'm trying to control myself from getting them from her. The longer we wait, the more time her captor has at getting away.

"Wednesday, I need to know. How did you get away?"

She places her fork into her bowl and passes it to me. "I was hoping to get a shower before we talked about it."

"Sorry, baby, but I think we all want to know—need to know." Nyx rubs her shoulders, comforting and reassuring her.

She takes one big deep inhale.

4

Catalina

"Wednesday, I need to know. How did you get away?" Cole looks at me with sorrow.

I place my fork into my bowl and pass it to Cole. "I was hoping to get a shower before we talked about it."

"Sorry, baby, but I think we all want to know—need to know." Nyx rubs my shoulders. I can feel his warm hands working my muscles and calming me down.

I close my eyes taking a deep, cleansing breath, trying to figure out where to start. My mind is one big jumble of a mess.

"Just start from where you want to. We won't rush you." Dorian's husky voice sent a thrill through my body. Probably not the time to be thinking these thoughts, Cat.

"Okay, I was working in the cemetery, taking my time. I had two bodies, and there was no rush for them. Guess that's my fault. If I didn't dog fuck I would've been finished

sooner. Maybe then he wouldn't have gotten to me." Three sets of hands squeeze my body. I look up at the ceiling when my eyes sting. I will not fuckin' cry. "I tried, I even grabbed my bear spray, but I fell into the grave during my run." Cole's finger brushes my hair away from my face.

"This explains the scratch, then."

"It doesn't hurt now. Glad it's not deep, but I'm getting used to head injuries." I let out a nervous laugh. We all know what happened the first night with them. I get them caught up with my escape trying to fill in the blanks and all of their questions.

"The only thing I'm trying to figure out is why he didn't have any demands or try to call anyone. Why kidnap you?" Dorian questioned.

"He says it's all part of the plan." Which I'm still trying to figure out what that means. He doesn't seem familiar to me. That's what's driving me up the wall. "Now he'll be waiting for me everywhere I go. He should've figured out by now that I'm gone."

"I think we should head back to that house and scope it out, and if he does return, I say we give him a Soul Stealers welcome," Cole growls, looking at me like he would burn the world down before he would let me go again. Too bad he couldn't look at me like that before this happened.

"Do you really think that's a good idea?"

"No offence, baby, this is the best idea. If we catch him, then this nightmare will be over right away. You'll be safe."

I place my hand over Nyx's heart. "I just don't want any of you to get hurt because of me. I'm not worth it." All three of them growl at me.

"Listen to me right now, darling. You are the most important person to me—us. We've met no one as unique as you. That's what I love about you. Trust me, if we wanted someone like everyone else, we would've picked a normal girl. But we want you because you are worth it. You are worth it because you never fake it with us. You show us your true self and are never afraid of who you are. So don't you dare say you are not worth it." Dorian crawls up my body and drops a kiss on the tip of my nose. "Do you understand me?"

"Yes," I say, blinking back tears. I've never had anyone that cared this much for me, let alone three people at once. It's too much for me to process. I go to stand, but Nyx stops me.

"Where are you going?"

"I just need some time to process all of this and a shower. I'm sorry. I just never had anyone on my team before. I don't know what to do."

"You lean on us. You trust us."

I look into Coles' deep blue eyes. "I trusted you, and you fuckin' stepped all over my heart. How can I ever trust you again?"

He dips his head. "You don't. I don't expect you to—"

"Good, 'cause it's not gonna happen. I forgave you once already easily, and I won't do it again, Cole."

I get up and start for the stairs. I have no idea where I'm headed. I've only been to two rooms in this house,

can't go wrong searching. My feet ache with every step I take. I take in the familiar hallway instead of going to the nasty all-white bedroom. I pass it walking into the room next to it. Pushing open the door, I take in the spice and citrus smell. From the scent alone, I can tell this is Nyx's room. I inhale deeply and relax the further I walk into his room. I take in how clean his room is. His room is beautiful, and the bay window is the perfect spot for reading or painting. I push away the curtains looking out to the empty dark street.

"What are you looking at, baby?"

The sound of Nyx's voice causes me to jump. "Sorry." Turning around to face him. "I wasn't snooping, I swear."

He walks closer to me, grabbing my hand. "I know, don't worry. Want me to start a bath for you?"

I lean into his chest. "That would be amazing." He rubs my back before heading into his insight. The sound of running water fills the bedroom. I stand at the door, watching him add Epsom salts to the water, swirling it around in the water. He must sense my presence because he turns and smiles at me.

"Get undressed. The water is perfect." He doesn't move and makes himself comfortable on the tub's edge.

I walk further into the bathroom. I pull my t-shirt over my head, dropping it on the tiled floor. I watch as his green eyes become darker. I slide my hands down my stomach getting a groan out of him. I turn around and bend over as I push my leggings down, showing off my ass.

"Fuck, baby. What I wouldn't do right now to be fucking that ass."

My pussy aches when he talks like that. I've never had more than a finger, so taking a cock makes me nervous. Except I trust him, I believe he would take good care of me and wouldn't hurt me. I slowly stand, running my hand up my legs. I've given no one a strip tease before, but the sounds he's making, I take it I'm doing a good job.

"You're killing me, baby." He repositions himself, and my stomach flutters at the sight.

I unclasp my bra, letting it fall to the floor. My nipples tighten either from the cooler air or from the way Nyx is currently examining me. I run my fingers along the seam of my thong, dipping lower each time. I'm about to slip them off when I stop.

"All right, big guy, out you get."

His eyes widen to the size of dinner plates. "Are you fuckin' kidding me? You get me this turned on to stop?" He stands, marching his way toward me. He's like a lion stalking his prey. I hold my position, never taking my eyes off him. "You know what I want, baby?" he asks when he gets right in front of me.

"No," I whispered.

He grips my chin, moving my face to the side. Running his nose alongside my neck, he nips his way toward my ear. I let out a small moan. When his hands slip into my hair, he releases my ponytail, running his fingers through it.

"That feels nice. Can I be honest with you for a minute?"

He keeps massaging my scalp. "Baby, I always want you to be honest with me."

I swallow to clear the knot that has grown. "I didn't think I would get out of that basement, let alone unharmed. My only thought was getting back here to you three, and I'm not sure what I would do if something happened."

He pulls me into his chest, rubbing his warm hands against my naked skin. "Shh, we wouldn't let that happen, baby. We would've gone to the world's end to find you."

The sob that left me was painful, shaking my body terribly. I honestly thought my captor would've hung me from the fuckin' rafters, leaving me there until they found my body. Now he's out there still, waiting for me. I should get Cole to scope out the house I left, and it's probably the only chance we have at finding who did this to me.

"Can you have a bath with me? I don't want to be alone at the moment." Nyx wipes my tears away when I look up at him.

"I would do anything you ask of me, baby." He steps back, pulling his shirt over his head. My eyes work over his sculpted body, he may be the smallest out of the three of them, but he's still very much built. Then I catch the piercings in each of his nipples. I raise my eyebrow at him.

He chuckles at me. "Don't ask. It was a dare. Don't dare me to do something. I'm gonna fuckin' do it."

"Is that a fact?"

"Get in the tub before I dare you to do something you won't be able to back out of."

I step into the hot water, lowering myself. I let out a moan when my entire body immerses in the water. Nyx steps up to the tub, fully naked. I can't help but lick my lips, moving forward, he climbs in behind me. The water sloshes over the side as his long legs wrap around mine. He runs his hands up my arms to my hair again, moving it out of my face. He leans down, kissing my cheek.

"I don't want you to ever worry about anything, do you understand? The three of us will take care of you even if Cole sometimes can't get his head out of his ass. He just has a hard time with the whole filter thing."

I shot him a scoff. "No shit. But I'm getting tired of being his punching bag. If he can't figure his shit out, I will not take it much longer. He's lucky that he gets a second chance. Usually, I don't believe in them, and if I recall, this is his third now."

"Lucky number three?"

"He better not blow it." I lean further back into his chest, feeling his heartbeat against my back. Closing my eyes, I've never felt more relaxed or at home.

"He won't. I trust him this time, baby." He tips my head back, getting my hair wet. "Let's not worry about him right now, and you need to relax and get some rest. We can worry about everything tomorrow."

I have a hard time concentrating. Nothing feels better than someone else washing your hair. I stifle a moan when he continues to massage deeper. When his hands work their way lower on my body, all thoughts leave the second his fingers pinch my nipples. I can feel him growing thicker behind me; I can't help but wiggle my ass.

"Careful, I might do something to that ass."

Oh, sweet Jesus. Yes, I want that more than anything. "Please, I want you so bad."

"Get out and get on that bed." His voice was husky. Usually, he was never one for being demanding. I shivered hard when I stepped out of the tub. Not sure from the air or from his words, I can't wait for what's coming. I lay on the bed waiting for him. He's taking his time getting his ass in here, and I'm getting more worked up the longer he takes. The bedroom door opens, and in walks Dorian.

"This looks entertaining. Mind if I join?" He walks over to the bed, kneeling just above me. His gaze sets my body on fire. I lick my lips when he runs his hands alongside my ribs. My stomach flutters when I feel Nyx's hands on my legs. Holy shit, this is really happening.

"Think you can handle both of us? Together?" Nyx asked between kisses.

I have to close my eyes to answer him, or I won't be able to concentrate. "What do you mean, together?" I've already taken them together, so why would he ask?

They both chuckle. "Both holes, baby."

"Holy shit."

"Spread your legs wide for me; your body is ours tonight, baby."

I do what he says, growing wetter by the second. Dorian pinches my left nipple, making me arch my back and dig my heels into the bed. Nyx takes that moment to drag his finger into my wet needy pussy. I let out a strangled

moan, waiting for him to touch me where I was most desperate, but he never did.

"Nyx, please." I whimper. I try to move my hips to reach his hand, but he tightens his hold around my thigh. Dorian takes pity on me by drawing a nipple into his mouth. Sucking hard, then flicking my nipple with his tongue. He bites my nipple, pulling it upwards before releasing it. I whimper before he heads to the other one.

I hear a bottle open, then cold wetness on my ass. I let out a gasp.

"Don't worry. I have to prep you first. Relax." I try, but I'm nervous. Dorian's hand slips between us, down my stomach. He finds my clit and starts rubbing it gently. I felt pressure in my ass, causing me to tighten up again.

"It's a plug. Focus on what Dorian is doing. Feel his fingers run along that pretty little pussy of yours." Dorian moves his lips along my collar, sucking hard in random places. The sensation of that and the pressure from both working me down below send me over the top. I plunge into my orgasm without warning, screaming my release, clenching my fingers into the blanket. When I finally relax, both guys are waiting for me.

Nyx crawls up on the bed beside me, cupping my face. "So beautiful. We'll take things slow, okay?"

I can only nod, my body is still tingling, and if I move my hips, I can feel the plug hit at a certain angle. "I'm ready for both of you, but Dorian is still overdressed." I look over at my blonde God to see him still fully dressed. He gives me a light chuckle before grabbing the hem of his shirt and slowly sliding it up his body. His sculpted abs display

a collection of tattoos on his torso. Once his shirt hits the ground, I'm already moving toward him. My fingers dig into the waist of his jeans, pulling him closer. I kiss his stomach, causing him to groan.

"Fuck…" His hands dig into my hair, pulling my head back. He leans down, kissing me deeply. Releasing me slowly, he steps back, unbuttoning his jeans. They slid off his hips, leaving him commando, his thick thighs flexing when he stepped out of his jeans. Nyx takes this moment to wrap his arms around my waist, pulling me back to the bed.

"Up on your knees."

I struggle to shift with the pressure building again. With every squeeze, the plug moves in and out of me. Nyx's hand runs along my ass cheek before he lands a loud smack. My pussy clenches, needing attention.

"I need more." I push my ass back until I touch Nyx. His fingers run along my slit towards my ass. I whimper when he lightly tugs at the plug. With a complete tug, I relax fully for him to remove it.

"Such a good girl. Think you can handle more?"

"Yes, I want both of you at the same time."

Nyx grabs the lube bottle squirting it over me and himself. His hand lands on my hips, pulling me closer to him. He runs the tip over my tight entrance and pushes forward slowly. I hiss when I feel slight pressure.

"You okay?"

"Ya, I'm good. Keep going." He pushes forward more, getting past the tight muscle. I take a deep inhale the further he pushes in. He pauses, giving me time to catch

my breath. I feel so full, and he's not even in all the way. Dorian kneels next to me. I take that moment to clasp my hand around his shaft. Nyx pushes the rest of the way inside the force, causing me to grip Dorian harder.

"Shit, darling." He hissed.

Nyx takes it slowly, not to overwhelm me, and I press back into him when he comes forward and need more. When he pulls out, I whimper at the loss.

"Don't worry. Dorian, lay down, baby, get on top." We do as he says. I crawl over Dorian rubbing my pussy on his cock. His hands come up to my breast, squeezing them. I reach between us, slipping him inside. With slow, controlled movements, I rock my hips forwards, worshiping his thick cock.

I never thought I would be back here, especially with both of these men. Getting kidnapped brings a new perspective to your life, that's for sure. If I never escaped, what then? Nyx lays a hand on my back, pushing my chest to Dorians getting me to leave my thoughts behind. He rubs my lower back while Dorian drives upwards, coaxing my orgasm closer.

Smack. "You don't come yet, baby girl. You wait until I'm inside of you first."

My pussy instantly clamps around Dorian. Nyx lines up behind us, making Dorian come to a stop. My toes curl, and I throw my head back when Nyx enters me fully. My breaths are coming out rapidly when he moves forward, and Dorian moves backwards. They work in tandem, bringing me to ecstasy. I tighten around each of them, getting growls and grunts in return. It's like feeling drunk.

My world is spinning, but I'm being held and secured. I know they won't let anything happen to me. I fall deeper into Dorian's chest, kissing his shoulder.

Dorian drives one final push before going still as he finishes with a deep moan, gripping my waist as he finishes deep inside of me. He kisses along my collar before touching my forehead. Nyx smacks me again before running his hand around my throat, pulling me to his chest as he pounds into me hard. I let out a stifled scream as I took him.

"I own this ass... *thrust*... do you understand... *thrust*."

I gasp when he lets go of me, and he goes, still shooting his cum in my ass. He slowly pulls out, letting Dorian do the same thing. Nyx rolls over onto his back, letting me curl into his side. Dorian turns over, trailing kisses down my neck. I kiss Nyx on the chest as my eyes grow heavy.

"Good night, baby." He leaves a kiss on my forehead.

"Good night, darling." Dorian leaves a kiss on the back of my head.

The last thing I remember before falling asleep is the sound of Cole's door closing.

5

Catalina

The next morning, I woke up alone. Not how I wanted to, especially after how yesterday went. Guess I can't have my cake and all that shit. Or, however that saying goes. As much as I don't want to leave this warm bed, I have to. I need to get my ass back to school and start figuring out who the hell is after me. I stretch my sore body popping cracks from my joints. Reluctantly, I climb out, searching for my clothes. I'll also need to head home to get clean clothes. I ditch mine to search through Nyx's dresser, finding a t-shirt and a pair of sweatpants. Pulling his t-shirt up to my nose, I take a deep inhale. It smells of spice and citrus, just like him.

I step into the kitchen to see Cole is staring out the window, drinking his coffee. He is not the person I want to be seeing first thing, especially after his rude dismissal a week ago. Am I still salty about it? Fuck yeah. I may have

let him have a free pass last night since everyone wanted information, but that dickwad can kiss the bottom of my feet now. He doesn't say a thing while I walk to the coffee pot and still doesn't say a thing as I sit down at the table. I do my business drinking my bean juice, waiting for Dorian and Nyx to reappear wherever they are.

"You don't owe me anything." Cole's husky voice cuts the silence of the room. "What I did to you was un-called for. I have a hard time dealing with my emotions sometimes. The thought of this being our fault doesn't sit right, and I didn't want you in the middle of it. I thought pushing you away would keep you safe." He finally turns with his head bowed, his shoulders slumped. He ran his hand through his already tousled hair. "I know I can't ask for your forgiveness, so when you're ready, can we try again?"

I focus on my coffee like it's the most crucial thing in the room, his words running through my head. He might have thought at the time it was the best thing, but he could've gone around it differently.

I drum my fingers on the table, thinking about how to explain things to him. "Cole, I—you left me wounded. Giving another chance will be your last one when I'm ready. For now, you're just a friend, nothing more."

He closes his eyes and nods. "I can agree to that. Thank you, Weds—Catalina."

"Baby, nice to see you up and wearing my clothes." Nyx leans over me, cupping my chin. Staring into my eyes, he kisses me gently on the lips. Before it can grow deeper,

he pulls away. Dorian comes up next, placing a kiss on my forehead.

"Morning, half pint."

I notice Cole slipping away to the stairs. Guess he doesn't want to hang around if he's only a friend now. "Where were you two?"

"Hittin' up the gym, needed to work off some pent up energy." Nyx goes about mixing a protein shake for himself and Dorian. "We have to figure some things out. We all agreed you're not returning to your apartment until this creep is caught. We can move you into the guest room." I go to interrupt, but he holds his hand up. "I'm not going to take no, so you'll do as we say."

"Is that so? I didn't realize that you are the boss of me suddenly." I cross my arms over my chest, staring up at him.

"Don't be like that half pint, it's for your own good, and you know it. So, we'll head to your place if you're ready."

I guess that's the end of that discussion.

Having all three guys in my tiny ass place is overwhelming, to say the least. I leave them to do their own thing. I'm not one to entertain. *Apparently,* I have a bag to pack. For how long, I'm not even sure cause if they think I'm letting them rule my life, they are sadly mistaken. I throw a bunch of random clothes in my bag, then wander into

the bathroom. I'm gathering the essentials when raised voices come from the living room.

The scene in front of me should only be seen on the football field. I'm surprised Cole and Dorian haven't fallen through my floor yet.

"What the fuck is going on!" I yell at all three of these dicks.

Their motions halt immediately. It would be comical in different circumstances. Dorian has Cole pinned to the ground. Dorian's biceps flex, trying to hold a struggling Cole still.

"Stop fighting me already," Dorian growled.

"You're not the boss of me, asshat. So, get the fuck off of me before I beat the shit out of you."

Dorian sinks lower to Cole's face. "I'd like to see you try."

"All right, that's enough, you two. Will someone tell me what the hell is happening? I leave for five minutes, and World War three breaks out." I give them both a disapproving headshake. I've never seen them fight before, especially like this.

Dorian pushes off Cole's chest, not without glaring at him. Cole gets up, dusting imaginary dirt off his pants. He brushes past Dorian knocking him back before he storms down the hall to the bathroom. I turn back to Dorian, raising my eyebrow, waiting for him to explain all of this shit.

With a huff, he finally spilled his guts. "He said a few things, and I flew off the handle, okay?"

"No, it's not okay. What kind of explanation is that?" I raise my hands in the air.

He goes to the couch, slumping in a heap, resting his forearms on his knees. "Cole was saying some shit about how he should've done more, and he was blaming himself. He was ready to storm out of here and do God knows what. That's when we started fighting, and I had to take him down forcefully."

"I've never seen anything like this before, baby. Cole has never acted out to this extent before." Arms wrap around my waist, and Nyx places gentle kisses against my neck. "I think he blames himself for everything that has happened to you."

I lean back in his embrace. "Well, he shouldn't. It wasn't just his fault if you really think about it. You guys ignored me, too. Somehow, I have forgiven you a lot easier." I mumble the last part, primarily to myself.

"I won't listen to that anymore. I was to blame, you understand." Cole's booming voice cuts in from across the apartment. "I shouldn't have done what I did, end of fucking story. I'll forever be making it up to you. No arguing. Grab your shit. We have to go." He marches to the door, leaving without another word.

Alrighty then, guess that's that. Coles is back to himself after probably giving himself a manly pep talk in the bathroom surrounded by girl products. Pinching the bridge of my nose, I leave Nyx's warm arms and grab my bag.

"Come on, let's get this show on the road. Mr. Grump doesn't like to be kept waiting."

"Damn right, he doesn't." Dorian comes up alongside me, grabbing my bag from my hand. "Get used to it, and Cole has mood swings worse than a woman."

Oh, trust me, I've noticed that, and we haven't even hung around that much. With one last look around, I leave my place, and I'll be so out of my element living with other people. I've been used to doing things my way that I don't know what to do with other people at home. The one thing I'll have a hard time giving up is the quietness—walking out of my apartment with my two men on either side, protecting me from preying eyes. I would have three, but Cole can't figure his shit out long enough. I noticed the growing number of blacked-out SUVs coming into town on the drive back to their place.

"That's for the mayor's meeting that's happening this week, and it's his turn to host it." There was an edge to Cole's voice that I couldn't place. I turned to face him in the rear-view mirror. His eyes darkened when they met mine. "We probably won't be around much this week. I need you to listen to what I tell you." Before I could tell him to fuck off, he turned his eyes back to the road. "Stay in the house when we aren't home, lock the fuckin door and don't answer it for no one. I'm serious, Catalina."

Pick your battles, Cat.

I have a feeling I won't be winning this one. By the time we pull into the driveway, I'm itching to get out of this car. I miss Johnny. The first chance I get, I'm getting her. I can't live without that car. Everything else, yes, but not my baby. I swear newer cars give me an itch—especially ones filled with tension. No one talked since Cole told me what

I would be doing. The only reassurance I had was Nyx caressing my thigh the entire ride. His hand drifted higher inch by inch, turning me on by the second. My body was hotter than hell, yet he wouldn't touch me where I needed him the most. I was beyond sexually frustrated when I walked into the house. I hear him chuckle from behind me.

"You think that's funny? You just wait and see what I can do to you, hot shot."

Arms are wrapped around me, pulling me into his muscled body. "You think so, baby girl."

I twist around, bringing my lips to his. "I know so." I palm his growing bulge getting him nice and hard. He moans when I kiss him. Just before he can hold me closer, I pull away and head for the kitchen.

"Get back here, you witch."

"No, siree bob. I told you I'd get you back. Go take care of that boner you're sporting." I shoo him away from over my shoulder.

"Un-fuckin-believable." I hear him mutter to himself on his way up the stairs.

Dorian is already prepping something to eat, which shouldn't surprise anyone by now. He's the momma bear of the family. We'd all starve if he didn't feed our asses.

"What ya cooking?" I drag a stool out from the island so I have first row seating.

He sets his pot down. "I'm going to make some minestrone soup from scratch."

A man that can cook and gives incredible orgasms. What else can he do?

"Who taught you to cook like this?" I watch as he brings all of his ingredients, outlining everything up in order. He was quiet before he answered me.

"It was my grandmother that taught me everything to know about cooking. I spent almost all of my childhood at her house. When she passed, I kept cooking, so I always held a part of her close to me."

"I'm sorry, Dorian. She would be extremely proud of you."

He gives me a small smile. "I hope so, half pint."

I watch him cook and send a silent thank you to his grandmother for teaching him everything she knew. When we all pile into the kitchen for supper, I notice Cole is somewhat in a good mood. At least when I smiled at him, he returned it. If he wants this to get further than the friend stage, he better get over the mood swings.

"I'm letting all of you know right now. I'm headed back to class tomorrow. If I don't attend, my scholarship is toast."

Cole stiffens, and Dorian stops chewing, but Nyx just beams with pride. That's because he gets the pleasure of sitting with me in philosophy.

6
Cole

This friend thing is complete bullshit. It's been three days since she's been back, and I haven't had her to myself since. How the hell am I supposed to get back to where we were if I can't even have a minute of her time? Having the mayor's stupid meeting also doesn't help. Henry has elected all of us to patrol City Hall. To top it all off, Catalina decided to leave without us knowing to grab her fucking car. I've never been more pissed off than I was when she skipped through the door, all while she smiled, swinging her car keys on her finger. That was until I flew off the handle and landed myself back in the goddamn doghouse.

I need to figure something out, and there have to be some clues on what to do cause god knows I can't for the life of me figure out what I'm supposed to do to make her want me. Being away from her again today isn't helping

me relax. That fuckin' creep can be around, and I knew we should've hit up his house the night she came home. I was too busy licking my wounds.

"I need a game plan, Cole. We can't be out here all night again. If nothing's happened, yet I don't think anything is going to happen."

That's another thing, Dorian keeps acting like king fuckin' kong ever since Catalina moved in, I'm not sure why he thinks he's suddenly the boss, but I'm not liking it.

"Do you think I like leaving her home alone? If Henry suspects us of slacking, then what? He already brought Conrad in, which I'm surprised he isn't up our asses on this job to make sure we're doing everything correctly." I lean my forearms on my handlebars, looking towards the City Hall.

Nyx scoffs. "Don't even get me started on that twat. There's something off about him, and I can't figure it out."

"I feel the same way ever since he was introduced to us. He's never to meet Cat." Dorian adds.

We all nod in agreement. There are some things I don't mind keeping hidden.

I was ready to call it a night when I caught something out of the corner of my eye. A black figure is climbing the fence onto the premise of the hall. I let out a low whistle to grab the guy's attention and nod in the figure's direction. We slowly dismount from our bikes. Reaching for my desert eagle cocking it when we cross the road, by the time we reach the fence, our mysterious visitor is already across the lawn, making his way for the door. I

give the guys commands to split up and deal with this guy however they see fit.

I head north, trying to round him up that way. When I notice another figure cutting through the west gate, I take off in that direction instead. Whoever these guys are, they aren't going to finish their task tonight. I've been itching to find a fight, and it looks like I finally found one. With quick light footsteps, I take off. I stop at the edge of the rock garden, finding the biggest rock I can. I pitch it toward his head. He didn't even know what hit him. His body falls forward, kissing the ground. Rushing towards him, I kneel on his back, pressing my gun into his head.

"Who the fuck sent you?" I growl, finger twitching on the trigger.

He struggles to break free, causing me to press more of my body weight on him. "I'm not going to ask again fuck face. Tell me now."

"Why the fuck should I? We both know I'm a dead man either way."

I dig my gun further into his head. "At least you'll know where this will end for you. But I'm not one to wear brain matter." I haul the fucker up by the back of his shirt, pushing him toward the others. A loud whistle comes from my left, and I steer us in that direction, pushing my prisoner along the way.

"Watch where you're digging that thing," Dickhead growls at me. Like he has a place to tell me what to do. I push my gun harder into his back, making him trip over his feet.

"Hey Cole, we caught two more creeping before they snuck in. What should we do with them?" Nyx hollers from up ahead. When I get closer, I can finally see the two captive cunts on their knees with their arms behind their head. With one final push, mine goes down next to the others.

"I'll call into Royce for him to bring the van. We'll bring them back to the torture room. Then get an answer that way."

I turn away, dialling Royce. When I explain everything to him, he tells me it'll be at least twenty minutes. Fucking bullshit, but nothing I can do about it. Now we have twenty minutes of holding these asshats here without being noticed. Easier said than done.

Especially in this town.

Of course, my prisoner is the only one who has to cause us grief.

"You should just put us out of our misery. We ain't gonna say shit. Either you do it, or I'll find a way to end us."

"Will you just shut the fuck up already, you're giving me a migraine." Nyx smacks him on the back of the head.

The more I think about it, the brain matter would've been worth it. He keeps talking shit as I tune him out. I'll have my fun with him soon. I think I'll let him sit in the room overnight. We've been gone too long, and I won't be able to concentrate knowing that Cat is alone. *Pop, pop.* The sound of gunfire has me ducking down low.

"What the hell is going on?" Dorian yelled.

"Fuck if I know, anyone hit?" I look around, gripping my gun—*pop, pop.*

"I'm good, you? Where the hell is that coming from?"

I finally take a look at the prisoners, and that's when I notice two are dead. Fuck. They must've had a team waiting somewhere that we didn't know about. Mother-fuckers.

"Grab him and fucking run!" I yell. I took off toward where the shots were coming from. Hell's if I'm losing my last captive before I get answers. Rounding the corner of the hall, I see a blacked-out van pulling away. I aim my gun and fire off a couple of rounds, and I shoot out the back windows before they disappear into the dark. Cunts. I make my way back to the guys to find them by their bikes. Thankfully Royce has shown up and is shoving the last dickhead inside.

"They got away, a blacked-out cargo van. Got a few rounds in it, didn't catch any sight of whose driving." I slump next to my bike, feeling lightheaded unexpectedly.

"Cole." Dorian's hand is cupping my elbow, stabilizing my sinking knees. "Man, you got shot."

I let out a small laugh. "*No,* you don't fuckin' say, bud." I look over at my arm to see the blood leaking all the way to my hand. Moving it makes me wince. "At least it was an arm wound and nothing else."

"Can you ride? I'll call the doc to meet at the ware-house."

"I'm good. Let's go." I mount my bike, pissed that we won't be getting home early now.

The house is silent when we all get home, and I wasn't expecting her to stay up for us. It's nearly three am. I'm tired, so I can only imagine how the other two are feeling. We're barely in the living room when the lamp is flicked on. There, sitting on the couch wrapped up in a blanket, is the beauty herself.

"What took you so long?" She surveys all three of us.

Dorian scratches the back of his neck. "We sorta had some problems. We should've called."

"God damn rights you should've called. What happened?"

I clear my throat. "We were ambushed, and I took a hit, no big deal. Head to bed Wednesday. You have class tomorrow." I head for the kitchen ending this conversation. I'm not one to dwell on shit. I need a stiff drink, the doc shot my arm up with local anesthesia, but I can feel it coming out.

"Hold up, Cole. What the hell do you mean you took a hit?"

I drove out a harsh sigh rubbing my eyes. "What does it sound like? I got shot in the arm." I point to my bandaged arm.

Her eyes go wide. "Shit, Cole, are you okay?" She rushes towards me, grabbing my arm gently. "How did this happen? Do you need anything?" Her violet concerned eyes meet mine.

"It's fine, don't fuss over me. The doc patched me up." I place my hand over hers, feeling the connection between us again sends a jolt to my lower stomach. If only she were ready to move our friendship to the next level. "Get to bed Wednesday, please." I kiss her palm before turning away. The less temptation, the better. I walk past a waiting Dorian and Nyx. It looks like I'll be sleeping alone again tonight.

My bed was already calling my name by the time I reached the top of the stairs to my floor. I painfully peel my t-shirt off on my way to the bathroom. No matter how much I want to pass out, I need to wash this night off. The steam from the shower quickly fills the room. Rounding my back to the shower, I tip my head under the running water when fingers trace across my stomach. I snap my head towards the opening to see Catalina wearing only a smirk.

"If you're in here, you know what that means don't you?"

She moves into the shower, brushing her tight nipples against my chest, arousing me more.

Her fingers slide further down my stomach, stopping at my pubic piercing. "I do, Cole. I could've lost you today if things had turned out worse. I can't do this anymore." She moves her hand lower, circling her hand around my shaft. I throw my head back with a moan. It's been a long while since she touched me. I almost forgot what she felt like. I grip the back of her hair, pulling her head back and making her groan, that sexy sound I love to hear. I lower my lips closer to her, tracing them with my tongue. She

grips me tighter when I nip her lower lip. Pressing my lips to hers, I never want to be anywhere else.

"Fuck, I'm going to make you scream my name." I reach for the handheld shower head switching the setting to pulse. "Hands on the wall, arch that back for me."

She lets out a small whimper when I run my hand along her back, getting her into position. "Good girl, it's gonna be fast tonight, but you'll still come for me, won't you?"

She nods. "Yes."

I kick her legs wider for me, her pussy on display. I run my finger between her lips and hips and kick back when I find her clit. Running the shower up her leg, she moans louder.

"Cole, stop teasing me."

I smirk. "Oh, little one, you would know if I was teasing." Her body stiffens with her oncoming climax when I pull away. She lets out a whine. I run the shower up higher, hitting her inner thigh close enough that she can feel the vibration on her pussy. I return my fingers, only this time I push them inside her.

"Oh, shit," she screams.

When she tightens again, I pull out.

"Okay, I get it." She trembles beneath me.

"That's me teasing you. Do you deserve to come?"

She nods. *Smack.* "Words, little one."

"Yes! I deserve to come."

I slam into her without warning, moving the shower head onto her clit. I have to grit my teeth with the hold she has on me already. I hold onto her hip as I unleash all

my pent-up frustration into her. I move the shower head closer to her clit to bring her closer to her climax.

"Cole, please."

"I know. Come for me."

I pound harder, feeling her walls clamp around me. I work harder through the resistance. When her body shakes, I drop the showerhead and grab her. I pick her up, kissing her as we both find our release together. Once we find our breath again, I let her down. She looks dazed but does so with a smile on her face.

"Please don't fuck this up again, Cole."

"I won't, I swear." Shutting off the water, I find her a towel. Once we are both dried off, we finally head to bed.

Tomorrow will be one busy day, and I'm thankful I have her back cause I'm going to need her more than anything.

7
Nyx

The smell coming from the torture room made me want to throw up Dorian's breakfast he cooked this morning. This motherfucker sitting in front of us decided to shit himself. Pulling my shirt over my nose, I walk further into the room, followed by Cole and Dorian.

"Jesus Christ, you are disgusting. If you think this will stop us from touching you, you're sadly mistaken. Maybe I'll rub your nose in it." Cole glares his deep blue eyes at the dickhole. He grabs the bolt cutters and walks over to the table filled with tools. I can see our friend shaking in his seat now.

"I still ain't talkin', so do what you have to. You saw what we do to our own."

Dorian moves closer, lowering his giant body to his level. "Wanna make a bet on it? You'll be squealing like a pig by the time Cole's finished with you. If he can't, then

there's two more of us." He wiggles his eyebrows. "Name, or I'll give you one."

Dickhole spits on Dorian. Wrong move. I can see the change quickly. With one move, Dorian's fist lands on dickhole's jaw, snapping his face in the opposite direction. I wince when I hear the distinctive cracking of a broken jaw.

"Spit on me again. A broken jaw will be the least of your worries." He wrenches away, coming back to my side. "Fucking cunt," he mumbled.

Cole steps up, opening and closing the bolt cutters, taunting him with a mischievous grin. "Talk. Who hired you to attack the City Hall when all the mayors are present at the same time?"

Tight-lipped. Staring straight at the wall, I guess he doesn't take us seriously. I move in, grabbing his hand and straitening his fingers for Cole. I have to fight to get at least one finger straight. Cole opens the bolt cutters positioning the finger in between.

"Any last words? You can save the finger."

We're met with silence once again—no warning from Cole. Bolt cutters snap shut, and a finger drops to the floor, followed by a red river. Screams fill our small room. If you had asked me three years where I would be, I don't think I would've answered in a gang. I also didn't know my family would've kicked me out over doing drugs once, and if you're wondering, they live in Eastwood. I moved in with Cole, then Dorian moved in after a short period. They treated us like strangers of the town, so we became them. We joined Soul Stealers; it became our outlet at

the time, and now I think we are all questioning Henry. His motives have gone out the window these last couple of months, more so weeks.

"Nyx, grab me a glove. I have something else to try." I don't even question him anymore, and he's in his element. Good luck getting him out of it. Handing Cole a yellow rubber glove, I stand back and watch.

"If you're done screaming like a banshee, you can tell us anytime now." He slaps the glove on, bending down to pick up some feces. My gut turns, and Dorian gags. Cole shows a cruel smile on his lips as he draws his hand closer to dickhole's mouth.

Dickhole's eyes double in size when they see the feces in Cole's hand. "S-stop this p-please." Sweat drips down his trembling face.

"Then tell us, it's that simple, or this goes in your mouth." His voice matched the hardness of his gaze.

A pathetic whimper leaves his mouth. "I d-don't know." Cole moves closer. "I swear, it was done over the phone. We were told to be at that location. We weren't really going to kill anyone. We were supposed to distract you three. That's all we were told."

Cold shivers race down my back. We left Catalina home alone for hours, something could've happened to her, and we would've gotten back in time. I'm pretty sure those gunshots were meant for us, not his men, as he told us. We better wrap this shit up so I can get to school, she may be safe there, but I'll feel a hell of a lot more relaxed with her in my sight.

"You have no names of who contacted you? Where did your men drive off to?" Dorian pushes for more answers.

But our guest has checked out, and the blood loss has taken over. I grab the smelling salts to wake his ass up. We aren't finished yet. He wakes with a jolt smacking his head on the back of the chair.

"Talk some more fucker. Where are your men?"

"Gone. I ain't sayin' anything more."

I turn to the guys. "I'm done. I'm headed to the school to check on Cat. I'll see you at home?"

"Yeah, we're pretty much done here. I'll let Henry know it was for fun," Cole tells me, flicking the glove to the floor.

I leave, sending Cat a text letting her know I'm coming back. She wanted to do lunch, but my guts were still slightly unsettled with Cole's plans. He would've literally eaten shit and died. I almost gag, thinking that as I mount my bike. We were so close to finding who was after her. If only dickhole had more information for us. Now she's never leaving my sight until he's caught. If he's already trying to set a plan in motion again, we have to be one step ahead of him this time.

I follow Cat into the driveway after school, and I want her on my bike's back. One day. I pull open her door, waiting for her to gather her things. She gives me a beautiful smile when she steps out.

"Long time no see, handsome." Wrapping an arm around my waist, we head for the house.

"How was the rest of school?"

She shrugs. "The same. I have another art project due before the end of the term. I can't complain. That means Christmas break, and I'm really looking forward to a break from school."

Christmas. I can't think of that shit right now. Halloween was last week, wasn't it? "A break will be lovely, wouldn't it? You deserve all the rest in the world, baby." I press a kiss on the top of her head. Guiding her through the front door, we're greeted by the scent of rosemary. Dorian must be cooking a roasted chicken tonight for dinner.

"Mmm, smells amazing. I don't think I've eaten this well in my entire life before." She kicked off the new boots that Dorian picked up for her, not without a fight from her. She wiggled her striped, socked toes at me, making me laugh.

"Come on, let's see what mom is cooking."

"He really is, isn't he."

Dorian and Cole were both standing at the island when we walked in, drink in hand. It's not normal to see them drink. That's how I know today was a tough one for them. I study them looking for signs of trouble, mainly if they talked to Henry. When I feel satisfied, I release Cat, and she moves toward Cole first. Reaching up on her tiptoes, she kisses his lips softly. When she turns away, he grabs her and presses into her again. I move towards the stove

to see what is cooking. It was about time those two made up.

"How did it go?" I lean against the counter, looking at everyone. Dorian has Cat tucked under his arm now.

"As good as you can imagine. He didn't say anything after you left, so I finished the job. I went and found Henry to give him the full rundown. That was a fuckin' joke. That goddamn Conrad had to be there sticking his nose into everything we had to say." Cole scoffed, moving to the fridge. "Can you believe he tried to tell me how to torture someone to get information?" Slamming the door closed, he cracked open his beer. That would explain the drinking.

"Why would Conrad be sitting in on this meeting with Henry?"

"That's what I want to know. Next time he says something, I'm not biting my tongue."

I think we need a meeting with Henry alone to see what gives with this Conrad guy. I thought he was only here to find the grave digger. He technically did his job, so he should've left by now. We've been doing every job that Henry has given to us without a fight, even if it's stupid.

"Either way, we completed it. I'm not going to think about it. We still have more important shit to do."

"Yeah, like, catch my creepy kidnapper," Catalina adds.

We all gave her a cautious smile, a silent promise that we hoped to fulfill. We need a goddamn motive as to why he took her. Usually, a kidnapper leaves a note or at least calls. This person did nothing. He said nothing to her regarding why he was leaving us in the dark and

no trail. Our only hope is if he makes another move, we better be around when he does.

"That's enough, suppers ready. We'll figure something out, but it won't be tonight." Dorian sets the food down on the table, motioning us to join. I'll have to agree. Without a game plan, we are sitting ducks.

"Supper looks wonderful. Thank you again for cooking."

Dorian cups her face. "Anything for you, darling." After dropping a kiss on her lips, he sits across from her. Cole parks his ass right next to her, grinning at me. Whatever, I'll let them have their time together.

"When are you going back to work, baby?"

She swallows her bite and wipes her mouth. "Actually, Dr. Deadbodies talked to me earlier about moving me to the lab. With the cooler months coming, he figured it would be better."

"That'll be all right then. Keep you in the warmth at least."

She gives me a slight shrug. "I don't enjoy working with other people, and they have a habit of casting me out before they get to know me." I see her side-eye, Cole. She hit the nail on the head with that one. He really did a number on her.

"What's not to love about you? You're sarcastic, you aren't afraid to speak your mind, and best of all, you're great in bed." We all let out carefree laughs.

"Well, if anyone else gets you in bed, they'll have me to deal with," Cole declares.

Dorian and I both nod in agreement. Cat rolls her eyes.

"Don't worry, three cocks are all I can handle. Trust me. They just happen to be attached to three incredible guys I don't mind hanging around with."

"Wow, hanging around. You make it seem like we're all just friends," Dorian said.

"Well, I haven't been on a date yet. All we do is fuck, so you tell me, are we friends, or are we more?" She asked, her face unreadable.

I didn't know we had to take someone on a date these days to classify as a girlfriend, and I thought it was a given when we kept seeing each other. I look at the other two for help with an answer, but they look just as frustrated as me.

Her face cracks, letting out a mouth splitting laughter, and her body shakes from laughing so much. "You... sshould've... sseen... your faces." She snorts, covering her mouth.

"You little witch." Cole goes in for the kill tickling her sides and getting a shriek. She tries to get away from him, but he's too strong.

"Help me, Dorian."

"Nah, you have this coming half pint. You are ours, and no one else's understood?"

Cole stops pulling her onto his lap and nuzzles into her neck. "I understand," she moans.

Gripping his shoulders. Supper now forgotten. Rising from the table, he walks into the den. I look over at Dorian, who watches them leave. I jerk my chin in agreement, and we both follow after them.

Cole already has Cat's top off, caressing her breasts, her head tipped back, mouth open as she sends out a silent moan. Dorian walks behind her working his hands under her skirt. I bit the inside of my cheek, and I do love when she wears her skirts and leg harnesses.

"Take the skirt off, but leave the harnesses on," I told Dorian.

He does what I say, dropping her skirt to the floor, leaving her in nothing but her black thong, knee-high socks, and her leather harnesses. Too bad she won't be getting completely naked tonight.

"Since you were a bad girl at supper, you need to be punished." I walk around her as Cole steps back.

"I'd have to agree. Tonight is all about us Wednesday. Get down on your knees and put that mouth of yours to work," Cole demands her, his inner dominance coming through.

She drops to her knees, waiting for our next move. My growing dick is pressing uncomfortably in my jeans. I step closer to her, and her hands quickly work, undoing my buttons. Her small hand wraps around my shaft as her other hand finds Dorian's cock. She strokes us at the same time while shifting her hips back and forth, looking for relief.

"Maybe you'll think twice about misbehaving?" Cole steps up, pumping his cock, and touching her lips.

"Open." He slides in until she pulls back. He snaps his hand into her hair, pulling her back. She grips me tighter.

Spit slides down her chin with how hard Cole is fucking her. The room is filled with groans and slurping sounds. The sight of them together brings my release closer. Her hand hasn't let up once. Cole groans, going still.

"Don't you dare swallow." He backs away, letting me step in.

I take over for her. "Open, I'm coming." I pump a few more times, my muscles contracting as I come in her mouth. My cum and Cole's cum mix together. "Fuck, baby, that's hot."

Dorian is next. He doesn't give her a chance to close her mouth. He shoots his load right away, groaning loud. "God, you're amazing."

"Now you swallow like a good girl," Cole told her.

I watch her throat work all of our cum down. I move her hair out of her face, kissing her deeply without a care in the world. "Do you think you deserve to come?"

"Yes," she whimpered. "Please, I need to come."

"Bend over then." She does what she is told. I slide her thong down, running my hands down her legs, barely touching her. Her pussy is dripping. "I love you in these." I run my hand over her leather harnesses.

"I know. That's why I wear them." She wiggles her ass, only for Cole to smack it. "Oh, fuck." He delivers another smack as my fingers enter her tight wet pussy. Dorian pinches her nipples. We all work together, bringing her an explosive orgasm. Her body is a trembling mess. By

the time we are done, she falls to the floor in a withering mess.

"Come on, baby, let's get you to bed." We have a busy day tomorrow. She mumbles something into my chest as I carry her to my bedroom. I lower her into bed, leaving a kiss on her forehead. I walk back downstairs to find the guys back in the kitchen.

"We need to find her kidnapper and soon. I have a plan, but you guys are not going to like it."

I fill them in on the plan, praying that it works.

8

Catalina

Walking into Philosophy with Nyx feels different to-day. I can't place my finger on it, but something is off with him. Last night he brought me to bed and cuddled closer than ever before. I should've known then something was wrong. Even his looks give it away.

"Are you okay?" I grab his hand, intertwining our fingers together.

He tightens his fingers. "I'm good, don't worry. Just thinking about stuff with the gang, that's all." He gives me a tight smile, then turns back to our substitute professor.

They filled me in on what happened to Davis and Adams, and I owe them so much I need to find some time to visit them. No one else would've even thought twice about searching for me. To be honest, no one knows I exist besides three, no, I guess five people now.

"I have work tonight in the lab—no need to follow me home. I'm not sure how long I'll be. I've never done this before." I bite my lower lip, wondering how many people I'll have to talk to tonight.

"Hey, you'll be all right. Everyone will love you." He pulls me closer, leaning his forehead on mine.

I absorb his positive energy, trying to see how hanging around other people will be good. "What if this blows up in my face?"

"Then we will be here to catch you, baby."

"Goes for you too, whatever's on your mind. I'm here for you." I gently kiss his lips before turning to face the front. I hear him groan and see him reposition himself.

The morning and afternoon dragged on, and I had nothing exciting in any of my classes happen. I was tempted to ditch out early to head to the lab but thought twice about it. I didn't want to be there longer than I needed to be. I also needed to find out why Nyx was acting so weird this morning, and I couldn't get it out of my mind all day. I tried texting him, but he left me unanswered. I assumed he was busy with classes. He was the only one that took schooling seriously. It was unlike him, though.

I took some time before heading to the lab to grab supper, I was going to invite the guys, but I needed a little *me* time; you know how it is. They can get a little over-whelming, especially since being kidnapped by creepy jones. My baby was always waiting for me in the parking lot. So glad she was fixed for me, running my hand along her black hood.

"Me and you for a while; let's go get some su—" Before I could finish my sentence, I noticed a yellow note under the wiper blade. With a shaky hand, I reach for it. I look around to make sure no one is around before unlocking the door. I have a feeling I know who this note is from. I'm not surprised it took this long for him to reach me. After sitting behind the wheel, I relock my door. With a deep, shaky inhale, I unfold the note.

Hello pretty girl,
I'm sure you're wondering why I waited so long to reach you, but all good things take time, as does my next move. The countdown begins now. Are you brave enough to find out on your own? Or will you need your three men to help you? Only time will tell. Tick tock, when will I strike again? Perhaps when a clock turns 12.
Until we meet again.

I refold the note, placing it in my bag. I stare at my bag like it's the plague now. What the hell does he want from me? Can't he at least give me that?

"Great, now what am I to do?" *Tell the guys.* I should be sending a mass text right now, so why aren't I? In a way, I don't believe he'll be attacking me anytime soon. I just want one night to be normal without the guys breathing down my neck. Can't I have that, at least? I promise to tell them when I get home.

Driving to the small café, I lost most of my appetite since finding that note. I keep repeating the last sentence over and over. What day will it be and what twelve?

Noon or midnight? The scary thing is, my creep could be anyone in this café. Without his mask on, he blends in so easily. I keep my eyes focused on the counter and quickly order my food to go. I'll eat in the car back on campus. That way, if a vehicle follows, I'll be able to spot it right away.

I grab my wrap and tea and leave. The streets are filling up with college kids leaving for the afternoon, everyone walking in groups chatting along without a care in the world. I'll have that soon—right? The drive back was uneventful, thankfully. I park right next to the back door under the light. I never noticed anyone following me, so maybe tonight isn't the night. That would be too convenient for him anyway, and he probably assumes I called the guys right away.

"You should've, dummy." They're going to be so mad. Luckily I have hours before that'll happen. I shove the rest of my wrap in my mouth, gather up my garbage, and head inside. Time to find out what all the fuss is all about working inside and with other people.

It turns out that working inside is only working with one other person, which isn't so bad. Riley works independently, so I don't have to talk to him like I thought I would. We've only exchanged about ten words so far. Two introverts working together are perfect. I also never

thought I would be the person wearing a white lab coat, but here I am. I even sent a selfie to the guys. They all suddenly came down with a cold that needed a doctor to look them over. I threatened them with rectal temperatures in return. It's mostly filing and collecting data from the cadavers I brought in. I didn't think I would ever see the Joe's again. Seeing them lying on the medical table instead of inside the body bag is weird. I never told Riley that I was the one that brought them in. He figures the school orders them in for the students. Oh, poor innocent Riley. He wouldn't last a minute out in the cemetery with me.

"Hey, Catalina? Could you help me with something, please?" Riley doesn't bother looking up from his work, which is what it's been like since I started. He's earnest about his work.

"Um, yep. One second." I finish up with my typing before I forget every detail entirely. Thank God, I'm pretty decent on Excel, or I would be fucked right now. Sliding my chair over to Riley, I take notice of what he's working on. "Dude, I'm not helping with that."

"Why not? It's perfectly normal."

"Normal for whom?" He's elbow deep in Joe's abdomen. I can honestly say I've never seen another person digging around in another before. I didn't think this was how it all went down.

He tilts his head to the side, giving me a smirk. His brown eyes illuminated under the light. "I have lived for this Catalina my entire life. I wanted to be worth something, and being here at this school, I finally can."

"You're worth more than you know, Riley, trust me." I pass him the kidney bowl as we get back to work. Neither of us speaks as we work simultaneously. You'd swear we've worked together for years. He's been a dream to work with, and I'll have to let Davis know I'm glad I took this job. Time flew by, and it was time to pack it up before I knew it.

"I'll see you later this week?" I ask while I grab my bag.

"You bet. I'll walk you out."

We both walk in the cool night. If I'm being truthful, I'm glad he walked me out. It's nearing midnight. My mood was slowly shifting to a damn near breakdown, and I needed to be somewhere private before that happened. He waves goodbye when I'm safely nestled inside Johnny. At full tilt, I speed out of that parking lot, trying to get home to my guys. I'm beating that clock no matter what. Tonight is not the night. No matter how often I told myself it wouldn't be happening tonight, I couldn't calm my nerves. My knuckles were white from gripping my steering wheel, and my heart jerked against its reins from all the adrenaline rushing through my body. Thankfully there weren't many people on the road because I was driving like someone ready to shit their pants. Trust me. I felt like I was.

The house came into view when I heard the sweet sound of a bike revving behind me. A grin sprang across my face. Of course, they would be watching my back even when I told them not to. They were pulling in behind me when I parked the car. I watched as they all dismounted their bikes. A pang of excitement hit me, waking up my

hungry pussy. I have to bite my lip before I spill out my deep dark fantasy as they walk closer to me. I damn near forgot why I was rushing home so quickly, for having them all around me staring at me like I'm their last meal calms me somehow.

"Fancy seeing you here." Nyx brushes his lips against mine before pressing them fully. Every time he kisses me, it's like he's leaving a piece of himself behind. He's the most thoughtful one. He knows exactly what I need without asking. This kiss is no different. He brushes my cheek before stepping back.

"Wednesday, how was work?" I give Cole a half shrug.

"Better than I thought to be honest. Riley and I work really well together, so I can't complain."

He runs his hand along the back of my neck. "Is that so? Another man moving in on our woman?" He pulls me closer to him, tipping my head back. "You only have three men remember that." Then he slams his lips on mine, taking all control. That's Cole always has to be in control, but I can taste his vulnerability. I tug him closer by his hoodie pocket.

"You're mine, all of you," I growl.

"Damn right, little one." I have to clench my thighs together to relieve some pressure on my throbbing clit.

"Fuck, I can smell how horny you are from here." Dorian comes up behind me, wrapping his arm around my waist and pushing me into his growing bulge. "Where's my kiss?"

I wrap my hand around his neck, pulling his head down to me as I tilt my head to meet his. Pressing my lips

against his sends shock waves down my body. This tall, muscular man may be gentle, but he'll do filthy things to me. His hands slip lower on my stomach, resting just above my waistband. I pull away breathlessly, closing my eyes. I can either tell them about the letter or strip them all naked. My head says one thing, and my slutty pussy is screaming the other thing.

"I have to tell you, guys, something important." I look at them, feeling nervous. "Inside, though."

Cole's gaze hardens instantly. "What happened?"

I can only shake my head. Dorian wraps both arms around me, directing me towards the house. I got this. I can tell them without breaking down, and it's not that bad. I have them for strength and support.

What could go wrong?

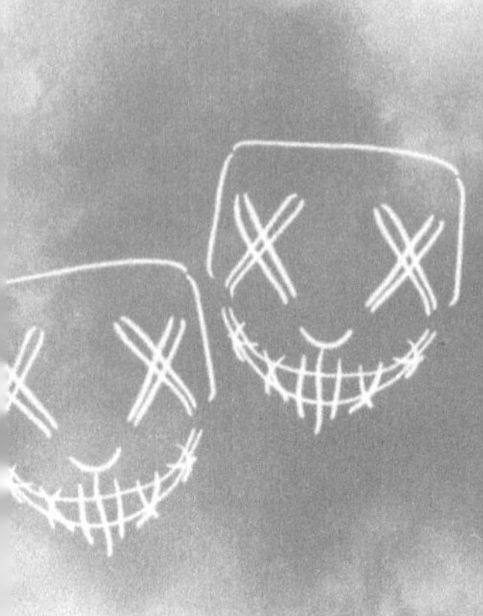

9

Dorian

Catalina is pacing the den, and I swear she's going to wear the floor out. When she told us she had something to say, I knew it was serious, but it couldn't be good for her to be stressed like this.

"Just take a deep breath. We're here for you. Lean on us." Nyx gently coaxes her.

She gives him a ghost of a smile, and that's when it hits me.

"Did he find you again?" I rise out of my seat and rush towards her. Bringing her into a tight hug. She nods her head. "Fuck, half pint. Why didn't you call?" I pick her up and walk back to my chair, and she curls into my body, looking at the other two.

"Tell us Wednesday, I'm going crazy here, and I need to know who to kill." Cole's fists clench and unclench in his lap.

"That's the thing, and I still don't know." She buries herself closer to me, needing comfort more than anything. "He left me a note on my car. It's in my bag if you want to read it. He didn't say much. Everything is all on the note, though."

Nyx goes for her bag, digging around until he finds that yellow folded piece of paper. I watch him as he reads it. He goes from his calm self to someone that would burn the world down. His eyebrows pinch in the middle of his forehead as he passes the note to Cole.

"The fuck, Catalina. How long have you been holding onto this?" His voice is laced with so much hatred, either towards her or her fucking stalker.

When he passes it to me, she finally answers. "I found it as I left school earlier, mid-afternoon."

What I read leaves me disgusted. This piece of shit violated her again and is now taunting her and leaving just enough clues that he's planning something but won't fully come out and say something. We need to find him, I know Nyx has a plan, he gave us a few details last night after we placed her to bed, but we now have to execute it fully. It was a good thing we followed her home tonight. If he were going to pull something, we would've been close by to save her.

"Why didn't you call or text one of us?" I question her, placing the note on the arm of the chair. "We would've been there in a heartbeat."

I could tell she didn't want to answer me. I rub her back, letting her know we're here no matter what. We won't be leaving just because she didn't need us.

"I figured he would be stupid to pull his plan off tonight, especially when he just delivered his note. He probably thought I called one of you. I wanted to, but in a way, I also wanted to handle this on my own. I'm sorry."

"Don't apologize. Call next time. This is serious. He still could've tried something, and we need to take everything he says seriously from now on," I told her.

Nyx moves closer, placing a hand on her thigh. "We're serious, baby. We can't lose you again. This guy didn't care about anything and didn't try anything until now to leave you a message out of the blue. That scares the fuck out of me."

"Same, and hardly anything scares me." Cole walks around me, placing a kiss to her forehead. "Don't fuckin' pull that shit again, or I'll have to punish you." She shifts on my lap, and I watch her swallow harshly. Earlier in the driveway flashes through my mind. We need to wrap this up before I strip her naked.

"One of us will always be with you from now on, either on the bike or in your car. You will not be travelling alone. You eat with us. When twelve o'clock comes around, all of us are with you." We all wait for her to say something. This is huge for her. I know how much she likes to have her space.

She closes her eyes and reaches out her hand, waiting for anyone of us to grab it. Nyx intertwines his fingers with hers. "I understand why you guys always want to attach yourself to me, but you really don't need to. You have a life too, and a gang to help with. You can't stretch yourselves thin."

"Don't you dare worry about us. We can handle it. There are three of us. Tag teaming is what we do well." Cole kisses down her neck, making her grind into my dick. I have to grip her waist tight to hold her still.

A groan slips past my lips as she grinds harder. I guide my hands under her shirt, touching her soft skin. I'll never get enough of her. She drives me crazy. She moans when Cole runs his hand around her neck.

"Tell us what you want." He uses his thumb to tilt her chin to the side. Lowering his face to hers, he plants small kisses along her jawline.

Breathlessly, she tells us. "I want all three of you at once, please I want to feel only my men tonight."

Cole walks away, heading, towards the desk, while I move her onto the couch. Nyx is already stripping his clothes. I pull her shirt off, leaving her in a pink lace bra.

"So beautiful. How did I get so lucky?"

She runs her hands through my hair, staring into my eyes. "The question is, how did I get so lucky? You're one of a kind, Dorian. You may look like you'll beat everyone up, but you're so gentle with me."

I let out a husky laugh. "That's because you're half my size. I'd squish you if I weren't."

"Whatever." She smacks me in the arm, but I barely feel it since she's smaller than me.

I love how we can easily joke, even during the most intimate times; it wouldn't work out if we took everything so seriously. I need some carefree time in my life, and I'm so grateful she's the one to bring it. I pull her leggings down slowly, almost painfully kissing her thigh as I go.

Her laugh turns to a moan, then a whimper when I pull away completely.

Cole finally comes back, holding something in his hand. "Can we try something? You can say no and use your safe words if you have to."

When I get a good look, I see its leather cuffs. My stomach sinks at the thought of her having a panic attack, but when I turn to her, I don't know any form of stress.

"I'll try for you guys. Red is my safe word," she says with determination. Nyx caresses her inner thigh, distracting her somewhat from Cole. He helps her sit up before removing her bra. Cole moves her hands behind her back, letting her back out still. When she doesn't, he places one cuff on.

"How does that feel?"

She nods. "Good, I'm good." She releases a breath. "You can continue."

He caresses the inside of her right wrist before placing the other cuff on, immobilizing her. "Still feeling good?"

Her breath hitches when he tugs at it. "I'm good."

I stand, gripping my shirt at the back of my neck. I pull it over my head, she tries to shift closer to me, but with her hands behind her back, she's having a hard time. I take pity and move forwards. Her lips land on my stomach before licking upwards. I wrap my hand in her hair, bringing her face higher.

"Want something else to lick?"

"Yes, please."

I undo my pants with one hand, pulling out my hard dick for her. I guide her head back down, waiting for her

warm wet mouth to take me in. I'm almost ready to lose myself when she hollows her cheeks, sucking me harder. I pull out, caressing her face, taking in her beauty. Before I get lost in her looks, I sit on the couch, letting Nyx move in.

"Hey, baby." He cups her face stealing a kiss from her, not caring that she was just sucking my dick seconds before. He strokes himself before brushing the tip over her lips. "Suck me as you've missed me." When she opens, he enters ever so slowly. She bobs her head, taking him all the way. She does this, getting a low groan from Nyx. Cole moves closer, getting on his knees and pulling her legs apart. Her pussy is so wet it's sticking to the sides of her thighs.

"Mmm, little one. Are you getting ready for us?" He throws a leg over his shoulder, getting his face nice and close to her aching pussy. The second Cole makes contact with his tongue. She makes a mumbled moan.

"Oh... fuck that feels good. Don't stop." Her hips move against Cole's face, and Nyx moves out of the way so Cole can shift onto the floor, taking Cat with him. "Sit on my face, little one." She kneels over his face, and he lets out a growl. "I said sit, not hover." He grips her hips and pulls her down. She lets out a loud scream followed by a moan. She tilts her head to the ceiling, eyes clamped shut as Cole eats her out.

I notice the bottle of lube on the couch. Placing some on my finger, I move behind her. I run my finger over her tight hole. While Nyx pinches her nipple, getting her to relax. When my finger is fully inside, her fingers tighten

into a fist. I gently kiss her back, and she lets out a greedy moan. Adding more lube, I slide in a second finger.

"Yes, baby, take him. Let Cole eat you out. Fuck, you look so hot right now."

"Such a good girl, aren't you." I can feel her inner muscle tighten around my fingers. I pump my fingers more, and her body grows stiffer, her breathing coming in faster.

"Don't stop. I'm right there!" she screams. Her toes curl, hands ball into tight fists. When she's finished milking my fingers, I withdraw them. Kiss her back when she slumps forward. Nyx catches her before she hits the floor. Cole moves her to the side, face covered in her wetness. I unclip her wrist, letting her arms free.

"You did amazing, baby." Nyx places a kiss on her forehead. "Got any more energy?"

"Always." She gives him a smile.

I move back to the couch, waiting for her. When she crawls over, I have to grip myself. She looks sexy, looking up at me between my legs. She licks her lips and takes over, stroking me. I let out a hiss from her touch. Her small hand doesn't even close around my thick dick.

"Get up here. I want that pussy." She straddles me, and my dick jumps when her pussy brushes against it. My hands tighten around her waist, pulling her closer to me. My lips press against hers, tasting her need. I lift my hips stretching her with my smooth head. "Fuck," I mumble as soon as I push inside. I dip my head, taking her tight nipple in my mouth. She rocks her hips, moaning when

she finds her motion. Another set of hands appears on her waist. When I look up, I grin at Nyx.

"This ass, baby. I'm dying to fuck it again."

"It's... yours." She moans.

I bring her closer to my chest, letting Nyx get better access to her ass. Holding her still, he pushes inside. The fullness of having him inside is almost too much, and we thrust, alternating our movements.

"Oh, fuck. It's so much."

Cole moves next to her, taking her hand to his dick. She takes him into her mouth. He wraps her hair around his hand, pressing her further onto his dick. She gags when he touches the back of her throat, and he doesn't let up. He holds her there until drool falls from her mouth. She takes a deep breath when he pulls out, only to do it again. All while Nyx and I push further into her pussy and ass. I run my hand over her sensitive bud, flicking it with my thumb, and she squeezes her inner walls.

Cole releases her. "I'm not coming unless it's inside that pussy. Now come for them, little one."

She lets out a small whimper. I thrust deeper and rub her clit in fast circles. Cole pinches her nipple, sending her over the edge. Her nails dig into my shoulders as she comes around us.

"Fuck, baby. Squeeze me harder." Nyx drives in harder in her ass as I pull out of her pussy. When I push back into her pussy, I feel her clamp around us.

My dick thickens, shooting my cum deep inside her. I groan into her neck, and I can feel Nyx grow thicker moments later, going still as he finishes in her ass. He

lowers his head on her back. We take a breather until Cole speaks.

"Get that pussy over here now before I slap it."

She clenches around us, and we groan. Our woman loves dirty talk, especially from Cole. Nyx gently slides out of her, causing her to whimper.

"Did I hurt you?" He looks at her with concern.

"No, you were amazing." She winks at him before moving to Cole.

Cole standing at the end of the couch, she doesn't even wait to be told what to do. She bends over with her ass in the air. With one quick smack on her ass, she spread her legs for him. He lines up and slams inside of her. He always did fuck like there was no tomorrow.

"Don't you ever hold information back from us again?" Another smack on her ass cheek. She moans louder, pushing back into him. If I didn't come already, the sight of both of them would throw me over the edge. The sound of skin smacking against each other, moans, and grunts fills the room.

He digs his fingers into her hips more when he reaches for her arm, folding it behind her back and grabbing her other one before locking the handcuffs together. He grabs hold of it tight before pumping harder, and a light sheen of sweat covers her skin.

"Cole, I need to come," she whines.

"When... *thrust*... I... *thrust*... say... *thrust*... so." He doesn't let up, even when her legs shake.

He pulls out, turning her over with her ankles over his shoulders. Pushing back in her, she closes her eyes, biting her lip.

He runs his finger between her slit. "Come for me, little one." She explodes around him.

Her scream goes horse after a few seconds, and he finally goes, still grunting his release inside her. We're all silent as they come back to us. He releases her legs, working quickly to remove the cuffs from her. Nyx comes into the room with a cloth ready to clean her. I have a blanket when she's ready to be covered. We worked her extra tonight.

"You did so well, baby. Let us take care of you now." She mumbles her answer, eyes already heavy with sleep. Glad we could take things off her mind so she could sleep tonight.

Cause come tomorrow, it'll be walking into the unknown.

10

Cole

I'm sitting in the kitchen the next morning, rereading the note that Catalina was kindly left. Looking for a hidden clue or literally anything to go on. I take another sip of my coffee, wondering how we are going to catch this guy. Nyx's plan was smart, but now we don't need to worry about catfishing a lunatic.

"What are you doing up so early?" Nyx's smooth voice breaks the quietness of the morning. I watch as he moves to the counter to pour a cup of coffee.

"Couldn't sleep. This stupid note has been eating away at me." I toss the note back on the table.

He takes one glance at it shaking his head. "I get it. We'll find him. Hopefully soon. I have a feeling it'll end in our favour and in our favourite room."

"Very optimistic of you."

He slumps in the chair across from me. "Have to be, and I don't want to think about any other outcome. Plus, it took us how long to get her. Finally, I'm not jeopardizing shit, man."

Which I understand completely, especially after the way I treated her. I had no right to be with her still. I will always blame myself for everything that happens to her.

"You have to stop blaming yourself, and I can see it written all over your face."

"What do you expect from me?" I get up, walk towards the fridge, and need a breather. I always hated to be confronted with problems I couldn't control, and Catalina was one of them.

"Cole, if she doesn't hate you, then it's not a problem. Stop trying to fix something that isn't broken."

I stare inside the fridge, looking for help. "What if I'm not good enough for her?"

"Well, I say that's bullshit. Because I think you are the most honourable person I know. So how about you stop thinking for me." Her gentle voice was strong yet determined to put me in my place. She stood in the kitchen's doorway, looking unamused yet still sexy as fuck.

Dorian comes up behind her, giving her a hug. "Pay no attention to him, darling. He only speaks bullshit anyway. Come on, and I'll make breakfast before school."

"I'd fuckin' say he speaks bullshit. If any of you second guess my relationship between us, I'll kick your asses."

I have to laugh and wave my hand in the air. "Remember what happened last time you tried to hurt me?"

She screwed up her nose. "That's because you're all fuckin' giants compared to me. It's not fair."

"What you lack in height, you make up in attitude, and I love that in you." I place a kiss on her lips, sucking on her bottom lip between my teeth, nibbling lightly before letting go. I smack her on the ass before walking to where Dorian is prepping breakfast. I hear her groan as she sits down.

⁂

Nyx drove with her to school while Dorian and I followed in the truck. We would've taken the bikes, but we felt we blended into traffic better this way. We usually never drive the truck to school, so if he was watching her, he didn't know what to look out for. I pulled into the far lot overlooking her car.

"Everything up and running?"

Dorian grunts at the lack of head space between the windshield and the dash. "Yeah, if anything happens, this should catch it. He shouldn't suspect a thing."

"Good, let's do this. Henry has a job for us later, too, so we need to time it correctly that we are home by midnight, or at least one of us is home."

He rolls his eyes as he steps out. I feel the same way. We can't be slacking on our duties, though. We signed up for this shit, after all. The walk toward campus was stressful, and we weren't aware of what he looked

like. He could be any one of these douchebags walking around. The scary thing is he knows who we all look like, my nickname for her. I'm hoping he hasn't figured out where we live yet. I scan every direction until I'm inside and can hug Cat.

"Be safe until lunchtime, I swear to God. I will burn this school down if I have to." Her small hands cupped my face.

"Cole, you need to worry less. I can see grey hair already." She tries to bite back a laugh.

I place my hands over hers. "That's not funny," I growl closer to her face. "You're asking for a sore ass little one." I watch her shift slightly, and I back away with a smirk.

"Jerk," she mumbled. She and Nyx walk toward their philosophy class. I'll be able to breathe a little easier for the next couple of hours. She'll be with him or Dorian.

Dorian and I go our separate ways, and I head to my lame English lit class that I've never paid attention to. If I graduate or not isn't a big deal to me. Henry's paying either way, so what did it really matter to me? I didn't want to be here. This class felt like it dragged. Who wanted to learn about old dead writers for two hours? I'm itching to get the fuck out of this stuffy room, and I need to make sure she's okay. I sent a text to Nyx, but all he sent back was a stupid thumbs up emoji. How the hell am I supposed to know what that means?

It's thirty minutes until twelve. I've come to the cafeteria early to find a table where we can sit and view the entire room. I'm not chancing dickshit today. I'm watching every entrance when Dorian walks in. He does a quick

scan when he sees me. He heads to the line. I get a ding on my phone, letting me know he'll grab everyone's food. I wait patiently for the only person I need right now. Moments later, I hear her laugh before I see her. The second my eyes land on her, hers turn toward mine. Even in the crowded room, she finds me.

"Hey, you. How was class?" She throws her bag on the floor, coming to sit next to me.

I wrap my arm around her shoulder, pulling her closer to me. "I hate school. I would quit if I could." I kiss her on the temple. "How was your morning?"

"The usual packed solid. I have that art project I need to finish or really start. I've been slacking a lot lately."

The aroma hits me hard, and Dorian chooses that time to drop food off. I pass her a pop and then a piece of pizza. She dives in like she's been starving for years. It's only been a couple of hours since breakfast.

"Slow down, baby. You'll choke."

She sticks her tongue out at Nyx, then chews. "What's the plan after school? I need to run by a drugstore to grab a few supplies your house lacks for a woman. I also need to stop by my place sometime this week for more clothes."

"You have Nyx for the rest of the day. Dorian and I have a job to do." It was the only thing I could think of without leaving anyone short-handed. Henry gets his job done. She's not left alone. I see him wiggle his eyebrows at her. Lucky asshole.

"Just stay safe. I'll see you when we get home." Dorian stands behind her rubbing her shoulders.

"Don't worry about me, big guy, I have my bear spray that I won't drop this time, plus Nyx will protect me, and if he sticks to his note, it's only midnight now that he'll attack."

He closes his eyes. "Still. Get in the house before then. We should be home by then, anyway." He leans down, kissing her forehead. He glances at me from the corner of his eye.

We better be home by then.

As we walk into the warehouse, Conrad greets us.

"Hello, gentlemen. I'll be working with you tonight. Henry wanted me to get a lay of the gang that includes you three—you're missing one." He looks around for Nyx like he's going to appear magically.

"Yeah, he sends his regards, but he has an assignment due, and if you know Nyx, he takes his school very seriously." I shrug, walking past him, toward Henry's office.

"Ah, well. I'll remember that. Always good to have a well-educated man working for us."

There he goes again, including himself in the gang. Henry needs to clarify some bullshit for us. Speaking of the cunt, he's sitting at his desk smoking, looking extra cozy, knowing he doesn't have to lift a finger tonight. This better not be another scam.

"Perfect timing, sit. I need to tell you all something. Where's Nyx? This includes him, too."

"Schoolwork." That is all I say when I sit resting my ankle over my knee. Dorian takes the seat next to me, sitting with his legs stretched out, looking comfortable but on guard.

Conrad takes the side of Henry grabbing a glass of whiskey. I try to keep my face neutral, but this smells fishy.

"I have a job for you, but I have some exciting news. Since Conrad has come on board, I've been stepping back and letting him take the reins."

News to me, he captures the wrong people, and you suddenly trust him more.

"I'm giving him the seat as acting VP. Since we've never had one, yet I give this gang rolls might as well have a VP. I figured if anything happened to me, we probably should have shit in order. What are your thoughts?"

I run my hand through my hair, blowing out a breath. Does he want me to answer that?

"I think it's complete fucking bullshit. You're going to ask someone that you know for what, a week compared to, say, Cole, that you've known for years. Fuck that shit." Dorians' voice shook with fury.

Guess he got his answer.

"Thank you, boy, but I wasn't asking you."

Dorian jolts upright, getting in his face. "Fuck you, fuck this gang. It's for pussies." He spits on Henry's desk. I dart up fast, grabbing the back of Dorian's shirt.

"Do you know what you're saying? If you want out, that means I still owe all three of you. That precious schooling that Nyx loves so much. I'll cut him off."

"Try it. I fuckin' dare you. Dorian and I are done with school, but Nyx is not. This gang doesn't deserve us, and you know it. Either figure that out, or we're out for good."

That could've gone a better fuckin' way, Goddamnit. We both walk out in silence. I'm trying to figure out how to explain all of this to Nyx when we get home earlier than expected. If we leave the gang, I have a good chunk of money saved. I can pay for Nyx without him noticing.

"Sorry about that. I can't stand being called a boy," Dorian says, slamming the truck door closed.

I clasp my hand on his shoulder. "I know. It's not your fault. That was sprung on us like a fart turning into shit. I didn't expect him to give Conrad everything if he kicked the bucket. What's up with that?"

He rubs his temples. "Think he just wants to go legit with the gang? Make it bigger than what it already is?"

"You mean to move from a gang and into an MC?"

He nods. He could be, *fuck,* he already technically made us the enforcers and calls himself the president. He wanted everyone living around the warehouse like one big family. He could be, for all I know, still. He could've tried doing it differently.

"Let's go home and surprise the shit out of those two."

"They are probably already halfway naked by now."

I fire up the truck heading home. If they are naked, I'm joining in.

11
Catalina

I've been stressing all day, and my gut was telling me something was going to happen. I knew it was wrong. Noon has come and gone without a hitch. Nyx and I are currently walking the halls of EU, heading to my next class, unfortunately, our classes are at opposite ends, so our goodbye is relatively quick.

"Stay inside until I grab you." He treads his hands in my hair, tugging my head back, his green eyes meeting mine.

"I know. You've told me a million times already. Trust me. I'm not leaving without you."

He tugs my hair harder; I hold back a moan. Now's not the place for this, although flashes of what we did in school weeks ago go through my mind, and I smile.

"Baby, get those dirty thoughts out of that head. You go to class." He places a quick kiss on my lips. "I'll be back in an hour to fetch this pretty ass."

I reach up on my tiptoes, pressing my lips to his. "I'll miss you."

"Miss you too."

He waited until I was in my class before he walked away. I turn to watch him walk away, getting a glimpse of his ass. I still don't know how I got to be so lucky. I find my seat, prepared to be bored for over an hour.

I'm watching the clock. Every second that passes is another second closer to getting out of this place. You'd swear I was doing time in maximum security, and my parole was coming up. I'm tapping my pencil on my paper, fixated on that damn clock. I don't know why. The professor can hold us longer if they choose to.

"Miss. Wilson." I have no idea why I'm even watching it. This professor is kind of a dick, anyway.

"Miss. Wilson." I continue to tap my pencil when it's suddenly ripped out of my hand. I look up to a very pissed off professor. I send him a nervous smile.

"Can I help you?" I asked.

"You can, by listening and actually paying attention, or you can leave the class. Doesn't matter to me. I get paid either way."

What did I tell you, dick.

"Can I have my pencil back, please?"

He blew his nostrils wide, narrowing his eyes at me. "Smarten up, Miss. Wilson, I won't give you another warning." He passes me back my pencil. I grab it, pulling it

towards me when he doesn't let go. We pull in opposite directions, I let go first, and his arm flings backwards.

"I don't need it, and I have a spare." I give him a smirk before facing the front. I have a feeling I'm not passing this class anytime soon. After giving me a stink eye, he walks away. I can feel eyes on me. I don't dare look around. I hardly ever bring attention to myself. What has gotten into me?

When the asshole professor finally releases us, Nyx is leaning against the wall across the hall. His long legs crossed at the ankles, his nose stuck in a book. He hasn't noticed that I've been secretly drooling over him yet. When he does look up, he shoots me the brightest smile.

"Hey, baby." He closes his book, tucking it back into his back. "If you're done drooling, we can head out."

My mouth drops open. "I was so not drooling." I retort. I walk away, wiping my lips just in case.

"I saw that," he hollered from behind me.

"You didn't see nothin'. Hurry up, hotshot." I turn around, skipping backwards, feeling happy. The smile on his face also makes me happy. I stop dead in my tracks. When he finally catches up to me, I grab his hand. "Nyx, you really are a kind person, you know that, right?" He raises one eyebrow in confusion. "I didn't think I would find myself in this kind of relationship, especially after everything went down between us." I cup his cheek, lifting on my tiptoes. My lips skimming his. "I love you so much."

His eyes shine bright. "I love you too, baby." His lips press against mine, letting me feel all his love. This is what I've been missing all my life. I've never felt anyone's love

before. He pulls me off my feet, swinging me in a circle. A small laugh falls out of my mouth.

"You're crazy, Nyx Thornton."

"Crazy for you. Come on. We have things to get done before the others get back."

You know what's not fair, being a girl. It's crazy expensive, especially in this small ass town. Throwing the box of tampons in my basket, I search for pain meds, nothing worse than bleeding, but let's add cramps on top of that.

"Fucking bullshit."

"What is?"

I jump at the sound of Nyx's voice. I tilt my head back to see him towering over me. "Being a girl, buddy. It's complete bullshit. Can I borrow your dick sometimes, and you take the uterus?"

"No can do. I'm rather attached to little Nixie." He readjusts himself to prove it.

I roll my eyes, tossing the pain meds in the basket. While we were cashing out, I noticed a sign on the counter.

"I didn't know the clock was broken. When did that happen?" I slip my debit card out to pay.

The cashier says, "Oh, that happened shortly after Halloween or that night. Probably a bunch of kids, to be honest. The construction crew will block the road, so I'd

advise you to go around the park, so you don't get stuck in traffic."

"Thanks, we will. Have a great day," Nyx tells her with a smile.

I take my items and head for the door. "Well, that's a shame about the clock. It was so old. Stupid kids always have to ruin everything, don't they?"

His hand falls on the small of my back as he guides me to Johnny. "That they do. We should've considered watching over main street more instead of going to the cemetery." He smiles down at me.

"Nah, the cemetery was a perfect choice." I laugh

We had to park down the street. The parking is outrageously busy today. It's like everyone did all of their Christmas shopping today. A chill runs down my back, and Nyx pulls me closer to his side. But even his warmth can't get rid of this chill. I feel eyes on me. It could be in my head since my creeper isn't caught yet. I relax a little when my car comes into view. I'm digging the keys out of my pocket when I hear Nyx let out a quiet hiss sound. I look at him, noticing he's stiffened up, furrowing my brows. I step away from him.

That's when I see him. His hood is over his head, casting a dark shadow over his features. His hand is pressed into Nyx's back, and things are taking a while to slowly register why he isn't walking away from the creep. When they do, I try to reach for the bear spray in my bag.

"Don't even, pretty girl. That bear spray won't work, or I'll shoot your boyfriend or one of them, I should say."

I halt my movements. I'm not placing Nyx in danger. It's me he wants. "You said noon or midnight. It's neither of them." I keep my voice steady, even though all I want to do is cry.

He tsk's at me. "No, you didn't read my note correctly."

"Bullshit, we didn't," Nyx spits out. He lets out another hiss when creep presses the gun harder into his back.

"You didn't, and I said when a clock says twelve. If you look at the town clock, I do believe it's set too—." He lets his sentence die off.

I already have a feeling what the clock says, and it's doomsday. My time is up. Everything we did, didn't matter in the end.

"What do you want from her? You had her once and did fuckin' nothing with her, you pathetic loser." Nyx doesn't see the hit coming for him, and before I can warn him, a fist contacts with the side of his face.

"Stop, please. I'll do anything you want. Just leave him alone," I beg, like my life doesn't matter. Right now, it doesn't. I need Nyx to get away. *"Please."*

My creep takes another deep breath. "You still don't get it, do you? You aren't important. You never were. Even after all these years, you still won't go away."

What the hell does that mean? He said I was important. Was it all a mind game? Before he can answer, Nyx turns so quickly, tackling him to the ground. I'm so busy watching them fight I forget we are in the middle of the sidewalk. The clattering of metal next to me makes everything come crashing down.

"Cat, call the guys now."

My hands fumble in my bag, and my mind has flashbacks to that night I ran from him in the school parking lot. I'm not alone this time. My guys are with me this time. I find Cole's name in my phone and hit call. I watch as Nyx and creep continue to fight. I kick the gun further away, waiting for Cole to answer his fucking phone.

"Hey, Wednesday. I thought you would be balls deep with Nyx by now," He lets out a deep laugh. His deep voice should bring me comfort, but it doesn't.

"Cole." I gasped out.

"Catalina, what is it." All laughter dies in his voice.

"He found us. We're on Main Street. please hurry." My voice shakes. I'm more worried about Nyx than I am about myself.

"We'll be there soon. Hold tight." The phone goes dead before I can say the words I've been meaning to say for a while now.

I glance back at Nyx to see him sitting on top of the creeps back, with his knee in his back and his arms restrained.

"What did Cole say?"

I shake my head. Right, Cole. "They'll be here soon, that's all he said. What are we gonna do with him?" I keep my distance, even though I really want to see who he is.

"Go sit in the car and wait. Lock the doors."

"I'm not leaving you." I shake my head, determined not to listen to him.

"Baby, please. Listen to me this one time," he grunts as the creep fights him again.

I walk backwards, never taking my eyes off them. My hand reaches back until it hits my car door, fumbling until I find the handle. I don't want to leave Nyx alone, but he doesn't give me a choice. I can only pray that the guys show up before something happens.

My eyes don't leave them for a second. I don't trust that creep at all. My phone rings, and I damn near jump out of my skin.

"Hello." I nervously answered. I didn't bother to check who called.

"Half pint, where are you?"

God, that husky voice. "Dorian, I'm in my car. Where the hell are you guys?"

"We're stuck in traffic, the fucking construction we didn't know about."

Oh, fuck. I completely forgot about that. My entire body wants to shrivel up. I turn to see Nyx struggle with the creep more and more.

"You need to hurry. What am I supposed to do?"

Nyx is thrown off the creep's face. I need to do something. I fling open my car door without thinking. I ignore Dorian yelling at me through the phone, and I run towards Nyx.

He needs me.

Right before I fling myself into the creep's body, he removes the hood, and I stumble, falling to my knees. I drop my phone, bringing my hands to my mouth. Tears threatened to fall. This entire time I knew who it was.

"How could you?" My voice shakes. My body wants to crawl in on itself.

"It wasn't personal—wait, it is," he recalls, tapping his chin.

Nyx looks complex. He doesn't know what to do. "Baby, you know this asshole?"

I close my eyes and slowly nod. Taking a deep breath, I turn towards the person I thought I wouldn't see again.

"I do. This is my older brother."

My brother, or as I like to refer to him as her older son, starts laughing.

"Haven't changed, have you? Momma was right about you. Such a slut aren't you."

Nyx's fist darts out fast, punching my mother's son in the face.

He laughs. "You always did need someone to fight your fights for you, didn't you."

"What the hell do you need? Why did you come find me?" I'm getting tired of him darting around my questions. I've had two years of freedom from that family. Why now did he come find me?

"Turns out Daddy Dearest loved you more than you thought." He rolls his eyes.

Two dark shadows cast alongside me, bringing me more strength to face the person who was supposed to be my friend growing up, the person who should've had my back, not beating me when my mother told him to. That's not what siblings are supposed to do.

I take a deep breath, willing myself not to break down.

"What does that mean? He didn't care my entire life."

He scoffs. I can feel Dorian stiffen alongside me. "Tell yourself what you need to. In the end, he left you every fuckin thing."

Cole places his hand on my shoulder. "What?" My mind is having a hard time playing catch up.

"God, you're really slow. Too many hits when you were younger. Father's dead. He left you everything, and I came to collect, except you are needed alive."

I sway on my feet, and Cole's grip tightens. "So, you stalk and kidnap me?"

He shrugs. "I figured scare you a little, before I tell you the truth."

"Are you fucking kidding me!" Dorian screams thunderously. Cole had to move to hold him back.

I'm at a loss for words. Why would my father leave anything to me? He did nothing my entire life to stop my mother and her ways. Was it the guilt that he felt, or was this some sick joke of his that he was playing? One last final hurrah from the grave, let's stick it to Catalina and give her some hope, only to take it away. Well, jokes on you. I don't want anything from that family anymore.

"Stop it. I can't do it anymore. Whatever he left me, just take it. I don't want it. I only wanted his help when mother would make you beat me. Even then, he wouldn't help me, and I don't want his help now. Take it and leave me alone. Never look for me again."

Her son has a huge smirk on his face like he just won the lottery. Maybe he did. I don't want to know what was left to me. "I'll get the lawyer to send the paperwork over and sign it, or I'll be back, Catalina."

He walks away, leaving me alone with my men.

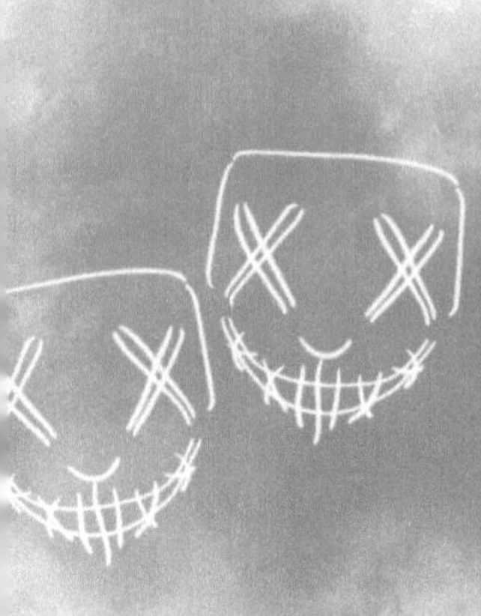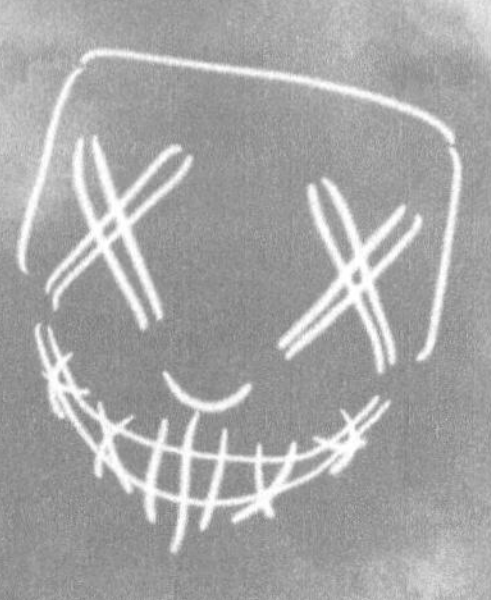

12
Catalina

I watch him walk away, all over some stupid inheritance that I didn't even ask for or want. I honestly didn't think my father had any money, and we didn't live as we did. Although my mother thought she should've been treated like the queen, she thought she was.

"Come on, baby, let's head home. It's been an eventful day." Nyx comes up, bringing me into a hug. I take in his spice and citrus smell. So glad he was with me today. "Love you."

"Love you too," I say into his chest.

"Wednesday, can we talk?"

"Now? Can't we talk at home?" I'm trying not to come off whiny, but I can't help it. I'm tired, and I want to curl up on the couch and relax with all three of them.

"Trust me, please." He reaches for my hand. "We'll catch up with you guys later."

He steers us toward his truck. We don't talk as we walk. He holds my hand the entire time, letting me know he's here for me. Once inside the cab, the first tear finally falls. I would blame it on PMS, but that bitch comes with a vengeance. This is for freedom. I'm finally free from my family once and for all.

"Hey, baby, what's wrong?" Cole brings me into his strong arms. His woodsy scent has always been my favourite smell. I cling to his shirt.

"I'm having a hard time with this, in a good way. He could've gone another way to get his stupid money. But it wouldn't be like him if he didn't torment me one last time, you know?" I wipe away my tears. I take a deep breath and pull away from him. "Sorry, you wanted to talk, and here I am, being a crying baby." I let out a small laugh.

He runs his thumb over my cheek, wiping another tear away. "Don't you dare apologize for any of this. I was so scared when you called. I can't lose you, Catalina." He lowers his lips to mine, kissing me so softly I could cry all over again. "I love you with all of my heart, and I would give up the world for you."

I close my eyes, absorbing all of his love. I kiss him deeper, running my hands through his hair. He lets out a low moan. "I love you too, Cole Valentine," I whisper over his lips. "Now, take me home."

Dorian's in the kitchen cooking and Nyx is lying on the couch when we walk in. This feels right. Now that I'm not in danger anymore, I can finally move back to my apartment. Even thinking about moving back in turns my stomach. I'm so used to being around these three that it'll be lonely again. I leave Cole and Nyx to seek my muscled man.

The kitchen is omitting a beautiful aroma. "Oh, my god. What's cooking stud muffin?" I make a show of wiping my mouth, getting a hearty laugh from Dorian.

"Nothing special, homemade burgers and fries."

I come up behind him, wrapping my arms around his waist. "Comfort food, exactly what I need. Thank you for everything you do, Dorian. I don't tell you that enough, and I'm sorry for that." He whips around so fast, gripping my chin.

"No. I need to apologize. I treated you like shit for a very long time, and I'll continue to grovel no matter what day it is. You are too special, not too." His blonde hair flops over his forehead, and I push it out of the way, his green eyes piercing into mine.

"I love you beyond the years, Dorian Prescott. You make me feel like I'm home."

"Fuck me, half pint. I've never heard those sweet words before. I can't believe you chose me to love." He caresses my cheek. "I love you, darling, for all the tomorrows. My life is complete with you in it."

His lips finally meet mine. I fist his t-shirt, moaning when his tongue dips into my mouth, swiping over my tongue. My pussy throbs with need. His hand dips down

my leggings, skimming the top of my panties. I let out a moan. I press up on my toes, deepening the kiss.

He picks me up, placing me on the island. I lean back on my forearms, watching him pull my pants off.

"Mmm, I feel like dessert first." He pulls my thong down, kissing the inside of my right leg all the way up. His tongue dips between my slit. "Tastes like heaven."

My hips rock forward, needing him more, and he sucks my clit hard. "Dorian," I gasp. He dips his tongue inside, grabbing my hips, he pulls me closer to his face. His tongue fucking me when his finger finds my clit.

"Fuck, you taste so sweet. Come for me." He dips his finger deep inside, swiping my g-spot. When he presses harder on my clit, my legs shake. My lower stomach cramps.

"I'm coming, oh fuck." He pumps harder, and I scream as I find my release, soaking Dorian's shirt as I do.

"God, that's so hot." He stares down at his wet shirt. I cover my face. I'll never get used to squirting. "It's nothing to be embarrassed about. I love it when you come all over my face. I love you." He kisses me deep, tasting myself on his lips.

"When's fuckin' supper?" Nyx calls out before walking in. "Well, I see what dessert is." He chuckles when he sees me on the island.

Dorian helps me off the island. I grab my pants and walk to the bathroom. These men are going to make me lose my goddamn mind. They are all so intense, and it's unreal that this is my life. Today has been too much

for me. Tears roll down my cheeks before I reach the bathroom.

"Get your shit together, Catalina Wilson. You're stronger than that family." I remind myself as I sit on the toilet seat lid. Propping my head in my hands. I take a couple of deep breaths.

"Come here, Catalina, Daddy has a gift for you, but you can't tell Mommy."

I smile so brightly at him that I come running across the living room. I never get gifts. Mother takes them and breaks them in front of me if I do. She tells me naughty girls don't deserve them. I've been trying to be good all week, to stay on her good side. I don't want any more beatings. Daddy pats the seat next to him on the couch.

"I know I haven't been a very good Daddy. It's hard some-times. Not everyone is strong, but we must try our best. Remember that, okay?"

"You're silly, Daddy. Where's my gift?" I'm bouncing up and down with so much excitement.

He laughs and roughs up my hair. "Here, sweety, happy birthday."

He passes me a bright pink-wrapped box. My fingers itch to unwrap it. I'm so nervous that we're going to get caught, I can only stare at it. He nudges my shoulder, encouraging me to open it. I finally tear the paper, revealing a beautiful baby doll. Tears pool in my eyes.

"Thank you, Daddy. I'll cherish her forever. Love you."

"Love you too."

Those were the last precious moments I ever shared with my dad. After my sixth birthday, he turned into a

shell. I hid that baby in the floorboards in my room so she wouldn't find it. To this day, that baby is sitting on a shelf in my apartment. I don't want to wish evil on anyone, but why couldn't it be my mother that died? Why did my dad have to stay with her? Why couldn't he just leave her? So many questions that I don't think I'll ever get an answer to. A gentle knock pulls me out of my past.

Before I can brush the tears away, Cole opens the door. I sniffle hard when he looks at me. In two big steps, he's pulling me into his chest. Without words, he's rubbing my back, pouring his strength into me.

"Everything will be okay, baby," he whispered.

I nod into his chest. "I know, it just hit me out of nowhere, that's all."

"Did you want another minute alone?" He tilts my chin up. Taking in my face.

"No, I'm good. I'm sure Dorian has supper ready by now, anyway."

He sends me a small smirk. "I'm sure he's full of his dessert."

I smack him on the chest. "You're only jealous because he got it first."

He growls low. "Not going to lie, I totally am. But I'm going to enjoy it later when I get the entire thing." He smacks me on the ass when I turn. I let out a laugh.

"So confident of yourself." I sass back.

He lifts me over his shoulder, hauling me out of the bathroom. I smack his ass only to get one in return.

"Put me down, asshole." I squeal when he tickles my side.

"Look what I found, guys," he lets out a holler, entering the kitchen.

They let out cheers. "I always loved my meals to go," Nyx said.

I struggle to talk with all the blood rushing to my head, and I push up on Cole's tight ass. "You're not funny, Nyx. Put me down, Cole."

He places me on my feet, holding me still. When I face the table, it's done up fancy like. They even found a white tablecloth. Black candles sit next to a bouquet in the middle of the table. This is what I needed to cheer me up, and the guys always know what I need before I do.

"What's all this?" I can't take my eyes off all their hard work, and it's gorgeous.

Dorian clears his throat. "We wanted to take you out on a date tonight." He doesn't finish his sentence; I can figure out why. It's been a lot to take in today.

"Thank you, this is really lovely." Nyx reaches his hand out for me. I take it as he guides me to my seat. I give him a smile. He winks at me as he flicks my napkin, then lays it across my lap. "Such a gentleman."

He chuckles. "For now, baby." He kisses my cheek, stepping back.

Dorian steps forward, placing my plate in front of me. I close my eyes, inhaling the aroma of the hamburger and rosemary fries. My mouth instantly waters. "Oh, Dorian, this looks amazing. Why didn't you go to culinary school instead?"

"I, school isn't for me. Enjoy half pint." He kisses me on the nose.

Cole places a glass of beer in front of me, and I side eye him. "How did you know I don't like wine?"

"I had a feeling you weren't into that shit. Who enjoys drinking fermented fruit?"

I burst out laughing. "I couldn't agree more. Give me a barley sandwich any day of the week."

He kisses me on the lips. "That's my girl. Now eat."

They all sit with their food and beer. As we eat and chat, I think about how this room is filled with love. This entire house is filled with love. It's everything I've always wanted.

"I love you guys."

All three of them look at me with so much love they don't even need to say it.

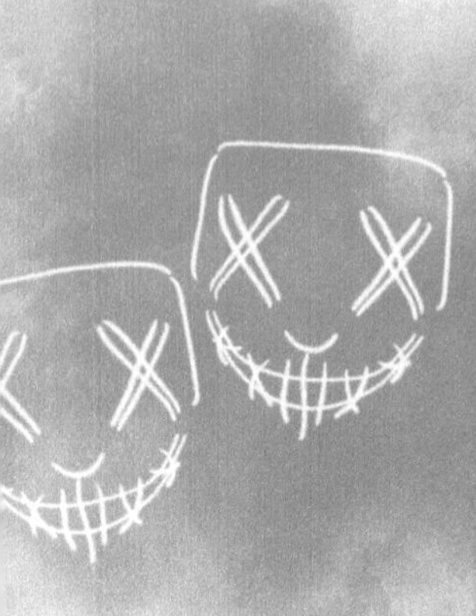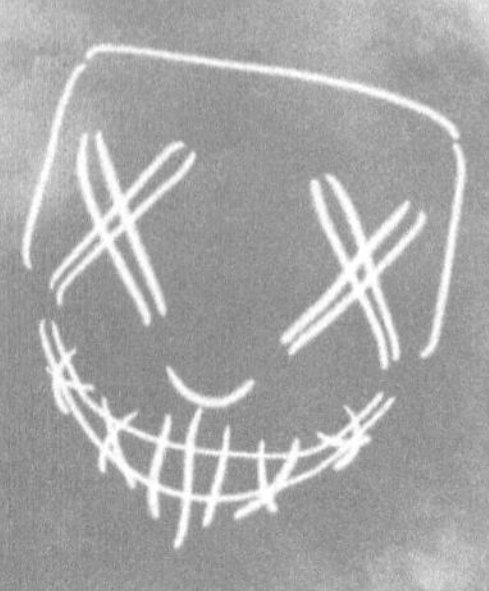

13

Nyx

What a crazy week it's been. It's the first week of December, and we're on our way to the lawyer who reached out to us. We made it known to Cat's brother never to speak to her. All this to keep her family away from her. I understand where she's coming from, but isn't she interested at all in what her dad had to say?

"I'm so nervous. I've never talked to a lawyer before." She straightens her black dress for the hundredth time this morning.

I grab her hands. "You'll do great. I'm here. Cole and Dorian are here. We have your back."

We all step into the office, never letting her do this alone. She'll never be alone. The look on the lawyer's face when he calls for her and we all stand is very priceless. The best part is she doesn't give a shit, and she doesn't care what others think. That's what I love about her. She

does what society doesn't expect. Who says you can't share one girl with your best friends? I'll never have to worry about either of us getting jealous of each other. We'll treat her with the utmost respect, especially Cole. He's finally figured it out. Just watching him now, holding her hand, walking down the small hallway. He's never going to screw this up again.

"Please have a seat. This won't take long. I was informed of what we would be doing." The lawyer gestures to the seats across from his desk.

Dorian pulls a chair out for Cat while we remain standing. We're only here for moral support.

"I'm very sorry for your loss, Catalina. As you are aware, your father did leave you as his only beneficiary. I also know that you want to turn everything over to your older brother, correct?"

"Yes, that's right. I don't want to know what he left me."

The lawyer adjusts in his seat. "Are you sure?"

She smooths her dress again. "Yes, if I'm not keeping it, it doesn't really matter to me now, does it? Please, I rather just get this done with."

He nods and goes through the stack of paper. "If you don't mind reading over this one, it tells you we are transferring beneficiaries between you and your brother. You won't be able to come back to claim anything down the road."

We all move in closer to read over her shoulder, and I place my hand on her shoulder, squeezing it gently. When she grabs the pen, I know this is something she's determined to finish once and for all.

"I feel so much more alive now. Is that a thing?"

We're all sitting in front of the fireplace in the den, listening to the wood crackle. We've been in here since we came home, and she told us it's her favourite room. It's easy to figure out why.

I run my hand along her thigh. "It's a thing, baby because you make me feel alive."

She looks up at me. "I feel like it's all a dream, and it's going to go away when I wake up."

"Never. You're ours just as much as were yours," Cole said, kissing her neck. She closes her eyes when my fingers run further up her thigh.

Dorian unzips her dress, pushing it off her shoulders. She pulls her arms free, only to be pushed onto her back by Cole.

"So beautiful, you know that little one."

She bites her lower lip and moans when my fingers inch closer to her entrance. I can feel her warmth through her panties. Inviting me closer. "Let's get this dress off you. I want to see you naked."

She pushes her heels into the floor, raising her ass up. I help shimmy her dress down her hip throwing it into the corner. I can't help but stare down at her.

"Are you wearing matching lingerie?" It's the sexiest thing ever.

"Oh, fuck little one." Cole unbuttons his pants, pulling out that pierced cock Dorian and I dared him to get done. He strokes himself. He took it a step further and acquired the pubic piercing. Cat's eyes glaze over when she sees it.

I remove her panties, dipping my finger into her core.

"Nyx, yes." She moans. Her hand grabs for Dorian, but he's already moving to her breasts. She moans again when he sucks on her tight nipple.

"What do you want, little one?" Cole asked.

She looks between all of us. "I want Dorian in my ass, Cole in my pussy, and I want Nyx in my mouth."

"Fuck, I love it when you know what you want." Dorian kisses her lips and then moves toward the desk. When Dorian comes back, he's naked and goes to lie on the floor.

"Crawl on top, face the guys." Dorian pats his stomach for her to sit on. She crawls over him, straddling him, and his cock bobs toward her wet pussy. He grips her ass cheeks. "Mmm, this fuckin ass of yours. I can't wait to be deep inside of it." Her hips rock forward.

Her fingers dip down to her clit, moaning as she circles her bud. I unzip my jeans stepping close to her.

"Are you ready for all of us, baby?"

"Mm, yeah. Please, I need you all."

Dorian hands her the bottle of lube, and she takes it, squirting some on his cock. Cole kneels between Dorian's legs, stroking himself. He pushes her onto Dorian's chest, taking the lube from her. Pressing a finger into her tight hole, she lets out a hiss. Her small hand wraps around

my shaft, pulling my eyes away from the show. I close my eyes, tilting my head back. The sound of her moans pulls me back. Dorian is pressing into her ass while Cole eats her out.

"Fuck, this is everything. Look at you. Take all your men." I wrap my hand around her hair, pulling her face towards my cock. She licks her lips opening wide for me. I groan when she sucks me hard. The vibration of her moans causes me to thrust further into her mouth. "Oh, shit, baby." I look down and see that Dorian and Cole are moving inside her, giving her the pleasure she needs.

"Such a good girl, aren't you, little one?" Cole pulls her hips closer to him.

She mumbles around my cock. "I'm gonna come soon." I push deeper into her mouth until she gags, and tears appear in her eyes. My balls tighten, and my body tingles. I thrust faster, throwing my head back, and I come down her throat. Slowing down, she swallows around my cock before I pull out. "Fuck, I love you." I give her a deep kiss before I sit down.

I watch the three of them; they move with each other, paying attention to each different needs. It's a beautiful sight. She screams, her release slumping more into Dorian's chest. Her black hair fanning out on his chest. Dorian lets out a loud groan going still. His eyes are closed. Cole is quick to follow, leaning forward and kissing her chest.

The entire den is filled with heavy breathing, and Cat's eyes are closing from exhaustion. I pull my pants on, heading upstairs to Cole's room. He's the one with the nice bathtub. I turn the water on and head into his bath-

room to grab a towel. I set everything up for her before I head back downstairs.

"All right, baby girl. I have a nice bath running for you. Let's get that nice ass of yours upstairs."

Her eyes light up. "In Cole's room?"

"Yes, that one."

She quickly gets up, dancing around with excitement. "I've been dying to get into the one."

"You never have to ask. It's there for your use anytime," Cole says.

She jumps into his arms. "Love you."

He narrows his eyes. "Me or the tub?"

She taps her chin; he tickles her side, getting a high-pitched squeal from her.

"Come before the water overflows."

I carry her up the stairs with her head on my shoulder. "Thank you, Nyx."

"Anything for you, baby."

It's a boring night. Cat had to work again, which I can't complain about. She's getting out of her shell. Working with another human will do her good. Despite what she told me about Riley, he doesn't talk much. Then again, she's not outside in the cold until spring. I will never dig up a dead body, give me a gun, and let me shoot someone any day of the week instead. I don't have to look

them in the eyes afterward. Just thinking about touching a stiff body turns my stomach.

I'm sitting at home when my phone rings.

"Hey, what's up?"

"I'm gonna pick Cat up from work tonight. Can you bring the supplies and meet us in the cemetery?"

"Does Dorian know the plan, or did you want me to fill him in?"

Cole chuckled. "He knows. He's excited."

Of course, he is. "All right, I'll meet you guys there."

This is one surprise Catalina won't forget, and there are some things we like to do to her to remind her of our beginnings.

Dorian and I are waiting in the far corner of the cemetery for Cole and Catalina to show up. My heart rate picks up as soon as we see those lights flicker across the tombstones.

"Cole, what are we doing here? It's cold and late." Her soft voice carries across the quiet night. I left Cole's surprise where he wanted it.

Dorian and I make our way toward them, her back facing away from us. She must hear the leaves crunch under our shoes because she swivels around. Her face breaks into a slow smile when she notices us.

"What do you say, baby? Wanna play a game?"

She bites her lip. "Yes, please, green." She drops the very first nickname she ever gave me.

My LED mask turned on with my green light shining in the night. Next to me is Dorian with his red mask and Cole with his blue mask behind her.

"You better start running, then, so we can catch you," Dorian told her.

She looks over her shoulder to see Cole swigging a pair of handcuffs. "Oh, fuck," she mumbles. She darts to the side, taking off fast.

We all laugh before we take off after her.

THEIR JOURNEY CONTINUES

C. L. EASTON

STRANGERS OF THE CROWD

STRANGERS OF EASTWOOD BOOK THREE

Prologue

Cole

"Will you shut the fuck up already?" I whispered.

I swear to God, working with your friends is complete torture.

"Sorry man, it's not my fault. It's cramped in here, and I'm a giant compared to you," Dorian hissed.

When I told Henry to figure his shit out with the gang and us, he did. It's now an MC with Conrad on board. It was an easy transition, although some were hesitant to want to switch. Most were excited. The town is a lot more welcoming to an MC than a gang. Dorian and I are still enforcers, Nyx wanted to quit and stay in school full time, but Catalina convinced him to stay in the club and school.

Instead of having him here tonight, it's Dorian complaining. I rub my forehead, getting frustrated. All we had to do was some recon. Another drug house has moved in, or so we suspect they have. We aren't sure, so we are

sitting in Catalina's Volkswagen. We needed a car that sorta blends in. We've been here for three hours, and not a single person has come to the door looking to buy.

"I don't think there is a drug house. If it is, then they do deals somewhere else."

"I would have to agree. Best tell Conrad."

The drive home no longer feels tiring. Catalina moved in entirely a couple of months ago. She had to wait till her lease was up. She wouldn't let us pay it out for her. She also made us repaint the spare bedroom to a dark grey and told us the white looked out of place in the house. She isn't wrong, but it wasn't our fault. We never had a reason to paint or decorate that room. However, she turned it into a bedroom with a small art studio for herself, and I'm so proud of it. The odd time, she'll catch me in there admiring her artwork.

Nyx is graduating at the end of the school year. Then we don't have to hear him talk about how he has to study all the time. Dorian likes to remind him he wanted to stay in school. That only turns into a fight, so when that asshole walks across that stage, you bet your ass I'll be cheering the loudest because this house will feel less pressure.

"Think Cat will be home?"

"I don't think so. I think she finally went back to work in the cemetery. Davis called her last night to tell her the happy news."

"Still, she digs up bodies for the school, and no one has figured it out."

That one is still hard to think about, such a petite woman hauling bodies out of a hole. "Maybe we'll pop over and visit. Send her a message and find out where she is. I would say invite Nyx, but this makes him turn into a pussy."

The Eastwood Cemetery was never my favourite place to visit, yet I find myself here more than I thought I would. We swung home to switch vehicles. I know she doesn't want her car to be seen there, and Dorian wouldn't stop complaining. It turns out Nyx also wanted to come. If he barfs, I'll never let him forget it.

I spot her before she sees us. She's focused on digging that she has yet to look up once. No wonder it was easy for us to sneak up on her more than once, including this time.

"Little one, check your surroundings," I growl.

Her head snaps up, eyes round. Her bandana covers the lower half of her face, but I imagine her mouthing the words *fuck*.

She pulls it down, grimacing at us. "Will you guys stop sneaking up on me? I'm going to have a goddamn heart attack." She pushes her shovel into the dirt, walking to meet us.

"Hi, baby." Nyx plants a kiss on her lips. "Miss me?"

"Always, love."

Dorian wraps her in his arms, pulling her into a tight hug. "Half pint, how's it going so far?"

"Amazing, I'm so glad to be back out here." She kisses him as he lowers her to the ground.

She swung around to face me, smiling brightly. "And you, dickhole. My surroundings were fine five seconds ago. How the hell can you sneak up on me all the time?"

I lower my head to her ear, taking her earlobe between my teeth and pulling it lightly. She moans in frustration. "I have my ways, little one. Trust me."

"I hate when you call me that."

"No, you hate when I call you that because it makes you wet."

She closes her eyes, taking a deep breath. "I love you, Cole, but not right now. I'm dirty."

Dorian and Nyx laugh. She drops her head and groans.

"You said it, baby, not us," Nyx says, trying hard not to laugh more.

"I love you too, Wednesday."

1

Nyx

Three years ago

The first year of college, and I have mixed feelings about it. Do I need a college education? Probably not, but what else am I supposed to do with my life? It's what's expected of me, and my parents want the best and only the best. I can't fail, or else my dad will be on my ass. I can't deal with him, and he's getting worse daily. I wanted to move in with Cole for school, and he quickly shot that idea down.

He also thinks Cole and Dorian are bad influences on me. He should know better. Dorian has been around since we were ten. I'm pretty sure he's not going to corrupt me. If anything, it's me that will be doing the corrupting.

The only thing he's worried about is me messing up his precious standings with the mayor. Like he doesn't know

his fuckin' mayor is corrupt. That shady fuck is the worst of them all.

"Come on, man. We're hitting up the gang before school starts. It'll be fun." Cole stands in my room, arms crossed, looking like the asshole he is.

"The gang? Why would we head over to the Soul Stealers?" Dorian lays comfortably on my bed without a care to give.

"Because I have word they are looking for recruits. It would be perfect for us."

"To be honest, I wouldn't mind. I need to get out of this house."

Dorian sits up. "Getting that bad?"

I spin around in my chair, looking at him. "You don't even know. You are so lucky your grandmother doesn't helicopter over every move you make."

I'll admit, Dorian's grandmother is the coolest grandmother I've ever met.

"Move it. This is going to be great. The leader, Henry, is the guy to see about signing up if we want to."

I've never seen Cole this excited, except maybe the first time he got laid. I've never seen a smile on his face that reached his eyes before—that was years ago.

"We best hurry before my dad gets back. If he catches us, I'm toast."

"You know, we can always take care of him if you want." Dorian grins.

"What's the point? With our luck, it wouldn't work, and we'll get busted."

We all head downstairs, and this house is too stale for my liking. Mom has a habit of keeping things looking like a catalogue, and it's disturbing. Everything has a place, and she would know if I moved anything. I'm going insane being here. This family thinks they are all socialites, and they aren't. All because of fuckin' Coleman.

The Soul Stealers compound is entirely insane. A large bonfire burns in the middle of the parking lot with what looks like the entire gang around it. Everyone is embarrassing one another and laughing; it's a perfect family.

"This looks amazing." Dorian's voice lights up from the front seat.

"I told you." Cole gives him a smug look.

Great, he'll never let us forget about this.

"We need to find Henry, and he'll tell us everything we need to know before we make our minds up." Cole steers the car near all the others.

Music booms from somewhere in the distance, and adrenaline rushes through me. I've never been excited to do something behind my dad's back. He would never think twice about looking for me here. Dorian wraps his arm around my shoulder, giving me a slight jerk into his side.

"Let Cole have his fun. He seems relaxed here, and I've never seen him like this in a long time. Don't worry about

your dad. I would love to see him come here with all these fine folks." He laughs.

"It's not so much him finding me. It's more when I get home that worries me."

"You could move out, and you are technically an adult now."

"I tried that. They said they would stop paying for my schooling if I did. It's so fucked."

Not that I want to be in school, but what else is there for me to do in this town? I can go to the EU, join the gang or move to the Southside. If my dad had his way, he would push me into politics.

As we near the fire, I watch Cole chat with an older man with dark hair, so this must be Henry. He turns and drinks his beer, watching Dorian and I close the gap.

"Henry, this is Dorian and Nyx." Cole introduces us. I reach out, shaking Henry's waiting hand.

"Good to meet you. What brings you by tonight?"

I nod in Cole's direction. "He pretty much dragged me out of the house and told us about you recruiting."

His eyes light up. "Well, I'll be damned. Three youngins want to join us. Follow me, and I'll introduce you to a few of the men and give you a rundown on how things are run around here."

All right, nothing seems sketchy so far. He introduces us to a few guys and tells us how the gang works and what would be expected from us. It looks like something I wouldn't mind trying. The only catch is—

"An enforcer? You want all three of us to be enforcers?" Dorian asked, brushing his fingers through his hair.

"I do. I think you guys would be perfect. Think about it." He heads back to the bonfire, leaving the three of us alone.

Cole stretches his arms sideways, spinning on his heels until he faces us. "I say we do this."

"Hold up. I think we should sleep on it. There is a lot to think about. Why don't we return to your place and relax a little." Dorian says as he starts walking to the car.

Cole follows him. "You wanna head back to my place? Why not yours?"

"Well, for one. My grandmother is there, and you have all the shit at your place."

"I'm down for that plan. I could go for a drink." This entire day is finally catching up, and I need to drown it out. Thank fuck it's Friday; there is no way I'm getting up tomorrow before noon.

"All right, fine. Luckily, that roomie of mine is gone. He's so annoying." Cole rolls his eyes before climbing behind the wheel.

"Cole, everyone is annoying to you," I tell him as I climb into the back seat.

"I can't help that. The world would be better if they weren't born with the stupid gene."

Oh, boy.

One thing about Cole is his attitude. He can't help himself. He always ends up ruining a good thing when his mouth opens up. Driving through Eastwood with the windows down and our music blaring, we are having the time of our lives. Dorian reaches under his seat, tossing

back a mask. I grin at the style—exes over the eyes and stitches over the mouth.

"Fuck going back to the dorm. Let's go to the Southside." I place the mask on, flicking the switch. The back of the car lights up green.

Cole places his mask on, lighting up in blue, and Dorian lights up in red. It's gonna be a good fuckin' night.

2

Dorian

The Southside. You would never cross the tracks and come to this side if you were smart. The Soul Stealers aren't the only gang in town. If we joined them, we would have more control over this town. Maybe it wouldn't be a bad thing if we did. Henry seems like a decent guy.

We pull into a vacant parking lot, and every business is boarded up from the lack of support from the neighbourhood. More drug dealers are moving in and creating problems even on our side.

I face Cole. "You think the gang would be a smart move?"

He looks to Nyx and then back at me. "I think it would be good. Enforcers, though?" He furrows his brow and shrugs his shoulders. "That's a big job, and he wants us? We're nobodies. What does that say?"

"That we're either stupid or willingly ready to take the fall for this gang." Nyx shrugs.

"Only time will tell. Here, I have something to celebrate." Cole digs in his front pocket. Nyx groans.

"You have a joint? Where the fuck did you get that from?" I pluck it from his fingers. It's been a while since I've smoked. It's something I rarely do. I can tell by the way Nyx is acting, he's not excited at all.

"One puff won't kill you, bud." Cole lights up, taking a deep inhale before passing it to me.

God, I missed this. I swear it only took a second before my body felt like jelly. Grinning, I pass it to Nyx.

"I'm not sure about this."

"I won't push it on you, and it has to be something you want to try," I tell him. I will never push drugs on someone else. Either you want to do it, or you don't.

Nyx nervously takes the joint and stares at it before placing it between his lips. The first inhale, I can already tell it won't be good. Even Cole starts to laugh. Nyx coughs as smoke blows out of his mouth.

"Should've taken a smaller puff there, bud." Cole laughs.

"Fuck you," Nyx rasps. "You cunts never warned me about the burn." He coughs again, rubbing his throat.

"Smaller inhales this time." I watch as he does what I say. He passes it back to me before slumping in his seat.

"Give him a few. It'll be entertaining as fuck."

Oh, that it will be. Nyx needs this tonight. I feel sorry for the bastard. Small giggles fill the cab as it hits Nyx at once.

"Awe, man, I didn't even do that much. How come you two aren't laughing?"

"Because, young grasshopper, we are seasoned pros." Cole takes another puff.

Nyx laughs. It starts low in his chest before he falls over in his seat and bursts out loud. I shake my head, laughing along with him. I have to wipe my eyes from the tears that fall. Even Cole is laughing so much that he's crying.

"Shit, he's fucked." I press my hand on my aching ribs.

"We probably should get him home before his parents' return."

Nyx laughs again. "Fuck those parents. I don't need them."

Yep, he's done for the night. We better pray that his dad isn't home.

The Thornton household always gave me the ick. The way Nyx's mom runs this house would've made me leave years ago. How he's kept sane is beyond me. Even the doormat is clean, not a speck of mud to be found. Nyx can't stop rolling around on the grass, pretending to make snow angels. I didn't think two puffs would affect him this much.

"Doooorian, the grass it's talking to me." He rubs his cheek deeper into the ground.

"No, bud, it's not." I shake my head, heading back in his direction. "Come on, up you go. Cole has the door open for us." I place my hands under his armpits, scooping him up. His brown eyes are bloodshot and unfocused; the next thing I know, his finger bops me on the nose.

His head falls backwards, and he bursts into laughter, stumbling back. I exhale slowly. It's like watching a toddler. Headlights illuminated the yard as they pulled into the driveway.

"Shit," Cole swore on his way over.

"Oh, no. Daddy's home!" the sarcasm dripping from his voice.

I have other words to use, but we'll go with his.

I watch Otis Thornton storm across the lawn, his face growing a lovely shade of scarlet with each step. I quickly grab Nyx, getting him standing and smacking his face.

"Smarten up. Your dad is on a rampage."

He sticks his tongue out and blows a raspberry. "I don't give a shit. Let Daddy-o come over." He snickers under his breath.

"What the fuck is going on? Out in public, of all things, Nyxon?" Otis grabs him out of my grip, shaking him. "Are you fucking stoned?"

"Are you fuckin' stupid?" Nyx leans into his dad's face.

A loud crack fills the air. Cole and I watch Nyx as tumbles onto his ass from the smack his dad landed on his cheek.

"You watch what you say to me, son." Otis squares his shoulders.

Cole goes to move, but I hold him back. "Don't," I whisper. "This needs to happen."

"Nyx is fucked up. It's not fair," Cole growled in his deep voice.

"Gonna beat me for all the neighbours to witness? That's one way to ruin the reputation you're trying to maintain, Daddy dearest." Nyx's tone mocked that of his dad.

Otis steps back. "No son of mine will be living in my house if he seeks the way of drugs."

Nyx scoffs. Getting to his feet, he moves forward. "It was one time. Don't act like I've done it multiple times. You can barely take a shit in that house without anyone knowing."

I advance closer. This conversation is getting heated, and if Otis tries anything, this is when he would. There are a few things that I'll put up with, but this isn't one of them.

"Otis, I think that's enough for tonight."

A mocking smile curled his lips. "Dorian, this isn't your place to say anything."

"No, but he's my friend, and I am going to look out for him. I'll bring him home tomorrow, and you two can talk about it when he's sober."

Otis doesn't say anything; he turns and walks away. The three of us stand there in silence, and I'm trying to figure out if he honestly kicked Nyx out for having done drugs once. It would be a little extreme if he did.

"I'll take you back to Dorians for the night, and we can figure this shit out in the morning," Cole says, turning and giving Otis one last glare before going to the car.

"You all right?"

Nyx storms toward the car. "I'm fine," he calls back.

He's anything but fine.

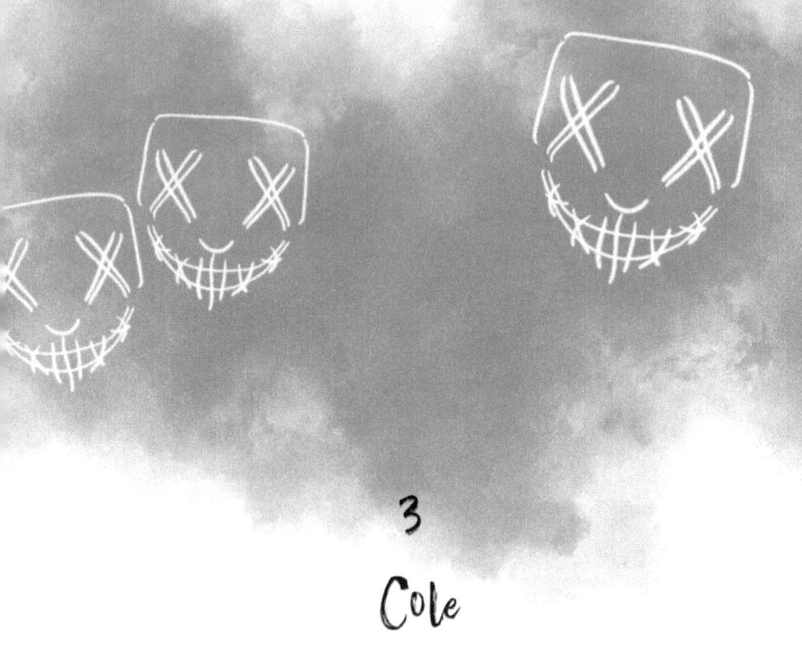

3
Cole

Things have taken a turn. I wasn't expecting shit to hit the fan last night with Nyx and his old man. You swear he was doing crack instead of smoking fuckin' weed. I never liked his dad; he came off with such an arrogant persona that I never cared for, even when I first met Nyx in grade eight.

Instead of having a chill Saturday, we are now helping Nyx pack his shit because no matter how much we all talked to Otis. It was a no-go to stay here. What a prick; he reminds me of my old man.

Nyx's mom didn't even try to stop any of this. All she did was sit back on that perfect cream couch and watch the entire argument go down. Makes me wonder if she even cares about her son.

"How the fuck am I supposed to pay for schooling, a place to rent and all the rest that I need?"

I toss his books in a box, trying to find an answer for him, only to come up with one solution. "Henry and the gang. What if we joined?"

"Seriously. Now's not the time for the gang bullshit, Cole." Dorian glares at me.

"Why not. It's perfect. We do a couple of jobs, get some money, and then we can move in together. I say we talk more with Henry and explain what happened."

"No, he's right. What could honestly go wrong? I'm already homeless if it's gonna shit on me, I'd rather it happen all at once." Nyx runs his hand through his hair, disappointment washing over his face.

He can think all he wants, and he isn't homeless. He's in between houses at the moment. Once we finalize everything with the Soul Stealers, things will start looking up for us.

Without a word, we all leave the house. Nyx loads the last box into the car before climbing into the backseat. There are so many things I want to say to him, but it wouldn't help him. Dorian shakes his head, not knowing what to say either.

We head for the compound first. The best thing to do is to get this conversation over with. If we aren't going to be a part of the gang, it's best to know right away. Then

we can worry about plan B. I have no idea what that'll be; I'm banking on this to go through.

Freddy meets us at the door, arms crossed. "Can I help you, gentlemen?"

"Uh, we need to speak to Henry," I tell him, never taking my eyes off him. For an old man, he's built.

His grey eyebrow pops upwards. "Does he know you're all here?"

Nyx turns to me and cringes. "No. We wanted to talk about joining."

Freddy nods. "I hope you are prepared for everything that comes with it. It won't be easy initially, but it's like family here. If you ever need anything, don't be afraid to ask." He moves out of the way. "Henry is in the office. It's down the hall, past the bar."

"Thanks," we all say in harmony.

My heart is in my throat with sudden nerves. If I'm nervous about telling him we want to join, how the fuck am I supposed to be an enforcer. I know what enforcers do, and having nerves aren't allowed. Rounding the corner, Henry is already waiting for us.

"Welcome, boys, follow me. I had a feeling you would be back." He heads into his office.

Dorian narrows his eyes at him. "Don't. He didn't mean it like that."

"He better not. I'm not a boy," Dorian growls, pushing past me.

I stare at Nyx. His face twitches. "Stop. We can't start shit before we even get into the gang, Nyx," I warn him.

He closes his eyes, giving me a slight nod. "For now, but you know how Dorian is."

Don't we all? There's a reason why he was always with his grandmother growing up, and his parents couldn't be bothered to raise him. They didn't know what they were doing when they had him and spent most of their time yelling at him.

It gives me flashbacks to my childhood. I was lucky enough to get out, but living in foster homes wasn't how I saw myself growing up. I wish someone had gotten me out before the memories were engraved deep enough. The only thing Southside blessed me with was getting rid of my old man.

I can't say I'm proud to be where I'm from, but it's made me who I am today. I'll always place those that I love first. Dorian and Nyx are more than friends. They are my family, and I wouldn't be here today without them. I'll do anything for them, and I'm confident they would do anything for me.

We just have to get through this meeting.

4

Nyx

I can't believe we joined a gang. I'm not gang material. I'll be the first to admit Henry's rules are a little strange. The fact that he wants all of us to go to school is the weirdest. But he says he'll pay for it, which I'm grateful for since my asshole dad has officially cut me off.

If it wasn't for Dorian's grandmother, I would be homeless. That woman, I'm not sure how I'll ever make it up to her.

I'm lying in bed when Dorian and Cole come barging in so much for a relaxing time.

"What do you assholes want?"

Cole falls onto my bed next to me. "Henry called. He needs us at the compound in thirty."

Dorian moves over the top of us until he's beside the wall.

"Fuck, man, lay off the steroids." Cole reaches over me to shove Dorian.

"Don't blame my big bones that your skinny, you little prick."

Cole snorts. "You could only wish you were this skinny. What the fuck does your grandmother feed you?"

"Apparently, more than your shitty ass foster parents."

I hiss, trying to sink further into the mattress. I wait for a fist to fly.

"At least I can say the word *parent*. Where the fuck are yours?"

Sitting up, I raise my hands. "That's enough. All our parents are trash, end of conversation. What does Henry want us for?"

"Buzz kill," Cole mumbles.

I haul off, punching him in the shoulder. "Kill that, you cunt."

Dorian groans. "Speaking of killing, I hope you are ready to put your enforcing tasks to work."

I glance over my shoulder. "Henry wants us to kill someone?"

"Welcome to the gang life, Nyx."

When I signed up, deep down, this never crossed my mind. What can possibly go down in this town? The things you never knew or wanted to know. I liked living in the shadows, if my dad only knew what was happening in this town. His son doing drugs once wouldn't be the worst thing.

The directions are clear. Henry doesn't like competition. We need to take care of it, either make them listen or make it permanent. Henry doesn't care what we choose, but if this asshole doesn't listen, we'll be back out here.

Southside is Henry's number one competitor. It's funny if you think about it. Does he honestly think all the EU students would be coming out here for drugs? Most of those kids are too preppy for these roads. They would shit their pants if they crossed that line.

Playing with my mask, the adrenaline is already rushing through my body. I didn't think it would feel like this, but maybe Cole was right. Joining the gang is what we all needed. I have enough built-up frustration that I need an outlet, and somebody's face is precisely what I need.

Cole wants to keep our identity covered for now, hence the masks. I don't blame him; we don't need a target painted this early in the game. We aren't even sure if we are staying in Soul Stealers. That's all I need, is to walk down the street and be gunned down. At least this way, no one knows who we are until our reputation is built. Between Cole and Dorian, I don't think many will mess with us, I'm not the best fighter, but fuck, if it calls for it, I'll lay them out.

Dorian drives while Cole checks his gun for the tenth time. Out of all of us, he's the one that was born for this. He may look like a preppy model douche, doesn't mean I want to cross him. Behind those baby blues lies a devil.

Cole sits sideways in his seat. "Once we get there, it will be a nut house. Henry probably wants a bullet in the guy's head."

"So guns a blazzin' is what you are saying," I confirm.

"Unless Dorian wants to blow the house up." Cole shrugs.

The corner of Dorian's mouth lifted. "I'm not opposed to that idea. Be quick, I packed the explosive."

"Of course you did."

Dorian grins at me through the rearview mirror. "Can't help myself."

The further we get into the area, the shittier the houses become. Every home should be torn down and this side of town forgotten. That would take a miracle. Coleman banks on this side for votes to stay in power. He's such a sleazeball.

We creep closer to our destination, and my heart finally gets the burst of adrenaline it needs. Reaching under my seat, I grab my gun. Henry gifted each of us a Desert Eagle for all of our jobs. I'm still not sure how to feel about it. Beating someone with my fist, yes.

But shooting someone? I'm still on the fence.

"Ready for this?" Dorian pulls the SUV over.

The drug house is down the block. People coming and going like the lion isn't hunting them. When a shiny Cadillac pulls up, we know shit's about to get real.

"This must be the big buyer. Should we hold back and see who it is?" I question, moving between the front seats to get a better look.

Cole leans forward, waiting for the driver to exit. "Who do we know drives a Caddy?"

There's only one name that comes to mind. "Coleman." I scoff. "What a piece of shit. No wonder he won't do anything about this side of town."

"Not like profiting off the poor even more." Dorian shakes his head. "I say we go in there and take care of Coleman too."

"You know we can't do that. We'll be charged with murder, without a doubt. We wait until he leaves, then take care of these pricks." I wonder what goes through his head some days. Nope, I take that back. I don't want to know anything in that pea brain of his.

Twenty minutes later, Coleman walks out, accompanied by none other than our dealer. If we're being honest, I can't remember his name. It won't be important come morning, anyway. The SUV is so quiet I can hear my heartbeat—every thump pulses through me.

"Get ready. The moment he pulls away, we move. Fuck the nice talk. If he's in bed with Coleman, this cunts a deadman." Cole doesn't look away from the front window as he speaks. "I suspect at least ten men inside—take them all out. Dorian can burn it down after."

The Desert Eagle feels like a thousand pounds in my hand. If I want to stay in the gang, I'll have to prove myself one way or another. In a matter of seconds, we are exiting the SUV and running across the street. The closer we get, the louder the house becomes.

"Masks on, when I reach three, storm in. Don't ask questions, and don't fuckin' die." Cole pulls his mask on, looking the part.

Dorian and I pull our masks down and stand beside Cole, waiting for the show to start.

"One... Two." He cocks his gun.

Cocking my gun, Cole advances on the front of the house, fucker could never count fully. Whoever was milling around on the steps caught sight of us, drawing their weapons.

"Who the fuck are you assholes, stepping up on us?" one prick speaks. He moves to the edge of the steps.

Cole laughs, aiming his gun. "Your worst nightmare." Pulls the trigger, shooting him in the chest.

Gunshots ring out.

Taking the back way behind the house, I plan to cut off anyone trying to escape over the fence and into the alley. Things are going a mile a minute; it's like a scene from a movie, not like being thrown into stuff from the get-go.

"Nyx, he's coming out of the house," Cole yells from behind me.

Quickly turning, we find our drug dealer making his escape. He can run, but he won't make it very far. I catch up to him, running into him.

"Where the hell do you think you are running off to, you chicken shit?" Pointing my gun at his head.

He snickers. "You're just a child. What are you gonna do?"

All that pent-up frustration that didn't get used on my dad comes to the surface. My fist lands a loud blow to

the cunts face. The pain is welcoming. Especially when the drug dealer hollers in pain.

"Fuckin' pussy. If you can deal the drugs, you can deal with the pain," I barked in his face. "Your operation is over with. I send regards from the Soul Stealers."

He covers his face. "No, please," he begs. "I'm just an errand boy. Don't you want the bigger fish?"

"Tell me who, and I won't shoot you." Pulling the gun away a little, waiting for him to answer.

He turns his head, eyes widen. My head barely turns before Cole shoots his gun. Blood splatters all over my shirt and mask.

Jumping back, I rip my mask off. "What the fuck, Cole! I almost had more information out of him."

"We don't have time for small talk, Nyx. Shoot, don't talk."

It wasn't small talk, you asshole. It would've been something to take back to Henry, a guaranteed stay in the gang. It would've been a big win if we took down the big man. Leave it to Cole to be trigger-happy.

"Come on, before you get shot." Dorian pats me on the back.

I shrug him off. "I almost had it, D." Closing my thumb and finger together. "This fuckin' close, and he ruined it all."

He lifts his mask onto his head. "There will be another chance, Nyx. It's our first job. We can't always go in full force."

They wouldn't understand. If this doesn't work out, I'd lose a lot. My entire life is riding on being in Soul Stealers. I'm not sure what my future would look like without it.

5
Cole

"Cole, this is a bad idea, and you know it." Dorian glares at me from across the kitchen table.

I give him a double shrug. "I know it is. You know it is. But it needs to be done."

"Have you told Nyx?"

"About that." I play around with my coffee cup, deflating the question.

"You idiot. He's going to find out, and it probably should be from one of us."

Rubbing my temples, I meet his green eyes. "No shit. Give me some time. I'll do it."

He chuckles. "Wanna pinkie promise?" He asks, wiggling his finger at me.

I'll figure out a time to tell him; he doesn't have to know now. We technically have two weeks before things go to hell. So, in all honesty, I have a week.

The front door crashes open, making both Dorian and I jump. He raises a brow, and I internally cringe; whatever happened can't be good. Nyx storms into the kitchen seconds later, covered in dirt and grease.

"Don't ask." He grunts on his way to the sink.

I'm gonna say his bike is acting up again. There are better times to tell him the news.

"Cole has some news for you," Dorian spits out.

"What the fuck?" I said, spreading my arms wide in disbelief. He threw me under the fuckin' bus.

Nyx turns to me. "What is it? It better be good."

I nod in the direction of the empty chair. This is def-initely a sit-down conversation. I wait for him to finish washing his hand and to sit before dumping this shit on him. I would've carried it around longer if I could, but Dorian is right. He needs to know, and I should be the one to tell him.

"Spill it, Cole. I have shit to fix."

"All right, fine. Henry got word from the mayor that purge night is a go this year."

"Nope, not doing it." He pushes his chair out.

I hold my finger up, freezing his actions. "We don't have a choice. The mayor is running for office again this year, and he thinks that he'll get another term if he does another purge night."

Nyx scoffs, rolling his eyes. "That's the stupidest shit I've ever heard. Why do we always have to get sucked into

politics? This is bullshit. How are we going to protect the town and Cat?"

"Well, for one. Half pint is not leaving this house on Halloween," Dorian states.

No fuckin' shit.

"Conrad also suggested that we—"

Nyx holds his hand up. "Nope, that's enough. I'm not having it."

"Listen to him, Nyx. It's important."

"You think handling club business for a town that doesn't give a shit about us is important? Get off that high horse, Dorian. The only reason I'm still in that stupid club is because of you, two."

I should've seen this coming. "We don't have a choice. We do what Henry tells us. You know the rules."

"The rules didn't help us when we needed them."

With that, he storms out of the kitchen.

"Well, that went better than I thought, to be honest. I'm sure he'll come around. We have a week before we have to figure shit out, anyway." Dorian shrugs.

"Glad you're the optimistic kind. I'm not sure he will be this time around. Henry really fucked him over."

"I'm headed out. Let me know when half pint gets home."

I wave him off, then head downstairs. I need to blow off some steam, and unfortunately, I don't have anyone to torture, so my body will have to suffice. Pulling my shirt off and tossing it onto the bench, I head over to the abused punching bag. I'm sure we could buy a new one,

but this one is well-loved. If you overlook the duct tape layers, it still works perfectly.

My gloves sit off to the side; I would wear them any other day, but today, I need to feel some pain. Henry is driving me up the wall with all this mayor bullshit.

The first hit is a welcoming feeling. I also hate how Conrad has weaselled his way so far into everything that he thinks he's now King of Turd Island. I land another punch, the worst thing about the mayor's newest idea. He wants Purge Night to be bigger and better than last year. Surrounding towns got wind of it after he met with all the mayors. He wanted more people to enjoy it.

Because that's what Eastwood fuckin' needs.

I swear our mayor is so detached from reality it's unreal. How he keeps getting voted back in blows me away. That should tell you how many people enjoy having him in the office to get this one night of the year.

I hammer harder and faster into the bag, sweat pouring down my back. I'm so far into my head that I never noticed somebody else had come down here.

"I would say you look hot, but what the fuck Cole?" Cat shakes her head. "Wanna explain to me why you didn't glove up?"

I can't help but give her a smirk. Her black hair is gathered up in a messy bun, and what I wouldn't do to tear that oversized sweatshirt off her. Those goddamn thigh highs only lead to what I want the most.

"Cole, upstairs now." She snaps her fingers, pointing to the stairs.

She's been cockblocking me for days now. This wasn't supposed to happen when moving your girlfriend in. She's driving me up the wall walking around wearing shit that shows off her ass. She does it on purpose.

And to add more to the fire, I follow her up the stairs, and I swear she adds more swing to her step.

"Sit. I'll get the first aid kit."

I give my hands a flex. They aren't that bad—bleeding, yes. But they could be worse.

"Here, place this on them. It'll help with the swelling. What the hell were you thinking, anyway?" She passes me an ice pack and sets up her little station on the kitchen table.

"I have a lot of shit going on, Wednesday. It was the bag or some asshole that I would come across on the street with."

Her violet eyes swept me up and down. "What's going on, Cole?"

"It's club business, so don't be telling anyone, got it?"

She rolls her eyes. "Who the fuck would I tell? The next dead body I dig up?" She grabs the antiseptic spray and then holds my right hand.

"You could've made a friend with Riley if you wanted to. We weren't stopping you."

Shrugging her shoulder. "I know. I guess I don't know how to make friends, and what am I supposed to do with him? I have enough guys in my life already." She chews on her lip.

"Wednesday." My fingers trace her chin as my thumb pulls her lip free. "Stop being hard on yourself. If you

want friends, make them. If you don't, that's fine too. But think about making one with Riley."

"Fine, don't think this worked from telling me what's happening with your little squad." Her little black eyebrow pops up.

"You better sit."

She backs away. "Shit, it's bad, isn't it. What has Henry done now?"

I pull her into me. "It's not like last time." I drop my head on her stomach. "The mayor wants to bring back purge night." Her hands run through my hair.

"What does that mean, exactly?" She tugs my head back.

"I mean, he's running for mayor again and wants a guaranteed vote back into the office. He wants a more phenomenal purge night than last year. Our job is to make sure it goes off without a hitch."

"It's gonna be worse, isn't it?"

I nod. "I think so. Dorian and I are concerned, but Henry doesn't seem to care."

"And Nyx?"

I take a deep breath before letting it out. "Cat. Things with Nyx and Henry are complicated, and I don't see them patching things up soon. But Nyx needs to realize that this is a job, and he has to do it without bitching. No one is thrilled about this, but we don't have a choice."

"When?"

"Like always, on Halloween night, he wants surrounding towns involved. We don't want you going out anywhere."

She steps back, crossing her arms. "Cole, don't start with me. I'm sure I can handle making my own choices, and besides, I learnt last year to stay inside on purge night because masked assholes hang around the cemetery."

I chuckle. "Yeah?" Moving toward her, I curl one hand around her neck and my other on her hip. "I'm pretty sure you love having those masked assholes around."

I watch as she licks her lips, sending my body into overdrive. I've had enough of her tormenting me. This ends now; lifting her, she wraps her legs around my waist. I move us to the kitchen table.

"I've had enough of you ignoring me, and I want what I want, little one."

She presses her heels into my back, pushing me closer. "Yeah, what do you want, Cole?" she asks, pulling up her sweater, showing off a pair of Halloween underwear.

I slowly slide my fingers up her thigh, watching her skin prickle with goosebumps. "I could spend all day looking at this pussy, little one." I slip off her underwear, getting a good look at her wet and waiting pussy. "Wanna know what I want?"

"Yeah," she whispered, her eyes craving with passion.

I move my hand to my jeans, unsnapping them. Slipping my hand inside, my cock is already dripping for her. My pants dip below my ass, exposing my cock to her.

"Mmm, I'll never get tired of seeing that." Her gaze lands on my piercing.

I give myself a nice long stroke, and when I flick the piercing, it makes my cock grow harder. God, I can't wait

to sink deep inside of her. Lining up, I smack her clit with my cock.

"I need you so bad right now, and this is what you get for making me wait. You're not going to come. This is your punishment." I drive into her with abrupt force, making her scream. Her body slides up the table. I have to pull her back into me. My fingers flex into her thighs, and I can't help but watch my cock disappear into her.

"Cole, I need you deeper."

"You'll take what I give you." I withdraw all the way, only to enter slowly until the head of my cock disappears again. I watch as her fingers work toward her clit. "Not so fast, I told you. You aren't coming." I wrap my hand around her wrist, raising it above her head. I reach down, grabbing her other wrist and restraining her.

I capture her mouth before slamming back into her hard. Her fingernails dig into the back of my hand, making me pound into her faster. Her little whimpers edge me further. The thought of her not getting to finish is my undoing.

"Fuck, little one." I drop my head into her neck, spilling everything inside her. "Fuck, I love you."

"Yeah, well, I hate you."

"That's because you're mad. Trust me, when Nyx comes back, he'll appreciate it." Kissing her neck, I slip out of her, watching my cum leak out of her. "That's a sight I'll never get tired of."

"This is why I cut you off all the time, dickwad." She half laughs, jumping off the table.

I fuckin' believe that. I may be hard to deal with, but it's not my fault. It's how I was raised.

"Don't get angry with me. This is your fault."

"Don't push your luck."

She narrowed her eyes at me, and I would be scared, but the last time she tried to hurt me, she only ended up hurting herself. I'll never let that happen again.

6

Dorian

I thought we were done with all this bullshit.

All Henry is doing is feeding into the mayor and giving what he wants. He's nothing but an enabler, and they both need to be stopped. If I have anything to do with it, this will be the last year for the purge. Throughout the entire drive, all I see are Coleman for Mayor signs. I had to refrain myself from running each one over. I respect my bike too much for that.

Pulling into the grocery store parking lot, I can already feel myself getting mad. I knew I should've just done online pickup. But they always fuck up my order and substitute my items with the most random things. If I want a potato, don't tell me I want a litre of milk instead. Those things are in different departments.

No one else in the house has figured out cooking be-sides Cat. Between the both of us, we feed the house, but

when we aren't home. The boys starve. It's not that hard to make a simple dish, fuck spaghetti is easy. I guess not everyone had a loving grandmother like I did. I miss her so much.

The stares I get walking up and down the aisle should annoy me, but I ignore them. Some are less keen on a biker club in town. It's no different from a gang, except for the cut I now wear every time I leave the house. It doesn't help that our logo is a giant skull with a scythe.

Every mom grabs their kid like I'm gonna snatch them and take them back to my perv van. If they only knew that we help find the dirty fuckin' pervs in this town. We do everything we can in the club to keep this town safe, then one night a year, it gets flushed down the drain.

You might as well call us hypocrites.

The whispers only grow louder the longer I take. If people think my shopping in the grocery store is con-troversial, just wait until the mayor drops his bombshell soon. Then we'll see who the bad guy really is in this town. All I want is for Cat to graduate then we can move away.

I'm almost at the checkout when I bump into some-body. Turning, I come face to face with Conrad. Great.

"Fancy running into you here." Conrad grins.

"Well, it is a grocery store in a small town. What do you expect?" Just because he's my VP doesn't mean jack shit.

His lips twitch. "Don't be like that. Henry told me you aren't excited about this Halloween."

Loosey lips Linda I see. Henry never could keep shit to himself.

"This is your first year here, Conrad. That's the only reason you're excited. Give it time, a few hours in, and you'll be over it, too. The only ones that benefit from it are the ones that have a fantasy about chasing women in the fuckin' park."

That doesn't sound good when I think about it, considering we chased Catalina last year. But that's different, we knew what we were doing, and it wasn't a sick fuckin' fantasy. And she wasn't a one-night thing.

"Either way, you need to be prepared too, Dorian. You are an enforcer for the club."

"Yeah, I'm well aware of my fuckin' job." Moving away, I move back in line. Fuck him. It's none of his concern about my life unless I have club business to handle.

I think we are still stuck in the mentality of a gang, and it's hard to transition from one mindset to another.

I always get excited seeing Cat's black Volkswagen in the driveway. I guess it was too much for Cole to shoot me that text. The sight of our house never gets old either, when Cat moved in, she made it her mission to plant a flower bed, and of course, she had to keep the dark theme. I never realized how many flowers come in deep shades of purple, black or dark red. It's beautiful, I'll admit, and I'm not a flower guy.

Climbing off my bike, I grab the groceries from the saddlebags. The neighbourhood is already starting to look perfect for fall; the leaves are changing, and the smell of fall is in the air. In no time, decorations will be out; I feel most sorry for those who don't decorate.

They'll be targeted first when the purge starts. The younger teens always vandalize buildings because they know the cops won't do anything to them.

There's only one rule: no murder. And shockingly, it's never been broken.

I'm barely in through the front door, and it's chaos.

"What the fuck do you want from me?" Nyx throws a pillow at Cole.

"I want you to fuckin' man up and do what's expected from you."

I spot Cat out of the corner of my eye, standing at the edge of the kitchen, shaking her head. I slowly make my way over to her.

Lowering my head, I whisper, "What's going on?"

She releases a sigh. "Nyx wants out of the club, to be honest. I think it was the wrong move to let him stay. He should've stayed out."

I walk the rest of the way into the kitchen, placing the bags on the counter. As the yelling continues, I pack the food away.

"Dorian, aren't you going to break them up?"

"No, darling. That is one fight that needs to happen. Cole can't always get his way. He needs to listen to others for once, I tried to tell him that Nyx wanted out, but he

wouldn't listen. I think the final push for Nyx was Henry fucking him over."

She walks over to me, wrapping her arms around my waist. "That's low and horrible. If you make a promise, the most you can do is keep it."

I tip up her chin. "Some things are meant to be learnt the hard way." I lower my lips above hers, slowly inching my tongue until it touches hers. Her mouth opens, inviting me in. Running my hand through her hair, I hold her still. Swiping my tongue against hers before closing my mouth, feeling her lips move with mine.

A loud crash comes from the living room before I can feel her body closer.

"Fuck."

"I told you to deal with them," amusement dripped from her voice.

"Watch it, half pint. I'm not their parent. The only person I'm going to punish around here is you."

She licks her lips and slowly rakes her eyes down my body. With a grin, she spins around and heads into the living room.

Goddamn her. When I walk into the living room, it's a mess. Pillows are thrown all over the floor, everything on the coffee table is scattered along the floor, and my eyes travel to the broken glass where Cat is standing.

She gently picks up the broken frame that held a picture of herself and her dad, and my heart breaks. As much as she didn't talk to her dad, I knew she loved him.

"Shit, baby. I'm sorry." Nyx reaches for her, crushing her close to his chest. "We didn't mean to break it, I swear."

"Let me go, Nyx."

He lets go, slowly backing away. I turn to Cole, a mournful look outfitted him. Good, I hope he finally fuckin' learnt a lesson.

"Wednesday?"

"Don't, Cole. Why can't you two deal with your shit without breaking other people's things? I'll be in the kitchen making supper if you need me."

I reach out to her, but she brushes me off. Turning back to the two assholes.

"What the fuck? Why do you always insist on starting shit for the sake of starting it, Cole? Can't you just leave it alone?"

"What do you want me to do?" Cole gets in my face. "I'm only trying to do what's best."

"For who? You or him?"

"For everyone," he spits out. "Why can't you think about everyone else for once."

I shake my head in disbelief. "What do you think I've been doing?" I point to Nyx. "He made up his mind, end of story. After Halloween, he's out. You got that?" I glance over at Nyx, who has been quiet the entire time.

"I can deal with everything until after Halloween. Sorry about the mess. I'll clean it up."

I wait until Nyx leaves before saying what I want to say.

"Cole, I'm worried about him. He's not the same since Henry fucked him over."

I watch him take a deep breath, kicking a pillow across the floor. "I know. It did a number on him. It fucked with his trust issues, and I'm unsure how to help him. I thought keeping him in the club would be the cure, but I was wrong. It's only made things worse. Every day, his demons are coming out."

"Perhaps what needs to be done is for him to get out. Only two weeks, and it's over. We'll tell Henry in the morning."

"Yeah, okay. We'll call a meeting and get it over with. I'm sure Conrad will have a field day with this."

Conrad can kiss my ass for all I care. He has no say in what happens until Henry leaves or dies. His opinion does not matter. Nyx deserves so much more than being in this club—everyone knows it.

"You need to go in there and apologize to Cat. A real one, Cole, not your bullshit ones that you always do."

"Whatever, asshole." He storms into the kitchen.

He was doing so well, but a tiger cannot change his stripes, and I shouldn't expect Cole to be a nice guy.

7

Catalina

I knew something was the matter with Nyx, yet no one would help him. His downward spiral has me worried. I want the fun, happy-go-lucky Nyx back. I miss him. But he's been gone for months now. This club has been sucking the life out of him, I'm not sure what the difference is between the club and the gang, but he needs to talk to me. Because fighting between everyone clearly isn't helping.

I slam down the pasta sauce, getting frustrated with the entire situation. Cole doesn't help things either, and he always has to act like the boss. For once, he can consider other people's feelings.

"Wednesday? Can I talk to you outside?" Cole's deep voice interrupts my ranting thoughts.

I don't bother answering him. Turning away from him, I head for the door that leads to the backyard. I con-

tinue walking until I'm halfway across the yard. I stand there facing the fence, breathing heavily, becoming more pissed off by the second. Cole's large hand lands on my forearm, spinning me around.

"Look at me, please. I'm not talking to your back."

His blue eyes pierce into mine. "The back is all you deserve right now, Cole. I can't believe you guys."

"One last job, and then he's out, I promise."

I laugh, shaking my head in disbelief. "Yeah, does Nyx know this?"

"He does. He agreed to it." He moves his hand down my arm, squeezing my fingers. "Listen. I'm sorry about your photo. Things got out of hand, and I didn't mean to ruin anything of yours. We shouldn't have fought like that."

"No shit. You idiots always do this. I'm getting tired of it, Cole. I'm not sure if I can take much more of it if I'm being completely honest."

I watch as his face crumbles. "Wednesday," he whispered in a rough texture. "What do you mean?"

I look at a dead spot on the grass. His finger lifts my chin, meeting my eyes. "Tell me, please, are you leaving me?"

"Cole, I don't know what you want me to say."

"I want you to say you won't leave when things get tough."

I hold my finger up, shutting him up. "When things get tough. Are you kidding me? Do you think this little fight you and Nyx had is when things get tough? Are you

shitting me right now?" I don't have to remind him what happened last year.

He tilts his head to the sky. "That's not what I meant." His eyes collide with mine.

"Then explain because the hole is only getting deeper."

He spins around, facing the house. "Fuck, Catalina. I don't know what I mean. I'm shit for words, and you know this."

And this is the problem. He won't express himself, and he refuses to open up. I don't know why. I only want to understand him better. After all this time, I hardly know him.

"I accept your apology, but I have supper to make." I brush past him, heading inside. I won't leave them, especially over a fight. But I swear if they can't figure their shit out fast, I'm unsure how much more I can take. It's taking a toll on me.

"You okay, darling?" Dorian asks as soon as I enter the kitchen.

"I'm not sure, and everything is so fucked I'm not sure what to do anymore." I drop my head into my hands, my entire body slumping forward.

Dorian wraps his arms around me, pulling me tight against his chest. "Stop. You don't need to worry about anything that happens in the club. It's club business, and it never should've entered the house. I'm sorry that we did this to you, Cat."

"It's not your fault, it's my fault. I gotta stop asking for details and stick to what I know best."

He steps back and grins. "Yeah, what's that?"

"Dead bodies."

"Oh, half pint. That's one reason why I love you so much. Let's forget about this and start supper."

He presses a kiss to my forehead before turning back to the stove.

Maybe he's right. Perhaps the club shit should stay out of the house, but when it starts to affect one of them, I can't help but get worried. These are my men—anything that happens to them happens to me.

Nyx walks in with the broom and dustpan. "I'm sorry, baby."

"I don't blame you, Nyx. I don't blame any of you."

"Well, you should. This entire thing is a fucking shit show!" he yells. His chest rose and fell on ragged breaths.

My heart breaks. Things were going so great up until Henry. Is it rude for me to think about digging up his body one day? So the students can examine what a piece of shit he truly is. Fuckin' karma is gonna come after me hard for that thought.

I watch Nyx walk away. This entire house is falling apart, and I don't know how to fix it.

"Half pint, let him cool down. Come, eat before you head to work."

He brings our supper to the table, setting it down.

"What cemetery are you at tonight?"

"Eastwood one."

Dorian cups my face, lowering his close to mine. "Please be safe. This time of year, everyone gets stupid."

I bring my hands to his. "I will, and I have the Bluetooth earbud, so if anything goes wrong, I can call you. I'll be safe, I promise."

"Don't make promises, half pint."

With a quick kiss, I pull out of his hands. "Don't be such a worried wart. No one hangs out in the cemeteries except loners, remember."

"Don't. You aren't a loner. Did you want me to come with you?"

"Nah, I think I need some peace for a while."

With a smile, he finally sits.

⸢⸢⸤⸥⸥

The medical department parking lot is vacant when I pull in. Even Dr. Deadbodies is gone. He's probably on his date with Professor Adams. I knew something was up when I saw Davis come into class out of the blue. Now, I hardly see him around the medical department.

I'm glad to be out of the house tonight. The guys need to get their shit sorted out without me being a referee.As much as I love them, I need some alone time.

The silence of the cemetery will be welcomed.

Parking next to the van, I grab my bag from the back seat along with the blue tooth earbuds from the ashtray. The guys would be pissed if I didn't have these with me. Ever since my stupid asshole of a brother kidnapped me,

they've been overly protective of me heading out at night. I won't lie, I've been nervous ever since.

I have to remind myself that I'm no longer in danger and can't keep living in fear. I'm taking all the precautions I can, and Cole even taught me a few self-defence moves. Not that I'm any good, but it'll be good for what I need. One good kick to the nuts will give me enough time to run.

I need to dig up three bodies tonight, and I'm glad they are all in the same cemetery. Not that going out to Eaglewood is terrible; the travelling is killing me lately, especially when Dr. Deadbodies fills my night with both cemeteries.

I think it's his way of getting back at me for being taken by dickhead Conrad.

The weather is warm tonight, not unusual for this time of year, but it also brings out clear skies. Clear skies are also my worst nightmare. The way the moon is out illuminating the area too much, giving me away; I need to be extra observant.

I pull the van as close as I can to the far end of the road. Being by the woods still sends chills down my spine.

"Grow the fuck up, Cat," I mumble to myself.

I stare into the woods, waiting for a shadow figure to jump out. This overactive mind will be the death of me. When I think no one is watching me, I head to the back of the van, where all my equipment is. Nyx suggested I get a little wagon to haul everything back and forth. But I think it would be more of a hassle in the end. I've been doing it this way for so long that I know how it works.

Counting the rows, I finally come across the grave Davis told me about. It's not the freshest, so I'll be digging for a while. I can only hope it's not a heavy body. Riley has been working overtime in the lab; with the cooler weather coming next month, we both will be inside again. I'll admit it was nice working with him, but I was glad to be outside once spring had arrived.

I stare at the grave and the packed-down dirt. Sweet fuckin' Jesus, this is gonna take me hours to get to the coffin. Shoving the shovel into the ground, I drop the rest of my supplies.

Releasing a deep sigh, I get to work.

The resounding thunk of the shovel hitting wood brings me sweet relief. I can hardly hold on to the shovel as my arms scream in pain. My lungs are on fire as I slump over the shovel handle, trying to catch my breath.

That's it. I'm telling Davis only fresh graves from now on.

I don't even think I can climb out of this hole, and here I figured I was on my game with all the workouts I was getting in. But I can't stay in this hole all night. Willing my body to work, I reach for the grass at the tip of the hole.

When someone's fingers touch mine, I stumble backward. I shut my eyes tightly when thoughts of my brother staring down at me wearing the yellow lite-up mask and memories of what happened last year race through my mind. Fear chases over my skin like an icy wave, my mind going completely blank.

"Baby," Nyx whispered in my ear, his head burrowed into the hollow of my neck as he pulled me closer to his

chest. "I won't let you slip into those memories. Breathe for me, baby. I need you here with me and only with me. Listen to my breathing and match it. Okay?"

I try with all my might to focus on his breathing. No matter what I do, flashes of him standing over me won't leave.

"Cat, it's only you and I."

I focus on Nyx's words and less on my thoughts. No one is here to hurt me, and I'm past all that now.

"I'm here. It's only you and I," I repeat.

"That's right, baby. How about we get out of this hole now, okay?"

I wait until he climbs out first to take a deep breath finally.

8

Nyx

Being a university graduate, I thought it would bring me more opportunities, but apparently, I should've chosen a better career because taking all those bullshit classes did little for me. I'm still stuck in the Soul Stealers.

Henry acts like he's the ruler of my life. Little does he know, no one rules my life except for me. I'm out of this club after Halloween, if he likes it or not. I can't be around somebody that goes against their word. I can't trust him after the hell he put me through a couple of months ago. And he is now doing the mayor's bidding to further his lifestyle. I can't be a part of that either.

If I think about it any longer, I'm gonna lose my goddamn mind. I need to escape from this house, and being around Cole isn't helping. He doesn't understand what I'm going through. He only has his mind set on one thing; unfortunately, it's not what everyone else wants.

His head is so far up his ass he forgets about the world and everyone in it.

There is only one spot I can think of that will help me calm down. Without a word, I leave the house. Climbing onto my bike, I rev my engine before taking off down the road. The wind feels wonderful on my skin. It's what I needed after fighting with Cole.

I let the road take me to my destination. The cemetery is quiet this late at night. I've been coming here since finding Catalina here last year. It's an excellent place to clear your head; no one is here to talk to you.

The moon gleams across the path on my way to the back of the cemetery. Noticing Cat's van parked, I park beside it and listen to where she is. In the distance, I can faintly hear the shovel crunching through the dirt.

As I near the hole, I notice her hand reaching the edge. Without thinking, I grab it to help her up. I didn't even think about what happened to her last year. My brain fuckin' glitched.

"Shit, shit, shit."

I quickly jump into the gravesite, pulling her into my chest. I do everything I can to pull her out of those horrible memories. She takes a deep breath by the time we get out of that goddamn hole.

"I'm so sorry, baby. I wasn't thinking," I apologize again.

She shakes her head. "Don't apologize. You didn't do anything wrong."

I cup her face, lowering mine to hers. "Listen to me. I should've known better. God, baby, I'm so sorry."

She whispered in a low, raspy voice, "It's not your fault, Nyx. I didn't expect to have that kind of reaction, that's all. Why, after all this time, does he still get that reaction from me?"

I stroke the back of her head, trying to give her reassurance. I have nothing to say because what can I say? Besides, give it time. Time doesn't heal all fuckin' wounds.

"Did you want to stay and help me with this body?"

I grimace. "Yeah, sure."

She backs up, laughing. "It's not that bad."

"Cat, my stomach is already turning. I don't get how you can do this every night and not be yacking in the bushes."

She pats her stomach and gives me a grin. "Made of steel, baby."

I blow out a breath, steel. That's what I need. I watch as she grabs the hooks from the tarp and walks to the grave's edge.

"I'll hook all this up if you want to haul the body up. I'm still too tired from digging."

"Yeah, I can do that."

She shakes her head before lowering down. My girl is the strongest person I know and never gives up. No matter what gets thrown at her, she still pushes forwards.

I help load the body into the back of the van, slamming the door shut.

"Did you wanna talk about earlier today?" Her violet eyes settle on me with concern.

"Not really, there isn't anything to talk about. It is what it is. I'm leaving after Halloween, and Henry can do whatever he needs to. I'm tired of it all. I should've left months ago."

Her warm fingers brushed the side of my face. "Nyx. You didn't know Henry was going to do that."

I turn away. "I should've seen it coming." I'm so disappointed in myself.

"Love. How were you to know he would cut your school finances off and then tell the Dean that you were responsible for everything?"

"Because when I signed up, he was all 'Education is number one'. What fuckin' bullshit. If he didn't care, then why get my hopes up. I almost lost everything." I slam my fist into the side of the van, breathing hard. I'll never forgive Henry for what he did. He knew how much going to school meant to me. It was an escape; no matter how much I didn't like going, I needed it. I needed to get out of my head and drown myself in those books.

Cat's hand lands on my shoulder, and I quickly wrap my hand around her waist, slamming her into the van.

"I just wanted to comfort you. You comforted me when I needed it."

Pushing her leggings down, rubbing my finger on her clit, getting her wet. Her sweet moans fill the quiet night air.

"I fucking need you more than I need to breathe right now."

She grips my forearm tight. "Nyx, I need more, please." She tilted her head back, exposing her neck.

I reach up, gripping her neck, watching her eyes flutter shut. I've always loved how her body responds to my touch. Her hand dips into my jeans, finger brushing against the tip of my dick. Brushing my lips alongside her jaw, working my way to her ear.

"I wanna hear you scream, wake the dead, baby," I whisper.

I turn her around, bending her over. She flattens her hands on the side of the van, pushing her ass out further. Yeah, she already knows what I'm after. Popping the button on my pants, I unzip just enough to pull my dick out. Running my fingers along the back of her thigh, I watch as her skin pebbles.

"Fuck, I love you, Catalina."

She peers over her shoulder, giving me a gentle smile. "I love you too, Nyx."

"Good, because I'm gonna fuck you like I hate you."

I line my dick up with her wet entrance and slam into her, making her walls clench, squeezing me tight.

"Oh, fuck." She moans.

Twisting my hand in her hair, I pull her head back and pound into her harder, getting beautiful noises from her. A day doesn't go by that she doesn't drive me wild. I don't know how I survived before her. I run my finger along the new tattoo on her ass cheek, three Halloween masks. Blue, green and red. Thank fuck a woman tattooed her because if another man had seen her ass, I would have lost it.

I pump harder just thinking about it. My fingers squeeze her hip, knowing tomorrow she'll have a bruise from my fingers.

"I need you screaming, baby." Moving my hand from her hair to her neck, her pussy squeezes me in response. "You like that, don't you?"

"Yeah, I love it when you choke me." She arched to meet my next thrust.

"Fucking." *Thrust.* "Perfect." *Thrust.* My fingers squeeze her neck tighter. "Fuck, baby. Your pussy is going to make me come."

Moving my hand from her throat to her clit, I rub fast, making her leg shake.

"That's it, baby, come around my dick. Let everyone know who owns it."

"Nyx, oh shiiit." She clamps around me hard, squirting as she comes.

I can't hold it in any longer. I spill deep inside her with a groan. I lay a gentle kiss on her neck before standing her up. Her legs shake, and she laughs.

"I think it's from digging the graves." She presses her lips to mine in a quick kiss.

"Haha, you're a funny one." I capture her mouth in a slow, saturated kiss. I begin to pull away when she locks her arms around my neck.

"Will you please talk to Cole? I don't like when you two fight. The tension is beginning to affect everyone in the house."

Her violet eyes plead with mine.

"I'll try, but Cole is pigheaded and always has been." You can't get a word in edge-wise with him. It's his way or the highway. Hence, why we're all still in the club.

She presses her lips to mine. "You can do it. Don't let him run all over you. You."—she pokes me in the chest.—"are not a doormat."

Where was she when I was growing up with my father? "Thanks, baby. Now, can we finish your work and worry less about me?"

"No. You can go. I can manage. Besides, I know how much you hate looking into the graves."

I rest my head on her forehead. "Thank fuck. It gives me bad mojo."

"Pussy." She laughs. "I'll see you in the morning."

"Please be safe." I run my hand through her hair before pulling her in for a hug. "Because I will kill anyone if they touch you again." I still regret not placing a bullet in her brother's fuckin' head that day on the street. I have nightmares of him coming back for her.

I wait until she reaches her next grave before I pull out. I figured I would take her advice and talk to Cole—what more damage could it possibly do to our relationship. Talking to him needs to be done in a certain way. Charging in like a wild boar will only end in another throwing match, which doesn't sound like a bad idea.

When I get home, I storm into the kitchen, where I hear Cole's voice. I don't bother saying hello, snapping my fingers and gaining Cole and Dorian's attention.

"You, asshole, to the basement. I'm settling some shit with you tonight."

He gives me a smirk. "Where the fuck were you?"

I can't help myself, I smirk back. "Banging your girlfriend, move it now."

Dorian snorts from his seat at the table. "I'm sure you were better than her other boyfriend?"

"Fuck you, asshole," Cole snaps. He brushes past me on his way to the basement.

"How is she?" Dorian asks.

I shake my head. "Tired of all our bullshit. I told her I would talk it out with dipshit but devised a better plan."

"Mmm, that explains it. I'll see you down there, eventually."

I race upstairs, finding my athletic shorts and changing into them. I find Cole warming up on the mats when I enter the basement. He's already panting—the disadvantage might just be mine.

"Get your ass in here, and you can tell me about Wednesday."

I finish wrapping my hands, shooting Cole a wide grin. Oh, I'll tell him about Cat, all right.

"Her pussy was begging for my dick, but that mouth." I lick my lips. "She had a few things to say about you."

I duck, missing his fist—always fighting with anger. "She told me to talk to you but figured this would be the best way."

He laughs. "She's smart." He's fast sweeping my feet from underneath me. I land on the mat with a thump.

"Fuck you, prick." I kick his shin, causing his balance to wobble. Jumping up, I punch his stomach hard. "I'm not taking your shit any longer, Cole."

"Is that so," he wheezes. A strand of black hair dangles on his wet forehead.

Adrenaline pulsed throughout my body. "Yeah, so next time a life-changing event happens, maybe let everyone have a say. You aren't my parent." My fist connects with his nose.

He wipes away the blood, laughing. If looks could kill, I'm sure my body would be a puddle of blood and a pile of bones. He takes a step forward, but thankfully, Dorian steps in the way.

"That's enough!" he yells, "Take your aggression out on the one that actually caused this."

"I'm so tired of this shit. I'm only trying to help." Cole rips his wraps off.

I grab a towel for his bleeding nose. "I get that, but Henry isn't listening, so it's useless." Handing it to him, he blots the blood.

"You two need to stop before you tear each other apart. Yelling and beating clearly aren't working. You need to beat Henry at his own game."

I flex my sore fingers. "What we need to do is get rid of Coleman."

That fuckin' mayor is no good for this town. Everyone needs to see what a douche he is. Exposing him is what we need to do before elections happen.

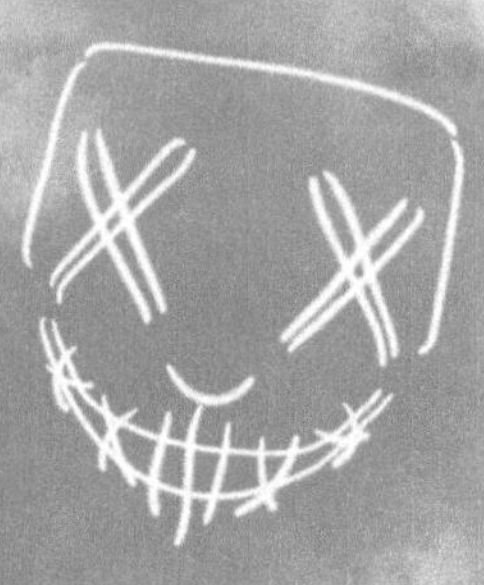

9

Cole

Nyx is right. The fighting needs to end. We're doing nothing but being complete assholes to each other when the enemy is out there causing a shit storm to our town. I dread coming to the compound for jobs now, knowing that Henry and Conrad are all about raving about the mayor and purge night coming up. Still not sure how it's our job to protect his ass.

I say let someone shoot the fucker.

That's actually not a bad idea. We could make it look like an accident. No one would suspect it if one of us went missing on patrol and shot him. We could act like the suspect outran us. *Oh, dang it.*

My phone goes off, and I roll over in bed to answer it.

"Yeah?"

"Good morning to you, too."

Henry, what a fuckin' lovely way to wake up.

"I have a job for you and the boys. Come down in half an hour, and I'll give you the details. Don't be late." He hangs up without waiting for me to reply.

I throw my phone somewhere on the bed; this is what I hate. The always-on-demand calls.

"You good?"

The one person I didn't think would stick by my side stands in the doorway, her dark hair piled high on her head with pieces framing her face, dark shadows smeared under her eyes. She looks irresistible wearing black booty shorts and a tank top.

I sit up in bed, patting the spot next to me. Henry can suck my dick for all I care. She comes first. "How was your night?" I placed a kiss on her forehead when she curled into my side.

"I'm so tired. I haven't been home long. The others are still sleeping."

Her body sinks into the feel of my arms wrapping around her. I don't want to leave. Panic furls deep in my chest at the thought of Halloween approaching.

"What about school? Are you headed in today?"

She nuzzles her head deeper into my neck. "I don't have class until later. Thankfully, it's my art class," she whispers quietly.

Her breathing evens out, and as much as I hate leaving her, I gently roll out of bed. "Love you with everything." I cover her with the blanket before heading to the bathroom.

Today will be stressful, and knowing Henry, it has to do with watching over the mayor. Here goes nothing. I'm sure the guys are gonna love this just as much as me.

The compound is busy when we all pull up. I think everyone is here, so this meeting is the top priority.

Freddy greets us when we step inside.

"You're late. He's going to lose his shit on you three."

"I had more important things to handle this morning."

Freddy grins. "How is our girl?"

"Working her ass to the grave, but she won't quit," Dorian scoffed.

Catalina and Freddy are two peas in a pod. You cannot separate them on Sundays when we get together. They became fast friends, and I love that.

"I'll have a chat with her on Sunday. For now, get your asses in there before Henry loses it." He nods to the hall. "He's in a mood, by the way."

"Perfect," Nyx mutters as he walks away.

I'm dreading this already. The second we walk in, the bitching will start. Henry will call Dorian a boy, and I'm not sure I'll be able to hold him back. It's the same old story.

Noise fills the hallway as we make our way to the meeting. The room falls silent when we walk in; scanning the room, my eyes land on Conrad, who grins at me. He has a punchable face.

"About time, boys. Only about," Henry looks at his watch, "fifteen minutes late. Sit down so we can finally start."

Dorian growls as he pulls his chair out. Spinning the chair backwards, he straddles it, crossing his arms on top of the back, narrowing his eyes at Henry.

Royce shakes his head, even though he knows this is bullshit. I might be able to persuade him to come with us when we leave. Henry starts talking, but I tune him out. My thoughts wander back to Cat. She looked beyond exhausted this morning. I feel most of it wasn't from work; it's from the added stress from all of our bullshit.

I'm trying not to bring it home, but like everything I touch, I ruin it. If only I wasn't always trying to out-think how my father raised me before child services stepped in. If only I was strong enough to remove those nasty memories.

Growing up in Southside, you always needed to think fast. If you weren't ahead in the races, you weren't eating that night. That's why I push the guys so much. I don't want them to end up in the gutter like I was. It took me years to get away from that side of town. Southside is rough; drugs are popular no matter who you are. Every other house would be a dealer or operation.

"Did you hear what I said, Cole?"

I blinked a few times, clearing my mind. "Yeah, I'm listening."

"So, you are good with driving Coleman around?"

The fuck did I miss? Why the hell would anyone wanna drive his ass around? Let alone me.

"That would be a fuck no."

Conrad shifts in his seat, and Royce straightens up. But Dorian and Nyx don't move a muscle. Oh, but Henry, his lip twitches just the slightest, and that left eye spazzes faster than a dog with the zoomies. I have to bite my lip so I don't laugh.

Henry stands, pushing his chair out with force. "You listen to me, you little shit. I'm the boss of this club, and what I say goes. You will do your job, or you'll suffer. Do you understand?"

I roll my eyes. "How the fuck will I suffer?"

He grins. "I would hate for anything to happen to that beautiful girl of yours."

I'm out of my seat along with Dorian and Nyx. "If you think about touching Catalina, I won't think twice about lighting your body on fire while you're still breathing."

"Then I suggest you do as I say." He leans further on the table, waiting for me to make a move.

Fuck! Fear and anger burn in my stomach. There's no way I'm letting him, or even Conrad, come anywhere near Cat. If I turn him down, he'll go after her. No matter how I play this, I have no choice but to do what Henry wants. He knew exactly what he was doing when he chose me.

"That's what I thought. You start tomorrow. Don't get Coleman killed." His eyes challenged mine.

"Don't ask for another fuckin' favour from me," I spat out. Dorian places his hand on my shoulder, giving it a squeeze.

"He understands. Nyx and I will be there to make sure he doesn't fuck it up." He tosses me a side-eye.

"What he said," I spoke lowly. Feeling defeated, what else am I supposed to do?

Conrad smirks. "I'll send over his itinerary and what he expects of you."

He gets what he gets. I'm not a fuckin' chauffeur. Maybe we'll get lost in Southside for fun.

I brush past Freddy without a second glance; I need out of the building—I can't think. The afternoon sun blinds me when I push open the door. I don't stop until I reach the firepit. Kicking the chairs over, I scream into the open air.

"We're fuckin' screwed. How are we going to protect Catalina and be with Coleman?" I turn to the guys, and they look just as scared as I am.

Nyx grabs me by the shoulder, pressing his forehead to mine. "We'll figure it out. Besides, Dorian and I can be with Cat when you are with Coleman. She never has to be alone."

"That's not the point."

"It is the point. Henry is only trying to mess with you. We won't let him get away with it." Dorian walks over, standing next to Nyx, placing his hand on my other shoulder. "We can do this together. We're family."

Closing my eyes, I take a deep inhale. I don't understand how they are so calm. They should be freaking out like I am. I need to see Cat now. My heart races with the thought of someone getting close to her again; for all I know, somebody could be watching her, waiting for the perfect time to strike.

Shaking off their hold. "I need to go, you guys can do what you need, but I have to go." I don't wait around for an answer. Moving quickly, I hop on my bike and peel out of the compound without a second glance. I'm losing faith in this club daily, and Nyx is right about one thing—leaving.

The ride to the University feels like ages before finally parking. The rev of two engines pulling alongside me doesn't surprise me either. I knew they would follow. Without a word, I storm off to the art building. That's what Cat said earlier; I hope that's where she still is.

"Why don't you call her?" Nyx says after storming into the building.

I didn't realize how big the art building was. Why are there so many different classes in painting on a canvas? Students give us a wide berth once they see the patch on our cuts, or it could be the look on my face that says. *Get in my way, and I'll fuck you up.* The Soul Stealers are now well known around town that we don't have to say anything for people to understand what we can do to them; it also doesn't help with that small *enforcer* patch on the chest. That usually makes people shut up.

"Because then she'll be freaked out, I'm only here be-cause my mind is freaking out, and I need to calm it down," I tell him.

I continue to peek into each class, looking for her. After a few nasty glares from the teachers, I dig into my pocket. Contemplating about that phone call to her. She has to be okay. With all these people around, how can anyone find her? We can't even see her.

How do we still not know where her class is after all these months? I never thought to ask, honestly. After leaving this place, I was done. She had Nyx.

"You ass, don't you know where her class is?" I address Nyx.

"No, not this year. Last year, she was down a different hall."

Dorian rolls his eyes and takes his phone out of his pocket. "Bunch of pussies." He hits a button and places his phone to his ear. His grin says it all. "Hey darling, where are you?" He nods. "Okay, stay there, be there shortly. Love you." He slowly places his phone back into his pocket and then looks at Nyx and me.

"Well?" I throw my arms up.

"Room 3458. Wasn't so hard, now was it." He punches my arm when he walks by.

For him, maybe I would've sounded like a mess, and she would've known something was up. I'm the asshole, not the worried wart. I can't do this again. We need a normal life for once. We walk around until we find her classroom.

Walking in, I wouldn't call it a classroom; it's a fuckin' studio. Bookshelves line the back wall with paint, paintbrushes and other necessary painting supplies. Another wall is filled with canvases of various sizes. I've never seen such a thing unless I took Cat to an art supply store.

My eyes land on her, and my chest finally feels relief. She sits in front of her canvas with a paint streak on her cheek, her black hair tied into a messy bun without a care in the world.

She scans the room, watching all three of us. "What's going on? You guys never come see me." She places her paintbrush in the water, swivelling on her stool to face us. "Don't bullshit me. What happened today, Cole?"

How can I tell her anything without throwing a fist through the wall? All I want is to bring her an ounce of happiness. I feel like every day, I'm failing. Why can't I protect her the way I see in my mind? It's like Henry knows what I want and sends a fuckin' grenade and explodes it without a second thought.

"Cole," her voice goes low. "Tell me now."

My shoulders slump. "Catalina, I need you to stay close to Nyx or Dorian from now on. Things have changed in the club, and I don't think you're safe anymore."

"Why?"

"Things happened. I'm not going into detail. Once you are done here, please come home." I get closer to her, inhaling her apple and honey scent. I dropped a kiss on her forehead. "Please, Cat. I won't be able to survive if anything happens again," I whisper against her skin.

She thinks about it for a while. "I promise."

I grip her chin, tipping her head back. "You best keep that fuckin' promise, Wednesday."

She laughs. "Or what?"

Dorian moves behind her. "Or you'll be punished," he whispers in her ear.

A small smile moves across her lips.

"You wanna be punished, baby?" Nyx strokes his finger down her cheek.

I love watching her get all turned on by all three of us.

10
Dorian

Deep down, I know what Cole is going through. We all want Catalina safe, but I have a feeling it's going to be a challenge. Watching her sit here with all three of us as we surround her is how I want her daily. She licks her lips, and I know exactly what she wants. Moving my hands down her waist, dipping into the waistband of her leggings. The heat from her pussy warms my hand; I don't need to guess how wet she is.

"Half pint, do you need to be punished?" I run my finger around her clit, getting the sweetest moan from her.

"Maybe I do." She grabs my wrist, pinning it to her body. "But unfortunately for you, the next class will be here shortly."

I rub my finger faster; a punishment is what she'll get even if I have a limited time. Her nails dig into my skin

the closer she gets to finishing. Cole moves to her side, sliding his hand under her shirt and cupping her breast.

"We need you to come fast for us, little one. Or you won't come at all until you get home."

Her head falls back, and Nyx takes the opportunity to kiss along her neck. Dipping my finger further down, I sink into her wet core, not stopping until I hit her g-spot.

"Fuck, baby. Seeing you like this makes me want to come in my pants like a teenage boy." Nyx continues to kiss along her jaw.

She laughs, but it becomes a moan when I stroke her g-spot faster.

"Fuck, Dorian. Don't stop, please," she begs.

"I love it when you beg me. How much do you want this?"

Cole lifts her shirt, exposing her breasts. Pinching her taught nipple, she squeezes around my finger.

"I want it so bad, please. I need to come more than anything."

Nyx hums. "Do you. Are you going to listen to us?"

"Yes."

"Are you going to do everything we say?" Cole asks. "Without putting up a fight?"

She's silent. I withdraw my finger.

"Yes!" she screams. "Please make me come."

"Such a good girl, aren't you?" I push two fingers in, pumping fast until my fingers are drenched. She comes fast, slamming her eyes shut; she moans our names. I'll never get tired of hearing her coming for us.

Cole fixes her shirt, trying to score those brownie points. When she looks at me, I lick my fingers clean.

"Thanks for the treat, darling. I'll give you something to lick off when you get home."

She smirks. "You wish, bucko, but work calls again tonight."

Cole glares at her. "You go with one of them or no work at all. I told you they stick with you no matter what."

She jumps off the stool, getting in his face. "I'm not an idiot, Cole. But I won't suck a dick when I'm trying to meet a quota. I already got my ass chewed out from the other day when Nyx rammed me in the cemetery. I have a job to do besides be a little fuck toy for you three."

I'm speechless. Is that what she thinks? Nyx takes a step back, looking at the floor.

"You could've said no," he mutters.

"You guys don't even take me on dates. What do you expect me to think.?"

My shoulders drop; I don't have an excuse.

Maybe one. We're shitty boyfriends.

Cole backs away, adding more distance. That worries me; Cole doesn't have to say words to say what he means. He's telling her what she's telling all of us.

"If you want out, there's the door, Catalina. No one is stopping you. You're the one that didn't want dates!"

She crosses her arms. "That's beside the point. And this is my fuckin' school. You can leave. You don't belong here." Her lips curl with disgust. I slowly move in, wrapping my arm around her shoulders.

"Cat, maybe we should talk about this when we all get home." I practically pleaded with her. She shrugs my arm off before storming to the door.

"Get out." Swinging the door open, she waits. "I mean it. You can't keep controlling me. This isn't how a relationship works. I'll be home after school."

Cole leaves first, not looking at her when he walks past her. She closes her eyes. When Nyx walks up to her, he pulls her into a hug. Her arms never leave her side. My heart breaks—the distance she's placing between us is slowly growing. I'm not sure what could be done to bring her back after this. I'm afraid she'll never forgive us.

Nyx whispers in her ear, but she never responds or blinks. Standing like a statue, I move closer, cupping her cheeks. I tilt her head back, staring into her violet eyes.

"Listen to me, Catalina. If I only wanted a fuck toy, I would've found anyone around this shitty ass town to fill that position. I wanted somebody to spend the rest of my life with, someone to have babies with. We would grow old and chase our dreams together. I chose you to be that somebody." Tears fill her eyes. "Why on earth do you think we act the way we do? We all love you and would do anything for you. But if you need time to find yourself, please take it. Don't think for a minute we won't be in the shadows, not watching over you." I breathe her in when I place my last kiss on her forehead. I leave her alone in that classroom with nothing but my heart and a fuckin' prayer that she'll return to us.

Cole and Nyx leave me alone while I wait for Cat to finish her classes. I wasn't kidding when I told her we would be watching from a distance. With the way Henry was talking, I don't trust that asshole. The way he's acting with this new purge has my hair standing on edge. I'm not sure what he gets out of it for opening it up to surrounding towns. All I can see is a mess coming from it, and I'm tired of cleaning up his and Coleman's shit.

A wave of raven hair flutters in the wind, and I instantly know my half-pint is finished for the day. I straighten up on my bike, waiting for her to get into her Beetle. She looks around, trying to find one of us, but she won't see me. I hid too well. Shaking her head, she opens her car door, tossing her bag in. With a defeated look, she climbs in. The second she leaves, I start my bike. Cole and Nyx are staying away from the house tonight; if she chooses to move out, there's nothing we can do.

On the ride to the house, my nerves are on fire. I'm not sure if my body is vibrating from them or from my bike. When she parks in the driveway, I stay on the street. Shutting my bike off, I remain seated until her door opens.

"Dorian, I don't need a chaperone," she calls from the edge of her car.

"I also told you someone would be watching you. Cole even said you wouldn't be alone. You need to start listening." I shrug, not giving a shit.

"I won't be long," she says as she enters the house.

I pull my phone out of my pocket. It's best to rip the bandage off fast, especially with Cole.

Me: She's leaving.

Cole: Jesus fucking Christ.

Nyx: For how long?

Me: I'm not sure. She didn't say much.

Cole: I knew this would happen.

Nyx: Maybe it's for the best. We have too much shit going on.

Nyx isn't wrong. But is she really safer out there without us? Where the hell is she going to stay? She gave up her apartment when she moved in with us. It's not like she has any friends she can crash with or family.

She exits the house carrying a hockey bag. That seals the deal. She's moving out. I hop off my bike, rushing to help.

She holds her hand up. "Don't. I got this."

"Where are you staying?"

"I called Riley. He said I could crash at his place."

Right. I guess she does have a friend, after all. Nodding, I let her finish hauling her bags to the car before I march over and grab her wrist.

"We aren't giving up on you. I hope you know this."

She takes a deep breath, closes her eyes, and slowly exhales. "I know, Dorian. But I think we all rushed into everything after what happened last year. Give me a week to think things through, please."

"A week, and then we're coming for you." I step back, giving her the space she needs.

"Thank you. I do love you. I hope you know that."

I give a small smile before I walk back to my bike. A week, that's all I'm promising, nothing more and nothing less. It'll be torture, but it could be worse. She could be gone forever.

Me: She's headed to Riley's.

Nyx: I'll follow her.

I get three dots from Cole, but he never replies.

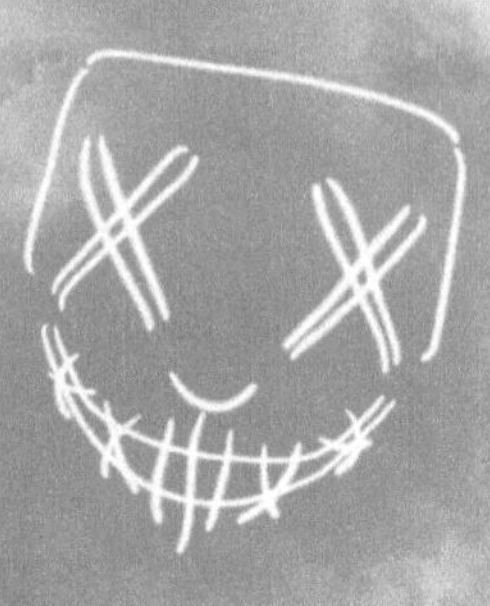
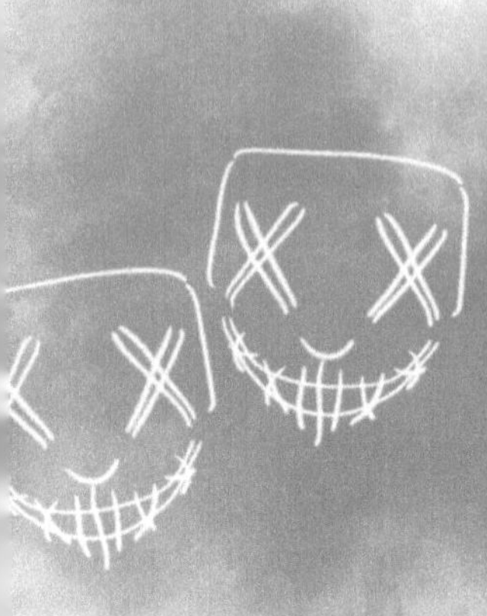

11
Catalina

I probably flew off the handle, but I feel like I'm never heard when they are around. As I pull into Riley's driveway, he's at the doorway, holding a mug and chocolate.

"What's this?" I ask when I get out of Johnny.

"I don't know what girls do after a breakup." He blushes.

Did I break up with the guys, though? I'm giving them a week to see if they can straighten up—I'm not even sure at this point. Maybe I'm doing them a favour and being less of a burden when they are stressing about the club and Halloween.

I grab the mug of hot chocolate from Riley and follow him inside. "Thanks again for letting me stay here. I didn't have anyone else to call."

He waves me off. "Don't worry about it. I'm hardly home, anyway."

His house is on the smaller side, roomy enough for two. You can also tell a bachelor has been shacking up in here. The living room is filled with his medical books, a small couch and a desk. He leads me into his kitchen and I hold back a laugh. Paper plates overfill his garbage.

"I don't do dishes. I barely cook, so hopefully, you can feed yourself."

"Don't worry. Dorian has taught me a few things." Just mentioning his name sends a ping to my chest. Riley stares at me for a second before he continues his tour. We walk down the hallway, and he points to the only bathroom.

"Sorry, we'll have to share."

"That's fine. I hope you don't mind girly shit lying around." I laugh when I look inside the bathroom. The countertop is covered with his shaving products, deodorant and absolutely no room for my things.

"Um, if you can find room."

I pat him on the shoulder. "It's only for a week. I'm not messy, don't worry."

He tilts his head. "Your room is this way. I keep it clean for when my mom comes down."

I poke my head in. His mom has to be the one who cleans it. The bed is made like a mom would do it. Or I would assume that's how a mom would make it. I was constantly yelled at if I didn't make mine a certain way, and if that didn't work, her son would come in. Shivers roll down my back with the thought of them.

Riley touches my shoulder. "You, okay?"

"Yep. I'll go grab my bags. I still have to work tonight." I try to cover my yawn.

"I'll help. My mom would tan my hide if she found out otherwise."

My plan is to dig until I forget. Nothing can sidetrack me tonight; a fuckin' earthquake could happen, and I still wouldn't stop. I know I can't change the guys, and never in my life would that go through my mind. But just for once, can't I be treated like a girlfriend? Maybe I'm asking for too much, and dating three guys simultaneously might be too much. Did they even want that in the first place? I'm thinking too hard, I'm getting a headache.

One Week Later
I'll be the first to admit living with another guy is hell.

"Jesus H Christ." I kick Riley's dirty boxers out of the way for the tenth time this week. "And you wonder why you're single still." All I want is a shower. Working and living with someone are entirely different points of view. I like the working Riley better; he's cleaner.

My phone dings from my bedroom. It could be Dr. Deadbodies or one of the guys. I'm in no hurry to talk to any of them, to be honest. My art project is number one and needs all of my attention. I have two months left of school, and I'm finished for good. Everyone can wait until

this afternoon for any answers from me. Besides, Davis knows where I'll be if he needs me.

On my way to the university, I stop at a small café for something hot to drink; when I walk past the window, a flyer has me stopping.

ANNUAL PURGE NIGHT FOR THE TOWN OF EASTWOOD HAS RETURNED!
HAPPENING THIS HALLOWEEN, BIGGER AND BETTER THAN BEFORE.
RULES FOR HALLOWEEN NIGHT STARTING AT 7 PM.
1. ALL ACTIVITIES END AT 7 AM
2. IF YOU ARE CAUGHT GOOD LUCK
3. ANYTHING GOES ON THIS NIGHT
4. TAKE NO PITY FOR THOSE THAT DON'T CELEBRATE
DON'T FORGET TO VOTE FOR MAYOR COLEMAN.

"What the fuck?" I can't believe people are hanging this shit up. How can the mayor get away with this still? This town is fucking crazy that's what it is. Do I still want my drink from this business? Do these people even know what goes on after dark? I certainly do. Look where that got me. I turn around and head back to Johnny, my mood turning sour. Thank God I can splatter some paint on my canvas today.

The only thing about that flyer that concerns me is the *anything goes.* What exactly does that mean? Before, it was to crave Coleman's sexual fantasies. Does he have another fantasy in mind this year? Purges usually mean one thing. To cleanse. What the fuck is he cleansing? He can't cleanse his dick every year.

I would like to cleanse him off this earth if possible. That's not a bad idea, actually. I have a few empty graves that need to be filled in.

I park my car with more attitude than needed; that sour mood won't be gone for hours at this rate. I wonder which guy tailed me today; it wouldn't be Cole, that's for sure. He has a way of making his presence known.

My art professor is a pain in the asshole this semester. I've been trying to get this piece done all week, but no matter what I do, it keeps turning out like absolute garbage. The colours keep muddling together, and I can't get the shading right. I'm tempted to trash it and start over, but with my luck, the clock will run out on me again. This piece counts for more than half my grade.

I should've done the stupid sculptor like I was planning on.

"Cat, you could combine the two."

My nosey neighbour points out. She's a slacker, so I wouldn't be taking her advice, but this time, she's kinda right. It would be wise. Cover up the shit mess with a blob of crap.

"Thanks," I mutter.

After painting my canvas black, I started sculpting something even darker, from which my childhood was created.

"You worthless child. You can't do anything right even after explaining it to you repeatedly." My mother snubs her nose at me.

"I'm trying, I swear."

"You're embarrassing me. Do you think your brothers would do this?"

I don't answer; most of her questions are traps. The teacher watches us from her desk, never coming to rescue me. No matter how much I try to plead for it. No one ever does. I'm used to saving myself for so long that relying on someone else only ends in disappointment.

"Mrs. Wilson, is there anything you want to discuss before the next parent comes in?"

Mother scoffs in disgust at me before turning her attention to the teacher. "Is she always this slow in class?"

"I'm sorry?"

"Her grades. They could be better. Her brothers never had such shit grades before."

My teacher stands there shocked. "I can assure you that Catalina is a brilliant student, Mrs. Wilson—"

"I find that shocking. Her head is stuck in the clouds. Her art isn't important and won't get Catalina anywhere in life. Focus her studies somewhere else."

My mother digs her claws into my arms, dragging me out of the classroom.

That was the day that I said fuck you and focused on my art. I stare at my sculptor on my table, and my hands shake. Even after all this time, I can still picture her hands and those long fingernails. I swear my arm throbs in pain at the memory of them digging into my skin.

My mind has to be tired if it's bringing up that memory. I was doing good at blocking her. It has to be the stress from the past week. I quickly pack up; my mind can't be

anywhere near this mess at the moment. When I reach my car, Nyx is waiting for me.

"Baby." Nyx pushes off my car—regret shining in his brown eyes. "Please come home." Meeting me halfway, he reaches for my hand. I swing it out of the way at the last second.

"I'm not sure I'm ready for that yet, Nyx. I have some more thinking to do."

His hand curls into a fist. "But you said a week."

"I know what I said. It's just." Pinching the bridge of my nose.

"You need more time, don't you?" His warm hand caresses mine.

How can I tell him I'm unsure about this relationship without sounding like a bitch?

"Hey, listen. We're here for you, no matter your decision, but you need to talk to us. Whatever you need, we all want to give it to you. Let me know when you want to talk." He drew me in, and I breathed his spice and citrus smell. I won't lie; I've missed how he can calm me down, and after today I needed this.

I can't get caught up in him. It's dangerous, and I need to keep an open mind. I step back, creating distance.

"Can I call you when I'm ready to talk?"

"Sure. You working tonight?"

I walk to my car. "Don't act like you don't know my schedule," I call over my shoulder.

"I know everything about you. You're my girlfriend."

"Prove it." I don't bother turning around.

"You like to keep everyone at a distance because you're afraid of being hurt. You hang around the dead because they keep your secrets. Catalina, you might think we don't pay attention, but you can't hide from us. We all want to be your boyfriends if that's what has you worried; we love sharing you."

Tears sting my eyes. It's not fair that he knew exactly what was bothering me. Here I thought I was a closed book. Yet he ripped me open and tore each page out one by one. It shouldn't surprise me. He's the one who knows me the most out of all three of them.

"I'll see you later, Nyx."

I don't have anything else to say. What can I say that he hasn't already?

12

Nyx

The week without Catalina felt like the Dark Ages. And now watching her leave isn't helping me either. Those lonely feelings are creeping in again, and I'm not sure if I'll survive them this time around. When this happened last time, I knew deep down we would get her back, but now, I have doubts. Something is eating at her, and she won't open up.

I follow her until she reaches Riley's, then take off to the house. There are a few things I need to discuss with the guys. Number one is how she doesn't feel confident in this relationship. I know for a fact she doesn't believe we all want her equally.

From someone who wasn't wanted, I know what that feels like; I would give her anything in this world and the one after if that's what she wants. But I can't do this alone. I want her with all of them, or it won't feel the same.

Storming through the door, voices come from the kitchen. It hasn't been quiet around here for days. I interrupt Cole and Dorian mid-fight.

"I talked to her today."

They both freeze. Cole stares at me. His blue eyes widen in shock.

"What did she say?"

Dorian runs his hand through his blond hair, tugging at the ends. "Please tell me she's coming home."

Cringing, I slowly shake my head.

"Fuck!" Cole roars, punching the countertop.

The trim busts off, landing on the floor. "Fuck this. She's coming home, whether she likes it or not. She's acting like a child."

"Cole, haven't you figured it out by now? She wants to be heard in this relationship, and you acting like a fuckin' idiot isn't helping," Dorian pointed out.

"To be honest, I think she feels like we never wanted to share her," I add.

"That's stupid," Cole and Dorian say.

I shrug. "It's the impression I got from her earlier. She's working tonight if somebody wants to take the night shift."

"I have to drive dickhead around as per my orders."

"Just finish Coleman off and be done with his ass. Have you seen the flyers around town?" Dorian asks.

I pull one out of my back pocket, unfold it, and toss it on the counter. "This shit. I found it at the café this morning. Cat was reading it. I can't believe he talked all these

people into hanging this shit around town. I wonder how many people are believing this shit."

"My issue is how many towns are going to take part in it." Cole reads the flyer, chewing his lip. "What happens when more people flock into town, and we aren't able to keep it safe like before."

"Then we do what we have to by any means." I shrug. "Besides, it's not like the cops are going to do anything."

Only two towns surround Eastwood, but how far can word spread that purge night is a free-for-all. This year is going to be bigger than anyone has expected in the past. With more outsiders, it's going to cause more issues; the one I'm afraid of is murder.

Catalina cannot go outside.

"We have one more week until Halloween. We should figure out what to do in the meantime with Catalina. Especially if she doesn't come home."

Cole glares at Dorian. "She's coming home. If she wants boyfriends, then that's what she'll fuckin' get." He marches out of the kitchen, and the front door slams shut.

"He's taking it hard but still won't talk about it," Dorian admits.

"Is that what you two were arguing about?"

Dorian walks to the fridge, opening it to grab a beer. He offers me one, and we sit silently for a while, sipping our beers. I wait until Dorian starts; whatever they were fighting about must've been serious if he hasn't spilled the beans already.

"Cole thinks we should take Coleman out."

"Out? As in," I run my finger along my neck.

Dorian nods. "Yeah, he figures since he drives him around, he'll have access to him on Halloween. The only issue I have is who's going to keep the town on track and Cat."

Where is the safest place for her? I can't even say the cemetery since that's where we found her. But we also knew about her last year. We had her in our sights for a long time. That's how we knew she was the one.

"What if she stayed with Riley for the night?"

"Is he trustworthy? Do we know he doesn't take part in the purge?"

I take another swig, that I'm not sure of.

Dorian finishes his drink. "Don't get me wrong, he seems like a good enough guy, and he's letting her stay with him, but I'm not sure."

"Cole will flip his lid if we bring it up. What if we kept her at the school? She still has access to the medical department. We drop her off. Her car won't be near the school that way. No one would know she's there."

"Only one problem." He looks at me, rubbing his chin. "Catalina."

She'll put up a fight worse than Cole will. But, like it or not, it's for her own protection. Even if I have to tie her down. Her ass is not going outside.

"I'll watch her tonight. Do you know which cemetery she's at?"

"She's in Eaglewood. I hate that cemetery. The fact that she's out of town, anything can happen there."

I'm still amazed that even after all this time, she has bodies to dig up. How doesn't this school have funding

for cadavers? How does this town have that many people dying? Something is happening here, that's for sure; it's got to be coming from Southside.

"When you go with her tonight, can you look for gang symbols on the bodies?"

"You have a suspicion about something?"

I tap my head. "Something like that."

That night, when Dorian comes home, he looks exhausted. I hoped he would walk through the door with our beautiful, gothic, loving girl. But she's nowhere in sight. My heart bottoms out when I realize she was telling me the truth earlier today. She isn't ready to come home yet.

"How did it go?" AKA any gang members in the dirt.

He blows a heavy breath out. "It went."

I motioned my hands for him to continue.

"Where's Cole at?" He walks past me into the kitchen. I follow behind, noticing how tense he is.

Whatever happened tonight can't be good. "He's downstairs. I'll grab him."

Opening the basement door, I call down for Cole; all that can be heard is his music being blasted. Flicking the light switch to grab his attention, he cuts his music off.

"Yeah, what?" he growls.

"Dorian has something he wants to talk to us about."

His weights slam down, and he appears at the bottom of the stairs, sweat pouring off his face. "This better be worth it."

I wait until he's closer. "Well, he didn't look happy if that makes you feel better."

He shoots me a glare. "Not really, Nyx."

When we enter the kitchen, Dorian is drinking whiskey. He slides the bottle toward us. "Here. You'll need this."

I pour two fingers' worth into my glass before sliding it to Cole. He holds the bottle; we rarely drink a lot because it reminds him of his father. Eventually, he pours some into his glass.

"Spill it, Dorian, what happened tonight." Cole doesn't even break eye contact as he slams his drink back.

"Nyx wanted me to check the bodies that half pint was digging up for markings." He takes a sip of his whiskey. "I don't think she ever paid attention to any of the bodies she dug up before. I even asked, and she just called them John or Jane Does. She never wants to think about what she's doing in case family members come looking around."

Okay, so everything sounds completely normal so far.

"So, why do you look like this then?"

"Because you asked me to check for gang markings, asshole, and I found them."

"Shit," Cole mumbles.

"On all the bodies she dug up?" I asked.

Dorian leans his forearms on the counter. "She dug up three bodies tonight, two females and one male. Both

females belonged to the Death Eaters. Cat had no idea what their markings looked like. The male was elderly."

"And Davis goes through the paper to find these bodies? Cause I highly doubt the gang will place obituaries in the paper." Cole points out.

"Unless they know someone is digging up the bodies and know it's a way of disposing of their members without the cops snooping around."

"Henry is still watching the cemeteries the odd night, too. He wanted me to keep an eye on it the other night." I mentioned, displeasure clear as day. I hated doing that job. I had no choice because I was sure Conrad had men following me.

Little did he know, I ensured Catalina didn't work those days. The 'Can't see you' texts are code, and it's been working.

"Do you think Henry knows what the Death Eaters are doing?" I stare at Cole.

He scoffs, rolling his eyes. "I'm sure that's where Henry is burying his dead, too. Where else would everyone go?"

Jesus, this entire time, Catalina has been digging up our members and not knowing it. She's lucky that she hasn't been caught. I don't want to think what Henry would do to her if he did catch her. My stomach turns the more I think about it.

"Where is Cat now?"

"I helped her at the school, then escorted her to Riley's. She wouldn't give me an answer as to when she'll be home. I don't think she even knows. We didn't talk much

about where we are headed, I followed her lead, and whatever she needed, that's what I did."

"Fuckin' pussy. She needs to be pushed in the right direction."

"No, Cole." I narrow my eyes at him. "That's what got us in a mess, to begin with. You and your bossy personality."

Cole shoves me. "I'm not bossy."

"You are bossy, you asshole." Catalina stood motionless at the entrance to the kitchen, staring at each of us.

"Wednesday." Cole steps closer. "You came home?"

She drops her bag. "I couldn't sleep, so I'm home."

Ten pounds of pressure fell from my chest. But I feel like she's about to drop another bomb on us.

13

Cole

When people say things are too good to be true, fuckin' believe them. Having Catalina at home is fantastic, but it's been two days, and she hasn't let any of us hold or kiss her. It's like living in the doghouse, and I'm trying to figure out what I did wrong.

All right, I know what I did wrong. I'm the worst boyfriend in the history of boyfriends, but she should know this. I'm not dating material; I have no account of a stable household. Give me an addicted father figure, and I can handle them; a shitty foster parent, no problem. But a girlfriend, I'm not sure what to do with them. I'm not a fancy date and flower-giving person.

I've tried googling ideas, but they all seemed so lame. Catalina isn't the type of person you take to the movies and dinner. I have a better idea, thankfully; I don't have

to drive dickhead around tonight, and she doesn't have any jobs.

I hope she likes this surprise.

"Dorian, can you make something for Catalina and me?"

He looks up from his phone. "Why?"

I rub my face, trying to keep my cool. "Because asshole, I don't need to kill her with my cooking."

He goes back to scrolling on his phone. "Well, no shit. But the question remains. Why?"

I can see the wheels turning in his head; he'll make fun of me and probably tell me how lame it is. Everything else I thought of was stupid and wouldn't be fun.

"Do it for her then. It would be a lot for her to go on a date."

"I would've done it, anyway. I wanted to give you a hard time." He throws his phone on the couch and gets up.

I, on the other hand, step toward him. "You sonofabitch." Punching him in the arm. "Don't be a dick."

He hisses, rubbing his arm. "Fuck you. Learn how to cook. Or I'll only pack enough to feed Cat." He heads for the kitchen, then stops. "Are you serious about killing Coleman?"

"Like a fuckin' heart attack."

"I'll get everything figured out; I'll talk to Freddy, get the torture room all setup, and make sure no one is around the compound for us."

God, Halloween is going to be one long, bloody night. And I'm going to love every minute of it.

I'm loading up my saddle bag when Catalina pulls into the driveway. A fishnet-clad leg kicks the driver's door open when I look up. Her black mini skirt shows just the right amount of thigh that has too much blood rushing to my cock.

Her violet eyes lock onto mine when she notices me. How she ever thought we never wanted her blows my mind; I would fight for her until the end of time.

"Cole." She looks at my bike, then back to me. "Where are you going?"

"Go get pants on. I have somewhere that I wanna show you."

She hesitates for a second. Staring at me, then the house. I'm not sure what she's expecting. I get that we always do things as a group most of the time. Or that I never initiate stuff between us, but I'm trying to be a better boyfriend.

"Yeah, give me a minute. I'll be back."

I'm nervous and excited. I've never taken anyone to this place before. All I can do now is wait. When ten minutes pass, I panic. Is she even going to come out? Dorian and Nyx are inside; they wouldn't talk her out of coming, would they?

I'm having an internal battle with myself. I didn't hear anyone sneak up on me.

"Ready?"

She still takes my breath away, no matter how often I see her. She's ready to ride with her hair braided to the side, a long-sleeved shirt, and black skinny jeans. Since

day one, I've been itching to take her out on my bike. I've just never had the time.

"I'm always ready for you, Wednesday." I strap her helmet on, brushing her cheek; she turns and waits. "You'll have to actually touch me on the ride."

Mounting my bike, I wait. Her legs press against mine, and it feels like heaven. This is where she belongs and nowhere else.

"Where are we going?" she asks after she wraps her arms around my waist.

"I want to show you something, so I figured I'd turn it into a date." I glance back to see her eyes widen.

"Oh. I would love that, Cole. Thank you."

Without a word, I start the bike and pull out of the driveway. I hope taking her back to Southside doesn't bring back horrible memories, but what I have to show her will hopefully make her understand me better.

Once you cross that line between town, it's a different ball game. I still can't believe I grew up here and that I didn't do worse shit with my life. The house that Cat was in when her asshole of a brother kidnapped her was burned down. Dorian couldn't stand the thought of having that place standing. I don't blame him. The way her brother did things still bothers me. Why stalk and kidnap her? The torture of her childhood wasn't enough, you had to continue even when she was happy. For what a couple of pennies, that's what bothers me. Why not just talk to her? She would've handed it over in a heartbeat.

Her grip tightens when we get further into Southside. I take her hand, placing it over my heart. It's steady, reminding her she's safe with me.

Turning down the street where my father tried to raise me, memories flood back.

"Hey, you little shit, hand me that bottle."

Dad's been on the liquor for three days, and I've been walking on eggshells. I've been doing everything possible not to be home, but the cops found me hiding behind the old junkyard and hauled me back. I hated those pricks. Why couldn't they haul my dad away? Things would be easier without him around.

"Here." I toss him his bottle of Jack. "Don't get too drunk. You have to work tomorrow."

His head snaps up fast. "The fuck you say to me?" Stumbling, he moves quickly. Grabbing me by my shirt, he gets into my face. His breath smells like stale beer. "You don't tell me what to do with my life, do you understand?"

"I can tell you what to do if I have to. You don't do anything around here anymore," I spit in his face.

Shoving me hard, I land on my ass. He stared down at me with his precious bottle in his hand. "You should've died alongside your mother. You don't deserve to be breathing."

I'm not sure if it was luck or not, but that asshole ended up being killed at work the next day. I think karma had a way of working its magic.

I park the bike across the street from the broken house. What once was a mint house is now painted in graffiti from the vandals having fun. Fuck, I hate this place

with a passion. It's another place I would love to see burned.

With a deep breath, I turn to look at Catalina. "This is where I grew up for most of my life." She takes in the house and the neighbourhood, not that there's much to take in. Every other place doesn't look any better.

"It's fine. You can say it looks like shit. I won't lie. Growing up here was shit."

"What happened after here?"

"I moved to a foster home until I turned eighteen. It was somewhat better than living with him, but they still treat you like garbage. They only want you for the pay cheque."

She bites her lip, looking nervous. I have a feeling I already know the question that's coming. It's something I never talk about.

"And your mom? You never talk about her."

"That's because she's dead, Wednesday." Her hand grips my bicep. "Don't feel bad. She died when I was three. A car accident, I think. We did not talk about here a lot in that shithole. Only when he started drinking, he always said that I didn't deserve to be breathing either."

"Jesus, Cole. How could someone ever talk to their child that way?" I stare at her, and she nods. "Right, never mind. I get it."

"But I have something else to show you. Hold on."

Pulling away from the nightmare, I take her to a hidden spot no one can find. It's deep in Southside that Dorian, Nyx and I would hide out in when we were younger. Taking an invisible roadway behind the junkyard, it's sur-

prising that it hasn't been overgrown with weeds yet. The gravel pit is precisely the same; I'm not even sure they use this place anymore. Most of the gravel piles have grass growing out of them, and the equipment has rusted to shit from the rain. And the fire pit we used to use is still here.

It'll be a perfect spot for Cat to finally relax and forget about the week of hell we put her through.

###

Dorian's lunch, of course, is over extreme. I would've been okay with peanut butter and jam sandwiches, but whatever. Catalina is happy, and that's all that matters.

"Why take me out on a date after all this time?" she asks, taking a bite of her pasta salad.

I mix my salad around, flicking the onions out. "It shouldn't be surprising that I'm not boyfriend material, Cat. I don't know anything about this shit. All I know is not to beat you. I don't know anything else."

She moves closer, taking my hand. "Cole, I don't expect the moon from you. I knew from the start that you didn't want anything to do with me. It was no lie that you had a hard time with us. And don't believe for a second I think your bullying shit is why you found me that night. I know better."

I'll admit it was a lame excuse, but in my defence, it didn't look good that she was creeping around at night to see an older man from school. There was something different about her.

"I wanted you to be mine."

She laughs. "You had a weird way of showing it. Did you have to wait until purge night?"

"Yes, how else would we know you had some kinks to work out."

Straddling me, she brushes a piece of hair out of my face. "I love this date. I only have one question."

"Okay."

"You aren't expecting anything from this date, are you?"

Stroking her cheek, I work my way down her neck. She swallows hard the further I dip. "There's only one thing I want, Catalina." Lying her on the blanket, I push her top up, exposing her breasts. "I want you coming."

Taking a nipple in my mouth, I bite it before sucking on it. Her hips raise to meet with my growing cock, and fuck does that feel amazing, but this isn't about me—I need to give her what she wants. Popping her nipple from my mouth, I take the other one, and her sweet moans fill the air. A sound I'll never get tired of hearing. But I need them a touch louder.

Moving my hand lower, I unsnap her jeans. "Tell me, little one. What do you want?"

She shifts, getting even closer. "What sort of tricks do you have in your bags?"

I grin, always up for an adventure. I have just the thing. Working fast, I open my saddlebag to find what I need. It doesn't take me very long. Oh, I can't wait to play; it's been a while since she let me do whatever I wanted. She doesn't disappoint either when I reach her. Lying naked

on the blanket with her legs spread wide, she's damn near dripping.

"Fuck me."

"Only if you want to."

I drop the rope and lube. It's been a while since I've tied her up, and I'm going to enjoy this.

"You remember your safe word?"

"Yes," she agrees. Getting on her knees for me. I run my hand along her collarbone, producing goosebumps.

"Perfect, little one." Grabbing the rope, we worked hard to overcome her fear of having her arms tied, and I couldn't be prouder of her. I tie her hands together in a cat claw. Once satisfied, I move her hand between her legs, lowering her head to the blanket. Wrapping the rope around her right ankle, I do the same to her left. I swirl the remaining rope until I finish it into a frog tie. Her ass is perfectly positioned in the air for my liking.

"Does this feel okay?"

"Um, yeah," she struggles to answer.

I tug the rope. "You sure? I can loosen or take them off."

"No, I love it. I want this."

Smacking her ass to be sure, her pussy becomes wetter. Spreading her cheeks apart, I run my finger around her asshole. "I'm fucking this ass until you come, do you understand?"

"Yes." She struggles against the rope.

Squirting some lube along her crack, I ease my finger in, working it back and forth. Pushing her ass toward me, I know what she wants. Ever since the first time she had anal, she's been hooked. Unbuckling my belt, I pull

my throbbing cock out. Adding another finger, she looks gorgeous with the ropes tied around her body.

Smacking my cock on her ass several times, I line up against her tight hole. Gripping the rope, my piercing pressing tight against her opening as I push deep inside slowly, the squeeze she has on me makes me pause.

"God, you're so fucking tight, I can't handle it." I pull out until the tip is left in, slamming back in; she moans, gripping the rope beneath us.

Without remorse, I pound hard into her, and I swear stars shoot across my vision the longer I go. I know this is supposed to be about her, but I can't help but enjoy it too.

"I love it when you're rough with me. Sorry that I've been a bad girlfriend."

I find her wet entrance and shove two fingers deep inside. "You've been a fuckin' brat is what you've been."

"Ahh, fuck," she groans, pushing her ass back into me, taking me deeper.

Stroking her g-spot, she clamps down on my fingers and groans louder as she reaches her climax. I want to see her squirt before I finish in her ass. Moving my other hand, I rub her clit fast.

"I want you to be as loud as possible when you come." Not letting up, I move both hands faster until her body shakes. She's so close, but she won't give in. Jerking my hips forward, I give her everything I have. All the sensations all at once. My body is in hyper-drive as her body clings to me.

My climax is rearing to go; if she doesn't finish soon, I will. Moving my hand away from her clit, I pull her hips into me, fucking her fast and hard.

"Fucking, come. I want everything you have." Pressing my fingers harder on her g-spot, she finally let go, soaking the blanket beneath us. Fuckin' heaven. Getting into a low squat and grabbing her shoulders, I can fuck her how I want.

"Cole, come in my mouth. I want to taste you."

"Anything for you, little one," I groan.

I don't stop fucking her until I'm about to explode. It feels too good to stop. Pulling out fast, I move in front of her, lifting her face up, and she opens wide. Her violet eyes meet mine as I shoot my cum down her throat.

"Fuck, Catalina." I moan.

I watch her swallow and smile at me. "Thanks, baby." Licking her lips, she gets every last drop.

I bend down, kissing her deeply. "I love you, but don't think I brought you out on a date so I could get my cock wet. I wanted to spoil you because I love you. Let me untie you."

The worst part now is that I'll have to take her home. It was nice to forget about the stress of everything for a while. But now the real work begins.

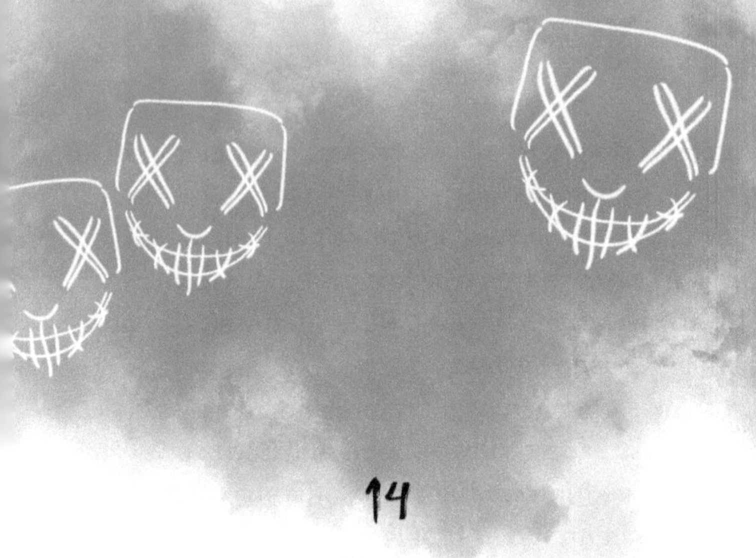

14

Dorian

I won't lie. I'm glad Cole finally took Cat out for a date, but at a time like this? Going to Southside could've been dangerous. Sometimes, he doesn't think, which drives me up the wall. I'm glad Cat was safe, but we have six days until everything goes down.

I'm only worried about leaving a trail behind. I know Henry; if anything, he'll watch us all night. I'm unsure why he has us around if he can't trust us. It's been this way for almost a year, and it's getting tiresome. Nyx has the right idea about leaving the club. It's not worth it anymore. The benefits aren't there, and we've been treated like trash since Conrad joined.

The *family* Henry once thought he had is gone. I don't even know what we enforce anymore.

Unfortunately for us, Henry had called everyone in for another meeting before the official fun starts. The

protocol is simple. He still wants everyone riding around the town's perimeter after sunset. I'm not sure why, it's going to be a madhouse, and there's nothing we can do about it. I hope he knows he just ruined this town.

"Everyone knows their job?" He looks around the table, and his eyes land on me.

"I think so. I mean, you are bringing more assholes into town, so expect murders, rape, and God knows what else. So have fun with the aftermath, but whatever." I shrug. It's not my fuckin' problem.

Conrad jumps out of his seat while Henry slams his fist on the table. The entire room falls silent. Cole and Nyx snap their heads at everyone else in the room. They wouldn't dare try anything.

Henry moves to me, getting in my face. "You're walking on thin ice, boy," he spits in my face. "I meant what I said earlier, and I'm a man of my word. Smarten the fuck up and do what I say." He turns to the room. "That goes for everyone here. If you don't want to be here, I can solve that. Do you think that cemetery is filled with town folk? Think again."

That's all the confirmation I needed. He and the Death Eaters also use the cemeteries as a dumping ground. Now, it makes me wonder if kidnapping Davis and Adams was a coincidence. Does Davis honestly get his dead body reports from the papers like he says?

"I want out after Halloween. I'm done with this shit." I stand to leave, followed by Cole.

"I want out, too. If Dorian and Nyx are out, then I'm gone. Sorry, Henry, but you've lost sight of everything

since I joined. This isn't the family I want anymore. You best find new enforcers because your so-called club is shit."

That target on Catalina's back has just gotten more prominent; I can feel Henry's eyes burning into the back of my head as I leave, but what else can any of us do? Freddy meets us outside, looking sad.

"You boys leaving me, aren't ya?"

"Sorry, man, we can't stay here." I pull him into a hug.

He cradles the back of my head. "Don't worry. I'm sure you have plans, and I agree with them." He pulls away, hugging Nyx next. When Cole hugs him, it breaks my heart. He's like a grandparent, and Cole has never had one before. Freddy has always been there for us; our Sundays were the best.

"Don't worry, boys, this shit won't last long. I'll join you in retirement soon. That girl of ours needs me. She'll lose her mind if she has to hang around you assholes all the time."

Laughter poured from everyone.

"Fuck you, old man. I was born an asshole. I can't change," Cole chuckles.

Nyx nods. "That I'll agree on. Don't worry, we'll look after her."

My nerves have never been this close to the edge before. Cole still has no idea that Nyx and I planning on shipping Cat off to Riley's. We probably should tell Cat, too. Then again, we have time.

Looking at our front door, maybe we don't have time.

"What the fuck is this?" Cole rips the note off the door.

"What's it say?" Nyx crowds around, resting his hand on my shoulder.

Cole scans it before looking at us. His face grows paler the more he reads. I snatch the note, getting impatient.

"If this is what a family looks like, you really fucked up. Good luck on purge night. K."

"Who the fuck is K?" Nyx takes the note, flipping it over.

That is what I would like to know. Conrad would do something like this; maybe he did and wrote a K to throw us off.

"Conrad," I growl.

Nyx thinks so hard his forehead lines crease deep. "There's no way. We left before anyone."

Cole paces the front yard. "He could've made anyone post it, but why the K?"

"Unless it isn't Conrad." Nyx stares at the note one more time.

"What makes you say that?"

"Think about it. Conrad doesn't do anything without Henry's say. Why would he post this before our meeting? Conrad is a coward. No one dares to come knocking on our door. Whoever this was has some major balls."

"Think it's someone from the school?" Cole questions, still staring toward the street.

"The question is, are we telling Catalina?"

"No," Nyx and Cole answer in unison.

That's what I figured. She's gonna hate us if she ever finds out that we are hiding something this crucial. "We hide it for now. If we get anything else, she needs to know. I'm not having a repeat of last year."

"Deal," Cole agrees.

Nyx nods. "I'll never place her in danger because we let our egos get in the way. But we need to figure out who K is."

"It has to be someone in the club that's pissed off with us for leaving." Recognition lit up in Cole's eyes. "Technically, Henry knew Nyx was leaving. Nothing stopped him from sending someone out here while we were gone."

He's not wrong. Nyx has made it known for a long time that he was leaving after Halloween—his time is almost up. I know it scared Henry at the thought of Cole and me leaving. Looks like he has everything to be worried about. Cole was right; it wasn't the family we first joined. It's funny that those were the words on the note.

"If it was Henry, then we take him out too." What's one more murder.

"Seriously, D. You want to kill two people in one night?"

"Don't act like we've never done it before, Nyx." I roll my eyes. He's a worry wart when he wants to be.

"That's different. We didn't have to kidnap them. We literally stormed the castle to kill them."

Cole scoffs. "Then we storm the castle and kill Henry, Conrad and Coleman."

"Woah." I hold my hand up. "Three, we're up to three now."

Cole shrugs. "Go big or go home, Dorian."

I can't believe I'm going to agree to this. If we want to clean up this town, there is no other way. We are enforcers and would be doing our jobs. One major loophole Henry didn't see coming. Now, we need a new plan for Coleman.

"Who's headed to watch Cat at school?"

"I will. I'm sure I'm stuck on dickhead duty still." Cole heads to his bike. "I'll send her home before heading out again," he calls over his shoulder.

Once his bike is down the street, Nyx and I are left to deal with his plan. How it will work is beyond me, but somehow, his plans always work, and I never think twice about doubting him.

"D?"

"Yeah, Nyx." I take him in. His face is serious, and disappointment shrouds his eyes when he turns to me.

"Do you think Cole is going overboard on the killings?"

"Coleman, yes. Not sure about Henry and Conrad. Then again, if we don't take them out, they could convince the next mayor or, even worse, run for it themselves. Who knows what they would do to this town."

He rubbed his hands on his thighs, shaking his head. "It's still bullshit, but whatever. If it helps you two and Catalina, I'm all in."

The resentment he houses for Henry will take years to get over. He still hasn't forgiven his father, and I don't blame him. Whenever I see Otis Thornton walking down

the sidewalk, the need to hit him with my bike is strong. Can't believe that prick has the balls to walk around and act like he hasn't destroyed his kid's life.

I'm thankful that my so-called parents don't live here. The best thing to happen was for my grandmother to take me in. I miss her every day. Cancer can kiss my ass.

She's the one who taught me more than my own parents. They only wanted the status of having a child; the thought of raising me was too much. No matter what I was doing, they seemed to be pissed off with me. Not a single day went by that they didn't yell at me. I can't fault my Grandmother; she raised her son the same way she did me. Some grow up to be assholes.

With the reminder of my grandmother, I head inside to start dinner. Can't have my girl starving when she gets home from school.

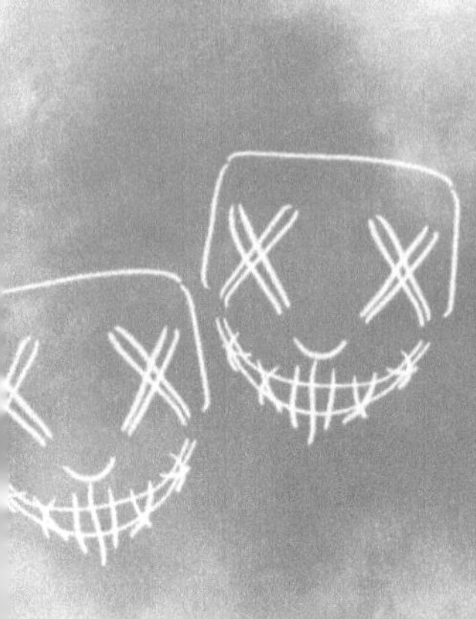

15
Catalina

There is something different with today. I can't place my finger on it, though, and it's driving me up the wall. All day in my art class, something in the back of my mind kept nagging me to check my car. I kept working on my sculptor and ignored it.

I could beat myself for being stupid. I'm beginning to think Johnny is cursed. Can spirits hitch rides? I'm starting to wonder if I brought one back, and it attached itself to my car. Bending to inspect the flat tire, I run my hand along it when I notice the puncture mark.

"The fuck?" I whisper.

Sticking my index finger in the hole. I haven't pissed anyone off this year. Okay, that's a lie, but Becky had it coming. There is only so much I can take before I snap, and she happened to find out the hard way. I'm not a slut for having three boyfriends. She kept telling everyone

who passed her how I spread my legs for every guy on campus. No matter how often I would say no to her, doesn't make me a slut, and that's not how it works, she wouldn't stop. I'm glad Cole taught me how to throw a punch because that blow to her face was impressive.

This has to be her getting me back. "Fuckin' cunt."

"Who's a cunt?"

My head whipped around at the sound of Cole's deep voice. Exhaling, I point to my tire. "The cunt that did this, poor Johnny, has no luck with tires."

Cole moves behind me, squatting to examine my tire. Placing his hand on my back. "Sorry, Wednesday." His thumb brushed up and down my spine. "Do you have a spare?"

Angling my head to look up at him. He's wearing a black hoodie with his club cut over the top. A deep sigh escaped my lips. He always looks so well put together, even if it's for a bike ride. While I'm dressed in scrubby clothes today, I look like Elmer, the homeless guy. Cole's deep chuckle pulls me out of my thoughts.

"Yeah, sorry, the spare is in the trunk." Cole gives me the signal to pop my trunk because who wouldn't think of doing so. Rolling my eyes, I open my car door and press the button for the trunk. I shouldn't complain. This would take me hours to do. Cole rounds the front of the car with my spare.

"This won't take me long, but are you sure it was somebody you pissed off?"

The muscles in my jaw twitched with annoyance. "Who else could it have been? I'm sure I broke Becky's nose, so it would've been her."

He smirks as he jacks up my car. "Those private lessons paying off, are they?"

"When you don't have your hands all over my body, they work. But seriously though. Who else could it be? Don't fuckin' lie to me, Cole."

He's quiet while he finishes up with my tire. That's how I know it's not good news. It was only a matter of time before the truth came out. Makes me wonder how long the guys have been sitting on this.

He brushes his hand off on his jeans and throws the jack back into the truck. Bracing his hands on the bumper, his eyes collide with mine. "Wednesday. This isn't the place for this type of conversation." His voice lowered, and his lip curled into a snarl. "When we get to the house, we'll talk. Drive."

Go figure, he could never tell me shit without backup. I'm unsure what will change with having the guys around; I can already tell this will piss me off. Guarantee it has something to do with them following me around.

If they think I haven't noticed them acting weird since last week, they are sadly mistaken. Purge day is looming over us like the plague if I know them. I'll be kept away like a princess in a tower. They forget that I'm capable of handling myself.

When the house comes into view, my knuckles are white from gripping the steering wheel tight. Flexing my

fingers, trying to get the blood flowing again. This conversation is already irritating me, and it hasn't even started.

"Out, now." Cole knocks on my window.

That man needs to learn patience.

The tension in the den is suffocating. I'm cool as a cucumber, sitting in the armchair waiting for anyone to speak. The only sound in the room is the clock ticking. Nyx stands by the fireplace with his hands in his jeans pockets. Not once making eye contact. When I look at Dorian, he's fiddling with his hoodie string. I mentally shoot daggers at him because he should've been talking first out of everyone.

Leave it to Cole to glare at me. I scratch my nose with my middle finger, getting a middle finger back in return.

"Can someone talk already?" I give them all one more look. "I'll tell you how this is going down. You three are going to work on Halloween night like you always do. You're all scared; I understand that. But treating me like a child isn't helping either. Stop keeping me in the dark."

"Fuckin' rights we care," Cole exploded. He rushes out of his seat, caging me into the couch. "Why the fuck do you think we keep doing what we do?"

I lean forward, almost touching his face. "I don't know? You don't tell me anything. For all I know, it's a way to control me."

He smirks. "You want me to control you? You would never leave this fuckin' house. Every time you do, something happens."

"I want you to start talking to me and treat me like a fuckin' equal."

He closes his eyes, resting his forehead on mine.

"Half pint, what Cole is trying to say is we are trying to protect you."

Cole hums. "Yeah, that." He kisses my forehead before backing away. "Sorry, but some things we leave out to save you the heartache."

Nyx still hasn't said a word, meaning there is more to say. Of course, this conversation couldn't be a simple one. They sure kept a lot hidden if they were still afraid to talk.

Nyx clears his throat. "We need you to stay with Riley on Halloween."

"Excuse me?"

"We won't be able to protect you, and we don't know anyone else you can stay with. Don't fight us, half pint."

I try to get up, but Cole pushes on my shoulder. "I don't like this idea either." He swings his head to the guys. "But they're right. Riley is your best bet," he grunts.

"Fine. I'll talk to him."

"Now would be nice. We don't have long." Nyx reminds me.

Cole hands me my phone, and I tear it from his hand.

Me: The three stooges need me to spend Halloween night with you if that works.

"Seriously?"

"It's rude to read others' messages. Cole."

Rye Rye: I don't mind. We can watch scary movies and plot revenge.

Me: Sounds perfect.

"He said it's fine."

"Good, I need to head out. Stay with these two."

Once Cole is gone, Nyx sits on the armrest. "Baby, we only do these things out of love. You know that, right?"

Dorian kneels in front, sliding his hand up my thighs. "We were only worried about what you would say."

What a lame excuse. They were only worried about getting their asses chewed out. Which I should be doing, but fuck, Dorian keeps sliding his hand further up my thigh, and it's getting hard to concentrate.

"How was school, baby?" Nyx runs his hands through my hair; closing my eyes, my head falls back.

"It was okay. It was after that sucked."

Dorian's fingers dip under my shirt, stroking my stomach, and I sink deeper into the chair. "How so? Us?"

Shaking my head. "No, someone stabbed my tire—"

"Excuse me." Nyx stands, eyes wide. "Were you hurt or anything?"

Dorian stops moving. "Half pint, this is serious. Was there a note or anything?"

My heart skids to a stop. No, this isn't the same as last year. My brother isn't coming back. He got what he wanted. These two are trying to freak me out so I don't do anything rash.

That's all that this is.

"Funny, I know what this is." I laugh, trying to get up. Dorian squeezes my sides.

"I'm not trying to be funny. Cole likes to hide shit from you, but things went down with the club. Cole and I are out after Halloween. Henry lost his shit and threatened you."

My cheeks heat from the rage that flows fast. Blowing out a breath, I try to control my words. "You don't think this was something I should've been informed of? Apparently, my time away did absolutely dickshit for you guys. Jesus Christ. Why must you keep me in the dark?"

"It was for your own—"

"Don't finish that sentence, Nyx." *For my own good*, I'm getting tired of hearing that. How is being kept in the dark for my own good? I'm at a greater risk of danger not knowing what to expect. I don't know what it is with these guys that they can't understand that.

"If it makes you feel any better, we did it out of love. We did what was best. At the time, we were scared, Catalina." Dorian backs away from me. "Don't hate us for trying our best."

"I don't hate you." Now I'm getting frustrated with them. "I'm having a hard time expressing what I mean here." Leaning over, I drop my head in my hands. "I just don't want what happened last year to happen again, is all. My car isn't an omen. It was a bitch from school, that's it, that's all. Now, I don't have work tonight. Give me a game plan for this evening."

Nyx sits back on the armchair, massaging my back. "If you say so, I believe you. But I swear to God, Catalina. The first sign of trouble this time, you call."

"I promise."

"Good, let's go make supper and watch a movie." Dorian heads out.

"Momma Bear is in a mood." Nyx jokes.

I can't help but laugh. I'm sure Momma Bear wanted to get lucky in the den.

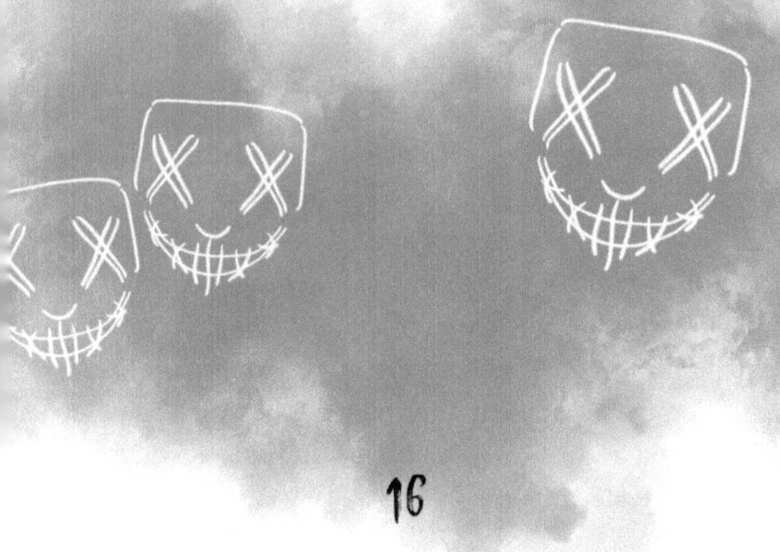

16
Nyx

One day until Halloween. The town is already on high alert. Most shops are prepping for one of the worst nights this town will ever see in their history. But who do you think allowed it? They did. They did nothing to stop it. Even now, no one has tried to boycott it. City Hall is vacant. The usual protestors are probably sitting at home, scared out of their wits, or excited. Honestly, it's hard to judge the people in this town. I'm not even sure about the surrounding towns ready to come in.

Henry made us come down first thing this morning for a debrief. Like I give a shit what he has to say. I ignored him; we had our own plans for tomorrow. He held his last meeting. There's not much I want to hear from him except three little words. *I was wrong.*

I park my bike outside of Riley's place. I need to have a talk with him before Catalina arrives tomorrow. I still

don't trust this guy; it doesn't matter if they work together or not. We're putting all of our trust in him. If anything happens to her, he's a dead man.

His place isn't something I would be bragging about, but then again, he is a university student. I wouldn't have the place I have now without the guys. Banging on the door, I pray this asshole better be up. When he doesn't answer right away, I bang again. I'm sure his neighbours aren't too thrilled.

"Yeah, hold the fuck up," I hear him yell. The door swings open, and I'm greeted by a wild-haired, boxer-wearing man.

He better not be dressed like this when Cat is around.

"Can I help you?" he asks with a yawn.

"Riley?" I ask to confirm this isn't some stranger danger's house.

His eyes peel open slowly. "Yeah." He licks his lips and rubs his hand down his face. "What can I do for you? It's a little early?"

I raise a brow. "It's after nine." Then again, why are we talking about the time? "Yeah, um, I'm Nyx."

He blinks slowly as if the brain is computing information at a sloth speed. "Right, right. Catalina's boyfriend. Not the asshole one."

Good to know I don't hold that title. Makes me wonder how much Cat and Riley talk.

"I came by so we can talk about tomorrow."

He waves me off. "No need. This place will be like Fort Knox. No one will be getting in; if all else fails, we could go to the school. Whatever you think would be best."

He seems too eager if I say so. "Staying here will be fine. Get some fuckin' decorations so your place isn't attacked. I swear if anything happens to her, kiss your career goodbye."

He smirks. "Maybe you could be the asshole."

"You have no idea. She isn't the only one that knows how to dig a grave."

He gives me a slight nod before I turn away. I'm glad Catalina has a friend, but something tells me not to trust Riley. He seems like a decent guy and all, but my gut is being a nag. My gut has never steered me wrong.

Okay. Once when, Cole cooked that chicken, but that was completely different.

The last thing I want to do is add another body to our growing list. It's bad enough that our game plan for tomorrow is stressing me out. The thought of the mayor's bodyguards catching us is what worries me. But Cole keeps reassuring me they all know him. Getting into his house will be easy.

All I know is this nightmare will be a thing of the past in no time.

I take the long way home. The changing leaves were always my favourite thing about this time of year. Doesn't help that Eastwood is housed between winding roads, making it fun to speed through on the bike. Pushing my

bike past the speed limit, the sound of the exhaust is music to my ears.

Passing the welcome sign, I make my way home. Having my freedom is great and all, but I need to spend more time with Cat. All this stress is weighing on me; only she can help me. Creeping down our street, I notice a white van parked across the house. I drive by slowly, studying the driver's side.

It wouldn't be weird if the driver's side wasn't empty. My radar is shooting red flares off. I quickly swing into the driveway and jump off my bike. Wasting no time, I run for the front door. Nothing else matters but getting to Catalina. My fingers tingle as I try to get the key into the lock; what if whoever was driving is in the house right now? I could be too late.

Trying to turn my brain off and not to think like that, the lock finally turns.

"Catalina!" I yell as I rush up the stairs. "Baby? Where are you?" Who cares if someone is in the house? Let them hear me. Reaching the landing, Cat stands with her bedroom door open, looking confused.

I rush to her, placing my hand over her mouth.

"Don't talk. It could be nothing, or we are currently being stalked."

Her violet eyes grow serious. She tries to mumble some kind of response from under my hand. With a roll of her eyes, she points to the window and throws her hands in the air.

"I'm not following."

"Mo, ssit."

I got that one. "Don't talk too loud." I drop my hand.

"Are you sure they aren't for the neighbour to rake the leaves?"

"I want to believe that, but when has Ms. Rita ever raked her fuckin' leaves, Catalina?"

"Touché. Have you called the guys?" She moves back into her room, closing her curtains.

Pulling out my phone, I open a group chat, sending the guys a quick SOS text. I move to her window and take a quick pic of the van. "You haven't noticed how long they've been there, have you?"

"No, you woke me up. I don't have morning classes today."

Probably a good thing. If she happened to go out, they might have followed her. All I can do now is wait until the guys show up—I'm not leaving Cat alone.

I make Cat crawl back into bed. There isn't much for her to do; the less she's walking around, the better.

"Did you search the house?" she whispers.

My head snaps toward her. "No. You were my concern." I scan her room, moving to her closet. Pulling the doors open fast only to be greeted by clothes. My chest falls in relief. That leaves the rest of the house.

"Lock the door behind me. Stay away from your window."

Not what I want to be doing. Then again, I need to make sure the house is safe. Checking all the rooms upstairs first, I head downstairs, listening for any unknown sounds. The house is silent as I make my way into the den. We should've invested in security, but we never

had a single issue with someone trying to break in. The thought of us being a part of the club usually worked at scaring people away.

The jiggle of the outdoor handle has me freezing. Drawing my gun, I flick the safety off. My heart jumps in my throat with every step closer to the door. Moving the curtain away just enough to unlatch the lock. With one deep breath, I point my gun and open the door.

"Jesus Christ, Nyx. It's me."

"Fuck man, I would've shot you." I back up, letting Dorian inside and locking the door behind me. "Did you find anything?"

"Nah, man, it's all clear. Whoever parked out there must be trolling us. Cole is out checking the van."

"I didn't hear you drive up." I make my way to the basement.

Step by step, we listen for any sound. Dorian nods in the direction of the furnace room. Keeping my hand on my gun, I move closer. This is the last straw. I'm calling to get an alarm installed.

"Clear," Dorian calls out.

I check behind the furnace and hot water tank. "Same."

"You didn't hear us because we parked down the street. Figured an SOS meant trouble. Guess we were right."

Cole greets us at the head of the stairs. "Where is she?"

I point upward. "Locked in her room."

"Kitchen now."

This can't be good. Add him, not wanting Catalina to hear. Cole presses his palms on the island. The anticipation is killing me.

"The van doesn't belong to the club." His voice was calm but had an edge of stress to it.

"Are you sure?" Dorian looks like he doesn't believe Cole.

Cole runs his hand through his dark hair. "Yeah, we always install a tracker on our vans. This one didn't have one."

"Well, maybe they removed it."

Cole shakes his head. "Freddy is the one that installs them. I called and asked. He's never heard of this van before."

"Do you think someone is on to us?"

"Conspiring again, boys?"

Fucking hell. She doesn't listen. "And you can't listen. What did I say?"

"I waited, then I heard all you three gabbing like three mother hens. Figured it was safe to come down. The van is gone, by the way." She opens the fridge to grab a bottle of water.

We're up and moving to the front window. Where the hell was the creep hiding? Cole moves to the front door, cracking it open slowly. With a huge swing, he steps outside. I point to Cat, making her stay in the kitchen.

"Whoever it was also left a present," Cole says from outside.

"How bad of a gift?" Dorian calls back, never letting Cat see past him.

Cole walks back into the house, holding a yellow LED mask. Cat gasped, dropping her water.

17
Catalina

It's hard to breathe.

The grip on my throat won't loosen up. No matter how often I try to take a deep breath, the weight of what Cole brought into the house lands on me. That van belongs to only one person, but why the hell is he back?

The whole point of him terrorizing me last year was to get what he wanted, and he did. Why all of a sudden show back up again.

"I don't like this."

"Same, half pint. Why the fuck is he back?" Dorian hasn't left his spot by the window since our gift arrived.

Cole and Nyx haven't left my side. I'm not sure what this means for tomorrow night. If anything, it would be safer; as far as I know, my brother doesn't know anything about Riley. I'm thankful that I don't have to work tomorrow. I'm not going through that again.

"It doesn't matter why he's back. We should've taken care of him when we had a chance." Cole's grip on my thigh tightens.

Nyx groans. "Cole, we can't add another body tomorrow."

"How many?" I dare to ask.

"Three," Dorian answers without a beat.

"Revenge requires more holes," I remind them.

Dorian smirks. "Good thing we know someone good at digging."

Oh, hell no. They can hit the road if they think I'm getting caught up in their shit. I won't even ask who they are killing because I don't want to know. Less is more in this case. I'll wait until the paper comes out, find out like everyone else, and pretend I'm not sleeping with the killers.

"Dorian, it's a good thing you can dig too." I shoot him a smug look.

"Don't worry, half pint, I wouldn't ask you to dig for us. I hope you aren't anywhere near what goes down tomorrow. I'm not even sure I want you to go to Riley's now."

"She can't stay here. Her brother knows she lives here," Nyx added. "Riley's is still the best bet."

Cole hasn't removed his hand or said a word. I'm afraid of what is going on in his head. If he thinks going after my brother will solve everything, he's wrong. More will only come. The only solution is to go after my mother. I need to figure out what the hell she wants. But being guarded

all day tomorrow isn't going to help me get answers. Like hell, I'm calling. She doesn't need to know my number.

"Nyx is right. She'll still go to Riley's tomorrow as planned." Cole raises his chin, looking at me. "No arguing."

"Wasn't going to. I actually agree. If my brother returned, it can't be for a sibling reunion."

I hear him take a deep breath before releasing it slowly. Leaning over, he kisses me on the temple. "Thank you." He stands, digging his hands into his pockets. "We should get some scouting done before tomorrow, and I want everything to run smoothly."

Dorian studies me from across the room. "I'm staying with half pint. You, two, can handle this."

"Don't leave the house. We shouldn't be gone that long."

Nyx leans over, kissing my temple. "Be safe. Love you."

I watch them both leave, praying they will make it back. If my brother is still at large, who knows what will happen if he does find them?

"Don't worry so much, darling." Dorian strolls toward me, dropping to his knees.

"I can't help it. If he's out there, anything can happen, Dorian. What if he finds the guys?"

He rubs his thumbs across my bare knees. Never taking his eyes off mine, I've always loved watching his green eyes change from a light to a dark shade of green. He's such a beautiful man.

"You're beautiful too, darling."

"I need to stop talking out loud."

He smiles. "It's entertaining when you do. I never know what will fall from those lips." Slipping his hand under my thighs, I lift my ass off the couch so that he can pull my sleep shorts off.

"I'm so glad we never lost you," he whispers as he kisses the inside of my thigh. "Don't ever leave us again." He places his hands between my thighs, spreading them open. He lowers himself to the floor before moving between my thighs.

With one long, luscious lick, my body shudders in response. I can feel him smirk against my clit. Running my hands into his hair, I grab a handful, tugging his head back.

"Keep it up, and I'll fuck you instead."

"Works for me, darling." He moves away, undoing his jeans; he yanks them down his legs. His dick is hard and dripping in pre-cum. "Come fuck me."

I'm not sure which is wetter, my pussy or my mouth. Dragging my shirt off, the cool air feels welcoming on my skin. I watch as he tugs his shirt off and lies on the floor, giving his dick a few strokes. With a curl of his finger, he summons me closer.

Crawling on the floor, I work my way up his body. When I reach his hips, he grabs hold of me.

"I want to feel your pussy around my dick so fuckin' bad."

The need I have for him overwhelms me. I'll never be satisfied; living my entire life with him would never be enough. Even the afterlife wouldn't be ready for us.

I plant my hand on either side of his head and smile. "Don't move."

"Yes, ma'am." I lean down, running kisses along his jawline. His only response is making his dick twitch.

"I said don't move," I demand, moving my hand between our bodies and grabbing his dick. "Do I have to punish you?"

He groans in pleasure. "Fuck, no." Flicking my thumb over the tip, he hisses. "Please, Catalina." His fingers dig into my hips when I don't move, and his gaze holds mine as I slowly sink. Every inch working its way inside. Our moans grow loud until I'm seated on his body.

"Your pussy is already choking me—fuck, you feel so good like this."

I grind my hips, and my stomach tightens. I won't last long like this. The stimulation on my clit will push me over too soon.

"It's okay. Come for me."

Ah, fuck.

He grips my hips tighter, helping me move faster. Slapping my hand on his chest, my finger outlines the newest tattoo, a little tombstone. It's perfect.

The faster we move together, the more the world melts away. No one else matters.

"Catalina." Dorian moans. And that's my undoing. I'm not sure what it is about a man moaning, but fuck is it ever sexy.

My nails dig into his skin, and my toes curl.

"Don't stop moving. I'm coming too." He thrusts faster, bringing another orgasm out of me.

"Dorian, shit." Pulling me into his chest, he works until he's breathless.

With a long groan, he finishes, spilling deep inside of me. "God, I love you."

Cole and Nyx didn't make it home until late. I still didn't ask questions. Three bodies and scouting can't be a good thing. I have other things to plan. The number one obstacle is Riley. As I pack my bag, I try to think of a plan, but nothing comes to mind. Riley will be watching me like a hawk, and I guarantee going to the bathroom will involve him following me.

For now, I need to act casual or the guys will suspect that I'm up to something. Cole will sniff my bullshit plan out before I can plan it. The thought of seeing my mother again makes me sick. I'm older, and she can't control me anymore.

All I need to do is keep repeating that to myself until I believe it. Whenever I think of her, the little girl in me cowers more within.

Today is the day. Daddy is taking me shopping for my Halloween costume after school. He told me I could pick out whatever I wanted. Sitting at my desk, my brain can't think about anything else except what costume I want. All I want is to fit in with all the other kids. They dress up pretty every year, and I want that.

With a broad smile, Daddy meets me in the parking lot, and I know he's keeping his promise.

"Ready, sweetie?"

"Yep." I jump up and down with excitement.

His laugh grows loud. "Wonderful, what are you going to be?"

I tap my chin. "An Angel."

"Sounds wonderful. Let's get going before it gets too busy."

The store is busy, but I found what I was looking for. The best Angel costume that I've ever seen. I didn't even enter the house, and my mother ripped the bag from my hands. My hand throbs in pain, but I don't dare make a sound.

"What's this?"

"It's a costume. I didn't think there was any harm in it," Daddy tells her.

Her face scrunches up in disgust. "She doesn't need a fucking costume. She won't be going out on Halloween. What has she ever done to deserve that?"

She stares at me, and it eats away at me. No one will tell me why she doesn't like me. When she moves toward me, I hide behind Daddy.

I grip my sweater tight. That woman has no control over me anymore. Fuck her.

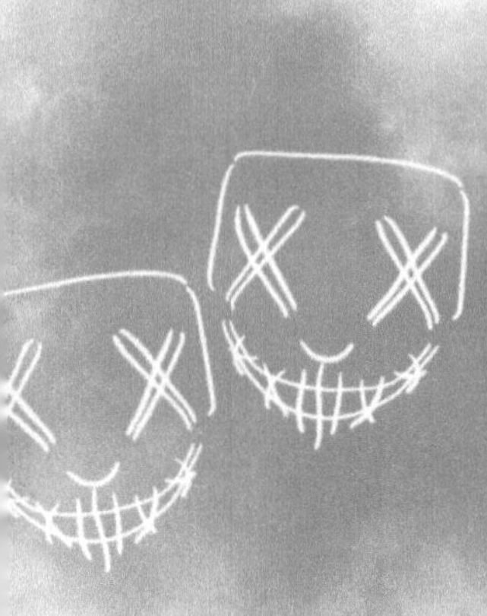
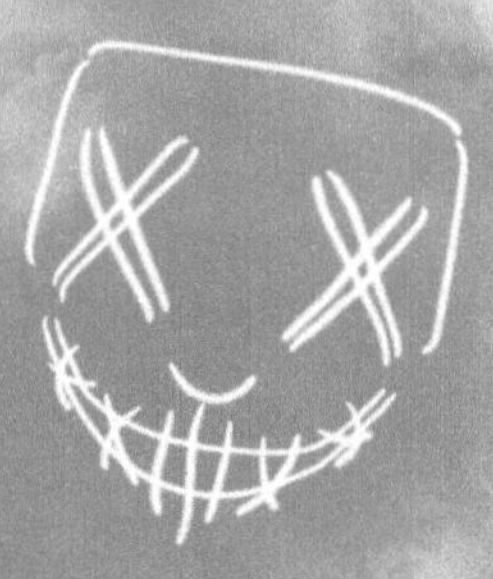

18
Cole

Halloween Day

The house is quiet as I make my way down both flights of stairs. I'll admit being on the top floor does get lonely. Catalina wanted her own room, and no one argued. We rotate rooms when she's up to it. I never want to intrude on her time, and it's been important to Nyx and Dorian.

It's hard to believe that tomorrow, this entire nightmare will come to an end. It feels like a decade since we heard about the stupid purge. I had to place my phone on silent. Henry kept blowing it up with pointless text messages. I'm not safe-guarding dick shit in this town tonight.

I head over to the patio doors and open the curtains. Taking a calming breath, our fuckin' guest came back throughout the night. All over the yard, red paint is splat-

tered on the new patio set, the shed, and a trail leading up to the doors.

"Cole?"

"Yeah, Wednesday?" I don't bother turning around. I was hoping she wouldn't have to see this or the message he left.

"He's coming after me again, isn't he?" She speaks so low that I hardly catch it. This time, I turn around.

"No, he won't be able to find you. I swear on my life, Catalina. He won't get you again."

I read his message once more. *This time the clock won't strike before I do.* Written in red paint on the patio window.

By midday, Dorian is growing grumpy. He spent most of the morning cleaning the red paint off the shed; that shit didn't want to come off. Our shed, which once was black, is now stained red. If anything, it's a sign of what's coming.

"Come on, Cat. We don't have all day. I thought you packed last night?" My patience is running thin.

"Hold that pierced dick will, yeah. I'm grabbing one last thing," she calls down.

Definitely wearing thin. She doesn't make my life easier, that's for sure. Then again, it wouldn't be the way it is without her. She bounds down the stairs carrying her

coffin-shaped weekender. Wearing her leggings and an oversized sweater, fuck she's beautiful.

"I'm ready. Who's driving?" she asks, heading to the front door.

Dorian grabs her bag. "I'll be driving. Cole and Nyx will be on their bikes, Cole leading and Nyx bringing up the rear. They will intercept at any sign of trouble, and I'll get you out of there. No one needs to know where you are headed. Any questions?"

She slips her boots on. "Only one."

"We're listening."

"What if he isn't working alone this time around? We have no idea why he's back."

Nyx pulls her into his chest. "Shh, nothing will happen. If that prick shows his face, we will deal with him."

"All we need you to do is have fun at Riley's and not think about tonight," Dorian adds.

I place a hand on her shoulder. "Let's go, Wednesday."

I didn't think this would be hard. Driving in front of the SUV, scanning every side road for a white van. I thought for a moment as we passed main street, I spotted it. It turns out it was a stupid delivery van. My mind is playing tricks on me. I hope Cat isn't stressing. Knowing Dorian, he'll make her feel at ease. The windows are blacked out so that even if her brother were to spot us, he wouldn't see her.

Riley's place is only a few blocks away when I spot a white van parked down an alley. I signal Dorian to keep going, and Nyx pulls up beside me.

"What's going on?"

I climb off my bike, nodding to the van. "I'll check it out. Stay here and make sure you can still see Dorian."

"Call out if you need me. Who knows what he's capable of."

I hope it's nothing and it's a random van. There's no way he was able to follow us, slowly creeping down the road. I stick close to the apartment building; you would've missed him if you weren't looking. He parked behind the dumpster, only his front end showing. It seems like the same van; then again, it has no distinctive marks to go by. Peeking through the driver's window, I see fast food wrappers spread across the passenger seat and spilling onto the floor. This wouldn't be his van unless her brother had eaten his weight in food in the last twenty-four hours.

Nyx is scanning the street when I reach him. "I don't think it's his." Mounting my bike, I take a look down Riley's street. Dorian parked across from his house.

"For sure?"

A nagging feeling in my gut appears. "Not one fuckin' bit, Nyx. But what the hell are we supposed to do?" I start my bike, which roars to life, ending the conversation. I need to make sure Catalina gets into that house safely before the shit storm arrives tonight. I'm hoping the visit Nyx gave Riley was enough to scare him. If not, the coincidences are going to suck for him.

Dorian meets us outside of the SUV, looking down the road. "I take it you didn't find him."

"Nothing. Move her fast to be safe." I rush across the street, pounding on the front door.

Riley pulls it open, looking nervous. "You guys love knocking loud, don't you."

"Later, have you noticed anything weird in the area lately?"

His brows pinch. "Ah, no. Nothing out of the norm. Why?" his voice rises.

I wave Dorian over. They cover Cat as they rush her across the street. Surprisingly, they didn't carry her.

"What's going on?" Riley asks once Cat makes it up the stairs.

She laughs. "It's Halloween. Get that fuckin' pumpkin outside." Riley mumbles under his breath but does what she says. Rules are rules, and decorated houses are safe in this town.

We all crowd in his front entrance, getting our good-byes in.

"Be safe tonight, all of you. I mean it. I won't be able to dig enough holes for the massacre I'll create. It'll be a cremation in the middle of town."

Her eyes bounce between ours, and I can feel the passion spilling from her words. I believe every one of them. She would kill for us, just like we would for her.

"Nothing will happen to us, baby." Nyx presses his lips to hers. "I promise."

"We always keep our promises, don't we, half pint." Dorian cups her head, tipping it back. She gives him a small smile. "Now kiss me." With a roll of her eyes, she lifts her toes, pressing her lips to his.

She wraps her arms around my neck, tugging me down. "I hate that you're so tall."

"I'm sure you do, except when you try to reach the mugs every morning."

"That's one reason why I need you to get back. How am I supposed to survive without coffee?" Her eyes tear up.

"You could lower the shelf, or we could get a mug tree." Wiping away a stray tear, she tries to smile.

"The mug tree sounds cool." I smash my lips to hers. I can't take her tears anymore. She's supposed to be the strong one.

"I love you, Wednesday. We'll go shopping when we get back."

"Promise?"

"Always."

Only a couple of hours until the night starts. We have some prep to take care of before we technically have to show ourselves at the compound. The first thing is to dig some holes in the cemetery. I'd rather have that ready to go, so dumping is quicker.

No one likes to be caught with their pants down.

We decided on Eaglewood; being away from everything tonight would be the best. Although we aren't sure how that will go this year, outsiders might find it too. God, this year is such a mess.

I'll admit Eaglewood is a pleasant cemetery. The massive iron gates that welcome you as you drive down

the road are once said to keep the souls locked in, or that's the rumour that was spread around elementary. Oak trees guard the surrounding property as far as the eye can see; some are as old as the cemetery, which dates back over a hundred years. But the best part is the entry road that circles the cemetery hides old and new gravesites. It's like an Easter hunt looking for old tombstones. Mausoleums are mixed within, housing the rich folks of Eastwood.

It's indeed a sight to see. Too bad assholes will be buried here tonight.

I park at the very south of the cemetery along the treeline. This is where some of the oldest graves are.

"This should do it. They shouldn't mind new bunk-mates."

Nyx looks pale. I guess he still can't handle this part.

"I'm sure the bodies are gone, bud. You can't even read the tombstone anymore." Dorian rubs the stone to prove it. "We won't even go down that deep, yeah?"

He swallows, lip curling. "Yeah, okay. But I'm shooting Conrad."

Whatever makes his little heart happy. But it can be satisfied after the work is done. We need to dig three holes before Henry figures out shit. I'm surprised he hasn't called yet; wondering where we are. Usually, he can't keep out of my life.

The first few hits to the dirt remind me why I hate doing this. Are we even gonna have the energy for tonight?

"What are we doing after?" Nyx wipes his forehead, panting. Someone needs to visit the gym more.

"I guess we have no choice but to listen to whatever bullshit Henry has to grace us with. Then we wait and strike."

Dorian stares off. "The quicker we do this, the faster we can get back to half pint."

"Agreed. Finish up, and we'll get out of here."

I can't wait to see the look on Coleman's face when he realizes it's his last purge, and it isn't how he expected it to go. No pussy for him tonight.

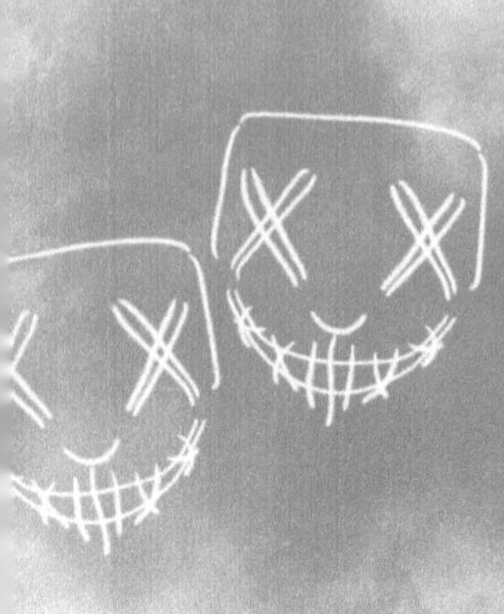

19

Dorian

One last purge. That's what I keep telling myself the entire time as I dig this hole. The mantra of the night, I feel. Whoever rooms in this hole better enjoy it. And lord have mercy on anyone's soul that finds these pricks.

The hours are ticking by, and we should do more than digging. But prep work is essential, and I get that, but fuck. The anticipation for tonight is killing me, plus leaving Cat alone. I don't fully trust Riley.

"We about done or what?" Nyx calls out from his hole. "I swear I saw a bone."

"Pussy," Cole yells back. "How can you kill someone but can't do this? Seriously, I wonder about you some days."

Nyx groans, followed by a loud thump. "I'm done. I can't do this anymore."

I stand, getting a better view, and his shovel lies on the ground outside the hole. Nyx is halfway out of the grave, covered in dirt.

"Honestly, they don't deserve to be buried any deeper. Call it quits, Cole." Bracing myself, I hop out. The three graves lie waiting, side by side.

Cole's phone rings, sending my heart rate flaring. In a way, I hope it's Cat, but I know it's Henry. It's time.

⸎

We swing by the house and clean up; the less suspicion we give away, the better. Three hours until the purge commences. I stand in the driveway, watching all the innocent kids go door to door, trick or treating as their parents scan the road. This isn't what this night is meant to be. How can kids be kids if danger is lurking hours from now? A little boy spots me from across the street, and his face lights up; he's dressed like a biker, and I wave him over. His parents look nervous but must notice the patches on Cole and Nyx's back because the kid comes rushing over.

"I love your bike," he squeals.

I bend down, resting my hand on my seat. "Did you want to sit on it?"

His eyes shine bright. "Can I really? It's so big."

"Place your foot on the peg and your hand on the gas cap; one big pull, and you'll be up." He does what I say,

and I lift him by his vest, getting him seated. His parents watch but never get closer.

"Wow, this is so cool. I can't believe you get to ride this all the time."

I laugh; his enthusiasm is welcoming tonight. "One day, kid, you can too."

"Cody, we should get going before it gets too late," his mom calls.

"Thank you, mister." He struggles to dismount, so I lift him using his vest. He runs straight to his parents. He leaves bouncing and talking up a storm.

"Nice, Dorian. That kid will have good memories for tonight." Cole pats my back.

"He'll get all the babes now and probably be a player come high school." Nyx laughs.

At least there won't be an MC for him to join.

The ride through Eastwood during fall is beautiful. You wouldn't know that it houses a large university. The small-town feel is what initially brought my grandparents here. It's also the thing that drove my parents away. They didn't like that everyone knew your business or the lack of shopping centres. For me, it was perfect. After Grandmother died, I sold her house. I couldn't bear living in it still—too many memories in the walls. A wonderful family bought it, and I'll drive by every once in a while.

"Dorian, how many times do I have to tell you not to play in the street? You and Nyx are going to get run over." Grandmother stands on the porch, trying to look mad. But Nyx and I both know she won't yell at us.

Nyx and I look at each other, trying not to laugh. "Grandmother, the street is empty. Besides, we move the hockey net when a car comes. We aren't babies anymore."

"Yeah, Mrs. Prescott. Sorry about your luck, but we are teenagers now."

Grandmother shakes her head. "You two will be the death of me."

She got diagnosed with cancer that year. She joked we caused it. She would roll over in her grave if she knew what I was doing now.

The compound is busy as we roll in; every member is here tonight. The only one I don't see is Freddy. Red flags sound off; he would've told us if he had left already. Something isn't right. Cole pulls next to me, scanning the crowd. But it's Nyx that speaks.

"Where's the old man?"

I keep scanning the area, hoping I overlooked him. It can't be that hard to find an old man. Not a sign of him. Only Henry and Conrad stand tall, smiling and waving at all those suckers.

"I can't find him. Do you think Henry told him to stay home?"

"God, I hope so. If he did anything to him. His death will be painful and fuckin' slow." Cole hasn't taken his eyes off Henry. "We better head over before he has an aneurysm."

The walk through all the guys usually feels like an accomplishment. This time, I feel like an enemy walking amongst them, wondering if they know our plans. The only one that does isn't here. I want to say if there were

any signs of trouble, Freddy would've called. He is stubborn, but not like that.

Henry sees us and grins. Asshole.

"Shoot me now. This speech is going to make my ears bleed. I can already feel it." Nyx stepped forward, hate gleaming in his eyes.

Cole stands next to me, arms crossed. "Let the bullshit fly." He speaks from the corner of his mouth.

Henry takes in the crowd almost like he's satisfied. He claps twice. A hush falls upon us all. And the prick looks pleased. President or not, he lost my respect.

"Welcome, everyone." The crowd claps, minus us three. "Yes, it is a time to celebrate. Coleman would've been here, but he is prepping for tonight. Now, our job is to ensure the town is safe, especially since it's open to the public this year. You are all aware of your jobs. Do you have any questions?"

Nyx goes to raise his hand, but Cole stops him. Royce lifts his. "I have one. What's the whole point of this purge night?"

The million-dollar question. Will he tell the truth or not?

Henry chuckles, a clear sign he won't tell the truth. That Coleman wants free sex without paying for it. So he would rather chase after an innocent woman and rape her. What a great so-called purge.

"The mayor wanted to try something new a few years back and called it a purge. I'm not sure why; it had nothing to do with purging. This year, he decided to have no rules; anything is open."

Royce doesn't look convinced. "Aren't the town folk concerned about all the murders and rape going on in town?"

"Listen here, boy. It's his town, not yours. Follow the rules, got it? Don't talk back." Henry's face turns a lovely shade of crimson, and it's comical. Someone finally had the balls to call him out on his shit.

Conrad steps forward, pointing to the far end of the compound. "Meeting's over. Go do your job."

Fun sucker.

He dies first, last to join first out. I don't make the rules, but I'll follow them in this case. I glare at the two cunts. Tick Tock, and then it hits me—Catalina's brother's warning from this morning. He said the clock won't strike when he does. The last time he struck was when the clock downtown was broken at twelve. Who the fuck knows this time. We need to get this done now.

Me: How is it going?

It's only been a few hours, but I need to confirm that she's doing okay.

Half pint: All good on the front. You?

Me: Not giving you details. But let's say Henry gave us his lame speech, and we didn't die from boredom.

Half pint: Thank God for that. Who would get me off if you did?

Me: Cat, I can't be walking around with a hard-on.

Half pint: Haha, it would be funny. I better go. Riley has the popcorn ready. Movie night starts soon. Please be careful. Love you, tell the guys.

Nyx nudges me. "What's wrong?"

"Hmm? Oh, nothing. Cat says she loves you guys."

"What else did she say?"

I let out a sigh of relief. "They are watching a movie and eating popcorn. Didn't mention anything else, which is good."

He bites his lower lip. "Yeah, or they haven't noticed it yet. The quicker we do this, the faster we get back."

The only other problem is Henry and Conrad are still hanging around, watching us. It's like they are trying to figure out why we are still here. It would be easier if they walked into the end of my gun while I pulled the trigger.

"Head for the bikes. Make it look like we're headed for our corner of the town. Once it's seven, we'll come back for these two." Cole salutes them before walking to his bike.

I leave without giving them any sort of acknowledgment.

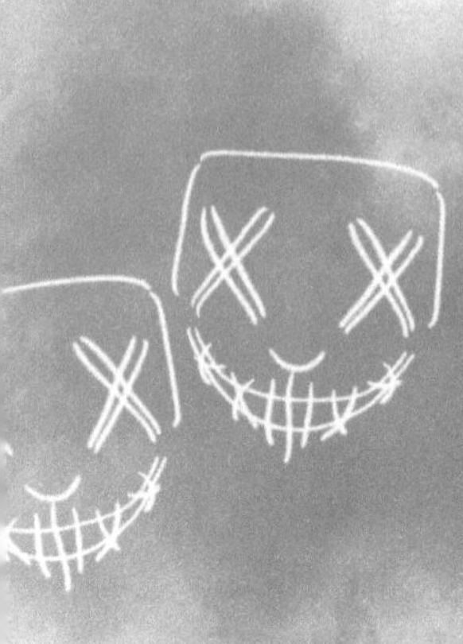

20
Catalina

I've been watching the clock, which is pointless; you'll know when it's seven. Minutes before, it'll be quiet and then all hell will break loose. I watch Riley check the window, and he sucks in a deep breath. I jump out of my seat, rushing to his side; gripping his arm, we watch the street flood with people wearing all sorts of masks.

"Jesus fuck." I watch as they carry weapons of all shapes and sizes—from machetes to baseball bats.

"I've never seen this before, Cat."

I move away, double-checking the front door, not that it matters. If anyone wanted in, a deadbolt wouldn't be stopping them.

"Riley, close the curtain and turn the lights off."

I turn the TV off, making the entire house dark. Maybe hiding at the school would've been the wiser choice. Then

again, I didn't expect this. The noise begins to pick up, and screams echo between the walls. Riley pales.

"We need to hide," I whisper.

He nods, pointing down the hall.

"We can hide in my closet. Do you think they got my neighbour?" His hand freezes on the closet handle.

My heart breaks. I hope not, but anything is possible tonight. "Let's get inside."

I thought I was scared when my brother kidnapped me, but this is much worse. These people won't think twice about killing or doing anything to you. They won't get punished for it. Unlike Cole, Dorian and Nyx, they asked if I wanted it. Whoever comes through that front door won't ask. I don't even think a simple Halloween decoration will stop them.

Riley squeezes my hand, it hasn't been over ten minutes, and the night is growing louder. If only the guys expected this, I could've been more prepared. I don't think anyone knew what to expect with more people joining. What the fuck was the mayor thinking? Did he want everyone in town killed?

"Cat, if we don't make it out of this—"

"Shut that cake hole. We will."

He sighs. "But if we don't, having one friend is nice," he says, the vulnerability in his voice.

I shift, feeling for his shoulder. I pull him closer. "As much as I hate working inside and with other people, working with you isn't that bad. Now, grow a pair. We ain't dying."

He laughs. "If you say so."

At least we aren't dying today. Not by some asshole in a hockey mask. If anything, I'll do the killing with a hockey stick.

I'm not sure how long it's been. My dumbass left the phone in the living room. I'm certain Riley has covered his ears; the screaming has gotten to him. I thought for sure that it would've moved on by now, but they keep coming. We have until the morning to deal with all this shit.

"Stay here. I have to grab my phone."

"I'll come. You shouldn't go alone."

We slowly make our way down the hall; an orange glow flickers behind the curtains as we round the corner. I feel Riley tense next to me.

"Where were you last year during the purge?"

"I went to my mom's. She has a cabin a few hours away."

I dig my fingers into his forearm, taking his focus away from the window. "It wasn't like this, I swear. This is new to me, too."

"I think we should get to the school."

And I still need to get my ass to deal with my brother and mother. But I can't leave Riley alone; the poor guy wouldn't survive. I point my finger at him to stay. I stick to the shadows, getting close to the window. If we can

leave the house without being spotted, we have a better chance of getting out of the neighbourhood.

I grip the curtain, taking a deep breath. The uncertainty of what lies behind them has a chokehold on me. But saving the guys is more important, and finding my brother is do or die. Moving the curtain enough that I can peek through, the street comes into view.

The neighbour's place across the street is trashed. The entire front of the house is spray painted, and the windows are broken. They had the nerve to toss the furniture outside. A small fire is burning in a barrel in the middle of the road, six feet away from another. I think another house is destroyed with a fire burning in the driveway. I feel sorry for the person who didn't park their car. It's now upside down.

People are still milling around, covered in blood. They seem to be patrolling the street like bodyguards.

"All right. We have three groups of five. All have weapons, and not one has a gun, so that's a bonus."

Riley laughs. "How so?"

"They can't shoot us while we run." And not a single person is wearing an LED mask. So he's not out there.

I head into the kitchen, pulling the silverware drawer open.

"Have you ever killed anyone before, Cat?"

"No, but that doesn't mean I won't. Find a weapon, Riley, and look confident when holding it."

He holds his hand out. "I use a knife in the lab. You should find a different weapon."

He has a point and probably has better luck locating veins than I do. With his help, I'm wielding an aluminum baseball bat. This will work perfectly.

"How do we get out of the house?" Riley peeks through the backdoor blinds. "They are everywhere. There's a fire out here, too."

What can we do? We are both victims if we leave like this. Riley heads to the living room, and I search the kitchen for something. I need a sign, and I'm almost ready to pray if I have to.

"Think Catalina, what would Lucy do?"

"Who's Lucy?"

"Um, Lucifer." I roll my eyes. How do people not know that?

"I don't think that's the saying. But I found these." Riley holds up two ski masks. Fuckin' ring-a-ling.

I swipe mine. "Told you praying would work."

"Ah, you didn't."

I raise my brow, and he doesn't need to know shit. I quickly braid my hair before tugging on my mask—this better work.

With a slightly panicked look on his face, I unlock the backdoor. "Walk casually until we can't, then run. Don't let go of my hand."

He nods. My heart is choking me. Never in my life did I think this would happen again. It's another nightmare, and I can't control it. Riley's hand tightens around mine, and cracking the door open, the cool air hits me. What was once filled with a crisp smell is now filled with burning wood and something else I can't figure out.

The coast is clear, and we slip out of the house; moving at a fast-paced walk, we get into the alleyway, and it's a murder scene. I weave my fingers between Riley, moving fast. Pools of blood lie all over the pavement; I'm afraid to look at the bodies, praying it's not someone I know. The revenge people have to do this is unreal.

"Jesus," Riley mutters under his breath.

We make it to the main street before we are spotted.

We might as well have a neon sign pointing at us. More people come out between the shops. The only thing saving us is we are the strangers of the crowd. They have no idea who we are. I have no hard feelings when I bash their heads in with this bat.

I twirl the bat in my hand. Riley stands tall, holding the knife away from his body, waiting for his victim.

"Well, what do we have here?" some slutty doll says. Can we pick any more of an original costume for Halloween? Her little group of slut dolls giggle. Gross.

Riley groans. I feel his pain. "Just nick the artery and let them bleed out."

He side-eyes me. I shrug. Lifting my bat, the head it is, then.

The slut dolls crowd around us, and then the wanna-be horror killers to do. Being in the middle of a murder circle doesn't feel like it would. Riley has his back to mine,

and his heart is beating as fast as mine. We slowly turn. Clutching my bat, I try to think of a game plan. The horror killers are men and will undoubtedly be harder to take down.

"Go after the girls. We need a pathway."

"Lord forgive me."

"I'm sure Lucy will welcome you with open arms."

He releases a deep sigh. "Not funny."

It's either now or we both die here. I step forward, and the air shifts. Don't fail me now, Riley. Without thinking, I rush forward to the first person to my right. With a giant swing, I wait until my bat connects with a body part.

A deep chuckle is all I get in return.

"I think you missed little girl."

Shit.

The ass wearing the hockey mask steps closer, his knife dripping blood. I swing again, aiming low. He yells out in pain.

"Didn't miss that time, prick." I swing once more. The cushion of his head silences the hollow ping from the bat. "Sorry."

I try not to pay attention to the blood spilling from his head or how it was a kid from school. Nope, just keep plowing through the bodies, Cat. Don't think about it—keep going.

I bend down to grab his knife just as a gust of wind blows over my head. Holy shit balls. I turn over, and it's a slut doll. She giggles.

"I almost had you, don't worry. She will."

Her words barely register before the sharp pierce to my right shoulder comes. "Fuck," I hiss, trying to reach the knife that's sticking out of my shoulder. My fingers shake as I try to touch the handle, and my stomach flips. I've cut myself plenty, but I have no words to compare it to this.

"It's a shame about your friend too."

Riley. No, she's lying. He's fine; he has to be. "Fuck you," I spit out. Slowly getting to my knees, I reach for the knife from hockey boy. The bitch that stabbed me steps forward, eye for an eye doll. I wait until she's right before me; this knife better be sharp.

One smooth slice and the knife sinks into the Achilles tendon of her left foot. She falls, screaming; the other doll helps to stop the bleeding. I try to stand, but my shoulder screams in pain. I need to find Riley. Trying again, I clutch my arm and stumble upward, biting hard in pain. I'm surprised I didn't break my molars.

The street is madness. What I thought were teams have now turned on each other. The distraction is welcoming if only I could find the person I needed. No matter where I turn, I can't locate him. Did he make it out?

I don't want to leave without confirming, but staying here isn't an option. My body jerks forward, a hand clenching my bad shoulder.

"Cat, we have to run."

I take Riley in. His ski mask is covered in blood splatter. I examine his body for any wounds. "You hurt?"

"No." His eyes focus on the blade. "Cat, Jesus. We need to go."

Thank God, because I don't think I could make it there alone.

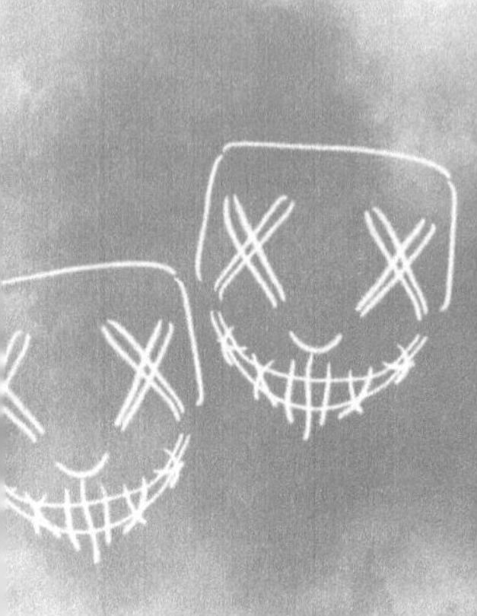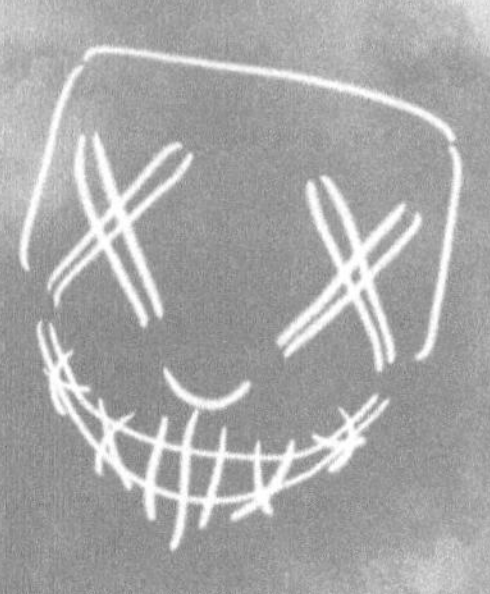

21

Nyx

I'm pissed when we pull out of the compound. Playing nice is one thing, but to stand there and watch all that shit play out tonight was wrong. What a stupid speech. I still can't believe out of everyone there, only Royce had the balls to stand there and speak out. If Henry wasn't on the kill list, Royce wouldn't see the end of the week.

As we drive through town, you can feel the shift. We take the outer road that leads to the high school, and people dressed in costumes already begin to enter the town. Who knows where they parked and if they will ever return to their cars. I am not on clean-up duty this year. Thank fuck for that.

I follow Cole and Dorian into the school parking lot. This night is gonna be one big nightmare.

"We'll double back for the compound. I think it's best to park the bikes at the gravel pit and sneak through the trees."

I like Cole's plan, but. "What if they left the compound?"

"Nah, those two are cowards. No worries there." Dorian winks.

"Figures. They're all for this shit, but can't even take part—" A blood-curdling scream fills the sky, cutting me off. Shivers snack down my spine.

That's not a good sign and a sound I never want to hear. I'm glad we left Cat with Riley safe inside. I can't imagine having her anywhere near this shit. She never needs to see what mess the town turned into.

"Let's roll before some ass decides to kill us. I have no idea how Henry thought we could control this." Cole shakes his head.

"Fuckin' hopes and dreams, man," D scoffs.

Even the back way to the compound is worse than playing a game of dodgeball. Every few feet, a dick in a mask would jump out in front of us, swinging their weapon, trying everything they could to slice our hands or legs. Barrels line the middle of the streets, burning what I hope is wood scraps. But I wouldn't put it past anyone if a body was burning instead. The stench is dead on.

The gravel pit was abandoned years ago, and the Soul Stealers took over it as a shooting range. At the odd time, teenagers will use it for parties, but that also involves someone coming to the compound and asking permission.

As suspected, it's vacant. Even during a purge, no one is stupid enough to come out here, even to hide. Climbing off my bike, I open my side saddle. We packed the essentials before leaving the house earlier—Our masks.

"Are you guys ready?" Yet again, who placed Cole in charge?

I cock my gun, sticking it back in my pants. "I'm good."

We wait for Dorian to answer. "D?"

He climbs off his bike. "Yeah, I was thinking of Catalina. You believe she's safe?"

I keep telling myself she is. If not, I'll go insane.

"She's fine. If anything happened, she would call." Cole walks away, shutting the conversation down.

I'll chalk it up to the stress of his short temper, not because that's who he is. Or the fact that we are under a lot of pressure.

We track through the bush, staying out of view of the compound's cameras. The closer we get, the faster my pulse races. I never thought this day would come, and leaving the club would bring me the freedom I needed. Turns out it was killing the president and vice president.

When we break the tree line, the compound comes into view. Cole gives us a signal to go left and stay low. We need to gain access through the torture room. It's the only room without an alarm, a fault all on its own. It's not

like I was ever going to say anything. It was handy when we dragged a body in and didn't have to worry about punching in a stupid code.

Lining up on the property line, we watch and listen. It's so dark; the clouds are covering the moon, working in our favour.

"Once inside, no one talks. Knowing Henry, the alarm will be set, and we have ten seconds before it beeps when we exit the room; if my assumptions are correct, he should be in his office. Conrad will be in his room with a hang around." Cole directs us like the leader he is. "One more thing," he adds. "Get out alive." He sticks his mask on.

I place my mask on. "Got it," I answer.

"Yep," Dorian agrees, sticking his mask on.

That's my main goal tonight: getting back to Catalina alive. If I come back like a slice of Swiss cheese, it doesn't matter. It's better than not breathing.

"Move out," Cole grinds out.

We scurry across the parking pad and the small yard. Resting against the garage wall, we double-check our surroundings. I watch the main entrance. Why wouldn't he have it guarded? Especially tonight of all nights. I take a step toward the compound.

The air cracks with gunfire, and before I can register it, the dirt in front of my foot flies upwards. Cole pulls me back against the building.

"Looks like someone is onto us," he hisses.

"No fuckin' shit," I pant. "I think I shaved off ten years of my life."

Dorian reaches for his gun. "Gunfight it is. My guess is Conrad."

Yeah, cause his aim is shit, plus Henry doesn't enjoy getting his hands dirty. We learnt that the hard way. I grab my gun, bending down to grab a rock. Time to see where the fucker is hiding. Cole nods, letting me know he's ready. My guess is he's hiding inside, shooting from the bedroom window. Pussy.

The third window in, the curtain moves. Bingo had a baby, and his name is... I throw the rock fast and hard. It shoots right through the window, and you can hear him yell.

"Move fast," Cole bellows.

We book it across the lot, flattening against the compound building wall. The door we need is only feet from us. Bending low, we move, Cole in the front and Dorian taking up the rear. I have no problem being the middleman. Commotion is happening within the compound's walls, guaranteeing Conrad has found Henry.

The door we need finally comes into view, and I'm unsure if relief is the word that comes over me or anticipation. The battle is only beginning.

"Light 'em up. I can't say what's expected, but shoot to kill." Cole turns his mask on, eliminating the night with a blue haze.

"It's gonna be a shit storm," Dorian says. Turning on his mask.

I just flick mine on, adding the green to the mix. I need one good shot. I'm over the thought of torturing these pricks. Cole rushes through the door first, and I pursue.

As expected, the inside is dark, but voices are heard, and they are panicking.

I've always enjoyed an excellent cat-and-mouse game.

"We know you're here. What do you want? We aren't taking part in the purge." Henry calls, his voice cracking.

That's right, be scared.

"I mean it, don't you know where you entered? This is the Soul Stealers. I can have you killed, and no one would care." He continues.

I think I figured out where he's hiding. I nudge Cole, nodding in the direction of the bar. Conrad is quiet. Your time will come, my pussy friend.

Circling the bar, Henry hasn't even noticed our presence yet. He's still yelling at us to leave him alone. It isn't until Cole laughs and Henry shuts up.

"Cole?" His head swivels, taking all of us in. "Dorian, Nyx?"

"Sorry, man, but no hard feelings, yeah?" That sounds sincere to me. If he's lucky, I won't spit on his grave.

"I did everything for you boys and this is how you repay me?"

"You didn't try to stop this from happening to the town. Have you even been out there to see what has happened so far? It's a gong show. A fuckin' nightmare, and for you to think we could protect anyone is unrealistic. You have your dick so far up Coleman's ass I'm surprised you can still piss. You are a disgrace to this town." Cole raises his gun. "I can't believe I looked up to you at one point."

Henry backs up, raising his hands in surrender. "Please."

"Nah, the fact that you still don't get it makes this easy." Dorian raises his gun, too.

I glare at Henry; something is still eating at me. "Where is Freddy?"

He laughs. "That old fuck? He didn't want a part of the club anymore. Said his old body couldn't handle it anymore. I told him to get the fuck out of here."

"Is that all? How did you know an attack was coming tonight?" I press for more; that ass is holding back, I know it.

He shrugs. "Maybe I made him talk, and there's no way he didn't know shit about tonight. Someone doesn't quit out of the blue."

I clench my teeth hard—that asshole. I leap over the bar, punching Henry in the face. "You prick. Do you feel like a big man, beating the shit out of an old man?" I slam my fist into his eye. It's not like he'll need to see again. He groans in pain, but it's not enough.

"I'm gonna fuck you up like you did to this town." Fuck, taking it easy. I grip his shirt, dragging him out from behind the bar; he scrambles to stop me, but I'm stronger when I'm pissed.

I toss him on the floor, kicking him in the ribs. He rolls onto his side, coughing. Grabbing his hair, I look into his non-swollen eye. Horror seizes him; he's not the man I once knew. I'm looking into the eyes of a coward. Releasing him hard, his head bounces off the floor. My fist flies; I can't tell you where it lands. All the anger I have housed inside is being released. My parents still won't give me the time of day, and honestly, if someone got

them tonight, would I care? Would they care if I didn't make it? Over something that happened years ago.

A hand squeezes my shoulder, pulling me from my thoughts. I look down, and Henry is a mess. My hand is a swollen, bloody mess.

"He's gone, Nyx," Dorian reassures me. "You okay?"

I take a couple of deep breaths, nodding. "I will be. One down."

22
Cole

I watch in horror as Nyx beats the shit out of Henry. The laid-back, reserved guy I grew up with since junior high is kneeling over Henry, using his fists as a weapon. Never in my life would I have thought I would witness this. I'm at a loss for words.

He's so disengaged from his surroundings that I wouldn't be surprised if he had no idea what was happening.

"Dorian, stop him before he regrets everything about tonight." I can't let him go much longer. He'll never recover.

Nyx sinks onto his heels, looking at his hands. The glow from his mask made the blood glisten.

"Shit," he mutters.

"You okay? And don't give me that bullshit answer. I'm *fine.* Seriously, what's going on in your head?"

He takes a deep inhale. "I was thinking of my parents and how it was so easy for them to forget about me."

"Nyx, you don't need them. It's been three years, and they haven't tried. We're your family." Dorian grips his shoulder. "We need to finish what we started."

Conrad, where is that snake? I'm surprised he didn't try shooting us from behind.

"Yeah, I'm good. Sorry for going off track."

I laugh and shrug. "Well, it wasn't the shootout, but he's dead." I think. I walk over, kicking Henry. I'm not sold. I aim, shooting him between the eyes. "He's dead now."

"Jesus, Cole."

"Don't act like you wouldn't double-check, D. Do you want this prick popping back up?"

He groans. "Not the point. Let's find the other prick."

Conrad can be anywhere in this place, and we should've split up as soon as we stepped foot inside. But Henry got under our skin as he has always done. I take off for the bedrooms and don't care where the guys go. We need to find Conrad before he leaves the compound.

Taking the stairs two at a time, I reach his room quickly. The door was left wide open; I've been in this situation before. I know he has a gun, and most likely, this will be the shootout Dorian wanted. With a deep breath, I poke my head around the door frame. His room is bare. I was expecting something more from a vice president. All that's in here is a bed and dresser.

Living the high life, I see.

The bedroom seemed empty, so I took the chance and stepped inside. My eyes slowly adjust, taking in the room.

The window is still open from where he shot at Nyx. If he was stupid enough, he could've jumped. Treading softly, I reach the window; looking outside, I can't see past the yard light.

Getting frustrated, I head to the room next door. I'll tear each room apart if I have to. He has to be here somewhere. The guys haven't called out, and I haven't heard anything, so they haven't found him either.

I storm down the stairs.

"Where are you, you fuckin' prick? Scared to face us?" I holler into the common area.

I spin around, stopping in front of the bar. Two sets of voices came from this direction when we first came in. There's a spot at the bar where the keg sits, and I bet any money he's hiding there. I silently lift myself on top of the bar, peeking over the ledge.

Dorian appears in the corner of my eye. I nod below me. Dorian moves to block the exit of the bar. I'm not sure where Nyx is, but if he needs a break, that's fine. I hold up my fist, counting to three. My third finger is barely up, and I jump off the bar, landing on the ground.

It's a risk; he could blow my kneecaps out.

A risk that never happened. "Where the fuck is he?"

"I searched everywhere, but he isn't inside." Dorian places his gun on the bar top.

This is getting frustrating. Where the hell did he go? Fuck this. I head to the main light switch, turning it on, eliminating the entire space. At this point, I don't care if anyone knows we're here. Lifting my mask, I get a better look at the place.

"Where can he go? I didn't hear an engine start."

"He could've left on foot." Dorian lifts his mask, looking toward the front door.

I shake my head. "No, he's on the property. Hiding, he knows what's coming. We need to find Nyx."

Dorian heads to the kitchen, and I go to Henry's office. We should've been gone by now; leave it to Conrad to delay us. I didn't realize how messy Henry's desk was. But I'm looking for one thing, shuffling papers to the side, tossing half-eaten sandwiches on the floor.

The desk drawer is locked, and that's how I know it's in there. I'm not searching that body for the key; giving it a good tug, the drawer pops open. Only he would leave it here, fuckin' idiot.

"Found, Nyx."

I jerked my head up. "Where?"

"He's in the garage."

I grab the set of keys for Coleman's place and follow Dorian.

The garage is lit up when we reach it. Stepping inside, Nyx is waiting for us.

He spins his mask in circles around his finger, shooting us a grin. "I found the fucker."

"Where? We searched everywhere for him." Dorian's voice went rough.

Nyx shakes his head. "You wouldn't believe it."

"Jesus, Nyx, we're wasting time." My patience is running thin, and the clock is ticking.

He points to the cellar door. "Down there. Scaredy cat won't come up."

Hmm. "I wonder why?"

"Well, I'm not sure we are friendly. He just doesn't want to play." Nyx grins.

Dorian stomps on the door. "Dick face, you still alive down there?"

Boxes fall over, and metal hits the floor. "I assume he is." Chicken shit. "Lift the door. If he doesn't come up alone, I'll drag the bastard up."

I stand to the side, aiming my gun, and Dorian does the same. Nyx reaches for the handle on the cellar door; he looks between us and nods. With a quick pull, it's open. My heart jumps when we're met with darkness. The worst part, the stairs are open.

"Be careful, Cole," D warns.

I turn around, taking the first step. Headed into the unknown, my heart is in my throat. Conrad could be watching me.

"If you jump me, I'll shoot you in the dick and leave you to die a slow and painful death."

"You'll kill me anyway, so what does it matter?" His voice echoes off the walls.

I reach the bottom step, and the hairs on my neck raise. He's somewhere near me. "Fuckin' rights, I'll kill you, but I'd rather do it when you're up there. Carrying your body isn't worth it."

My eyes take forever to adjust to the dark, taking tiny, quiet breaths. I wait until Conrad moves. Feet shuffle to my right, turning, a fist enters my view. I'm too slow at dodging, and my eyes water from the pain. *Sonofabitch.*

Conrad chuckles. "Not so tough in the dark, are ya?"

I wipe away the blood. "Oh, I'm tough. I don't have to take cheap shots."

"No, that's Nyx, isn't it."

That's a low blow. He's lucky I didn't send Nyx down here. "Face me, and we'll fight man to man."

He emerges from behind the pile of boxes, and I have to resist the urge to shoot him in the head.

"Drop the gun, Cole."

I laugh. "Drop yours first."

The clang of his gun hitting the floor is almost a relief. Somehow, I don't trust him. The thought of dropping my gun kills me. I'll kill him later. Dropping my gun, I stare at him.

"Are we gonna finish this or what?" I ask through gritted teeth.

Conrad steps forward. I need to control myself no matter how much I want to beat the shit out of him. He rushes for me; I think he forgot that I'm the club's enforcer. Grabbing his arm, I swing him around, jabbing him in the kidney. He falls to the ground, crying out in pain.

"Remember your place. You think you can win against me?" I punch him hard in the jaw, knocking him out. "Pussy." I whistle for the guys.

"What's wrong?" Nyx yells down.

"I need help to get him up the stairs."

Dorian slides down the stairs. "Jesus, I can't see shit. Where are ya?"

"You're almost on top of me."

"You did a number on him." Dorian kneels next to me.

I roll my eyes. "What I wanted to do was shoot him and leave him down here, but we would've had to haul him up either way."

I collect my gun and grab Conrad by the arms, and Dorian grabs his legs. Lift and shove; I don't care how it gets done.

"Cole," Dorian grunts. "Think of a better plan next time."

I hike Conrad's arm higher over my shoulder. "I'll keep that in mind for next time."

Coleman's death will be quicker and easier.

We move Conrad into the torture room. Now, it's a waiting game for him to wake up. Nyx rechecks the time.

"How hard did you punch him?"

I cringe. "I'm not sure. I didn't think it was that hard."

He shakes his head, leaving the room. Dorian glances at me and shrugs. I gave up asking questions about what Nyx does; I rechecked Conrad's restraints. The last thing I want is for him to get free when he does wake up.

"I'll wake him up, move." I back up in time for water to be splashed all over Conrad.

Conrad wakes with a deep inhale.

"Nice, watch out dickhead." Nyx throws the bucket at Conrad's head.

Conrad is slow at reacting and doesn't see the bucket coming. His head snaps back from the force. We all couldn't help but laugh.

"That was hilarious, man. You should've seen your face," Nyx snorts.

I head to the table we have filled with tools. I want to make this last, but I want to return to Catalina. I grab a pair of pliers. I'll cause him some pain before ending his shitty life.

"Fuck you, Cole," Conrad spits out.

I wave the pliers in his face. "Are you sure? I can fuck you with these if you want?"

Dorian holds Conrad's head back, knowing what I'm planning. Nyx digs his fingers into Conrad's jaw. Conrad fights us when I bring the pliers closer to his mouth.

"When was the last time you saw the dentist?" Conrad screams louder the closer the pliers get to his teeth. His body shakes in the chair as I clamp down on his back molar. Needing leverage, I kneel on his leg. With a tight hold, I pull. Blood pools in his mouth, but I keep going. Dead people don't need teeth. His screams die down, and the fight leaves his body.

"Think he's had enough?"

Nyx chuckles. "I always knew he was a pussy. Never could tough it out. End his miserable life."

I move away, and Dorian drops Conrad's head. Blood drips onto his shirt.

Conrad mumbles something.

"Sorry, didn't catch that?"

He lifts his head. "I said fuck you," he slurs.

Dorian sighs. "Even after ripping half your teeth out, that's your comeback?" He shakes his head. "Ever wonder why no one gave you respect in the club? No one cared about you." He walks backward until he reaches the table. "Did you want to pick the weapon, or should I?"

His eyes flashed with fear as Dorian grabbed a knife. Dorian slips his mask back on before heading in Conrad's direction again. Nyx and I follow, surrounding Conrad.

Dorian cups Conrad's neck, touching foreheads. "No hard feelings?" With a quick jerk, he sinks the knife deep under his ribcage, driving it into his heart. Conrad gasps for air.

"How are you feeling, D?"

"I'm getting tired of this night already. Two down."

We're only getting started.

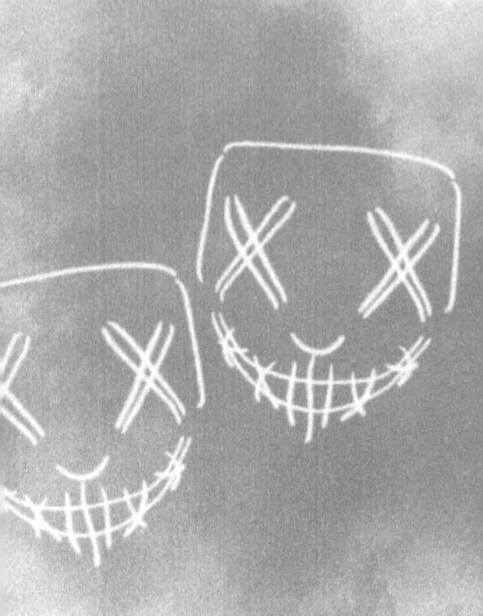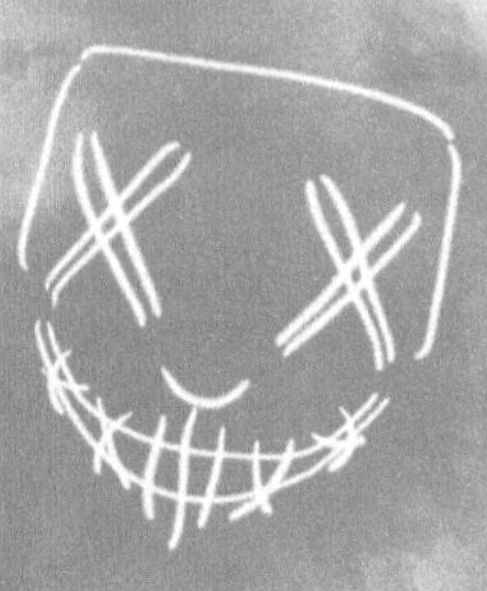

23
Dorian

I can't wait until I'm back in bed, wrapped in the warmth of Catalina. When I signed up for tonight, I wasn't expecting it to be so hard. I can't blame Freddy; what Henry did was unexpected. That completely blindsided us. To go after an old man for what we had planned. No wonder why Nyx lost his shit.

I'm trying to resist the urge to beat him as I roll his body in the tarp. I gave this man three years of my life and got nothing in return. Fuckin' nothing. Not a lick of respect; he couldn't even call me by my first name. Always *boy.*

I hate when it's time to go with my parents. I love staying with Grandmother. And she spends time with me and doesn't yell when I do something wrong. They haven't even picked me up, and I can already sense what's coming. I don't understand why they keep trying to be my parents when they don't want me. I've known since I was five that they didn't

care about me. I'm not stupid; a kid can tell when they aren't being loved.

"Dorian, sweetheart. Your parents are here." Grandmother pokes her head into my room.

My shoulders drop. "Do I really have to go? You're his mom. Tell him no."

She steps into my room, kneeling on the floor next to me. "Listen to me. This won't last forever. One day, when you're older, you can make your own decisions. The world will be your apple. But until then, you'll have to spend time with your parents."

Tears sting my eyes. "I don't understand. They don't like me. Why do they keep doing this to me?"

She cups my face. "I'm not sure, sweetheart. But you are loveable. I love you, and we can only hope one day they grow up before you do."

Who knew she was right? It only took them years to figure their shit out. That's when I realized I wouldn't let anyone, including this asshole, control my life. I dump Henry in the back of the van.

"Asshole," I mutter.

"Doing alright?" Nyx asks.

I chuckle. "I honestly don't know. Nyx. The past keeps coming up, and I swear I'm holding on by a thread."

"I know, this night is almost over, and we'll never have to do this again. One more, and then we can get our girl."

God, I can't wait. I need her so desperately right now.

"Here." Cole drops Conrad's body into the van. "We need to move out before Coleman changes his plans for the night."

The ride back into town is quiet until we hit the *Welcome to Eastwood* sign, and I'm blown away. The sign is burning. I'm at a loss for words. The further we drive, the more destruction unfolds. I've never seen so many stores destroyed and people running for their lives.

"Cole, this is unreal." Nyx weasels his way in between Cole and me.

"Thank the fuckin' mayor."

"I would hate to be caught in that. Your chances of surviving are slim to none." I keep driving, trying to weave between people.

The road to the mayor's place is dark, which doesn't sit right with me. His road is lined with light posts, but everyone is broken.

"Something is wrong," Cole finally speaks.

"Think someone else got to him first?"

Oh, let's hope. Our job will be easier. I just don't like surprises. Cole was sure Coleman would be bunkered down in his house, but maybe he fled early on. Pulling into the driveway, it's clear that someone has come through. The front door is wide open, and the windows are smashed out.

"Fuck," Cole hisses.

We jump out of the van and rush for the door. Stepping inside, we freeze. I've been killing people for years, but this, I've never seen anything this gruesome before.

"Holy shit, what the hell happened?" Nyx walks deeper into the house, stepping over a dead body.

Two bodies lay on the living room floor. There is blood splatter up the white couch to the ceiling. No sign of Coleman yet. We follow the blood trail into the kitchen, and I'm shocked Nyx hasn't barfed yet. If Coleman is in this house, he's got to be dead. The amount of blood can't be from the two bodies.

"I say we search upstairs. If he did escape, I would be shocked." Cole rubs his face, his mouth forming a grim line.

"I almost want to ask questions, but in a way, I don't. You have to be a sick bastard to do this." I understand we pulled Conrad's teeth out before stabbing him, but those bodies were stabbed more times than necessary.

Nyx groans but turns for the stairs. "I swear if he's still alive, I'm not waiting—I'm shooting on sight."

Coleman can't live like the peasants in town, his staircase splits with the left side entering his office and the right heading down the hall to the rest of the rooms. I head for the office; I'm getting so tired of searching for people. His office is empty, minus all the blood from somebody venturing in here; I'm about to walk to his desk when Cole yells.

"Dorian."

Please say they found him. I head in the direction of Nyx and Cole's voices.

"I swear, Cole, I'm done. I can't keep doing this."

"You have no choice. We all agreed we would do this. It's not over until Coleman is dead."

I walk in, finding them arguing over Coleman's body.

"Is he dead?" I ask, walking closer.

"No, he's passed out." Nyx turns to me. Someone did us the favour and tied him to his bed for us.

I slap Coleman across the cheek, and his eyes spring open.

"W-what's going on? Release me." He pulls at his restraints.

I roll my eyes. I took my gun out, resting it between his eyes. Coleman stops moving, and his eyes grow wide. "I wanted to shoot you on sight. I'm tired of this night, and it's all thanks to you. Why couldn't you just find a fuckin' hooker and call it a night? Why invent a stupid night like this? Are you happy with how it turned out this year? Do you know your downstairs is painted red?"

"Of course I'm not happy," Coleman scoffs. "I wanted this town to be a place for others to visit and talk about. Who wouldn't want to visit a town that offered a night of fake purging?"

"Fake purging. Are you kidding me?" Cole's voice turns sour. "You know what the guys do in this town every Halloween? It gets talked about all right, but not for the reason you want. You disgust me."

Nyx closes his eyes, taking a deep inhale. "I can't imagine what went through your head to think this would be a good idea. Your wife's pussy not working, or she finding it someplace else? Is that why you wanted this? You know

what? Doesn't matter anymore. You're done. Dorian, just shoot him already."

"No, please, you can't do this."

I'm over this shit. I pull the trigger ending his life and the bullshit he has over this town.

"About time. What a bunch of bullshit, not even an apology." That's what pisses me off the most. Not an ounce of regret. Whatever, it's done.

"Are we leaving the other two bodies?"

Cole steps to the window, looking out. "I'm not touching them. Whoever stumbles in here tomorrow morning can deal with that issue."

It's almost a relief to be getting to the cemetery. Our task is complete, and once they are in the ground, we can finally get back to Riley's and grab Catalina. This nightmare will be over. I'm not even sure what hour we're at.

I'm glad we chose the cemetery out of town. It's still quiet out here. Doesn't surprise me. There aren't people to fuckin' murder. Realistically, we could've brought Cat out here, and she probably would've been safe.

"We'll do this quick. I'm worried Riley's place might've been attacked." Cole stares out his window.

Nyx whispers, "I fuckin' hope not."

I hop out, heading for the back doors. Nyx greets me with a small smile. "Almost over bud."

"I know. Thank God we dug those holes already."

We each take a body and start dragging. With a big kick, the body drops into the hole. I salute the cunt and grab the shovel. I'm halfway filling the grave in when I hear leaves crunch behind me. I look over and see the guys freeze.

I go to reach for my gun. "I wouldn't do that, Dorian. Or you two."

I peek over my shoulder to see two guys standing there with LED masks on. One is yellow, and the other is orange.

"Catalina's brother, I'm guessing," Cole asks.

"Brothers, where is she?" Orange-masked dickhead says.

"Like we would fuckin' tell you, little assholes." Nyx laughs. "Are you shittin' me? What the fuck do you want, anyway?"

They laugh in return. "I don't think you have an option. Momma, have at it."

Momma? What the hell does that mean? A loud buzzing noise comes behind me, the painful bite into my neck. "Ahh, fuuck." I try to scream. My teeth clench tight, and no matter how much I fight, my body falls to the ground; when I look above me, a woman with blonde hair grins at me. My body jerks like a fish out of water.

She kneels down next to me, pulling out a pair of cuffs. "I would apologize, but there's nothing to say."

I have plenty to say, you fuckin' bitch. You wait until I can move again. You'll be in a hole, too. I look past them, noticing the white van. Motherfucker.

24
Catalina

I've never been in this much pain before. Every step I take feels closer to the ground. Riley has been amazing, and how he escaped without being killed still blows me away. He still won't tell me how many people he ended up killing. I don't think he wants to think about it anymore than I want to. Which, honestly, works for me. I want to forget about this night. The school comes into view, and I'm relieved.

We've been lucky and have been able to dodge a few crowds of clowns running around. I think they had other things on their minds, thankfully. It's getting harder to tell who wants to murder and who's just out trying to ruin the town.

"Can you hold yourself up so I can unlock the door?"

I nod. "Yeah, I'm good." Resting my head on the wall, I wait. The knife is still sticking out of my shoulder, and

I haven't been brave enough to pull it out yet. Riley wouldn't touch it.

Riley guides me inside, heading for the lab. "I'll try to fix you up, but I'm no doctor."

"That's fine. I'll try to be a good patient. But no promises."

He leaves to find his supplies, and I try to distract myself. My thought wanders to Dr. Deadbodies. I hope he's safe tonight. I should've sent him a text or something. It's not like I've had many people to check on.

"All right, I found little, which surprises me, considering this is the medical area. Then again, I don't have access to every space. Don't bleed out on me." He touches the knife, and I hiss. "Fuck, don't. I don't think I can do this."

"Yes, you can. Please, Riley. I need you too." Shivers rolled down my back.

He rubbed his temples. "Yeah, okay." He grabbed some gauze and some antiseptic. "Should we count down or?"

"Pull it on three." I clench my teeth and wait for him to count.

"One...Two." And he pulls.

My stomach turns, and my body falls towards the floor. Riley's hand slams hard into my shoulder, and his other stops my body from going anywhere.

"Catalina? You with me?" his voice uneasy, almost fearful.

I try to answer, but I'm so dizzy. Maybe we should've left the knife until the morning and gone to the hospital.

"Riley," I slur. "I'm not feeling so good."

"Stay awake. I can't do this alone. We made it this far, but I have to stitch it closed and—" He's quiet.

"Yeah?"

He clears his throat. "I don't have meds to freeze you."

Balls. "Do it, can't hurt any worse than the knife." I need to think of other things, but it's hard when I know what's about to happen. I need to know if the guys are doing okay. I should've asked more questions about where they were going; It's club business as far as I know.

"We need to take your sweater off."

Oh, holy hell. "Just cut it so you can work. I'm not taking it off."

"I don't have anything to cut it with." I raise a brow staring at the knife, and he cringes. Thankfully, it's not a favourite shirt, or I would be extra pissed.

"You need to hold this." He grabs my hand, making me press the gauze to my wound. He pulls the collar away and starts cutting away; he swears when my wound is fully exposed.

"How bad is it?" I try to take a glance down, but the world spins.

He ignores me and grabs the needle and thread. "I'm gonna start now." He nods like he's trying to convince himself more than anything.

I nod fast and grip the table. I will myself not to pass out and be strong for the guys. I need to find them still before my brother does. Every time Riley pokes me with the needle, I become light-headed and dizzy.

"Riley, I'm gonna pass out now."

"Shit."

My head bobs forward, and then it's black.

The throbbing in my right shoulder wakes me. I'm praying this night is over; it has to be morning. I try to sit up.

"Fuck."

"Yeah, you are down an arm, remember."

My eyes fly open, and Riley sits beside me, looking like death. "How long was I out for?"

"Not as long as you've been hoping for. Thirty minutes tops. But you're all stitched up, and I never want to do that again."

"Thanks." I sit up. Where did I put my phone? "Have you seen my phone?"

"Ah, I think you left it at my place."

The one thing I meant to grab, and I completely forgot about it. They could've been trying to call me this whole time; I'm so stupid.

"Cat, you can call them from the phone here."

I laugh at him. "You know, this is why you're going far in life, my friend."

"You're also in pain, and that brain isn't working. I'll help you off the gurney."

I call Cole first, and it rings and rings. Not wanting to be that girlfriend, I call Nyx next. When he doesn't

answer, I'm starting to get worried. Come on, Dorian has to answer.

It rings twice and connects.

"Dorian? You there?"

"No, pretty girl. Dorian is a little tied up at the moment."

My heart stops. No, it didn't just stop. My soul left my fuckin' body.

"What's wrong? Not excited to hear from your big brother?"

The sound of his voice sends chills down my spine; deep down, I knew my brother would go after the guys. But in a way, I wish he would've come after me.

"Where are they?"

"What makes you think I'll tell you so quickly?" his voice shook with fury.

Every muscle tensed. What's the point of this conversation, then? If he won't tell me jack-shit, how am I supposed to read his mind if he won't help me?

"Jesus Christ, just tell me what you want then."

"You sure do act strong when you're on the phone, Catalina."

Riley places his hand on my shoulder, squeezing it. "Just tell me what you want?" I swallowed the lump that formed.

"I want what's owed to Momma."

"What?" I shoot Riley a puzzled look.

"Oh, don't act like you don't know. Meet me at the house." The line goes dead before I can answer.

"Cat? What's going on?"

I would rather stick needles in my fingertips than return to that house. "Riley, my psychotic family has kidnapped my boyfriends. I need to go get them."

His eyes shifted nervously in my direction. "You can't go back out there. Are you crazy?"

I might be losing my goddamn mind is the problem. I swore I would never step foot in that house again; there was never a reason to. I don't understand what he means by *what's owed to her*. I gave them everything last year when Dad died.

"I have to. Are you coming or staying?" I can do this alone if I need to. I'll be worried about him, don't get me wrong, but I can't stay.

He rubs his face and groans. "Cat, I can't let you go alone. You were fuckin' stabbed a few hours ago. What if you passed out again? Not happening. I'll drive. The van is parked out back still."

"Thank you, Riley."

I'm unsure what's worse—the drive through Eastwood, watching people destroy it for fun or the drive back to my hometown. I'm trying my hardest to keep the memories at bay, but they keep pressing to break free. Returning to Laketon is proving to be the worst memory of all.

"You grew up here?"

"Unfortunately." Passing my old high school almost makes me laugh. Even though I lived in my car, I survived the tough times. My family didn't beat me down.

But when that baby blue house appears, pain grips my heart. I should've come home at least once more to visit my dad. Or at least called him. I'm still wondering why he left all his money to me and how he acquired all of it in the first place. Was it from guilt? If that's the reason, then I'm glad I signed it over to her. But I signed it all over, so why are they coming after me again?

"What's the plan once we get in there?" Riley asks parking across the street.

"I'm not sure. Her sons are horrible people, Riley. You need to watch yourself in that house. They'll most likely be keeping the guys in the basement. We need to get to them."

Whatever they have planned, they can do it without the guys. This is between me and my family.

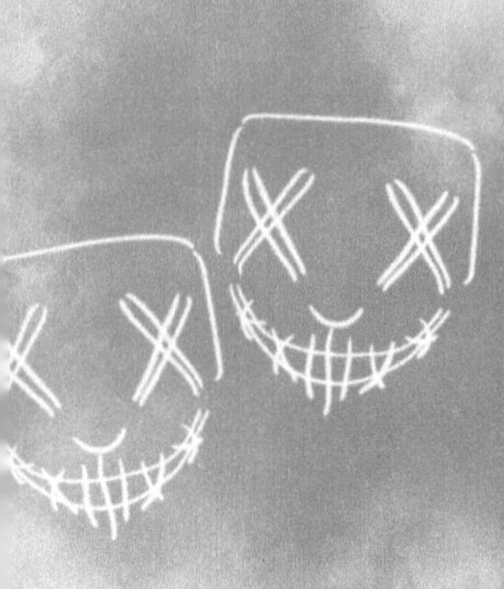

25

Cole

Never in my lifetime would I think I would be kid-napped. I find it funny if I think about it hard enough. Kidnapped in the fuckin' cemetery. It's ironic, isn't it? I can't figure out where we are. I watched in horror when Dorian went down by a stun gun. I was helpless, then Nyx went down, and I knew it was over.

Now we're stuck tied to a pole in a musty basement somewhere. I jiggle my hands once more, trying to break the handcuffs.

"Cole, fuck off already. They aren't going to break." Dorian spat out, drawing in a deep, harsh breath.

"How else are we supposed to get the hell out of here, Dorian?" My anger rose with every word. If he doesn't help, then I'll do it alone. Nyx hasn't spoken since he woke, and I'm getting worried.

Nyx turns, his cuffs clanging on the pole. That's the most we've gotten out of him this entire time.

"Nyx, please talk to us. We know this is killing you, too. We will get out of this," Dorian begs him.

We're greeted by silence.

"Nyx, he's telling the truth. The kidnappers have a plan. It's only a matter of minutes before they tell us what it is." I try to reason with him.

He ignores us.

"Hey, you assholes, come down here and talk to us like fuckin' men!" I yell. I'm tired of this bullshit. If they want us, they better start answering our questions.

The door swings open, slamming against the wall. Heavy footsteps descend the stairs.

"Will you shut the hell up? You'll wake Momma up."

Is this dude for real? His momma? He's worried about waking his mommy.

"You still live at home with your mommy. Aww, that's cute." I tease him.

The ass wearing the orange mask storms to me, punching me in the stomach. All the air escapes my lungs, and my body tries to fold in on itself, pulling tight on my shoulders.

"Sonofabitch," I cough.

"Watch what you say about Momma or I'll cut your tongue out." He spits out, anger radiating off his body.

"That's enough. You'll soon find out what I need from you three. Until then, keep your mouths shut," the Yellow masked asshole says.

For the likes of me, I can't remember her brother's names. She never refers to him by his name. I've only read it once on the lawyer's documents when she signed over the inheritance. I raise my eyes and smile at him.

"I'd watch your back if I were you."

He gave a brief laugh. "Yeah, and why's that?"

"Because your sister isn't one to be fucked with anymore."

I'm not playing around anymore, and I hope Catalina never finds out where we are. This will send her into a state of panic. Her brother doesn't need to know, but Catalina is stronger than last year. The three of us will get out of this together.

"Fuck you, Cole." He slams his fist into my ribs. "I guess you'll have to wait and see."

A sharp pain shoots up my side and my body sags.

"Cole?" Panic in Dorian's voice raises. "Get the fuck out of here, assholes. If you can't tell us what you want, then leave us alone."

Their footsteps pound up the stairs. Leaving us alone once again.

"I'm fine. It's not like I haven't been hit a few times before. I don't understand what they want. Is it a trap for Wednesday?"

Nyx groans—the first sound since we've been down here.

I jolt awake from the voices from above.

"What's going on?"

"I'm not sure. They started a little while ago. Whatever is going on, they aren't overly happy about it." Dorian tilts his head, watching the rafters.

I rest my head on my shoulder, looking at Nyx. His head is dropped down, staring at the floor. He hasn't made a peep since we figured they wanted to lure Wednesday here.

The basement door flies open.

"He can stay down there with them. I don't care." A female voice yells.

We all watch the stairs, waiting.

"Hurry the hell up, or I'll push you down the stairs."

"Keep your hands off me, and I'll be able to walk, you asshole."

"Riley?" Dorian whispers.

No. It can't be.

"I have a new roommate for you dickheads," The cunt in the Orange mask tells us.

Riley rounds the corner, and I'm at a loss for words. I'm so confused and don't understand what is happening. He must see something and shakes his head slightly. Orange mask shoves him so hard that he falls to the cement floor.

"I'll guess that'll be your home. I don't have time for your bullshit. You shouldn't be here." He tears his arms up, and a popping sound explodes in the basement. Riley's voice cracks as he screams. But dickhead ignores his

cries and ties his hands to a metal rod. He shoots us a glare before storming up the stairs.

We're left in silence as Riley draws in shaky breaths. Luckily popping a shoulder into place is easy; it's getting out of the handcuffs that are proving to be a pain in the ass.

"Riley? Doing all right?" I cautiously ask.

He draws in a deep breath, lifting his head. "Not really. But I'm not bleeding, so that's a plus."

That's good. "Wanna tell us what's going on?"

"Like, why the fuck you're here," Dorian adds.

"Where the fuck is Catalina, Riley?" Nyx lashed out. Pulling hard on his cuffs, trying to get to Riley.

Fear twisted in my gut when Riley turned pale. That answers the question.

"She's upstairs," he spoke, the words barely reaching me.

Nyx loses it.

He bangs his cuffs on the pole and screams for them to let Cat go. My heart can't take anymore; a piece breaks off with every scream. The need to be with her and to hold Nyx is killing me.

"Nyx, we'll get her. I swear, even if it kills me, we will get her."

He yells once more. Then he turned to me, and his eyes darkened with pain. "Don't make promises you can't keep Cole. I'll burn this house to the ground with all of us in it if I have to."

"Riley, what do they want from her?" Dorian asks the question that I've been thinking the entire time.

He shakes his head. "They never told her. They only kept saying they wanted what was owed."

"The fuck does that mean?" Nyx spits out.

"She didn't know either. She said she paid them." He shrugs and then cries out in pain.

The inheritance money? She signed that over. What the hell is going on up there?

"Can anyone get free?" I ask even though I know the answer.

"No," they all say.

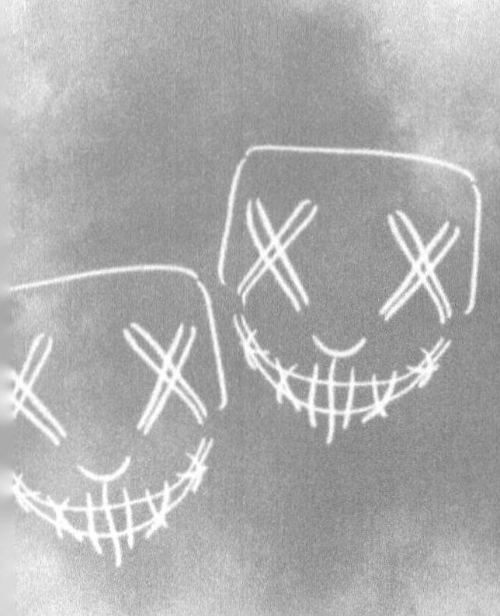

<h1 style="text-align:center">26</h1>

<h1 style="text-align:center">Catalina</h1>

I knock on the door, and I can sense doom lurking on the other side of the door. Riley, Jesus. He should've stayed behind. I'm placing him in the worst situation of his life. The purge will resemble child's play compared to what greets us behind this door.

The door swings open, and I'm face-to-face with him. His mouth twitched into a knowing smile. One that said, I still have control over you.

"Well, if it isn't the slut. Welcome home. Momma missed you." Then his eyes look past me and harden. "Who the fuck is this?" he spits out.

"A friend."

"Get the fuck inside now." I bite my lip as he grabs my sore arm, dragging me inside the house. "Tell your friend to join us."

I stare at Riley, and thankfully he follows.

The house hasn't changed at all. The same beige paint on the walls tells me she hasn't changed her taste and thinks beige goes with everything. He keeps dragging me until we reach the living room. I'm surprised they changed the couches. It must've been with the money they collected.

I let out a laugh.

"What's so funny?"

"Oh, nothing." Riley moves next to me, and my brother's heads snap at him.

"Is this another one of your boyfriends?"

Riley goes to answer, but I give him a nudge. "Don't worry about him. What do you want?"

Then I smell her daylilies and peonies. Her scent hasn't changed, and it sends chills down my spine. I don't need to turn around to see the anger and hate on her face. I can feel it on the back of my head.

"Well, if it isn't the daughter and her? What is he?"

"No clue. They won't talk."

Fuckin' rights we won't talk. If they can't tell me where the guys are and why I'm here, then we don't speak. Highways work in both directions, assholes.

"Catalina, where's the rest of the money?" she asks pleasantly.

I want to vomit. I raise a brow, confused. "I signed over the paperwork a year ago. Perhaps you spent it?"

She struck faster than I thought she would. The crack of her hand on my cheek stings the same. "Watch your fucking mouth." Her voice rose with each word. "I know there's more money. Where is it?" she yells.

"I don't know what you're talking about," I said through clenched teeth.

"Get him in the basement with the others. If she doesn't talk, we'll make her."

Her sons grab for Riley; I yell and dodge after them. Fingernails dig into my fresh stab wound, and I fall to the floor.

"Riley, I'll get you. I promise," I grit out.

"Don't worry about me, Cat." He fights his way, but my brothers shove him to the basement door.

Mother laughs. "Don't be so foolish. You won't be saving anyone in that basement, you little whore." Her fingers dig more, drawing blood from my wound.

I'll fight for those men down there. I'm not the same girl who left this house three years ago. She knows nothing about me. I'm not being ruled by them anymore. Screams come from downstairs, and my heart lurches. What did they do?

"Guess they couldn't help themselves after all. You best remember that, Catalina. Now speak before they do the same to you."

"I don't know anything." I managed to suppress the tears swelling in my throat.

She shoves me away. "Don't lie to me."

I want to apply pressure to my shoulder, but that would satisfy her. I will myself to stand without flinching. My only other thought is where the other two youngest sons are.

"Where are Quinn and Lane?"

She scoffs and rolls her eyes. "Don't mention their names to me. They are nothing to me."

I see the ivory castle walls are falling. Or beige, I guess. "Aww, did they realize their mother is a bitch?" I've waited years to say that to her.

Her face turns a lovely shade of crimson. "How dare you speak to me like that in my house."

"What's wrong, Momma?" Both brothers come racing toward her.

She points at me. "This whore called me a bitch."

I need to channel my inner Cole. I'm stronger than before, and these assholes have my boyfriends locked up in the basement. I still need answers, though.

"What money are you guys talking about? Why are you dodging my question?"

My mother storms down the hall, leaving me alone with the devils.

"What did you do to Riley?"

They both laugh, and goosebumps rise along my skin the louder they laugh. "That guy had what was coming. He won't be a problem anymore."

Hollowness hit my stomach; this is my fault. "You'll fuckin' pay for this." I blinked the tears back. They both shrug. It was as if an electric current had gone off. I leapt through the air, going after my oldest brother, screaming as I tumbled us over.

"You douche waffle, you're lucky I don't fuckin' shoot you between the eyes," I shout in his face. I haul off and knee him in the nuts. "You won't be needing them." Then spit on his face. He yowls in pain. Before I can register

anything, I'm thrown across the room, landing on the floor in front of the couch.

I turn on all fours when my brother kicks me in the ribs. Falling to my forearms, I gasp for air; he pulls me up by my hair, getting into my face.

"You miserable bitch."

"That's enough, Kyle and Royce. We have things to discuss first."

I've never been thankful for that woman in my life until now.

"Fuck this bitch. I say we just end her life. We don't need her," Kyle slowly gets off the ground, holding his wounded nuts.

"How about you show me my boyfriends, before we talk anymore," I wheeze out. "Without the masks, you cowards."

They look at her, and she nods. Of course, she will.

Kyle leads, still limping. I hope I bruised them. Royce shoves me, and I need to walk slowly. I'm trying to think of a plan here. Only one comes to mind. I glare at the witch as she holds the basement door open for us.

"Hurry up. We don't have all night."

"It won't take long. I'm sure her guys will convince her to give it to us," Kyle tells her.

I'm getting angrier by the second they don't tell me. I hate going to the basement; it's dark and stinks. Holding onto the handrail, I take my first step, there are thirteen, and I need to time this correctly, or I'm fucked. Hitting step five, I brace myself and kick Kyle as hard as I can down the stairs. He has no time to correct himself; all we can do is listen in the dark as he hits step after step. The finishing hit is to the cement.

"The fuck." Royce finally flicks the light on, and we stare at Kyle motionless at the bottom of the stairs. Impressive. After all this time, it was the stairs that got him. "Catalina," he growls.

"I didn't do it. It was dark, after all."

"You best get down these stairs before I help you." His warm breath fanned the back of my neck.

I quickly race down the stairs, stepping over Kyle and making the turn. I want to break down and cry. All three guys are cuffed to the same pole I once was long ago.

"Wednesday."

"Half pint."

"Baby."

They all greet me, but it's their voices that break the dam. I collide with Nyx first. Sobbing into his chest. "I thought I lost you." I ignore the pain shooting from my shoulder. It's about them, not me.

"Shh, baby. Fuck I wish I could wrap my arms around you." I place a kiss over his heart, feeling it pulsing.

I move to Cole, and he groans when I wrap my arms around his waist. "Did they hurt you?"

"It's fine." As he spoke, his eyes stayed fixated on mine.

"It's not. If he isn't dead, I'll kill him." They hurt him, and I'm glad I pushed my brother down the stairs.

His brows lifted in surprise. "It's hot when you talk like that, but do nothing stupid."

He tilts his head, but he's still too tall. I can only reach his chin. "I love you."

He shoots me a slight grin and a nod.

"Half pint, find the key, then come back to me."

"Dorian."

"I'm good. I need you safe, and it's not down here."

I glance over my shoulder to find Royce glaring at me. He steps closer, shaking his head. That's not a good head shake. I back away from the guys, moving deeper into the basement.

"Catalina, I think you owe me," he taunts, moving closer.

Nyx sees him first, and his eyes shoot wide. "Royce?" They know him.

"Hello, fellas. No hard feelings about the club or anything?"

"Seriously? Did you join the club in hoping to track your sister down?" Cole tries to wiggle out of his cuffs.

Royce shrugs. "I mean, it worked. We found her, didn't we?" He keeps coming my way. "But now it's her time to see Momma and explain how she killed her favourite son."

I stumble backward, crashing over a body. "Riley," I cry out.

"Cat." He gives me a faint smile, and beads of sweat run down his forehead. What did they do to him?

"I'm coming, Catalina. You have no place to run."

I'm torn. Do I stay and help Riley or try to get up the stairs? Why didn't we pack any weapons before we came? I search the floor for anything sharp; the douchebags only tied Riley. He can cut himself away.

"Run, Cat," his voice was small.

"I can't leave you."

"Do it."

A hand grips my ankle, pulling me away. Too late. I'm caught.

27
Catalina

Royce drags me away from Riley. The fear in his eyes matches mine. I try to kick his kneecap with my free leg. The guys cheer me on, but it does nothing for me. My fate is sealed. I should see where it goes, but once she finds out, I killed Kyle. I don't think I'll be making it out of this house alive.

"Kyle? Royce? What's taking so long?" She calls from above.

With Royce distracted, I take my chance. I haul off and kick him hard in the knee. He drops my leg, and I scramble to get up. I only make a few feet away before my head jerks back.

"I don't think so. You can tell her what you did." He drags me backward to the stairs.

"Cat, baby, don't stop fighting. We'll find a way to get out of here." Nyx locks eyes with me.

"Remember what I told you, half pint," Dorian yells.

Royce drags me up the stairs, and I try to step on each step, but he's going too fast, and I miss them. He has a good grip on my hair, and the sting burns. I crab walk just to keep the pressure off my scalp.

Royce tosses me to the side and slams the door shut. I can hear Cole yelling through the floor. The pain rips through his voice.

"Momma."

"Where is Kyle?" She looks around like he's going to pop up.

Royce points to me. "She killed him. Pushed him down the stairs."

I stare at both of them and grin. "One down."

Royce's mouth twisted into a snarl. "You stupid whore, you'll pay for this."

"Royce, did she just say that?" She breaks into a sobbing mess. I roll my eyes; I'm over this. They don't scare me anymore.

I do, however, need to run. The basement opens to the kitchen, a slight design flaw, but it works in my favour. I race for the drawer with the knives. Pulling the drawer open, I find it empty. I run my hand deep inside, trembling when I touch nothing.

I grip the drawer, pulling it hard with a hard swing. I connect it with Royce's face. The vibration radiates up my arms. I watch as Royce staggers back, falling into the fridge. I'm positive his neck snapped. Fingers dig into my forearm, twisting my body to face her.

"I knew I should've killed you when you were a child. I never wanted a daughter. They only bring trouble, and look what you are doing to my family," she said, her tone full of steel.

"Me? You are the problem. You couldn't even tell me why you kidnapped my boyfriends. You kept giving me the runaround. What do you expect me to do?" I bit off each word, spitting them back at her.

She screams in frustration, letting go of my arm. "I got a letter in the mail a few months ago saying the lawyer had a mix-up, and you never signed all the money over."

"What money?" I snap. I move toward the living room.

"Don't act like you don't know, Catalina. Your father loved you more than he did me. Sign it over, and I'll release those boys of yours."

I shake my head. Not happening. I need her gone, too. Wait. Maybe I can twist this around.

"Fine, show me the paperwork." She shoots me a satisfying grin like she won the lottery. Maybe she has. I couldn't tell, ya.

I follow her to the office, Dad's office. Her son's pictures are still hanging in the hallway. And not one of me. It doesn't surprise me. I don't even think she took a single one of me when I was growing up. Stepping into his office brings back memories, and that's all. She changed everything in here.

She walks around the desk, grabs the folder, and passes it to me. She drops them in front of me when I don't take them.

"Here, read these and sign them. I want you gone. You ruined everything."

"Before I sign these, release the guys." I don't even look at the papers. She has two options, the way I look at it.

"Why, you little bitch."

She shoves me hard in my shoulder, throwing me off balance. Falling to the floor, I see the devil in her eyes. It's then I know who killed my father. He was trapped in this hell like I was.

"You killed him for the money? How did you know about it?"

Her mouth twitched. "Don't be so foolish. I knew for a long time he was hoarding his cash." She steps closer. "There was no way I would live the rest of my life like the middle class." She lets out an uncontrollable laugh. Bending down, she gets into my face. "I would never lower myself like some people."

Her hand moves to the back of her pants, pulling out a gun, and every nerve in my body froze. There is no way this is how I'm going out, especially if I made it this far. Fuck her. I will my body to listen to me. I need to fight to save the guys; they need me.

I'm needed.

I let out a scream and reach for her wrist; she's so shocked she staggers back, I get up and wrestle her for the gun. Her claws dig into my wrist, and it goes numb. My right arm is growing weak, and I force myself to use every cell of strength. Clenching my hand, I haul off, punching her in the stomach. She tears her fingers from my skin,

leaving red marks behind. The gun tumbles to the floor, and my heart lurches.

"You'll pay for everything, Catalina," she hisses, smacking me on the cheek.

My eye waters from the smack; I should've seen it coming. She always went for the face.

"You hit like a girl." I drop to the floor, grabbing the gun. Lying on my back, I pull the trigger.

It's quiet. I stare at her, blood running down her pink blouse from where I shot her in the heart. She makes a slight gurgle sound, tumbling to the floor.

I move closer. "Where are the keys?"

"Catalina," she coughs, blood splatters on her chin.

"Answer the question." I point the gun at her head. "Please, tell me."

Her eyes slowly fall shut. I kneel, giving her a shake. "Tell me where the keys are."

"Fuck!" I drop her like a bag of potatoes. "Fuck you. Couldn't give me one thing before you left."

I have to hold back the kick I want to land on her. Let the dead rest. Right. Those rules don't apply to me. With a grin, I spit on her. "Have fun in hell." I turn to leave when I remember those stupid papers. I'm kind of curious; swiping them off the desk, I rush for the guys.

I'm halfway down the stairs when hushed voices greet me. All I want to do is cry because I'm not sure how I'll be able to free them. Stepping over Kyle's body, Nyx sees me first.

"Baby? What's wrong?"

"I can't free you." I pressed my fingers to my lips, holding back a cry.

"Yes, you can. All you need is something that can cut the cuffs. No one said you need the keys," Cole's deep calms me.

I take a deep, calming breath and turn to Riley. I owe this to him.

"Riley?" I race to his side, taking him in. "Riley? I'm so sorry."

"It's not your fault, Cat. Stop it," his voice cracks.

I check his wrists out and think I can get him untied. I look back at the guys, and Dorian nods. I nod back and go ahead and start untying him.

"This is gonna hurt, Rye Rye." I free his wrists, and his arms drop. He lets out a blood-curdling scream. "Fuck, I'm sorry. What do I do?"

The guys tell me what to do, and I get Riley into position. I hope he forgives me after this. I grab his arm, place my foot on his side, and pull. His grunts make me want to stop, but I keep going. The slip of his shoulder into place is a relief, not only to me but to Riley.

"Thank fuck," he groans.

My body is slowing down, but I can't let the guys see it. I bypass them and go up the stairs again. I have a feeling those keys are in her pocket. She wouldn't trust Royce or Kyle with them. I take the stairs two at a time, rushing down the hall. I stop in the office doorway, trying to catch my breath.

"Please have the keys." I slowly walk to her side, swallowing the lump. I bend down, reaching for her pant

pocket. You would think with all the dead people I touch, I would be used to this. But I want to vomit. Deep down, I'm waiting for her eyes to pop open and her hand to reach out and grab me.

"Hurry the fuck up, Catalina," I tell myself. My blood spikes when my fingers dip into the pocket.

Nothing.

I reach over her body, digging into her other pocket. The clink of keys gives me a jolt.

"Thank you, Lucy."

I run back toward the basement, slowing down on the stairs, or I'll be like Kyle.

"I have the keys," I yell, racing to Nyx first.

"Good job, baby. I can't feel my arms anymore."

I reach on my tiptoes, getting the key in. I work fast, trying to get him free. When his arms wrap around my waist, I feel a part of my soul reconnecting. Giving him the key, I backed away. My body officially finished for the night.

I sink against the pile of boxes, trying my hardest to stay awake. I look down at my shoulder, noticing fresh blood. *Oh shit.*

"Catalina," Cole said, dropping to my side. "Wednesday, what's wrong?" He gently lifts me into his lap. "She's bleeding," he yells.

"What do you need?"

"We need to leave."

I curl deeper into Cole's chest, blocking everyone out. I wanna go home.

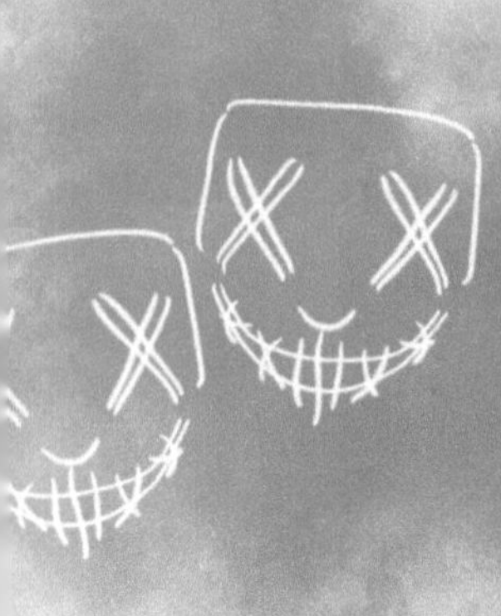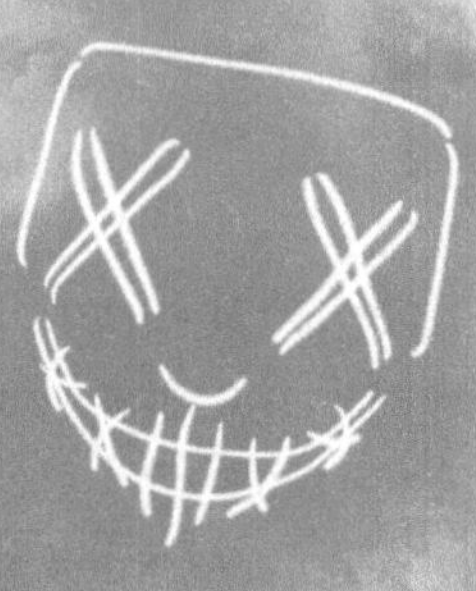

28

Nyx

We survived the night. That's all that matters. I can't believe she placed her life at risk for us. I would've been okay with dying in that basement. I was at peace hanging there until I died. Watching Cole carry her up the stairs breaks me. She never once complained that she was in pain; her only worry was getting us out.

I help Riley up, bracing his arm. This guy has gone through hell, too. He has proven himself to be a loyal friend to Cat. I don't wanna say my chat with him had anything to do with it, but I'm just sayin' it had something to do with it.

The thought that she had to kill her family also doesn't sit right with me. That should've been something that we had to do. Those images will haunt her for life. She needs support right now, and I'll gladly give it to her once we get home.

"I parked the van outside. The keys are in my pocket," Riley tells me when we reach the top step.

"Back pocket?"

"Who places keys in their back pocket?" he shot back, raising his brows.

"I swear if I touch your dick." I reach into his front pocket, staying away from his inner thigh. "Riley, perhaps it's the other pocket."

"Bud, you're the one that dove into that pocket."

I take a deep breath, trying not to punch him. "Cole, take Cat outside." I need her out of this house fast and Dorian to burn it down. The fewer memories for her, the better. I dig into Riley's pocket quickly, and he chuckles.

"That's my dick," he whispers.

"Ah, fuck no." I pull out fast with the keys. "You're a dick."

He flinches when he shrugs. I can't think about his dick; I need to think about getting out of this town and getting everyone home. I push him to the front door, following the guys out.

Entering Eastwood, I'm in shock. It's way worse than we left it, and it makes me feel a little better knowing that Coleman is dead. I would be more excited about it if Cat would wake up. She passed out in Cole's arms and hasn't woken since.

The streets of Eastwood remind me of a zombie apocalypse. The fires left the coffee shop, where we usually met Freddy every Sunday a charred mess. Devastation all over town, and I can't look anymore. Trying to get to the hospital takes longer than expected. The cops are all over town detouring traffic; I'm surprised they wanted anything to do with us after yesterday.

"It's going to take forever to see a doctor," Cole complains about the tenth time since we showed up. The waiting area is filled with people sporting every injury.

"There's nothing we can do about it; she's breathing, and that's all that matters. She worked herself hard and is exhausted, Cole. She'll be fine," Dorian tells him before walking away.

The only lucky one was Riley; a nurse was able to sling him up, and then he went home. Cole was insistent on getting Cat checked over by a real doctor. Her shoulder stopped bleeding, but he's overreacting. She's alive and well. If I don't tell myself that I'll explode.

"Catalina Wilson," a nurse calls.

We all stand, walking with Cole. The nurse blushes as she studies us. Sorry, sweet cheeks, my heart is taken. She raises her hand, stopping us.

"Only family allowed."

Dorian broadens his shoulders, stepping close to the nurse. "She's my reason to breathe every morning, my motivation to never give up, so don't tell me only fuckin' family."

Her eyes widen in shock. "I'm sorry, but rules are rules, sir."

Oh, shit. I move fast, placing my hand on Dorian's shoulder. "Hey, big guy, we're making a scene, and Cat needs to get back there. We'll wait out here. Cole will be with her the entire time. Yeah?"

He shrugs me off. "Yeah, whatever." He storms off to the exit.

"Cole, please."

"I will, don't worry, stay with D."

I bury my lips into Cat's hair. "Wake up soon for me, baby." I squeeze Cole's arm, turning to chase after Dorian.

I find him outside, sitting on the bench. I feel his pain; we're all worried and pissed. It's natural I also get that, but fuck, I want to be with her.

"Nyx, I don't wanna talk." He speaks before I sit.

That works for me.

I'm not sure how long we've been out here, but my ass has gone numb. When I look over, my world stops. Her eyes gleamed with tears as a smile spread across her face. Cole cradles her arm, helping her across the parking lot. Her face isn't as pale, and relief floods through me.

"Catalina, baby." I took off toward her. Wrapping my arms around her waist, I bury my face in her neck, breathing her in. "Fuck, baby. You had me scared to death."

She wraps her arm around me. "I'll never leave you, love. I swear." I pull away, and her violet eyes blaze into mine. I stroke her cheek, feeling her body tremble.

"I love you, Catalina. But I swear to God, if you pull this shit again, I'll pull you over my knee and spank you." I threaten her.

Her lips fall apart. Running my thumb over her bottom lip, I tilt her head back. "Now kiss me." She blinks and licks her lip and the tip of my thumb. I lower closer, gently wrapping my hand around her neck, pressing our lips together. "I meant what I said." I kiss her once more, sensing Dorian behind me.

"Darling. Don't do that to me again, please."

Of course, he makes his quick and sweet.

It's been a week since shit hit the fan, and Cat has been home. She's been healing slow and steady, and I can tell it's killing Cole. He wants her back to normal so he can return to his normal routine, which we don't have.

The town is still being cleaned up. The body count is over fifty and rising. More bodies are being found as more rescuers dig through the rubble. They found Coleman's place empty; he's presumed to be missing.

Missing in a hole, more like it. I'm sure they'll find him. Eventually.

Cat was determined to return to school and wanted to finish her work and graduate next month. I want to be positive and think that'll happen, but honestly, I don't think it will. Her shoulder has limited mobility, and her

art pieces demand lots of work. We try to head in after classes and help her, but we aren't very good at it. I think we cause more of a headache than anything.

The worst part is that she's been off work this entire time and is going stir-crazy. Davis told her that with all the bodies that came from purge night, she isn't needed at the medical department.

"Catalina?" I open her bedroom door finding her laying on the bed. "Can I see you downstairs?"

A smile tugged at her lips. "You're seeing me now."

"I know, but downstairs would be better."

"All right, give me ten."

I give her a thumbs up and race downstairs. The guys are in the den setting up.

"She's coming down. Are we ready?"

Dorian lights the last candle that lines the mantel, and Cole dims the light. The room is all set for her, and I hope she enjoys herself.

When she walks in, she's speechless. This was our way of saying thank you for saving our assholes. She never should've done that, but we'll forever be in her debt.

"You guys." Her hand shook as she reached for me. "Thank you, love."

I gently gather her into my arms. "You never have to thank me." I shift her to Dorian.

"Thank you, sweetheart." He bundles her in his arms.

"Thank you, darling."

She stares at Cole, and tears fall. "Dickhead," she whispers.

"Wednesday, come here." He spreads his arms wide. He drew her in, closing his arms tight. I never would have thought Cole would become the softy. He pulls her back, wiping her tears away. "No more tears." He presses his lips to hers.

I move behind her, lightly skimming my hand under her shirt. "Baby," I breathed into her ear. Sliding my hands upwards slowly, so slowly, her body presses into mine. "Be patient." Her back arches, pressing into Cole, and he groans. Kissing along her neck, I torment her before cupping her breasts. She moans as Cole kisses her again, and I pinch her hardened nipples.

"Let's get your clothes off. Dorian is waiting for you." Cole steps back, reaching his hand over his head, he pulls his shirt off. Cat licks her lips and blinks slowly. She grabs her shirt and pulls her arm out, and I help her with her sore shoulder.

"If it hurts too much, we'll stop."

"I'll be fine, and I trust you guys." She grabs my shirt and pulls it up. I bend the rest of the way so she can pull it off. She flicks my nipple piercing, and my dick twitches.

"Get on the floor and start sucking Dorian's cock," Cole demands.

She drops to her knees, and Dorian steps before her, stroking his dick.

"Relax your throat, let me all the way in." He brushes the tip along her lips before she opens, taking him in. "Ah, fuck." Holding her head, he thrusts, making her gag.

I can't take it much longer; kicking my jeans off, I fist my dick with every thrust Dorian makes. I watch Cole move

to his knees, smacking Cat on the thighs as she lifts up. Fucker gets the first taste.

"Ride my face, little one." He moves between her thighs, and she sits like the good girl she is.

Her muffled moans only make Dorian breathe heavier. Fuck, it never gets old seeing her like this. Her fingers dig into Dorian's thighs as Cole grips her tighter. Her head falls back, and a silent cry falls from her lips.

Cole rolls her over, kissing her lips. "You taste like fuckin' candy." With a groan, he slips inside.

"Cole, please," she begs.

"I got you, little one." Lifting her legs to his chest, he drives in hard.

The sight of her is beautiful. I'm unsure where our future will go, but I hope it'll be forever. The three of us will never let her out of our sight again. I can promise her that even if that involves moving towns.

"I need you to come." Cole's voice interrupts my thoughts. I watch her toes curl, and he pulls her into his hips. "Good fuckin' girl, come all over my cock." Cole groans, leaning forward and kissing her. He slowly pulls out, and his cum drips out.

Dorian lays down, stroking himself. "Finish sucking me off." Dorian meets my eyes, and I know what he wants. Cat crawls over him, getting in between his leg, and I shift behind her moving her ass in the air.

"I'm gonna fuck you from behind and drive your throat down on D's dick, don't come up for air until you swallow all his cum."

"Okay."

I kneel behind her, gliding my hand over her ass, smacking it. Walking my hand along her spine, I sink into her hair, pulling her head back. "Open your mouth." She opens wide, and I look back at Dorian and slowly lower her head, making her take him all. Dorian's mouth pops open, and his eyes roll back.

I grab my dick, smacking it against her clit. The need to fill her roars inside of me. Slamming into her, my head spins from the sensation of her muscles clenching around my dick. *Fuck.* Our bodies shift forward, and all three of us moan. Dorian digs his hands into her hair, pulling her down more on his dick. I drive her hips into mine.

"Shit, she's taking it so well," Dorian hisses, flexing his hips, getting even deeper. She gags as I push her forward.

"So... Fuckin'... Well." I drive into her, needing her to come. I brush my finger over her clit, causing her walls to clench. I groan at the tightness. As I lung into her again, she explodes. I drive in harder, prolonging her climax.

"I'm coming. Get ready." Dorian groans.

Thank God, 'cause I can't hold on much longer, her hand weaves between our legs, squeezing my balls, and I see stars. I dig my fingers into her hips, thrusting long strides as I come.

"Fuck, baby. That was intense." I rest my head on her back, breathing hard.

We're all a puddle of bodies on the makeshift bed we created, and I couldn't think of any other place I'd rather be.

Epilogue
Dorian

Five Months Later

Spring has officially come to Eastwood. It's been a crazy last couple of months. With Catalina finishing school with her art degree, it's been a busy time here. An art dealer saw her collection at school and offered her an exhibit at the Darkscape Gallery in the city. It's been complete madness around the house while she works. We turned the shed outback into her workshop and hardly see her now.

I'll never complain she's happier now. The cops came to the house two weeks after Halloween, telling her that her mother and brothers were dead. Then, a lawyer showed up, explaining that she had more inheritance. She told the lawyer to find her other brother's and give it to them. She was done with them.

As for the club, once word spread about Henry and Conrad, everyone went their own ways. It's been peaceful.

"Dorian, I need your help out back." Cole pokes his head through the patio door.

I also have to deal with someone becoming domesticated. Out of all of us, I wasn't expecting it to be him.

"What are you doing?" I step outside and bite the laugh back. A patio set is spread out on the lawn in pieces.

"I can't figure it out." He runs his hands through his hair, tugging the ends in frustration.

I let the laugh out. "Have you read the instructions?" I shrug.

His face drops. "Seriously? You don't think I tried that? It's all in Swedish." He waves the paper at me.

I snatch the paper from him. I doubt that he probably didn't even try. Why is it so thick? Flipping through each page, I try to find the English. "You know what, look at the pictures."

He shakes his head in disappointment. "And you bitch at me? Un-fuckin' real."

We're halfway through the chair when I hear her laughing.

"Don't start with me half pint."

She walks to the box, shuffles through the mess, and picks up another booklet. "Wouldn't it be handy to have the instructions?"

I shoot Cole a glare. "You asshole. They had more booklets in there."

"News to me."

Somehow I don't believe that; I feel he didn't want to build this shit alone.

"Come on guys, I'll help and make supper after." Cat grabs a cushion, tossing it at Cole's head.

"Watch yourself, little one." He chases after her.

Nyx walks out of the house, catching her mid-stride. Her laughter rang out, and I couldn't help but laugh with her.

"Where's the fire, baby?" He wraps her legs around his hips, and her arms naturally wrap around his neck.

"Cole is the fire," she says over her shoulder, looking at Cole.

He shoots her a smirk. "Ain't that the truth."

"Only in your dreams, hot shot. Can we finish these so we have somewhere to sit tonight?"

Nyx walks over, setting Cat down. "I have other plans for the new patio set." Smacking Cat's ass.

"I wouldn't mind eating pussy off the table for dinner," Cole adds.

Cat throws the instructions at us. "Build fast."

THE END

About the Author

Hello, loves! I'm a Canadian romance writer who's all about the steamy and dark stuff. Horror books, movies, and music? Yes, please! I have a little true crime obsession, but I'll just call it research and pretend it's normal.
If you crave love stories that push the limits of lust, trust, and desire, you've come to the right place.

Follow me for exclusive sneak peeks, giveaways, and behind-the-scenes glimpses into my writing process. And if you want to keep up with my latest releases or connect on social media.

Let's dive into the shadows together, darlings.